Forbidden Arabelle

Dear Brian,
  I hope you'll like
the swashbuckling
world between these
pages. Thank you, my
friend, for your interest

Mellyora Ashley

in my writing!
  God bless yee!
  love,
  Mellyora Ashley

All characters in this book are purely fictional, and have no existence outside the imagination of the author except for the following historical characters portrayed or mentioned:

King George II

Lord and Lady Chesterfield

Captain Ligonier, Royal Military Academy

William Chamberlain, Cordwainer,

Ancestor of Belinda Curwen-Reed

Colley Cibber

"Sing to Me Only With Thine Eyes"—Ben Jonson, 1573-1637

"It was a Lover and His Lass"—William Shakespeare, 1564-1616

Some phrases of the times used for Aunt Claracilla's letters came from *The Newest Polite Letter-Writer.*

This book was printed in the United States of America.

To order additional copies of this book, contact:
Xlibris Corporation
1-888-795-4274
www.Xlibris.com
Orders@Xlibris.com
56046

Also by Mellyora Ashley:

A Lady in Disguise

A Zebra Regency Romance, Kensington Publishers,
New York, 1990, ISBN: 0-8217-3107-6
It received a front-cover endorsement by
DAME BARBARA CARTLAND, who said:
*"This is a charming, delightful costume romance with a plot
which keeps one surprised until the end."*

Baron Buffoon

A comedy play in four acts,
Set in Lord Chesterfield's London, 1752

To inquire about Mellyora Ashley's books and plays, or to send
her your comments and reviews, write to her at: PO Box 220,
Yamhill, Oregon 97148 USA.

Dedication

To Belinda Curwen-Reed

As soon as our pen friendship began, I knew we were kindred spirits. You have my undying love and thanks for all your research help, and for showing me treasures all over England and Scotland with Robert, Felicity, and Douglas. For your beauty, wit, and laughter, spiritual kinship, and loyal friendship, I dedicate this book to you, dear Belinda.

My Special Thanks

To Glen for lovingly supporting my writing with your great idea, and for your skillful artistry on the cover.

To Landen for your willing help in so many ways. I rejoice in the splendid, adventurous person you are, and will always be glad when you come home.

To Julie Richeson for reading this story and telling me your thoughts, especially where you laughed. You're a priceless friend.

To Mary Stevens-Zarich for your amusing and insightful remarks as you read this book. You spurred me on, dear friend-of-my-heart.

To Peter Drinkwater of Warwickshire for Georgian letters, real face patches and their meanings, and answers to my questions on historical themes throughout our thirty-two-year pen friendship. God bless you!—you're a treasure-trove.

To Michael Bosshardt, my Civil War reenactment Captain of 4th Texas, for sharing your encyclopedic knowledge of swords and dueling with me, and for your enthusiasm over my novels.

To Ashley Nuico, my wonderful representative at Xlibris, and your twenty-three colleagues who voted unanimously for this title.

To Philip Sarthou at Xlibris for your great help and generous spirit.

Thank you so much, everybody!
It's fun to share this writing process with you.

Contents

Forbidden Arabelle

England

1752

Chapter One

A Coach Full of Men

"Do you know who *I am?*" Lady Bastwicke demanded, her close-set eyes snapping in fury.

The stolid coachman, wrapped to the eyes in a snow-encrusted scarf, merely stared defiance at her, dangerously uninterested in who she was.

Lady Bastwicke enunciated as though explaining to an idiot, "*I* am the Viscountess Bastwicke! And *you* must take me to London! And my daughter with me."

Arabelle, warming her hands at the inn's fireplace, marveled at her mother's aggressiveness. Could she really force a stranger to do her bidding by such means?

The coachman eyed the Viscountess from under his crop of grey eyebrows and declared, "I cannot do it, Madam."

Lady Bastwicke shoved a chair noisily over the floorboards and hissed, "What insubordination! Obey your betters, and open up two spots in that coach at once!"

Arabelle lifted her fur muff to her face, hiding her chagrin. Her mother could have asked this coachman gently for the favour of a ride. How would she ever gain his cooperation in this abrasive manner? After all, he was not one of her servants to command.

The man drank deeply from a tankard, then slammed it onto the refectory table. "I told you, Madam, that I have three gentlemen, a tailor, and no extra seats!"

Undeterred, Lady Bastwicke put her beak of a nose to the frosty window, eyed the situation outside, then whirled to point at him before he escaped out of the door. "That commodious vehicle holds more than four persons, surely! Why do you even consider taking those people—a tailor, you say!—if not us?"

"In this blizzard, few stages dare to run," he threw back. "A military man must return to Woolwich according to his Captain's orders, so I put myself at his service, seeing I have three teams of horses between here and London. But other folk, especially women," he spat, eyeing the grandiose specimen before him, "should stay put!"

Lady Bastwicke exploded, "I am not *folk!* Or a mere woman! I am a Viscountess, man! My outriders tried and failed to dislodge my own coach from a snow bank. You stay and listen to me! It is already past midday, and the snow falls thicker than ever. I demand seats in your coach for myself and my daughter. She is already nineteen, and must—I repeat *must*—enter London Society this week, do you hear? There is nothing else to be done!"

The coachman snorted and cast the Viscountess a thoroughly disgusted look. "Enter Society! Not in *my* coach!" he growled, and took his last bites of bread and Cheddar.

Lady Bastwicke, yanking on her orange kid gloves, told Arabelle icily, "Let us be off." To the man, she said, "I already ordered my outriders to put my trunks in your boot."

At that, he turned menacing and threw his muffler across his neck, flinging chunks of ice over her. "Then I shall order my guard to toss them into a snow bank!" he roared into her face. He stomped across the uneven planks of the common room, making them vibrate, and plunged out the arched door into the white world. The door slammed and shuddered behind him.

Arabelle hurried to her quivering mother, whose small green eyes spat fire as she furiously swiped melted snow from her chin.

"Listen, Mother." Arabelle was forming a daring idea. "I shall go and ask the soldier who hired the coach if he is willing to accommodate us. If he is, what objection can the coachman then have? He will make a higher profit . . . *if* he can squeeze us in."

Lady Bastwicke pushed Arabelle to the door with sudden determination. "Go! Ask, of all things! Be forceful. After all, if you had not insisted on breaking our trip to see your useless Aunt Claracilla, we would not be in this fix."

Arabelle winced. "Yes, Mother."

"You've forgotten already. Call me *Madam*, not *Mother*."

This, Arabelle had discerned, was to keep the public thinking, whenever possible, that the Viscountess was not old enough to have such a grown daughter. "Yes, Madam. If I do not return, please follow me."

Lady Bastwicke grasped her arm again, painfully. "Make sure you do not introduce yourself to any men in that coach. We are far above them, and do not forget it. No talking to that military chap beyond asking for space, mind."

"No, Madam."

Out in the quiet world, Arabelle took a deep breath of frosty air. The gold letters on the wine-red *Aynscombe Stage* were nearly covered by the fluffy snow that had fallen during the change of horses. Two blindered wheelers were already in the tracks of the former team, with ostlers hooking their traces. A red-nosed groom held four collared Percherons that snuffed out puffs of air, their dark manes and tails vivid in the whirling whiteness. Lanterns cast iridescent orbs of light at each corner of the coach with its snow-banked wheel spokes. Arabelle could not see through the steamed windows, but she hoped that the occupants would be more civil than their driver.

The coach door creaked open. Arabelle saw a gentleman's head emerge. He had sleek, white hair pulled back into a queue at the nape of his well-shaped head. When he turned, she saw a smooth forehead and black brows that marked a dramatic contrast to his white hair. He looked to be in his mid-to upper twenties. Arabelle had never seen such an arresting man, so handsome, vital, and fit. One of Boucher's paintings, which she had admired at a Canterbury exhibition, came close to portraying such a paragon, but this one lived. His midnight blue coat accentuated his wide shoulders and swung past shiny boots as he kicked down the steps. He placed a black three-cornered hat on his head and spoke to the guard.

That individual held a silver horn. He cupped a hand to his mouth and bellowed, "Coach!" It was the signal for passengers to board.

The moment had come for Arabelle to address the man before her, for surely he was the military personage for whom the coachman ventured forth in such a snowfall. The grandeur of the man's confident bearing made her heart thump. What could she say? She had not envisioned begging for space from a man with such an air of command.

Her mother's words thrummed through her head: *There is nothing else to be done!*

He bent to reenter the vehicle. Soon he would be gone. And there went her mother's outriders, trotting away through the falling snow to deal with the Bastwicke carriage, deeply stuck in a snowdrift.

"Sir?" called Arabelle, hurrying toward the *Aynscombe Stage* despite her qualms.

The man placed a white gauntlet on the doorframe and ducked back out. What a way he had of cocking his head as he searched the whirling snow for who had spoken.

"Sir," she repeated, "would you possibly—" Drawing near, she met his interested look and felt so awestruck that she lost her train of thought.

"Would I possibly . . . *what*, my beauty?" his voice caressed her.

With astonished pleasure, she asked, "Would you have room in your coach, Sir, for two stranded ladies? We need . . . that is, we would *like* to reach London tonight." She felt a prick of guilt, for tonight signaled a theatre party that her mother simply had to attend. Arabelle's eyes nevertheless played over his sculpted face with hope.

For a moment he gave her no reply, just looked at her thoroughly as though drinking her in.

Arabelle gave him a little curtsey. When a horse snorted, she looked up into the man's black-lashed eyes. Was that a twinkle lurking in their blue depths?

"Yes, Miss," he said with feeling. "We certainly have room for *you*."

She blushed, and felt a dangerous thrill in accepting his offer.

The coach door next to them flew open and slammed against the body, knocking snow down like a waterfall. Within the vehicle, three men's noses turned, and fascinated eyes regarded her.

The enravishment of Simon Laurence was quick, and unlike anything he had ever imagined. This dark-haired beauty made him want to know her in every sense of the word. How did she do it? He looked at her. By the power of a lively, appealing spirit that peeped at him from behind long lashes and a tender blush—that was how. Was she the desired dream that he so badly needed, hovering here before him in the ethereal whiteness? Surely so, for her hazel eyes seemed too fixed upon him in sweet curiosity to be real. But glorious reality hit him sharply in the leg as he backed into the iron coach step.

"Let me enter first and help you up," he said, an elated timbre in his voice.

She glanced toward the inn over her shoulder, and then flashed him a dazzling smile. "Thank you, Sir; you are a most benevolent gentleman. It surprises me to receive such help from a stranger."

Oh, how he wanted to help her more! What incredible fortune had brought this cheer-producing beauty to his hired coach on this unlikely day? "As I said, you are infinitely welcome." He viewed the curves of her face, framed by a burgundy hood with a dark fur lining. The seductive power of her eyebrows alone was enough to cause men to drop what they were doing to appreciate. What, he wondered with racing pulse, did she look like beneath the sweep of burgundy cloak?

As soon as she put her trusting hands into his, he felt himself flooded with the need to sing the song, *I have found her! I have found her! The woman my heart doth crave.* But he kept it to himself. He fought to ignore the sick accusation that pierced like a dagger to his midsection. *You already have someone,* it thrust home brutally. He resolved to ignore the guilt that bled in drips upon this new and pristine dream.

He steadied her on the slippery step. Her slender fingers in pink gloves tightened around his, making him proud to know that he could protect her. A pink silk skirt appeared as her cloak parted. He saw one shapely high-heeled pink patten over a matching shoe, and caught a glimpse of her slim ankle stockinged in pink. A swirling gust of snowflakes blew her hood back from her long, dark hair, revealing her graceful neck.

She smiled her thanks at him. Simon's heart did a drum roll as the lantern light glistened on her lips.

The other three men had scrambled aside or half to their feet in the confines of the interior, trying to make space for the dark-browed beauty with the enquiring eyes. They fell to their seats like dominoes as she passed through the doorway. The cool smell of snow came with her, sifting like sugar off the folds of her burgundy cloak. A sprinkling fell onto Simon's glossy boots, and he felt the thrill of privilege.

"Do join us, *Mademoiselle*," said Sir Pomeroy Chancet, his throaty voice throbbing with delight. In his early thirties, the Baronet was full of youthful zest as he exclaimed, "What a glorious treat for us!"

Simon winced at that gentleman's overt reception, then said, "Sir Pomeroy, why not let the lady face forward?" He gestured that Sir Pomeroy should vacate his place and sit opposite her.

The obtuse Baronet, however, whisked his purple gauntlets off the seat, twitched his rump sidewise, and with an elegant gesture and an acquired French accent, said, "Of course she shall face forward. A window seat, *Mademoiselle*? 'Tis the most scenic side of the Maidstone-London Road." He grinned widely and patted the place he had hastily contrived for her next to himself. She sank into it with a grateful smile.

Simon, resuming his former place on the backward seat opposite her, heard his brother, Radford, clear his throat in curiosity. The other two men looked from her to him and back. Simon veiled his eyes to hide the fact that he wanted to sit next to her as well as they did. As he watched her dipping dark lashes on which snowflakes lingered, he realized that across from her was by far the best place to be. It would be a rare treat to feast his eyes on her for even a mile.

To think that God had made such a beautiful woman! And all Simon could do was gaze at her for the space of a journey.

Chapter Two

Forbidden Arabelle

Abashed by the attentions of the men shifting about on her behalf, the Honourable Arabelle Lamar tried to relax against the tufted grey squabs behind her shoulder blades. She said, "I want to thank you gentlemen. You are the kindest strangers I could ever hope to meet." Self-consciousness then overtook her for saying so much, especially against her mother's orders.

"We are? How positively gratifying to hear that," said the startling Sir Pomeroy at her side. His rouged lips moved enthusiastically as he continued, "I must declare that we are simply transported to have you!" He had the oddest combination of lively brown eyes under lazy eyelids. He amended saucily, "Have you join us, I mean."

From the other side of him, a man laughed softly, then chided, "Tut, tut, Sir Pomeroy!"

He retorted, "No scolding me for the enthusiasm we all feel. I am much the most expressive of you lot, so I am sure I but divulge with candour the palpitations of us all."

Arabelle laughed.

If sounds through the nostrils counted as laughter, then all the men laughed with her. The expression of mirth through the nose came from a serious-looking, thin man in her diagonal corner. He quickly returned to his sketching, but she could not see what his subject was.

To her left, she eyed Sir Pomeroy and marveled at his pale lavender wig with three neat curls up each side and a purple satin bag holding the queue at his nape. Frothing at his neck was an expensive lace cravat. His purple embroidered coat had a long matching waistcoat and knee breeches, and his purple cape was lined in sheepskin. Golden *fleurs-de-lis* embellished his purple gauntlets and a black patch in the shape of a crescent moon graced the corner of his eye. Arabelle had never beheld such a decorated man. She felt that her eyes were opening to what Aunt Claracilla called The World.

Arabelle did not know many young, single men besides the minor gentry, merchants' apprentices, farmers, and tenants who attended church on Sundays, and who spoke to her or doffed their caps at every opportunity. She knew more about middle-aged and elderly men such as her father, Lord Bastwicke, who occasionally visited her, and her beloved Uncle Trent, Lord Shepley, in whose home she had lived for eleven years. Most of Uncle Trent's visitors were married men, or older widowers and bachelors who provided no fuel for her romantic imaginings. At the country parties she had attended when she lived with her uncle and aunt, young neighbour men were only there as occasional country dance partners, participants in parlour games, and fellow singers at the pianoforte.

Uncle Trent and Aunt Claracilla had closely protected Arabelle, for that had been Lord Bastwicke's main request when he relinquished her and Genevieve to their care. While the girls lived with them at Fawnlake Hall, Uncle Trent and Aunt Claracilla were to forbid any entanglements with men who might form designs upon them. Arabelle and Genevieve must be strictly reserved for high society marriages. Arabelle's marriage now loomed before her in this move to London; in fact, it was The Reason for it. Lord and Lady Bastwicke would determine who was right for her after they introduced her into the highest realm of Society.

Therefore, Arabelle had had little opportunity to know any gentlemen outside her family's approved circle. She grew curious about the man beyond Sir Pomeroy who had just rebuked him. He was a good-looking man with light laugh lines at the corners of his dark-lashed eyes. He wore his chestnut brown hair pulled back into a club as simple as the military man's was. The style was unpretentious and masculine on both of them. The simplicity of it featured their high cheekbones and straight noses. "Welcome," he said to her, bowing his head.

She bowed and smiled in return. She saw in his smiling blue eyes a further resemblance to the soldier whose gaze she kept avoiding. While he had a heart-stopping effect on her, this second version was easier to face. His suit was not military, but smartly cut of dark green wool with *Alençon* point lace forming his cravat and wrist ruffles.

As she heard the guard outside rumbling things in the boot, she felt a sudden panic. Would Madam never come? Would she not be furious if the stage left without her, conveying Arabelle to London in a coach full of men?

Across from Arabelle, the glossy boots moved, causing her to look at him. "I shall make bold to introduce myself," he said, his black eyebrows lifting for her permission.

She remembered that this was strictly forbidden, but there was no way she could deny him. Besides, she very much wanted to know his name. Bravely, she looked him in the eyes and smiled.

He put his hand on his heart. "I am Simon Laurence. At your service." He sounded as though he meant it.

Simon Laurence. What a name to roll over her tongue in private moments. She bowed her head in respectful acknowledgement, and her heart beat fast.

At the silence that fell, she realized that the men were all looking at her. What now? It was her turn, but her mother had warned her fiercely not to introduce herself.

"I am Radford Laurence, Simon's elder brother," spoke the gentleman with the chestnut hair, tactfully filling the breach.

"Not wanting to be outdone, I am Sir Pomeroy Chancet, Baronet," added the man in purple. "No brother to those two, let me assure you. That man shooting looks at you from his corner is my tailor, Mr. Dupper. We returned from France via Dover two days ago. He made me look superb at Versailles. None of these old rags for the Marquise de Pompadour." He eyed Arabelle coyly while he gave a shake of the elegant *Point de France* lace at his wrist.

Arabelle's lips twitched. Unable to stop herself, she said, "Your appearance in that illustrious gathering must have drawn general applause."

The Laurence men laughed, and Simon met Arabelle's fleeting glance with a twinkle of admiration.

"Why, *thank* you! What an angel!" crowed Sir Pomeroy, glancing at the other men with pride.

Mr. Dupper industriously measured with a ruler on the topmost of his sheaf of papers. Arabelle could see that his project was a knee-length waistcoat on which he busily drew buttons at perfect intervals. He counted with silently moving lips. He drew three more circles and whispered, "Thirty!" He looked up, blinked at Arabelle, and said, "Oh, yes, Sir Pomeroy applauded his appearance assiduously and without reserve at Versailles. That is what the Hall of Mirrors is for."

Sir Pomeroy sputtered at him in surprise, while the Laurence brothers roared.

Arabelle laughed, too, but looked kindly at Sir Pomeroy to prevent him from feeling wounded.

"Yes, I am Felix Dupper, Miss," added the tailor with the latent wit. "I am privileged to meet you, I'm sure." He bowed his grey wig at her matter-of-factly. He had a heart-shaped face with almost no chin to behold, but a very broad, lined forehead. Hastily he drew embroidery in scallops down the edge of the buttons. He had a flair with his pencil, she could see that.

Arabelle had now met them all. She was afraid she appeared rude by not introducing herself; but hoped they understood that a single woman did not plunge into acquaintance with a bevy of strange men if she had any pride at all.

To make more room for her seat partners, she squeezed in her collapsible panniers, which held her gown out fashionably at her hips. *False hips*, they were called. *False formality*, she thought, regretting that she could not freely converse with the men. They all interested her; one certainly more than the others. To busy herself under their scrutiny, she unwrapped and pushed hot potatoes she had bought from the innkeeper's wife into the pockets of her fur muff.

The guard with the horn passed the window, peering at the wheels and axles, preparing for departure.

Arabelle, in earnest worry now, asked Simon Laurence, "Do you, by any chance, see two trunks sticking out of a snow bank?"

His searching looks through all the windows followed by his lazy smile were well worth her query. "None yet, Miss." His eyes alerted. "Is that what our coachman threatened?"

She nodded ruefully.

"How dare he! I will punish the scoundrel." He gripped his elaborate smallsword and made as if to lunge out after him.

A delighted laugh escaped Arabelle, and the look he gave her was nigh on a wink. He asked Radford Laurence to open the door and call the guard. When the man appeared, Simon Laurence asked, "Did you take on two extra trunks?"

"I did, Sir. I cannot get the boot quite shut. I had to strap it. That be the reason for the delay, Sir."

"Good man. Handle that baggage with care."

Arabelle saw that the form of her mother finally appeared through the white slanting snowfall.

From kitty-corner came a heart-felt groan. "Another one?" Mr. Dupper cleared a spot on the clouded window and leveled his quizzing glass. "I don't believe what I see! Yonder woman still wears an infernal farthingale!" His eyes protruded in extreme disgust. He gestured over Arabelle. "Why, even you, Miss, sport panniers—hen's baskets—but *that* one! She comes sweeping upon us like a gargantuan broom."

Sir Pomeroy threw back his head and screeched up and down the scale with laughter.

Mr. Dupper put his forehead to his hands and moaned, "Women! Think they would use the heads the Lord gave 'em for somewhat other than such ludicrous—"

"Hush, man!" warned Radford Laurence. "She is arrived." He pushed the door wide to admit Viscountess Bastwicke.

The extremely thin, bronze-cloaked woman gripped his proffered hand with her orange glove, and, in gaining the step, nearly pulled him out of his seat. In a high pitch, she observed, "Daughter, I see you have found us accommodation." She regarded Radford Laurence down her pointed nose and released his hand. "What an insufferable coachman! He knew I must get to London tonight. I told him often, and with emphasis. It was not until he learned I am a Viscountess that he—botheration!" she exclaimed, red-faced with exertion. "These stage coach doors are so diminutive! Much narrower than what I am accustomed to." She heaved sideways, this angle and that until her orange gown, flat at front and back, but with an immensely wide shelf beneath her elbows, burst at last through the portal and past the men's knees with creaks of protest.

Arabelle had suggested that her mother give up her wide court farthingale, which made her hip line eight feet across, for everyday wear. Believing she conceded to fashion, Lady Bastwicke had taken one that was six feet. Then Arabelle had urged her to adopt the new mode of smaller, collapsible panniers that ladies now lifted to pass through tight spots as Arabelle and the new generation wore. But Lady Bastwicke was not about to take any more advice from a daughter. Her magnificent wide skirts rendered her noticeable, and gave her such a sense of power by causing people to back away or jump aside for her wherever she went, that she would likely wear them to her deathbed.

Of necessity, the men had half-risen again. Simon Laurence stood tallest, the shoulders of his greatcoat brushing the ceiling, his white head bent. Arabelle admired how his wig was so well made that no hairline showed at all. No powder sprinkled from it, either. She saw a midnight blue solitaire in the black ribbon that tied his queue. All the details of his military accoutrements showed care and precision. She sincerely hoped her mother was not delaying his arrival at Woolwich.

When the Viscountess finally maneuvered her snow-dusted grandeur inside, she aimed her derrière into the vacant spot between the offended tailor and their benefactor. The men ended up in the corners as far as it was possible to be without their heads out the windows, and her gown still covered their laps.

Mr. Dupper's face mottled in fury as he struggled in vain against the burden of her snowy bulk banking down and scattering his patterns onto the wet floor. Arabelle warred between sympathy and mirth as he and Radford Laurence retrieved them. She caught Simon Laurence's eyes gleaming at her as if to ask, *Do you find this a ridiculous sight?*

The door wrenched open and more snow swirled in. "What in thunder?" the coachman bellowed, making Arabelle jump. Under his icy outcrop of eyebrows, his eyes bulged enormously, for there preened Lady Bastwicke, settled between the soldier and the tailor, taking her half from the middle in a majestic manner.

Arabelle knew she must halt any further altercation between them. She reached into her pocket and offered the coachman the coins clinking in her hand. "I will pay you now, Sir. How much is our fare?"

Noisily fuming and wheezing at Lady Bastwicke's perfidy, he craned his bundled bulk round to look at Arabelle. Too overcome with wrath at her mother to even speak, he waved Arabelle's money off. "Nothing from you, Miss."

Ignoring her mother's beetling stare, she appealed to Simon Laurence. "Will you please tell me the price of the fare?"

"You need not pay a thing, Miss. I already divided the cost amongst us men. This coach is paid for."

"Oh, you are too good! Nonetheless, I must pay a little something for us as well." She pressed her money into the coachman's damp glove. "Here," she said. "Thank you extremely. You are very understanding to take us up."

With a gruff voice but softened eyes, he capitulated. "Just as long as the one who hired this coach is agreeable."

Simon Laurence lifted an eyebrow and murmured, "Most agreeable."

Still seething at Lady Bastwicke's defiance of him, the coachman threw her his parting shot. "But my cattle don't need the extra weight!"

The Viscountess drew herself up, filling with histrionics. Her mouth opened as the door clanked shut. She leaned and hissed a whisper at Arabelle, though everyone could hear, "Why on earth did you give him so much? He was an extremely offensive oaf!"

Simon Laurence said smoothly, "Because she is wise."

"Excuse me?" Lady Bastwicke attacked him with a querulous ring.

"There are few drivers who would risk driving us to London in this weather." To Arabelle, he said with approval, "Your extra payment will stand as a well-deserved gratuity."

Clearing her throat in warning, Lady Bastwicke regained his attention from her daughter. Endeavouring to stare him down, she enunciated, "My daughter is forbidden to converse with strangers."

Arabelle felt hot abashment flood over her.

"Please pardon me," he returned with utmost gentleness. How noble he was to counteract her mother's offense with such forgiveness, Arabelle thought.

From the driver's box, the coachman bellowed, "Sit tight!" The guard blasted eight lively notes on his horn. Arabelle could just see grooms whipping the loincloths off the leaders first, then off of the other horses. The guard vaulted to his seat next to the coachman while a groom stepped on behind. The team bolted forward, and snow squeaked under the large wheels as the coach joggled laboriously into the road, bumping its occupants together.

Sir Pomeroy Chancet produced a mint-smelling paper, which he unrolled and held to Arabelle's notice in what seemed to be gleeful disobedience of Lady Bastwicke's rule. "Will you accept of a peppermint stick?" he whispered to Arabelle jauntily.

She would have taken it because it would have been unthinkable not to when offered so charitably, but Lady Bastwicke shook her head emphatically. "*No*, thenk you!" The tight-mouthed frown she gave each man in turn made it abundantly clear that they were not to accost her daughter in any way.

Yet, had Lady Bastwicke but noticed, Simon Laurence communed with Arabelle in many ways throughout the journey. Now he excused himself to the Viscountess, and, with deft movements, doffed his double caped greatcoat. He was warmed, no doubt, by her velvet cloak and quilted mohair gown. Removal of his coat revealed a well-fitting uniform. His lace jabot fell over a dark blue *justacorps* that contrasted with a white waistcoat and breeches. What well-shaped muscles he had above his long black boots. He was obviously a physically active man. A silver-corded baldric that slashed across his chest held his sword. Arabelle put up her hand to ward off the ornate silver scabbard, but it did not swing any closer. He had every movement well under control despite the jostling of the carriage. After he reseated himself beneath her mother's suffocating finery, he positioned his etched sword upright, and Arabelle felt his boot touch her shoe.

She wondered if he could have avoided it. By the look of his innocently downcast eyelids, she knew he could have.

Instantly she chastised herself. Surely she was wrong. Must she be so charged with awareness of him that even the contact of his boot on her shoe spelled high drama?

Settled once more, Arabelle's unsettler withdrew a book from his coat and adjusted his white cravat ends within his waistcoat. As he opened his volume, he lifted his eyelids lazily and smiled at her.

Arabelle could scarcely breathe because he was so attractive and daring. She dropped her gaze for fear he would see evidence of the thrill that infused her. When she looked up, her mother had turned a suspicious stare upon him.

His fixed his attention studiously upon his book. His dramatic black brows rose at pyramid angles and feathered out. Arabelle thought he looked independent, genteel, and what else? Intelligent, in control, and secretly mischievous. It made her wonder what life with such a man would be like.

Lady Bastwicke presently grew bored, and broke her own rule without compunction. "Witness my predicament," she said to Radford Laurence, interrupting the men's discussion about the snowfall. Smoothing her pale red chignon with its jet beads clinking from hanging ribbons under her black lace cap, she informed them, "We were forced to leave our comfortable coach to take this common stage, all because no one had cleared the approach to Fawnlake Hall, my brother-in-law's estate." Contemptuously, she sniffed. "I assure you that such is never the case at our estate."

If only she would keep quiet, thought Arabelle.

"I see." Radford Laurence nodded to her, rubbed his thin-gloved hands rapidly together, and blew on them.

Arabelle fumbled inside her muff and offered him one of her hot wrapped potatoes.

"Ah! That is most generous of you, Miss, but I cannot take it from you. Surely you need it yourself."

Despite her mother's eye-popping glare, Arabelle pressed the potato into his hand and said, "Please take it. I have more, and I am perfectly warm with one in my muff." Then followed the embarrassment of accepting his gratitude. He really was very nice.

Though Madam kicked her, Arabelle daringly asked, "Would anyone else like this one? I do not need so many." She could not make herself look at Simon Laurence.

"Daughter!" snapped her mother, trying to silence her.

Sir Pomeroy leaned against Arabelle's shoulder and looked at the potato in its small cotton blanket. "I would be so very, completely honoured, dear lady," he crooned, "to take this warm little potato from you." He tenderly took it from her hand. "Such welcome warmth," he added meaningfully, his pupils wide in his dark brown eyes so near to hers.

Lady Bastwicke looked daggers first at her scandalous daughter and then at Sir Pomeroy. He and Lady Bastwicke had not been introduced. Arabelle wondered how her mother's behaviour to him would change if she but knew he sported a title. Arabelle could not make it known to her because Madam herself had strictly warned her against introductions.

The coach horses pulled the wheels through the silent, snowy world of drifts and overhanging branches from which snow dislodged and fell down the windows. While the others occasionally conversed, Simon Laurence's glances not only spoke to Arabelle but also appeared to discern things about her. What did he see? Could he tell she was fresh as a gooseberry and on her way to London for her social début? Had he discerned that her mother was carting her thither to display her in the elite marriage market? She vowed not to tangle with his speculative looks again, for those facts humiliated her.

She could not keep from looking at him for long. When a wheel lurched into a puddle of broken ice and everyone jounced onto his neighbour, Lady Bastwicke's elbow cut him in the side. Arabelle noted how quickly he repressed his grimace of pain. His smile forgave the Viscountess though she did not ask. Lady Bastwicke tittered in a silly way as she lifted her ear from his shoulder.

Arabelle silently groaned at the impression her mother was making. The tailor actually rolled his eyes for Radford Laurence's benefit, and that gentleman retired, grinning, behind his newspaper. Sir Pomeroy gave a guffaw and as quickly repressed it, his eye crinkling up as he eyed Arabelle sidewise to see what she thought. Avoiding that trap, her eyes roved back to Simon Laurence.

A surprising dimple played in an odd spot in his cheek when he lowered his head to resume his reading. Arabelle could hardly wait to describe him to her sister, Genevieve. But how could she, in mere words, do him justice? She studied the sculpted lines of his face, the defined cheekbones, and the handsome jaw. She could run her eyes over him forever and continue to receive pleasure. But she would not have forever—only this trip to London.

He caught her looking at him. Her admiration must have been apparent, for he appeared slightly abashed but pleased—almost as if she had told him to his face that he was glorious enough to slay any woman. Hotly, she turned her attention to the window, but that was futile, for snow flurries whirled against the glass and left little to view but the dark bulk of a passing horse and rider. Within minutes, the air cleared considerably, and she fixed her eyes on the sight of Lullingstone Castle with snow-laden roofs on the left. Soon the churning wheels rumbled over a bridge, whereupon Crockenhill Castle hove into view on the right.

"Did you drop this, Viscountess?" Simon Laurence inquired. He offered a folded missive to Lady Bastwicke after a particularly nasty series of ruts.

Arabelle's heart jumped. The thrice folded ivory paper had *Arabelle Lamar* flourished across it in black ink.

Her mother snatched it up. "Ah! Mercy me, did that leave my possession? One of so many letters." She thrust back her cloak and felt through the slit in her orange petticoat to the pocket that hung suspended inside her bentwood farthingale. "How appalling. This letter did work its way out." With a glance over the military man's face and uniform, she simpered, "Thenk you."

He bowed his head and looked away.

Arabelle marveled. How *did* he keep a straight face?

With a showy flip of her arm, the vainglorious woman next to him handed the letter to her beautiful daughter.

So, thought Simon, having read the inscription, *her name is Arabelle Lamar.*

"A footman gave it to me while you were tipping Lady Shepley's servants," said the mother, as if to point out to them that she was of the tipping-servants class.

Simon saw Arabelle Lamar's natural blush deepen to a rosier pink. He was gratified to note such sensibility in her. It was clear that she wished her mother would not air her affairs to them all.

A yearning coursed through him as he watched the beauty's long, dark lashes drop. *Arabelle Lamar,* he said silently, *if I could, I would make all of your affairs . . . mine.*

Her angelic presence would waft through his memory for the rest of his days. Thinking of London, he turned to the window with a bitter sigh and an anguished question: *Why, dear God, did I finally meet her now?—when it is too late?*

Chapter Three

To Corrupt the Innocent

With a hot flush creeping up her cheeks, Arabelle gave attention to her letter. The wine red wax seal bore Lady Shepley's candelabrum crest surrounded by the words, *Walk in the light as He is in the light.* It seemed a long time since Arabelle had lived in that blessed household, but it was, in fact, five months. How different her life was now that she was under her mother's jurisdiction.

Aunt Claracilla and Uncle Trent had taught Arabelle and her sister, Genevieve, to pray for the love of Jesus toward their fellow creatures—not only toward the people they liked, but also toward their enemies. Being taught from the Word, the girls had enjoyed a secure and happy life with Trent and Claracilla, Lord and Lady Shepley, who loved them. It was the worst day of their lives when they had to leave them.

Arabelle's father, Lord Bastwicke, had come to fetch her and Genevieve home to his Kent estate. To go with him was not the bad part because they esteemed him. He had visited them several times a year when they lived with his sister, Claracilla. But, three months after they left Aunt Claracilla, they heard that she lost her voice to a debilitating disease.

Following that tragedy, which Arabelle and Genevieve felt like arrows to their tender hearts, Viscountess Bastwicke, their real mother, breezed back into their lives like a perfumed cyclone. Arriving from the Continent, where she had gallivanted for years between trips to London, she tried to take up her old spot as their active mother. Instantly, she threw them into emotional chaos.

After a series of inquisitions in the drawing room the sennight after her arrival, she took them back to Fawnlake Hall to visit Aunt Claracilla. It became apparent that Lady Bastwicke wanted them to see the aunt they had been "torn away from none too soon," as she sarcastically phrased it.

"See?" she crowed as Arabelle helped Genevieve climb tearfully into the coach for the return to Bastwicke Chase. "That woman, whom you wish you still lived with, is a nothing! She is now dumb. She cannot say a word, not a single word! I almost wish this had happened to her years ago, considering all the damage she has done to both of you. Stop that horrific blubbering, Genevieve! We are coming to the village. Do not let anyone see you in tears! They will think I am maltreating you." Whereupon she pasted a queenly smile on her vermilion lips, and her coach wheeled slowly, as instructed, through the High Street so that all could admire the Viscountess of Bastwicke, who had returned to grace their environs.

Jostling along in the dim coach toward London now, Arabelle missed Aunt Claracilla with a pang as she began to read her flowing words on the creamy paper.

Fawnlake Hall
January 22, 1752

My dearest Arabelle,

How heart-moving it was to see you, my precious niece! I am so glad you came so late that your mother agreed to spend the night here. If only I could have spoken. Never, since I lost the use of my voice, have I wanted it more than today. This is why I stay up to write to you.

These past five months without you have been difficult in the extreme, for, after keeping you as my own for eleven years, I feel such a loss at having you and Genevieve gone. Your Uncle Trent feels the same. We concede that you are your mother's and father's, but we will always keep shrines for you in our hearts.

Since you are off into the world, a place replete with every kind of vice, give me leave to offer you instruction with regard to your conduct in London. You will move in high society, where your personal charms and endowments of mind will attract many admirers . . .

It seemed as if the occupants of the coach held their collective breath, wondering what her letter said.

Radford Laurence leaned forward and glanced at her face.

Sir Pomeroy's peppermint breath breezed onto her now and then as he sang a little love ditty to the dry amusement of the other men.

Eyeing him, Lady Bastwicke looked exceedingly irked, but could not find how to rebuke the man for singing.

The tailor rigidly endured every jolt from his corner, with her bulky gown smothering his designs and preventing his industry. He stared woodenly at Arabelle's missive.

Who knew what Simon Laurence did, for Arabelle could not look at him. Suddenly she felt too hot to bear sitting so any longer. She undid the silk cords of her fur-lined cloak to let blessed air flow onto her neck.

Sir Pomeroy left off singing in mid-stanza.

Arabelle quirked an eye at him to discover why, and saw that his rouged lips hung loose as his eyes widened upon her fashionably low, square neckline. Simon Laurence looked upon her and appeared to be undergoing an avid sensation. If that were not enough, the insistent stab of her mother's eyes told her she had made a big mistake.

Arabelle readjusted her cloak so the fur again prickled her bosom. Feeling hotter than ever and not daring to look at anyone, she returned, discomposed, to her reading. *Every moment I spent with you, listening to you and watching your combined good sense, sweetness, and beauty, I admired you so much that I know everyone else will, too. But where men are concerned, I heard a warning bell within my head.*

One of the huge wooden wheels jerked so violently into a hole and up again that the tailor, the Viscountess, and Simon Laurence pitched up out of their seats.

With no warning, Arabelle felt the unaccustomed weight of a man—Simon Laurence!—catapulted onto her, one of his hands unavoidably landing on her shoulder. While everyone else made noises in the chaos, his cheek slid across hers. His silky hair grazed her forehead as he caught himself with his other palm on the squabs behind her. Pinned by him in such a heavenly way, Arabelle locked eyes with his blue ones. For that instant, they were so close that she could have counted his eyelashes. His breath upon her face and his hand cupping her shoulder would resurrect dreams of him for the rest of her days. She realized later that she sighed in bliss.

Seeming very pleased by that, he backed himself slowly, slowly off her knees. "I am sorry!" he said aloud. Lowering himself to whisper in her ear as he adjusted himself, he added, "Truly, I'm no such thing."

Her eyes lifted to his in delicious shock.

The rest of the passengers disentangled themselves with grunts, exclamations, and apologies. Mr. Dupper was beside himself with intense perturbation, for Lady Bastwicke had wrought further havoc, ripping two of his designs with her heels. She had apparently knocked noses with Sir Pomeroy, for he was rubbing his while tears watered his eyes. She screeched recriminations at him, and pushed upon his lavender knee breeches, fighting to regain her seat and her dignity.

Arabelle wondered what Madam her mother would say if she knew he was a Baronet. She would never use him so roughly. If she changed her behaviour toward him upon such a pronouncement, it would be too ludicrous to bear. The Viscountess categorically assumed that these were all common men since they were using the stage instead of private carriages.

"Well, fie!" she expelled when her dress again battened down her neighbours, "I told you your coachman is an infidel. How shall I ever survive this trip? I wish it were well over."

Not I, thought Arabelle. She wanted it never to end. If only her mother were not here. She must not waste precious time over that regret when she could enjoy the unusual pleasures of the journey.

It was uncanny, but she still felt Simon Laurence's grip on her shoulder after he sat down. She felt that they lived in a secret realm, though squashed against the other passengers. She ached because the tantalizing Simon Laurence was destined as a memory, for this coach ride had to end tonight in London. There, her parents would present her to the high-ranking men and women they would allow her to know. That circle would not include this mysterious man with his wealth of compelling qualities—oh, no. Any man to whom her parents attached her must have a title and very heavy coffers.

Grateful that she had something to do besides face the glances of the four men and the disapproving glares of her mother, Arabelle returned to her letter. *Where men are concerned,* she reread, *I heard a warning bell within my head.* Aunt Claracilla had told her to beware of the snares of men. Of what could those snares consist?

Your large fortune worries me, for it will attract far more admirers than you need or want. Your arduous business, dear girl, will be to distinguish the one type of suitor from the other, and make a due difference between him who makes love to your person and he whose affection is centered solely on your marriage portion.

Arabelle gathered, from reading novels and from chats with her aunt, that a man who *made love* to a lady could do it most ardently through a motivator called *lust.* That, she gathered, was not necessarily the same as love. How she longed to ask Aunt Claracilla to explain the difference. She could never imagine asking her mother about such things.

In their transactions with each other, some men keep up an appearance of integrity, while with regard to us, under cover of gallantry and charm, they put into practice every stratagem and deceit they can conjure up to corrupt the innocent and betray the unwary.

They do? Arabelle's mind reeled. She could not believe it of Uncle Trent or her father, but this Sir Pomeroy Chancet, with his provocative eyes and effusive flattery . . . well, it was just possible. Even now, he was trying to read her letter. She angled it away from him, toward the light from the window.

She could not imagine the Laurence men doing anything of the sort, however. Radford was reading his newspaper, neatly folded to two columns. His face looked so noble, serious, and responsible that she felt he was a respectable man of the highest order.

Simon, with his head leaned back, his eyes closed as if taking a rest, looked quite loaded with good characteristics. What's more, they culminated in his attractive expressions and in the confident, easy way he held himself. He caught her admiring him, for she saw a narrow gleam of humour between his double fence of lashes. His odd dimple played for an instant.

Her pulses pounded at her temples, and she hastened to read on. *Beware, and God bless you, Arabelle.* "Buy the truth, and sell it not;

also wisdom, and instruction, and understanding." Proverbs 23:23. Pray for wisdom that God will lead you to that one man He has prepared for you, dearest. Accept no other through spontaneous whims. Be not deceived by anyone.

Your most affectionate
Aunt Claracilla

Arabelle's mind reeled. What a jewel of a missive from her wisest of aunts! Arabelle considered the advice to pray for that *one man*. She must believe that God was even now preparing him for her, and her for him.

Glancing over the closing lines, she wondered if her mother was the *anyone* by whom she should not be deceived. How could she possibly deflect her domineering mother's commands?

Or, did her aunt mean men whom she would want to trust, but whom she should not?

When Arabelle raised her eyes from her letter, Lady Bastwicke's fingers beckoned imperatively, so Arabelle had no choice but to relinquish the letter into her hand.

Chapter Four

The Roar of Rapids

Lady Bastwicke's lips moved and her forehead rose into a washboard of lines as she read the letter. Her lips worked irritably. Likely what irritated her most was that Claracilla presumed to advise *her* daughter. She at last folded up the letter with an incensed huff and, with difficulty, maneuvered it into the pocket hanging inside her farthingale.

As Arabelle watched it disappear, so did Simon Laurence. He raised an eyebrow at Arabelle and cleared his throat into his fist. She wondered if he had seen any of the words. It was possible because her mother had held it out far in front of her in order to focus on it. He was too much of a gentleman to have spied, but he may have seen the gist of Aunt Claracilla's warnings. Tonight in Bloomsbury Square, Arabelle would tell her seventeen-year-old sister all about this magnetic man whose eyes gleamed at her one minute, and showed his understanding nature the next.

Earlier in the week, Genevieve and the infants, Lenora and Jerome, had left for London with the servants whom Lady Bastwicke sent ahead to prepare for her arrival. Genevieve, who had pitied Arabelle's having to stay and travel with their mother, could never have imagined what kind of a journey Arabelle would make.

After they left Bastwicke Chase yesterday, Arabelle had fretted for some time how to ask her mother to stop and spend an hour or two at Aunt Claracilla's home. Arabelle and Genevieve had made her a small unicorn tapestry with a japanned frame for her birthday, and Arabelle had wrapped it to deliver on their way. Her mother could not rightly refuse when she produced the package as the gates of Fawnlake Hall loomed ahead.

Lady Bastwicke had displayed annoyance as she viewed the intense devotion between her daughter and Claracilla. There were kisses and tears upon parting. With a full heart, Arabelle had hugged the dearest woman in all the world and blurted out, "Will you please come to us in London?"

At sight of her mother's broiling face, Arabelle knew it had been the wrong thing to ask. Aunt Claracilla had shot her a heart-tugging look of regret. Now if Arabelle could get the letter back from her mother, Aunt Claracilla would, in a sense, go with her to London. She needed her aunt's wisdom and counsel as never before. She needed to reread what she had warned her about men. Because her mother's ideas and advice were feckless, reckless, and worldly compared to her aunt's, Arabelle feared what lay ahead. She felt like an oar-less rowboat beginning to spin in a plummeting current with the roar of rapids ahead.

The coach jostled on, the blizzard ceased, and a slant of sunlight cast purple shadows onto the soft world of snow. It lasted for the half hour before sunset. While her mother looked the other way, Arabelle lifted her eyebrows at Simon Laurence and glanced toward the warm colours painting the sky.

His face lit with appreciation. He looked out and expelled, "I declare, this is the most beautiful sight." He flashed a white smile pointedly over Arabelle. He took her breath away.

Radford Laurence and Sir Pomeroy, looking from the vivid sunset to Arabelle, agreed.

Lady Bastwicke, shading her eyes from the directness of it, complained, "It's too bright."

Simon, his dark blue eyes gleaming with highlights in the shadow of his corner, said, "The brightness of the view is a glad sight after winter's gloom."

Radford added, "Especially when you have lived in dismal darkness for so long."

"True," returned Simon, looking at his brother. Arabelle detected that they shared deeper meanings, and she longed to know what they were.

When Simon raised a blue book, the faded gold letters gleamed enough for her to make out: *Rules and Orders for the Royal . . .* something, which she could not see because his fingers covered the words, then *Directions for Teaching the Theory and Practice.* He inserted that volume into his haversack and opened a red book. He read for a minute, and then lifted faraway glances to the window. He did this so often that Arabelle knew he was committing passages to memory. Sometimes he looked tickled by something, and his merry eyes met hers.

After Lady Bastwicke gave him and his book a few blatant stares, he asked her genially, "Would you care to read a play, Your Ladyship?"

"What play is it?" she asked, snatching it and looking at the title. "Why, it is Molière's *A Would-Be Gentleman!*" she crowed, looking Simon Laurence up and down, coquettishly assessing him. "I read this before, but it is a good one, so yes, I shall indulge as long as the light holds." She found the first page, held the book at arm's length, and soon her lips were moving, for she could rarely read with still lips.

Arabelle wondered if he had been memorizing lines from the play for a reason: for a performance. It certainly seemed so; and if so, it was generous of him to give the script to her mother. How she would love to ask him where he would read or perform the play, and what he did in His Majesty's Army. There was no end to the things she would like to know about him.

It would also be interesting to quiz Radford Laurence and the flamboyant Sir Pomeroy. How did they occupy their days? Did they have women in their lives? Did they love?

The very thought in respect to Simon Laurence made her feel a pang. A man the likes of him would surely have women galore flocking after him. He looked so impressive in his midnight blue coat and eggshell waistcoat and breeches. Added to his manly form was that smooth white hair pulled back with such dash, leaving his profile as vital and strong as Caesar's on a Roman coin. He was full of mystery and intriguing qualities, not the least of them his demonstrated kindness and forbearance.

If only her mother were not so iron-willed in her snobbery, Arabelle could have asked him and each of these men in turn about their lives. Lady Bastwicke would only allow Arabelle such discourse when she reached London, and then she would undoubtedly push her into it—but only with the proper men. Would any of them prove as interesting as these appeared to be?

Radford Laurence, snapping his newspaper, said, "The King is patronizing the composer, Handel, more and more of late."

Mr. Dupper, lifting his quizzer on its chain around his neck to read the other side of the newspaper, remarked, "He has lost much of his eyesight, I hear."

Sir Pomeroy tut-tutted over what a tragedy that was, and wondered if Handel would be able to write any more music.

As the miles rolled by, Simon Laurence declined to speculate on that or any other news, though Radford and Sir Pomeroy tried to draw him into conversation. Once he gestured that he would rather not talk across the Viscountess, which Arabelle thought was considerate since her mother's eyes had drooped closed while reading the play. Arabelle reached forward, just as Simon Laurence did, to catch the book that slid from her slackened grasp. He looked glad to snatch the opportunity to hold Arabelle's hand around the book.

She gave a breathless laugh of apology while his eyes caressed her. His intimate regard from those glinting dark eyes caused her to drop one of her gloves on the floor.

He took the book from her, and, with a peep at her sleeping mother, stooped to retrieve Arabelle's glove. Very slyly, he eyed her, then kissed the glove on its way up.

She received it in her naked hand with discomposure. Her heart raced as she molded it back onto her fingers. She would forever keep this glove that he had kissed.

She busied herself by rearranging her velvet cloak over her skirt. When she finally looked at him again in the dimness, she saw his sparkling regard, yes, but something deeper, too. She perceived that he had chosen his moment brilliantly to commit such an act as kissing her glove while sitting next to her dozing mother. Only Radford could have seen it, if indeed he had. When Arabelle glanced at Radford, he smiled at her, but she could not tell what he thought.

Mr. Dupper had closed his eyes in futility. He and Lady Bastwicke were in danger of cuddling their heads together in sleep, for she was leaning his way more with every left turn. Arabelle was very amused at the sight.

Simon Laurence, alerted by her lip-curving mirth, observed the situation and laughed silently with her.

Sir Pomeroy, who had been struggling to polish his silver shoe buckles with his lacy handkerchief all the while, looked up and joined in on the stealthy merriment, even raising his hands as though directing musicians, willing the two to conk heads together. While doing so, he cleverly dropped his handkerchief onto Arabelle's lap. Then he noticed it with surprise, picked it up with thumb and forefinger, and grinned at her suggestively. "Do excuse me, fair one," he whispered. "It was such a temptation to drop onto, and pick up from, your tempting person. It's *Argentan* lace, made in Burano, Italy," he impressed upon her in a whisper.

As Arabelle smiled in appreciation, Lady Bastwicke's head cracked against Mr. Dupper's forehead. She woke with a snort, and he with an enraged curse. She snapped a censorious word at him. He cringed back into his corner, rubbing his lined forehead and muttering with a vengeance.

Radford covered his face with his hat, and Arabelle saw his eyes crinkled in laughter behind it.

"Welcome back, Your Ladyship," said Sir Pomeroy magnanimously.

"Back from where?" she retorted, and pruned her lips together, staring him down.

"Dreamland, was it, Viscountess?" Sir Pomeroy's eyes slid teasingly to Mr. Dupper, who scowled at him from his ignominious prison.

Suddenly clarion notes sounded from the guard's horn, and the coach bumped and swerved.

"Are we slowing?" asked Lady Bastwicke.

"Yes, to change horses, Ma'am," said Simon Laurence. "We are due to halt briefly at a coaching inn in Bromley."

Radford peered ahead. "It looks like the replacements are in readiness for a quick change. I hope I have time to buy a newspaper."

Simon said, "Of course. Let's have refreshments quickly served to the ladies."

"Indeed, yes."

Arabelle smiled appreciatively at each of the Laurence brothers, touched by their care. They smiled back, each with handsome lips and twinkling eyes, causing her to marvel. *My cup runneth over*, she thought. *Truly, this is living!*

"Assist me out," said Lady Bastwicke imperiously to Mr. Dupper, who, aghast, scrambled out and turned grudgingly to hand her down. When she and her gown had finally exploded through the doorway with alarming shrieks of hidden wood, she turned and beckoned Simon Laurence to escort her to the thatch-roofed inn. Simon vaulted gracefully out of the coach to comply.

Two ostlers covered the steaming horses with loincloths while others unhooked them and led them to the stable. They emerged leading fresh horses, and relayed them into their places. Arabelle admired the gleaming-eyed Morgans nickering and tossing their brown heads.

A lamplighter touched a torch to illuminate the courtyard, just in time to highlight one of the coach's occupants to his satisfaction. Sir Pomeroy stood accepting the homage of stares from the people dining at the diamond-paned windows of the candlelit inn. Displayed under the lamp, Sir Pomeroy paused, his black tricorne with glittering braid setting off his lavender wig and purple finery. He said to Arabelle as he received her down from the coach, "How transporting this is! I ask myself, why did I bother to go to France? The rural scenery and the opportunity for exquisite moments prove far better here." He ogled her up and down, and flourished his tasseled walking stick as they walked smilingly, in state, across the snowy flagstones.

The publican swung wide his door for them. His hot fare was a turkey pie and apple tart, hot mead and good, strong tea with plenty of cakes, he said. Arabelle and her mother had a private parlour allotted to them, arranged by the considerate Laurence brothers. The men went to quaff their tankards and take their meat pies in the public room.

When Arabelle and her mother went on to make their hasty ablutions, Lady Bastwicke said, washing her hands in a china bowl, "This episode will be something ridiculous to tell all my friends. I cannot wait for this insupportable ride to be over! You, however, must not mention this to a soul, do you hear?—else you could be ruined. I will not breathe a word that you were with me, and rubbing shoulders, literally!—with common men. I believe the one next to me is an *actor!*"

"Is he not a soldier?" Arabelle asked, but her mother was already passing down the narrow hall with difficulty, trying to uphold her dignity after her gown caused a three-legged table to topple over.

At the clarion call of the coach horn, Radford and Simon met the ladies at the door. Despite the fact that she had just scorned him in words, Lady Bastwicke grasped Simon's arm and simpered up at him.

Radford appeared, behind their backs, to risk his chance, and he smiled at Arabelle invitingly. She put her hand through the crook of his proffered arm, for she liked his courteous manner. She turned her eyes to the grand pair of shoulders before them, and admired the confident way Simon moved in his tall boots, and how his profile looked when he handed her mother up with helpful expediency. She did not know how he did it, but he cleverly aimed the wide gown into the coach with a minimum of trouble.

Under the snowy trees near the courtyard wall, upon whose top several inches of snow gave the look of icing, they all resumed their places in the *Aynscombe Stage.* Mr. Dupper had made a run for the outdoor privy, and was jogging back clutching his three-cornered hat to his head, his skinny knees pumping as the shout of "Coach!" went up.

"This is absolutely outrageous!" exclaimed Radford Laurence when they rolled away onto the dim road. He leaned toward the carriage light outside his window, reading the front page of *The Daily Advertiser.*

"Oh, do please," urged Sir Pomeroy, "read me something outrageous."

"This is no light scandal, Chancet," said Radford severely. "Can you believe it, Simon? Last week, a *third* lady was abducted from a London drawing room!" He shot his brother a look of disbelief.

With a darkling look, Simon expelled, "No! That is terrible! Absolutely horrendous!"

"Another one?" queried Lady Bastwicke.

"What is it all about?" pressed Sir Pomeroy. Arabelle, too, wanted to know.

Lady Bastwicke leaned toward them and effused, "Two daughters of peers were abducted in London—from a salon and a rout party, was it not? Have you not heard?"

"No, Your Ladyship, I have not heard. I have been in France. Tell, tell! It sounds terrible—gruesome!"

"My husband told me that two of his friends in the House of Lords had their loveliest daughters kidnapped! They have not been seen since!"

Radford exclaimed, "Oh *no!* They traced them through Dover and Calais. The information is sketchy, it says, and the King's courtiers have no clue as to the abductor's identity."

Simon said, "They must be found! And the abductors severely punished."

Radford, still reading, said loudly, "They discovered that the heiresses were, and I quote: *sold to foreign princes.*"

"Truly?" shrieked Lady Bastwicke. She covered her mouth in horror.

"Oh no!" breathed Arabelle. "That happened in London Society?"

Sir Pomeroy asked, "And now there's been a third one taken?"

Mr. Dupper asked, "How can this be prevented from happening again?"

Lady Bastwicke lifted her pointed chin and concluded, "One cannot be too careful with one's daughters when one is a peer. I am well aware."

"I heartily agree with you," remarked Simon, frowning from her to Arabelle.

"I would take extra good care of this one," said Sir Pomeroy, patting Arabelle's forearm.

Lady Bastwicke cleared her throat, not knowing what to do with him. Looking around from one man to another, she snapped, "I am doing so! The best way to protect her is to forbid my daughter to have any exposure to men, and forbid all men to even think of setting their sights on her, except for those we approve from the Court circle, closest to the King."

Arabelle was flooded with embarrassment.

Sir Pomeroy said, "Indeed, yes! That is . . . wise of you, Your Ladyship. Although," he added, fingering his chin and frowning, "it seems that since the women were abducted from the highest circles, that could be precisely where the danger lies, don't you think?"

Lady Bastwicke bestowed a fiery glare upon him.

The Baronet shook slightly against Arabelle, and hastily lifted his tricorne hat from his lap to examine the inside. Behind its brim, the two of them, hidden, exchanged looks.

Thereafter, he leaned onto Arabelle as they rounded corners in the twilight. This had happened with more frequency the darker it became. She had to stiffen her elbow into his side to keep him from cuddling right into her waist and staying there.

They reached London two hours after starlight; hours during which her left arm grew sore from fending off one male while her emotions whirled over the presence of the one across from her. She already lamented their imminent parting of the ways.

The *Aynscombe Stage* at last wheeled north on The Borough through Southwark at a slow crawl. Arabelle tried to stretch first one cramped foot out and then the other without being conspicuous. Her mother, peering out the window past Mr. Dupper, did not see and certainly did not hear her small gasp when Arabelle's ankle was suddenly caught fast between two leather boots.

Arabelle widened her eyes upon the possessor of them, but he kept reading with his book turned to catch the lantern's rays. He had captured her, and was enjoying it very much. What an actor he was, for anyone else looking at him would detect nothing at all out of the ordinary.

She dared not move, for to struggle in any way would draw the others' attention and create the most awkward scene. And he knew it. She almost felt like laughing. She could do nothing but leave her trapped leg between Simon Laurence's boots while her heart thundered erratically. He had her; and she felt a mixture of vivid emotions while trapped by this amazing man. Striving for dignity, she lifted her brows and tried to give him a fiercely reproving look. That did not bring her intended effect.

He turned a page, and gave her a gleaming squint between black lashes. With a smooth lift of his hand, he blew her a discreet kiss off his lips.

Arabelle closed her eyes and held her breath. He made her feel so very desirable.

Slip-sliding out of the press of carriages and slush of the busy London thoroughfare, the coach swerved right, and the steaming horses clip-clopped wearily into the first courtyard of the George Inn. There they halted. Soon the grip on her leg must cease. Was she daft? Could she possibly want to stay there like that, with Simon Laurence trapping her close to him so daringly in the dark?

Ostlers came running to the horse's heads. Arabelle glanced out at the old candlelit inn. With black walls and white spindled balconies, it rose to four stories on three sides of the courtyard. Beyond was an archway that led to more stables, as evidenced by the horses emerging. Warm light glowed in many windows all around them, and doors opened and slammed on voices, singing, and activity from various public rooms.

Arabelle felt Simon Laurence loosen his hold on her. She saw the white of his smile in the dimness as he released her.

With a shaky breath, she pulled her foot back under her petticoat. Her cheeks felt hot, and she realized full well that she had been living a clandestine adventure. What glorious moments to recall and savour. She shot surreptitious looks at him, trying to memorize his face. She would welcome more adventures with this imaginative and compelling man, if only it were possible.

The travelers unbent. Mr. Dupper, out first, was obliged to turn and give his hand to Lady Bastwicke; she expected it. He twitched his nose in annoyance as she forced her gown out, first attempting one strategy, then another, until he had to help her by yanking the extremity of her farthingale to get it to pop noisily out of its confines.

Surprisingly, he presented her with a card. "Here is my direction, Ma'am. I sew for discriminating women as well as gentlemen. I make panniers in the newest mode, collapsible for the greatest convenience." With that, he sheered off, leaving the Viscountess staring after him with her mouth ajar.

Radford Laurence made his smiling exit next, saying, "Good-bye, ladies. It has been a pleasure to travel with you."

Arabelle smiled and bowed her head to him.

With a special smile for her, he doffed his hat and went.

The air carried the oddly familiar, sweet scent of hops. Arabelle knew that her father stored and traded his crops at a George Inn in London. Could it be this one?

Sir Pomeroy, after smoothing out his crumpled cape, poked his head back in and, since her mother was not privy to his words, said, "I shall look you up. What is your name, you lovely thing?"

She flushed. "I am forbidden to tell you."

"Forbidden! How piquant that makes you! Nev-er fe-ar," he said in singsong, "I know your father is a Viscount. I shall seek you out." He gave her a perky-eyed leer.

"Good-bye!" she whispered firmly, smiling behind her muff. She could not imagine that he would ever do so, and she did not want to encourage him. Her mind had already reverted away from him as he bowed a handkerchief-flourishing *adieu* and made an elegant leg to her.

Her heart began to pound, for Simon Laurence had slid sidewise on his seat. He hesitated, but saw Lady Bastwicke peering their way, so he kept his eyes on the woman and moved himself out of the coach. Arabelle quickly reached for his dramatic black tricorne hat with its white edging. The rakish black plume tickled her chin. "Oh, Simon Laurence!" she breathed, and held it there, her heart thumping, until he turned back toward her. She dropped it to her lap, watched him adjust his sword scabbard, and looked back over his shoulder. Lady Bastwicke stood not a dozen feet away, but her back was turned as she spoke to someone.

Simon leaned into the coach with a smile, so Arabelle handed him his hat. "Why, thank you." He set it handsomely onto his head, where the plume arced in a dashing curve. Then he enveloped Arabelle's hand in his. She took in the beauty of his speaking eyes for a heart-stopping moment.

"Come . . . forbidden Arabelle." His compelling voice and glistening eyes invited her.

She sighed from the depths of her heart.

In spite of his recent hijinks, he handled her tenderly, guiding her down the round step to the snowy cobblestones. The more views she had of him from different angles in different light, in the piquant situations he contrived, the more of her he claimed. When she heard him say her name, it added an intimate dimension to what she kept collecting as future memories of him. Now his strong supporting hold made her want to stay near him, and let him hold her more. She had never felt such a wish for any man before.

Under the gimlet eye of her mother, she thanked him formally. He bowed to them each in turn.

Arabelle's breast constricted as their ways parted. Why did her mother have to oversee their good-byes? Any minute he would disappear, and in this vast city, she would never see him again. What was the point of living? That thought stuck in her heart, like a monumental truth, as soon as it came.

She saw Simon and Radford talking together. She pretended interest in a latticed shop window near the public room door so she could blink away the tears that stung her eyes. She chided herself for impossible wishes. She did not know Simon Laurence. They had not been allowed a proper introduction, and never would be, because he was but serving in His Majesty's Army, and not a member of the peerage.

Beneath the sign of Saint George in armour slaying a dragon from the back of a wild white horse, the Laurence brothers shared animated words, nodded, and clapped each other on the backs. They must be taking their leave. They seemed to be as close as she and Genevieve were.

Arabelle heard her mother imperiously tell someone to unload her trunks and hire her a post chaise from the premises. Then she side-stepped down through the inn's main door, bidding Arabelle to follow. Maneuvering her gown grandly up a wide, open staircase in the midst of the three-storied black oak interior, Lady Bastwicke turned right up the next flight. She leaned over the rail and asked Arabelle embarrassingly, "Do you have to go?" She pointed upstairs.

"No, Mother. I will wait here." Arabelle blushed; glad that only a serving maid had heard, though the inn was full of noisy people in both directions. Her mother loudly accosted the maid, and ordered her to follow and assist with her gown, never mind her tray of tartlets.

When Lady Bastwicke had disappeared from the square gallery above, Arabelle looked back out through the window. She saw Simon Laurence pointing out his trunk in the boot. After the guard tipped it to the paving stones, Simon strolled toward the door behind which she hid in shadow. He flicked a chain in his waistcoat, pulled out a gold watch, and consulted it close to the lamp. It was obvious that he had some wealth since he owned a watch.

Arabelle snatched at a boy who was passing near her with a pitcher. "Go, please, and tell that uniformed gentleman to come inside for a drink of . . . what is that?"

"Mulled ale, Miss."

"Tell him that it's compliments of the house. Please? Here, I will pay you. But do not tell *him* that!" With a firm look, she stuck a coin into the boy's hand.

He nodded in understanding, set down his pitcher, and dashed outside to tell Simon Laurence he could have free mulled ale if he would but step inside.

What had she done? She could not watch her order carried out. She did not know what to do or where to go. Her heart thumped fast, knowing that she could, in another minute, face him again. Would he suspect her? How mortifying that would be. Madam would be awhile washing up and combing her falling wisps, or so Arabelle devoutly hoped as she eyed the staircase.

The outer door opened, letting in a draft of crisp air. Bowing Simon Laurence inside, the boy said, "I will run to the taproom for glasses, Sir," and cast Arabelle a hazardous wink.

With her face guileless, she turned and lifted her gaze from Simon Laurence's etched sword to the planes of his handsome face. It was now or never.

"Simon Laurence," she said his name shyly, "I wish to thank you with all my heart for your kindness in bringing us to London. I am sorry for all the inconvenience you so patiently . . . suffered." She grinned, meaning her mother's gown all over him, the wood farthingale poking him in the side, and the elbow jabs.

The odd dimple appeared in his cheek and his eyes gleamed with comprehension. He reached out a hand toward her and looked ready to say something when the impish boy glided toward them and triumphantly presented two tankards of ale. Arabelle wished him continents away, and Madam, too, for she heard her high above them, querulously making her way to the landing. Arabelle cared for nothing in the world but to hear what Simon Laurence had to say.

"Let me assure you, Miss Arabelle Lamar, that you were no inconvenience," came his tender voice. Setting the pewter tankards on a shelf, he moved her deftly behind a floral-painted screen and out of sight of the staircase. How thrilling it felt to have him touch her waist and hide her so clandestinely. "Thank you for making this the trip of a lifetime," he said. "God knows my heart needed sunshine, but I never, ever expected any so brilliant; or so beautifying. Thank you!"

With a burst of pleasure, she returned, "You are welcome!"

"I am?" He looked glad and suddenly predatory.

Simon let go of Arabelle Lamar's hand and whipped off his gauntlet. Knowing that he was stealing moments in both of their lives, he reached up and cradled her smooth cheek in his palm. A wave of longing rushed through him. With loving pressure, he gave her a romantic tribute straight from his heart. By the astonished look she gave him, even though her face melted against his hand for an instant, he felt distinctly that she was saying good-bye to him.

Her tremulous eyes locked with his, and he wanted, with every fiber of his being, to plead that they see each other again. She put her hand over his upon her cheek, and squeezed it. He caught his breath at her response, and would have pulled her to him, but the sound of her mother's heels on the wood stairs above forced him to drop his hand from Arabelle's face. He lifted his tankard to her and backed smoothly to a doorway.

Simon Laurence drank his ale to her—intently and silently toasting her. He bestowed a searing look upon her before he ducked through the low door and into the crowded public room.

"Ohhhh!" Arabelle sank weakly against the wall.

Lady Bastwicke hove into view above, dominating the staircase with her melon skirts. Arabelle had never felt more devastated to see her. "We must be home before eight, Arabelle." Her perforating voice galvanized Arabelle to move out from her hiding place behind the screen so Madam would not redouble her volume in searching for her.

As she grandiosely descended, Arabelle had a view of her pinched nostrils and jutting chin. "Ah, there you are, girl. I go to see David Garrick in *The Medley of Lovers* with the Devonshires tonight," she said loftily for everyone's ears on all three floors. "We must be off this instant."

When three men approached the bottom of the stairs, casting admiring looks over Arabelle, Lady Bastwicke added, "How grueling it is to travel without servants! Never will I put up with these emergency arrangements again." She halted on the steps just above her daughter. "I see you bought yourself something to drink. What about me?" She looked offended.

Arabelle reached up and gave her the mulled ale. "This is for you, Madam."

"Oh. Well, give it to me then; I am parched. A-ha!" she said, swiveling to peer through a window, "apparently they have found me what I hope is a decent post chaise." She gulped a few times and plunked down the tankard on the nearest table. "Make haste, girl."

Arabelle did not follow immediately, but lifted her fur-lined hood at a round mirror, which, as she hoped, reflected the public room into which Simon Laurence had gone. She sneaked a long, last look at his handsome white head through the glass. If her mother knew about her emotions, or had seen him caress her face, she would raise the rafters with shrieks and recriminations.

He drew admiring glances from the room full of noisy travelers, not only because of his uniform and dramatic white wig and black brows, but also because of his military bearing. His was a tall figure whose shoulders and well-shaped legs would be the envy of every man Arabelle knew. He could pass for the very cream of the aristocracy—the aristocracy of Arabelle's wishes, at least. Who knew what hideous men actually populated it? She would see for herself all too soon.

At the sound of her mother's annoyed voice, Arabelle tore her gaze away. As she passed the public room doorway, she did not want him to see her now when her face felt about to crumple. Giving a good-bye touch to the screen that had secluded their precious hiding place, she put her soft fur muff to her trembling lips and followed her mother out into the stinging snow.

Chapter Five

Acting on an Impulse

Simon . . . Laurence. Arabelle savoured his name on her silent lips as she lay on lace-edged pillows, her arms thrown up and her long, dark curls spilled across them. The morning sun brightened the pink and yellow silk tester above her, its bishop-sleeved drapes lined in rose and yellow around her, adding to her cheerful thoughts. "What a man!" she breathed.

Next to her, Genevieve drew a waking sigh and yawned.

Arabelle let go the twisted bedpost and pulled down her languid arms, hoping her sister had not heard. Energetically, she kicked off their yellow silk coverlet.

"Don't!" Genevieve snatched for the sheet, yanked it over her shoulder, and snuggled into a tighter ball. In a sleepy voice, she mumbled, "Put the covers back on me; I'm cold." While Arabelle tucked them around her, Genevieve opened an eye and yawned again, then asked, "Who is *What a man?*"

Arabelle had planned to tell her about Simon Laurence, but she had kept him her private treasure for three days. "He is my dream," she said, for that was what he seemed now that she was back to daily reality.

"Too bad," murmured Genevieve sleepily. "It sounded like he was someone special."

"More than special. Now it is time for you to get up, Genevieve." Arabelle patted her sister's apricot-blonde curls, long and tangled below her nightcap. "Do you recall the first thing Madam our mother said to you when we arrived in this house from Kent?"

Genevieve blinked up at her, trying to think. "She said a lot of unpleasant things. Do not remind me."

"But as a result of seeing your ill-fitting gown that night, she made an appointment. She is taking you out early this morning to be fitted for new corset bodices."

Genevieve groaned, and covered her face with her hands.

Arabelle flounced to her knees in her muslin nightdress, faced her sister, and imitated Lady Bastwicke. "Why, Genevieve," she said, flipping her wrist and pointing, palm upward, "you look positively wanton in that flat corset. You are too young to be popping out like that. You look like a peasant."

"Arabelle, I cannot help it!" cried Genevieve. "All my corsets are flat. And Madam pops out of hers on purpose, so why did she have to make a spectacle of me? She humiliated me!"

"She should not have pointed it out in front of the servants. It is such a painful business. I remember."

"I do not want to go for a fitting."

"Since you need new ones, why not?"

Genevieve's hazel eyes snapped in outrage. "A man will have to measure me!"

"Why a man?"

Genevieve propped herself on an elbow and said, "She had a card from a tailor she just met."

Arabelle's eyes alerted. "Could it have been a Mr. Dupper?"

"Yes; Dupper, Dupper, stitch for your supper. She sent him a note yesterday, asking him to come to the house, but he sent one back saying he only sees clients in his own receiving room. So she gave in crabbily, and wrote to say we will appear in his rooms this morning." It amused Arabelle to know that Mr. Dupper had scored one on her mother by achieving her patronage.

Genevieve slid down the side of the high bed to the steps. "I suppose she would not waste a single minute for fear someone might see me in my present state of indecency. I do not understand!

Aunt Claracilla said we are never to let strange men touch us. Do you not remember?"

"Yes, she told us they will always be dying to, and trying to," Arabelle finished with a roll of her eyes.

Genevieve laughed. "So she did!"

"Apparently she knows." Arabelle added thoughtfully, "She is still very lovely."

"So why do *I* have to stand in a room with a couple of tailor's assistants gawking at me, and let some eager-fingered Dupper put a measuring string around my chest?"

Arabelle lifted her shoulders helplessly. "Because Madam our mother will be present, I suppose."

Genevieve screeched, "That makes it acceptable?"

"I do not like it any more than I like a doctor poking and prodding me all over. Just slap Mr. Dupper's hands if he gets too familiar."

"I will!" vowed Genevieve, looking as though she would relish doing that.

"But he didn't look to be a womanizing type to me," murmured Arabelle, recalling his dry appearance and devotion to his task. "But, you never know."

Genevieve, with a sound of exasperation, threw a small book of sonnets at her.

Arabelle unlaced her chemise at the bodice front, drew it over her head, and prepared for her morning bath. She blessed the famous Lord Chesterfield, for he was responsible for her daily ablutions. Since Lady Bastwicke longed to cull a friendship with the celebrated Earl here in London, the whole Bastwicke family now followed his example by bathing their whole bodies nearly every day. To anyone she could, the Viscountess made it universally known that she and her family bathed *à la Chesterfield*. People who heard it for the first time were mightily taken aback. Some warned Lady Bastwicke that it was detrimental to human health, and that they would all suffer for it. Lady Bastwicke merely turned up her pointed nose and pretended to be in His Lordship's inner circle and above their understanding.

Genevieve padded to the window, looked down on Bloomsbury Square, and said woodenly, "When I have children, I will not dump them on someone for eleven years and then take them up again, like old dolls forgotten. I could never expect them to love me after that."

"True. But I know God meant us to have Aunt Claracilla and Uncle Trent."

Genevieve nodded. "I am glad He did that for us, now that I know what our real mother is like."

For that period, it had suited Viscountess Bastwicke to flit about on the fringes of Society, from London to the Continent, and to every country house party to which she could wangle an invitation. Arabelle overheard her aunt and uncle discussing Lady Bastwicke, who was determined to raise herself and her husband into the highest echelon in London: the Court circle. Because it took all her energies to do it, she did not wish to look after encumbrances such as children. "No joys of maternity for her," Uncle Trent had bitterly remarked. Trent and Claracilla were not blessed with children of their own, so the two girls received their undivided adoration.

Despite her social campaign, Lady Bastwicke bore two more children: a girl named Lenora, now five, and two years later, their only son, Jerome. He was the precious heir to the Viscountcy of Bastwicke. The infants began life in the nursery in Bloomsbury Square, and it was not until last spring that Arabelle and Genevieve lived in the same house with them at Bastwicke Chase in Kent.

Their melding as a family came to pass when Daniel Lamar, Lord Bastwicke, returned from his second largest estate in Wales, and put his foot down on his wife's gadding. He told Uncle Trent that he deplored his fragmented family life. He, who had visited Arabelle and Genevieve several times a year, collected them and moved them to Bastwicke Chase. The estate had a fine Tudor mansion with forty tenants and a thousand acres of orchards, cattle, sheep, and hops. Lord Bastwicke planned to settle into country life there, with occasional trips to London. It was past time, he said, to reconstruct his family.

Therefore, he summoned his wife home from Liege, Belgium, where she was gadding at the time. In no uncertain terms, he reminded her that their eldest daughter was nineteen and overdue for her entrance into Society. He wrote his wife to get back where she belonged and to "act like a mother for a change." Aunt Claracilla confided all of this to Arabelle.

A horrendous five months followed. Lady Bastwicke descended on them in a hurricane of society anecdotes, affectations, and plans. She opened twelve trunks of foreign fripperies, and took over the lives of her eldest offspring with a vengeance.

After the first shock of receiving their frivolous mother into their midst, Arabelle and Genevieve daily pined more miserably for Aunt Claracilla. Lady Bastwicke openly deplored everything about her grown-up daughters and their rustic employments. When she caught them pruning filbert trees in the orchard with the head gardener, she gave them such a tongue-lashing about their station in life that they dared not resume any of their pleasant outdoor activities. It seemed that nothing useful they had ever learned at Fawnlake Hall was right in the sight of Madam their mother.

Arabelle had enjoyed a chat with an old tenant farmer over a stone wall one day. Upon her return to the house, she was still chuckling at his joke when she received such a flea in her ear from her falcon-eyed mother that she dared not be friendly in her presence when she met tenants or villagers after that.

With a sigh at those memories, Arabelle yanked the pink velvet bell pull. "Genevieve," she confided, "I need Aunt Claracilla. I feel afraid."

"Of what?" Genevieve looked at her anxiously.

"You know this mystery man I have to marry?"

"No . . . but the one who, hopefully, exists? What about him?"

"I do *not* want to marry him."

Genevieve's bafflement intensified. "Why ever not? You don't even know who he is."

Arabelle endeavoured to explain. "No man can be as exciting as the man—"

As she left off speaking, Genevieve, her face alight with interest, asked, "What man?"

"Of my dreams," Arabelle breathed. Revolving across the carpet as in a dance with half-shut eyes, she relived the moments in the coach when he, catapulted into contact with her, said, *I am sorry!* and then whispered, *Truly, I'm no such thing.* What other man would be so deliciously daring?

"You have much better dreams than I do," observed Genevieve with wonder.

Thinking of her ankle trapped between his boots, and the heart-stopping kiss he blew off his lips in the dark made Arabelle drop her lashes and savour those intimate tributes. And he had removed his gauntlet to caress her face behind that screen . . .

"Arabelle! Tell me what you're thinking!"

A loud *rat-tat* sounded on the door, and in walked the girls' menacing abigail, carrying towels.

Genevieve pointed straight at Arabelle and whispered. "Tell me later! I mean it!"

Three maids staggered in under the weight of two pails of hot water apiece, and splashed them into the two bathtubs behind the embroidered screens. The hour of bathing and toilettes passed with the aid of their dour Scots abigail, Bertha Blumm. Bertha was deemed, by the agency from which Father had hired her, to be of a nature that would keep young ladies safe, and behaving prudently. She was certainly intimidating enough to ward off men, with her red-grey hair scraped back from a ruddy complexion, her small, russet-lashed eyes, and her large frame and jutting jaw. The sisters never discussed anything important in front of the maids, and certainly not in front of Bertha. They had learned that she not only told their mother everything, but that she also added her own negative opinions.

Arabelle kept Simon Laurence a tantalizing secret as she poured dippers of warm water over her shoulders. From behind the other bathing screen, Genevieve kept leaning her head back and throwing her quizzical looks. It was evident she knew that something extraordinary kept transporting Arabelle far beyond the mundane motions of bathing and dressing.

As soon as the maids had garbed her in a clean chemise with a wide, scooped drawstring neckline edged in fine lace, she put out her feet to have her silk aqua stockings rolled up onto her legs. She tied her own pink ribbon garters to her preferred snugness while a maid brought her a linen under-petticoat. Then her oval-ended light blue linen panniers were tied on by ribbons around her waist and at each of the ends of whalebone hoops to bring them each together. To cover that came the outer petticoat with pink ruching across the front where it would show, and over that came an aqua and pink striped *robe ronde* over-gown with sleeves and a wide skirt split in front. Over all, her bosom was laced into a pink faille corset.

With her hair combed and her cheeks rosy, Arabelle hurried up two flights of the airy, oval staircase, her hand on the cherry wood rail. She looked up at the mural of cherubs painted across the dome high above the chandelier. It was airy, and the pale blue walls had been repainted. She saw more paintings from Bastwicke Chase, mostly rural scenes that her father had collected, arranged upon the walls. Was he trying to bring a bit of the countryside that he loved into London?

Veering from the staircase at the second landing, she glided along the oval gallery and into the nursery, calling, "Lenora! Are you here? And where's my big, strong Jerome?"

A naked three-year-old with an embroidered cap on his damp hair ran giggling out of the nursery and threw himself into her arms. She kissed Jerome, and hugged him round his arms and soft bottom. "Mmmm, you smell so good. Did you have a splashy bath? I hope you did not get Fanny all wet."

"Yes, I did. I splashed her hair and cap and nose." He giggled and clung round Arabelle's neck. He let go, and with his blue eyes sparkling into hers, said, "I sailed my red boat. Sailed it over my shins. Then I sank it with my feet." He wriggled down, crying excitedly, "Oh, oh, come see, Arabelle! The kittens' eyes are open!"

Fanny, the nurse, curtseyed from the doorway and beamed fondly at Arabelle, her arms laden with Jerome's change of clothes.

"Clothes on first, Jerome," called Arabelle. Between them, they caught and dressed him by the fire. When they let him loose in a clean shirt and over-dress, Arabelle followed him to the purring white cat on the hearth rug. She was nursing four kittens and blissfully blinking her green eyes. Jerome wanted to detach a kitten in order to show Arabelle its eyes, but she bade him wait a little.

He nodded, saying, "I'll let the kitties finish their tea."

In pranced five-year-old Lenora with her blonde hair looking dark honey-coloured as it clung to her cheeks in wet locks. She squealed at sight of Arabelle, who pulled her onto her lap in the rocking chair. Asking Fanny for a comb, Arabelle worked at Lenora's long tresses until they were free of tangles.

"Are you going to a ball soon, Arabelle?" Lenora inquired, head cocked.

"To many, I expect. I must dance with men I do not know." She made a horrible face.

Jerome, lying on his back on the rug, laughed from his belly. "You look like a gargoyle!"

Lenora said, "But you will like the beautiful men, Arabelle. They will be like princes in my picture book. I saw some of them dressed splendidly downstairs when Madam held a drawing room. Genevieve said they will *love you.*"

Arabelle stopped combing. "Oh? Why?"

Lenora clasped her hands and exclaimed, "Genevieve said you have the fairest face in London. The men will die for you." She flipped up her wet, spiky lashes and questioned with big blue eyes, "Why do they have to die for you?"

"They won't die, silly goose. What else does that imp, Genevieve, say?"

"She says that she is ugly. She sticks her tongue out at the mirror. She says she will never be pretty if she lives to be ninety. I do not think she could be prettier when she's ninety, do you?"

Arabelle giggled. "No. She is growing up, and looks luscious as a peach already. She is anything but ugly."

"Leastwise not as ugly as Fanny," whispered Lenora. "Fanny has maps on her face."

Arabelle clapped her hand over Lenora's mouth. "Who told you that?"

Against Arabelle's hand, Lenora's lips moved. "Madam our mother."

Arabelle frowned and whispered, "That's appalling. What if Fanny walked in and heard you? We should thank God for sparing her from the smallpox. Most people die from it. Her marked face does not matter in the least. She has nursed you and Jerome so well, and you love her dearly, don't you?"

Lenora nodded, shamefaced. Impulsively, she said, "I am sorry. I love Fanny. And I love you, Arabelle."

Jerome, holding a kitten by the stomach, ran and dropped him onto Arabelle's lap. "I love you, too, Arabelle." He grabbed her with fervent little arms.

With her heart full, she picked up the kitten and lifted Jerome carefully onto her panniers and gown. Then she took up Lenora on the other side, and rocked both children, kissing their temples. They brought her more kittens to cuddle, and, with them mewling and clawing over their combined laps, they sang the *Twenty-Third Psalm* together. "The Lord is my shepherd, I shall not want . . ." Jerome, watching her and Lenora's lips, joined in when he remembered the words. "He leadeth me in the paths of righteousness for his name's sake . . ."

Arabelle thanked God for this little sister and brother, and that she could spend time with them. Though she pined for Aunt Claracilla, these little souls were sweet consolation. She would continue to teach them all the good things she had learned. When they sang, "I shall fear no evil," she prayed that she would keep faith that God would sustain her in the unknown London Society, "for thou art with me," was the assurance she clung to.

Lenora had set her thinking of the men who would soon be foisted into her life. *Beautiful men,* she called them. Could any prove as beautiful in any way as Simon Laurence?

Resting her chin on top of Jerome's cap, she alerted when she heard the clip-clop of hoofs and coach wheels start up below the house. She set the children down and moved to look down on the Square with its trees and flagstones, its people, dogs, horses, carriages, and carts. She waved through the leaded pane and blew a kiss at Genevieve's woebegone face looking up from the coach window. The Bastwicke town coach rumbled away, taking the Viscountess and her daughter to Mr. Dupper's establishment. The groom and the guard hopped onto the back perch, their gold and blue coats matching those of the coachman and the pair of outriders. It was important to Lady Bastwicke that all impressions of her family indicated an exalted position. The outriders looked excessive in town, but Lady Bastwicke always employed an equipage, even to travel a few streets away. The outriders' practical tasks were to clear the road for her carriage, and to brandish their swords if any danger threatened Her Ladyship.

Arabelle had succeeded in staying behind. She had assured Madam that she had all the clothing she needed. Although she would liked to have given Genevieve reassurance during such traumatic business as having her blooming figure recognized, Arabelle had something she needed to do. She wanted her mother well out of the way. Despite her palpitations, now was her chance.

It was convenient that her stalwart father had traveled to Bastwicke Chase to listen to the concerns of his tenants and collect the quarterly rents. He had spent the past three days with his family. He had made their games and outings so cheerful, especially on Sunday, when they all, excepting Lady Bastwicke, went to church. Afterward, he bought hot cross buns and chocolate to drink from a familiar street vendor, and they ate them on the ride home.

Lenora and Jerome had climbed all over Father in the coach. He let Lenora pinch his nose while he honked like a goose. When the traffic halted, a Puritan woman walking by stared at Lord Bastwicke with disapproval. Hijinks and pleasure were sins to Puritans, and never more so than on a Sunday. He was in a coach, traveling, but of course, she did not know that they had come from church. One did not undertake journeys on Sundays.

Jerome had giggled, and then grown scared and serious. "Hush, Father! You must be good or else." He pointed at the Puritan woman glaring back at them.

"Or else what?"

Lenora, who knew a great deal, said, "Or else she'll whack off your nose like they did to the stone effigies in the churches."

Lord Bastwicke considered this, crossing his eyes and looking down his nose. "Well, mine could use an inch lopped off. How about if I laugh again?" and he put his window down and leaned back his head and roared heartily toward the Puritan woman's back. Jerome giggled, then hastily covered his mouth, his eyes huge. "No, no, Father! I like your big nose. Keep it on! Keep it on!"

Genevieve critically surveyed it from the side. "Well, it could use a little carving, but we're so used to it huge like a pickle that—"

"That's enough!" roared Lord Bastwicke, pinching Lenora's little nose. "I think I'll pickle yours. Yum, yum."

Arabelle always enjoyed the relaxed times with her father, and it was a rare treat to have the family, minus Lady Bastwicke, together in that cosy way. Arabelle felt security in looking at her father's set chin and remarkable profile. His character was well stamped on his lined forehead, and his bristly black eyebrows gave him distinction. The wig he wore today was of the finest quality, powdered white through the sausage curls at each side, and thick and smooth from crown to pigtail.

He seemed serious after the servants served supper that night. "I feel we are on the brink of change in this family," he remarked, glancing wistfully at Arabelle in the circle of golden candlelight. "It is time to look for the best husband this land can produce." He smiled tenderly. "For you, my dear," he said, passing a hand over her hair, "I doubt that there will be anyone superb enough—in my estimation, at least."

Arabelle's mind instantly saw Simon Laurence. *There* is *someone.* She longed to tell Father about him, but knew that, though he loved her dearly, she could not persuade him to look upon a soldier as a suitable suitor.

"My, my!" Lady Bastwicke said waspishly. "How you do vaunt the girl!"

"Oh, Father," said Arabelle, earnestly looking into his large grey eyes, "it is all so different here in London, with strange people and bewildering ways. I wish you could stay and escort me through my trials."

He sipped his wine and set down the goblet. "Arabelle, my pet, you have no need for concern. Trials, indeed! You will be welcomed everywhere. What is more, you will enjoy yourself at all the drawing rooms and balls. You shall even meet the King, for we intend to present you at Court in a fortnight. Will that not be a stellar day for you, hmmm?"

Lady Bastwicke said, "Aye, the husband-hunt is on." She feigned a yawn. "I shall keep my eyes open for someone. All we need is a title and deep pockets, and Arabelle will be set up right fine. Those are our criteria. It should not be an impossibility." She snapped open her black lace fan and waved it languidly.

Genevieve looked askance at their mother, and then shot a wide-eyed look at Arabelle.

Despair flooded through Arabelle. Visions of foul-breathed old widowers with costly rings on their black-nailed fingers wavered through her mind. She shuddered. Breathing deeply to calm herself, she bowed her head and prayed for deliverance from such a husband. When she looked at Genevieve, she saw her thin fingers clasped tightly together under her linen napkin. Arabelle gave her a loving look, knowing her sister was praying for her, too.

When the family began to ascend the stairs for the night, Arabelle turned and clung to her father.

"How smooth a face," he said, patting her cheek and smiling fondly. "You're such a lovely girl. I shall be proud to launch our first daughter before the eyes of London."

Lady Bastwicke was mounting the stairs ahead of them to where the steps split and doubled back to form an oval. As she came around to face them, Arabelle looked up and saw her mother sneering down at her.

Father had not seen it, and he lifted an amused black eyebrow and boomed, "Everyone will be amazed. Amazed that we could spawn such a stunning and intelligent creature—eh, Lady mine?"

Arabelle glanced covertly up at her mother. The whites of Lady Bastwicke's small eyes had flared. "Daniel! You are highly offensive!"

Her husband tried to retain his jocular vein. "Regina," he called laughingly, "you know I married you for your looks, not your brains, my dear."

"Yes!" she threw back maliciously, "and I disappointed you. I am smarter than you thought."

Genevieve tugged Arabelle's skirt. Arabelle knew what she was thinking, for they had discussed it, shocked by the fact that their mother could not live without constant adulation. Father rarely gave her the kind of compliments she wanted, except when she reminded him. Yet Madam could not stand to listen to compliments about anyone but herself; and this, they had discovered, included her daughters. Instead, she relished any chance to ridicule them. Her complaints ranged from their lack of knowledge of her important friends' names to the girls' habit of being naively truthful when affectation or prevarication were called for. "In French Court circles," she told them, "no lady ever says what she thinks. That is vulgar and utterly boring. You must develop the right way of speaking." When they asked what the right way was, she had snapped impatiently, "Oh, fie! You have *everything* to learn!"

The girls had eyed each other with apprehension.

"You must cultivate wit," she had remarked another day. When they pressed her for details, she never could explain how such wit was to be cultivated. They did not think she had much of it herself.

Arabelle was rarely able to display any free-spirited, natural conversation in front of her mother, for she always felt inhibited. As a result, Lady Bastwicke often faulted her daughters' lack of conversation. She also condemned the girls' habit of confiding in each other. Arabelle and Genevieve treasured their confidences. There was no way their mother could ever succeed in stopping them.

And their education! That remained a sore point. At Fawnlake Hall, Arabelle and Genevieve had studied diligently with Uncle Trent, who knew chronology, history, geography, Latin, and agriculture. Aunt Claracilla taught them to read English and some French, to memorize from the Bible, to paint in watercolours, and to write a beautiful hand. She schooled them in lace making, embroidery, country dancing, singing, and playing the harp and pianoforte.

Lady Bastwicke thereafter warned, "You girls must hide what you know from books, or no man will ever offer to marry you. No one in her right mind would have taught girls history, geography, and all that mathematics! Bah!" She had turned on Arabelle. "I suspect you read Latin as well, but you have not admitted to it, have you? You translated an inscription on the church cornerstone for what's-her-name's little boy, I heard you. If you girls let any of that creep out of your mouth in London, you will be finished! Utterly! Do you hear me?" She had grabbed each of them painfully, her eyes alight.

"Yes, Madam!" they had cried.

Arabelle prayed for love in her heart toward this mother of hers. It was impossible to manufacture any. She had never known what to do with that verse, *Love your enemies,* because she had had no enemies . . . until her mother blew back into their lives.

Now, since Madam had driven off with Genevieve, Arabelle knew her time had come to be daringly assertive. Her mouth went dry as the broad-shouldered Bertha, another new enemy, rumbled into her chamber, squeaking floorboards and asking what she was about. The forty-two-year-old spinster had to accompany her wherever she went. Arabelle knew it would be tricky to keep her from knowing what she was up to, but she told her to fetch their cloaks and hats, for they were going out. She hurried away, ignoring Bertha's queries and sounds of opposition.

Arabelle thought over her plan as the coach wheels rolled the two of them out of the wide expanse of Bloomsbury Square, and from New Oxford Street onto Kingsway.

"This is not the way to Mrs. Chittering's," Bertha said at once, reaching for the check string to put the coachman right.

Arabelle stayed her hand. "Let him drive where I directed him, Bertha."

"Are we not going to the singing lesson your mother arranged for you?" Bertha demanded.

"It is early yet, Bertha. My lesson is set for two o'clock."

"In your diary, I saw it written down for one."

"I changed it."

Bertha crossed her arms and challenged, "Why?"

Arabelle felt a flutter of unease. However, she must do what she needed to do, demolishing any hitches along the way. "I had to move my singing lesson back because I must make an inquiry at the firm where my father does his hops business. It is important, and must remain a strict secret, Bertha. There is deadly competition to sell for the best prices, and if too many growers try to sell when the price is good, the brokers may stop buying altogether. That would be disastrous for us."

Bertha squinted skeptically at Arabelle.

She lifted her chin and looked out the window to dismiss the subject. When they halted in the busy yard of the George Inn, she let Bertha follow her into the coaching house, but told her to stand against the wall since the line was only for those who had business to conduct. As Arabelle gained the booking counter, Bertha was forced to remain out of earshot. This was exactly how Arabelle wanted it.

A round-faced official with a white wig slightly askew called, "Next!" He looked up and his face brightened. Not expecting a lady, he straightened his wig and posture and said, "Good day, Miss. How may I help you?"

Lowering her voice, Arabelle said, "Please, I would like the address of a certain passenger on *Aynscombe Stage* number seven, which arrived here last Thursday evening." She said in an under voice, "His name was . . ." Her heart thumped as she pronounced, "Simon Laurence."

"Miss, I regret to tell you we do not give out information about our passengers. It is a strict rule."

"Oh! But . . ." She had to think quickly. "I have something which I must . . . send to him," she improvised.

"Ah." He blinked his eyes in a friendly way. "What is the item?"

Arabelle, caught unprepared, said, "I expected to take his address and send it to him myself."

"Ah. But since I cannot give you his direction, perhaps you will allow me to send it for you. What is the item?"

"It is . . ." She frantically searched her mind. With him watching her, she opened her carpetbag and fingered the items inside. It still had family outing paraphernalia from their coach ride. There was nothing at all among the hot chocolate jug, Jerome's toy horse, and Lenora's mittens that she could possibly use—except one item. She arranged her body so that Bertha could not see, and passed the box quickly over the wood partition to the clerk's side.

The man received it, bewildered, and opened it by lifting the gold latch. "A Nine Men's Morris? A game?"

"Yes. A rather expensive one," she assured him. It was made of ivory and jet, and set in a mahogany box, as he could see.

Over his spectacles, he eyed her kindly. "Fine, then. If you will leave me a sixpence, I will have it delivered to the gentleman without delay."

Arabelle glanced back at Bertha, whose eyes suspiciously raked the proceedings. Drat the spying snoop! She was moving closer through the milling crowd by degrees. Arabelle tried to look as though she was in good charge of the business. Recklessly, knowing she would have to deal with unknown consequences later, she said to the clerk, "That will be the best solution."

He riffled through a book. "Please write your name and direction here. I must include it to the recipient with this package so he knows who sent it."

Arabelle, heart beating fast, took his pen and dipped it into the ink he pushed forward. This signing in a book should look official to Bertha.

"Miss Lamar?" the clerk read, his eyes wide. "Not Viscount Bastwicke's daughter!"

"Shh! Yes."

"My lands! Miss Lamar, I am tremendously sorry. I do hope you understand that I must keep passengers' information private. It is a rule for everyone's protection. I would not withhold any service from you were it within my power to do otherwise."

"You did your duty. Thank you."

He ripped out and tucked her address into a pigeonhole marked *Immediate* and put the game in after it. "Your father is a benevolent man, Miss Lamar, and a credit to the Lords from all I hear. Furthermore, he is a most valued client of ours. I am gratified to tell you so. I will have the game delivered without delay."

She withdrew politely from his nodding, beaming regard.

Nervous at what she had done, she collected Bertha, deflected her questions, and went on to her lesson. She sang a few scales and trilled "Drink to Me Only with Thine Eyes." The lyrics set her reliving all the looks she had received from Simon Laurence. Over the harpsichord's top, Mrs. Chittering praised her for wonderful expression.

On the ride home, Arabelle scarcely heeded Bertha's insistent queries as to why Lord Bastwicke would rely on his daughter's discretion over hop sales. At her third foray into the topic, Arabelle tried not to snap as she said, "Father trusts me. The prices fluctuate, and no one would suspect a young lady of entering that inn with intent to sell." There. That should silence her. It seemed to.

A sudden fear prickled Arabelle. "Bertha, do not mention this to my mother. She might let it slip to friends whose men folk raise hops on their estates."

Bertha grudgingly met her eyes, and Arabelle could see she knew this to be true about Lady Bastwicke. "She might, at that."

"Then, if you value my father and his ability to keep you employed for any period of time, keep absolutely mum."

As the coach wheels halted in front of her door, Arabelle tried to quell a stab of unease over what she had done. Whatever would Simon Laurence think when he received that Nine Men's Morris from her?

Chapter Six

Corset Bodices

"Genevieve!" called Arabelle as she pressed the ornate lever to their bedchamber suite. She was coming from the small greenhouse conservatory, where she had directed a manservant to cut flowers for the dining room table. She had been obliged to first run upstairs to check which gown was laid out for her mother to wear at dinner. Her task was then to choose flowers to match or complement it.

From out of their sitting room with its lacquer work chairs, painting table, and needlework frames, Genevieve emerged in response to Arabelle's call. She was looking self-conscious, and wore a new corset bodice of ivory brocade with gold embroidery that fit her very well, and went well with the gown that Genevieve already owned in ivory, gold, and a warm Pomona green. "This pretty corset was already made up, but the lady who ordered it never claimed it, so Madam bought it from Mr. Dupper on the spot."

Arabelle praised it, turning Genevieve around to admire. "What a sweet fit on you." Slyly, she asked, "How *was* Mr. Dupper?"

"Oh, quite cordial to me, but he escorted Madam to another room almost as soon as we set foot in the place. He closed the door, but I heard her arguing with him about farthingales versus panniers. Really arguing."

Arabelle smiled knowingly. "So the brangle goes on. Who won?"

"She didn't buy any."

"I'm not surprised. What happened with you?"

"I was taken off to a fitting room by a thin, whey-faced man who looked like Mr. Dupper. His nephew, as it turned out. He worked down Madam's list for all the garments I need. He had his assistant, a young woman, remove my outer garments so that I was left standing there in only my chemise!" Genevieve eked out in a whisper, "And he took his string with all his inch knots on it, and he measured everything! Even round my legs! He was annoyingly quick. I tried to grab the string off my chest, but he got it on again and wrote down the measurement, and whisked it around my waist by sneaking from the back. He had a slobbering grin, too! I tell you, I shall *never* go back there! I shall kick and scream!"

Arabelle, weak with laughter, gave her a hug. "My dearest dear! What you had to endure should not have to happen to any young lady. But it is over now, and it does not sound as humiliating as certain sessions I have endured."

"Oh, but that was not all!" Genevieve looked portentous with news.

"There's more?"

Genevieve pressed Arabelle's arm. "Remember that door I mentioned on the opposite wall? The one that Mr. Dupper closed?"

"Yes?"

"Well, one next to it opened as soon as that odious Dupper nephew clattered out with his information. From that other door came a fine-dressed gentleman, just turning to take up his hat from the fitting room table."

"Oh, my! What on earth did you do?"

"I gasped. Then I shrieked, quietly!"

Arabelle met her eyes, agog. "Then what happened?"

Genevieve recounted painfully, "I just stood there in my chemise and stockings and stared at him with my heart pounding. It was awful! It was pure death! I did not know a man was in that room all the time they were measuring me. He could even have been looking through the keyhole! I never dreamed some stranger could walk in on me undressed like that. I *hate* London!"

Arabelle gripped Genevieve's hands. "This is terrible. What did the man do?"

Genevieve blushed. "He said, 'Excuse me, little beauty, but I have been trapped in there for half an hour, waiting for my chance to leave without disturbing you. When I heard those footsteps cross the floor and die away, I thought the room was empty at last.' That is what he said, Arabelle, and he bowed low, and flourished his hat at me, and tried to leave without staring too hard, you know. But he did eye me up and down once more, because I do not suppose he could help it, being a man, as Aunt Claracilla told us. Then he said, 'Good-bye, lovely girl. I hope to see more of you.'"

Arabelle dropped her jaw. "*More* of you?"

"I retorted, 'No, you will *not* see more of me!' and then I was really embarrassed because he burst out laughing."

The girls laughed in quavering shock, ending with a wail from Genevieve's throat as she finished, "He bowed then, and blew me a kiss! Oh, I could have expired on the spot!"

"I imagine so!" averred Arabelle, vastly interested. "What did he look like, this bold, brass man?"

"Tall and handsome, and a bit reserved."

"*Reserved?* Behaving like that?"

"He was, really; I could tell. But the daftness of my standing there with practically nothing on jerked him out of his boredom, or whatever he lives in, don't you see? He had spots of colour on his cheeks, as if he were delighted and surprised and embarrassed all rolled into one."

Arabelle threw her head back and laughed. "Yes, I see!"

"Don't laugh!"

Arabelle kissed her and smoothed back a red-gold tendril from her temple, securing it in her chignon. "I am sorry. You had an alarming day. But one good thing came out of that experience that I can see."

"Whatever could that be?"

Arabelle put a hand on her hip and leaned toward her sister, chucking her chin. "You were told you are lovely and a beauty by someone other than me, which better lead you to finally believe it."

Genevieve looked as though she could not deny the lift that the man's compliments had given her.

Irrepressibly, Arabelle asked, "Did that give you a dashing man to dream about for yourself?"

Genevieve turned away with the wisp of a smile, but would not admit it.

Tibbs, the butler, delivered a folded, wax sealed missive to Arabelle in the music room the next day as she finished stroking and plucking the harp for the three Misses Kingsley and Lady Bastwicke. Arabelle's heart skipped at sight of the unfamiliar, masculine hand. She waited until her mother was the one talking, and slipped out of the chat-filled room with her letter well hidden in her corset bodice.

Though her mother had absently seen Tibbs approach Arabelle, she was now busy telling her guests the high prices of two brilliant blue and red vases that a certain nobleman had bought her at a glass blower's in Venice. She never listened to her daughters' musical efforts, anyway. Arabelle rushed upstairs to read her missive.

Her heart gave a leap. It said *Miss Arabelle Lamar* in an attractive, masculine hand in black across ivory paper. She knew that, had she opened this at the harp, her mother would have marched over within minutes and read without compunction over her shoulder, or even snatched it from her to read first. As it was, Arabelle would have to fork over this *billet* in due time if Madam knew about it.

Arabelle dashed to a long window, slipped behind the tasseled pink curtains, and examined the small crest in the silver sealing wax. The motto said, *Serve to Lead.*

Her pulses pounded. She worked the seal up from the paper carefully so as not to break it. Breathlessly, she read:

Royal Military Academy
Woolwich
January 27, 1752

Dear Miss Lamar,

  My delighted thanks for the Nine Men's Morris, which I received through Mr. Smith-Aynscombe at the George Inn. I will not speculate on why I was the lucky recipient of this fine game, but I know you had a reason, which you will reveal to me one day. I am grateful to have, by this means, your address.

> *Let me say that I found the greatest pleasure in my trip to London. The vision I beheld was the most breathtaking of my life. I see it daily, hourly . . .*
>
> *What is more, I perceived that you are a pure and noble young lady, but I also saw that you have not the inane kind of innocence that would close your mind to imagination, or your heart to experience.*

> *I am*
> *Your admiring servant to command,*
> *Senior Cadet Simon Laurence*

Filled with astonishment, she clasped the page to her breast, flung wide the curtain and spun in gladness. He wrote to her! And so quickly. He did not condemn her for sending the game. She threw herself onto the settee and reread every word. *Lucky recipient . . . greatest pleasure . . . vision most breathtaking of my life!*

That perception he expressed about her *innocence*—what was she to make of that? What did he insinuate? Did he express approbation for her wild impulse to contact him with the game? Or was it gentle criticism? No, she doubted that, for he had behaved very audaciously himself.

She feasted her eyes on his words, his dashing style of forming them, and then held the precious letter to her nose. He had touched this paper, he had written these words . . . to her.

After some minutes, part of her stung with shame. Was she found out for a fool? He was puzzled about the Nine Men's Morris. She had behaved in the most forward manner by sending that to him out of the blue. Aunt Claracilla would cringe to know that she had boldly courted the attention of a strange man of whom she really knew nothing. But Arabelle knew in her heart that she could never forget him.

She admitted that he had paid her some very special compliments. Her eyes sparkled, for she could see them in the gilt-edged mirror. She felt as euphoric and uplifted as she looked. It amazed her to read that he signed himself *Your admiring servant to command.*

"Why are you looking so *a-ha?*" Genevieve demanded, treading quietly across the carpet to study Arabelle.

Arabelle jumped and whirled. She held her letter inside the lace table skirt behind her, hoping her sister had not seen it. "Am

I?" Trying to appear nonchalant, Arabelle grabbed a rabbit's foot with her other hand, dipped it into her powder box, and ran it over her face, but soon she was half smiling, thinking of him again.

"You are always dreaming about something intriguing," Genevieve accused her, crossing her arms and leaning against the tall French *armoire*. "Tell me about it, Arabelle. I told you my catastrophe."

"Oh, Genevieve, it's complicated. It all relates to the burden I carry. I am expected to align this family with a wealthy, titled husband."

"I am, too, eventually. What is wrong with that?"

Arabelle whispered, "What if I do not want a . . . titled husband?" She faltered as she thought of Senior Cadet Simon Laurence of the Royal Military Academy. True, it was a great honour to be part of that institution, but never would military prefixes—unless possibly the title of Admiral—be high enough to make Arabelle's parents embrace such a man as a son-in-law.

Genevieve looked baffled. "Why would you not want a titled husband?"

"I would not mind the title, except . . . what if I fall in love with someone who has no title, or no vast amounts of money?" She swallowed and could not meet her sister's eyes.

"That would be a tragedy of astronomical proportions in this house."

"Amen," Arabelle concurred. Even though her dowry was large, her father would never consider aligning his daughters with men of less than substantial fortunes.

It was not the moment to tell Genevieve about Simon Laurence. Maybe it never would be. She forced a bright look. "You look so fetching in that corset that you should go let the Misses Kingsley see you. You are much prettier than any of them."

Blushing a little, Genevieve looked over her shoulder in the *armoire* mirror. "It would not take much to look better than those three," she scoffed. "Are they not all over five-and-twenty? Ancient maidens! Thanks a heap!"

Arabelle laughed and waved her off, saying, "Whisper to Madam that I do not wish to come down. I have an unsettled stomach, but tell her I can take care of myself."

Alone again, Arabelle's breath quickened with the butterflies that unsettled her insides. Her mother must never see this letter. Hastily she penned a line to herself from her new dancing-master, saying their lesson would be an hour earlier than planned the next day. If her mother believed that, Arabelle would welcome the extra hour to do as she pleased. She folded and crumpled the contrived letter slightly and left it on her *escritoire*. Madam could pounce upon that one.

She tucked the letter from *him* deep into her corset bodice, where her heart beat against it the rest of the day and all through the night.

Chapter Seven

Intrigue in High Circles

"Cadet Laurence reporting, Sir," said Simon, saluting his white-wigged Commanding Officer from the open doorway. He always found Captain Ligonier's office the most inviting spot in the Academy. A generous fire perpetually crackled there in winter, and the smell of coffee pervaded everything in the room, even the papers that left it, for the Captain kept a bag of fresh-roasted beans behind his desk next to his grinder.

The Captain swung his chair around, gave Simon a crooked smile, and set a steaming cup of coffee on the desk. "At ease, Laurence. Close the door, sit down, and join me in a cup."

Simon thanked him and took the seat indicated. He sipped the good, strong brew and exhaled with pleasure, eyeing the red-coated Captain who drew so much of his respect.

"I have new orders for you, Laurence," he said, riffling through a sheaf of papers.

Simon cocked an eyebrow with interest. "Yes, Sir?"

"I am sorry to say that, as of tomorrow, your big day, you will no longer be a Senior Cadet at this Academy, beneficial though your tenure has been to us all. Even the greenest, rowdiest cadets listen to you because they admire you, and respond to your teaching style of leadership. You have proven yourself as officer material. I ask you now officially: Is it still your desire to serve as an officer in His Majesty's service?"

Simon responded emphatically, "Yes, Sir!"

"Glad to hear it, because the King needs you to undertake a mission. That is why I plan to make you a Lieutenant in a private ceremony this evening. Other than your obvious merits, you are older than other Senior Cadets, so if their fathers envy your quick promotion, they can look at the facts. Any questions? You have earned your epaulettes with honour."

Simon felt gratified. "Thank you, Sir. Did you say this is a mission for King George himself?"

"Yes, Laurence, His Majesty chose you personally."

Simon felt bemused. He did not think George II knew anything about him.

Glancing at a report, the Captain's face grew sober. "Three young ladies, comely daughters of a Marquis, an Earl, and a Baron, were abducted from social functions in the last two months."

"I regret to say I heard the horrendous news, Sir."

"It is unspeakable. Their fathers are frantic. They joined forces and took the matter to the King. After a meeting with his cabinet, His Majesty sent a message to certain of us officers. He asked for a special man to undertake the task of ferreting out the villains who abducted the heiresses. I wrote a report on you, Laurence, because you meet their specifications for innovative courage, tact, subtlety, and a list of other attributes I shall show you some day. I include your acting ability."

"Oh?" Simon grinned and looked down at his gleaming boots.

"I submitted my recommendation to His Majesty's cabinet, and *voila*, you are the man the King selected."

Simon said under his breath, "I am in your debt, Sir."

The Captain waved that off. "Nonsense."

Simon asked, "What would His Majesty have me do?"

Captain Ligonier leaned across the desk. "Spy," he hissed. "I can see by your face that this appeals to you."

"It does indeed." Simon's enthusiasm was whetted by his genuine concern over those appalling abductions. To spy it out could be exciting. Challenging. Dangerous.

"You performed brilliantly with those wild cadets when I had certain suspicions. Thanks to you, they toe the line these days." Captain Ligonier smiled. "Added to all you have learned per our agreement when you were chosen by the Master General to begin your career here, I know you will gather evidence with your own brand of finesse."

Simon laughed. "It will be my pleasure, Sir."

"What is convenient is that you have the entrée to the highest echelons of Society. That will aid us immensely in planting you where we need you. You and your brother receive frequent invitations from the *crème de la crème*, so we want you to accept as many of those invitations as you can. Find those villains who abducted beautiful virgins and sold them to foreign princes, and all England will salute you. The King, the courtiers, and I are counting on you, Laurence. Just let me know what you need."

Simon Laurence stood, opened the door, and saluted. With a full heart, he responded, "Yes, Sir!"

"Arabelle! The Countess of Chesterfield is here! Do you hear me? The Countess of *Chesterfield,* for mercy sakes! And Corisande Wells, her cousin. Get up! Make haste!" Lady Bastwicke, glorified to giddiness by the vaunted title seated in her drawing room, shook Arabelle urgently by her hip and shoulder.

Her mother had apparently achieved a *coup,* thought Arabelle through a sleepy haze. The Countess of Chesterfield, wife to England's former Secretary of State, was actually in this house?

"Up now, Arabelle! Put on that cherry and white brocade with your Venetian Point lace tucker, and the new chemise with three tiers of sleeve lace. Bertha, forget the chocolate! Arabelle has no time to drink that now. You must dress her, hurry-scurry! Wait until you see whom Corisande Wells brought with her!—the most elegant man ever! You won't believe it."

While Arabelle looked askance, her mother's expression turned coy. "Oh, la, his melting eyes!"

Arabelle moaned from the depths of the bed and clutched her abdomen. "But Mother, I am not well."

Lady Bastwicke's shrewd eyes raked over Arabelle. "Bertha, give her a powder for her cramps." Notwithstanding, she ordered

Arabelle to "Hurry up! Look your best! No showing pain." She pinched her orange cheeks at the mirror, looked flirtatious in her thoughts, and hissed as she left, "Remember: show some wit, and smile at him, for heaven's sake. Since he is so infinitely suitable, you must sparkle, Arabelle!"

Arabelle dragged herself up and blinked at her looming abigail.

Bertha chuckled as she handed Arabelle the cup of hot chocolate and echoed jeeringly, "Sparkle?"

Arabelle, who never wore a nightcap, pushed back her tumbled hair and gave a wry grin. "When I look and feel like this?" She sipped the hot, sweet chocolate until it was all gone, and relinquished the blue porcelain Spode tray and cup to a waiting maid.

Later, as she submitted to Bertha's head-jerking hairbrush, she marveled at how much the success of her mother's "drawing rooms," or fashionable home gatherings, meant to Lady Bastwicke. There was a race in Society to host and attend them.

To this day, her father had not given his own levée, the masculine version of the drawing room. He attended many given by the King, the latest having occurred at Hampton Court Palace. Lord Bastwicke complained at having to wait hour upon hour for the royal dressers to finish with the King. Last week, there were some of Lord Bastwicke's friends in the antechambers, which made for good conversation. But when there were not such acquaintances present, he waited in time-wasting boredom until the doors to three inner chambers opened. Then His Majesty strolled out from one to the other to greet his courtiers—if he showed himself at all.

On the days when admitted into the anteroom that housed the grand, empty throne which His Majesty never inhabited, Lord Bastwicke and the other peers had to bow to it, and then wait. The last time, the King surprised them by poking his head in. Finding a dozen men speaking softly there, His Majesty actually joined them. He prosed to them in heavily-accented English until, exhausted by the effort, he slipped back to the safety of German. His interpreter was harried to distraction, trying to keep up with his fits and starts from one guest to another.

"When someone asked the King if the rumour is true that he is going to marry again," reported Lord Bastwicke to his women-folk, "His Majesty whirled around and bellowed, 'Dat is vun big lie!' That

was the highlight of my three hour's wait. And since then, I saw the
episode in caricature in a coffee house window."

Lady Bastwicke clapped her hands in glee at this episode with
the King, and ordered her husband to persevere. "You were actually
there, and now the event is famous! Ooh, I have such a juicy bit to
tell all my friends. Did they draw you in the cartoon? You would be
most recognizable, so I hope they did. If not, we can get another
artist to draw one with you in it."

"No, no, no!" boomed her husband. "Leave me out of it,
Regina!"

"Viscount!" her voice arrested him as he sidled toward the
entrance hall. "You want to be very much in it, so do not even
think of shying away from the King's doings." She opined that if
he but put in frequent appearances, and launched himself in the
most genial way to the King's notice "like Lord Chesterfield has
done with tact of late, even though the King used to hate him, why,
the reward will be entrance to the Bedchamber, and therefore, the
Inner Circle."

Lord Bastwicke was weary of it all, and said so.

With tears of frustration, his wife continued to badger him to
hold his own levées. "And learn German, for pity sakes."

"Why on earth should I? The King knows English perfectly well,"
Lord Bastwicke retorted. "He is just lazy. As for levées, heavens!—it
would abash me to keep my friends waiting outside my bedchamber,
or to invite them by card to come in to converse, and choke, while
my face is buried under the cone while my wig is powdered. Levées
are a dashed silly nonsense!"

"It would boost your consequence!" cried Lady Bastwicke.
"Witness my own prospects."

At the theatre, during the interval, she had at last managed an
introduction to the Countess of Chesterfield. In their conversation,
Lady Bastwicke invited her to attend one of her drawing rooms,
and to bring along the distant cousin who now lived with her. She
thrust herself on a par with the timid Countess by declaring that
she, herself, had a daughter she must bring out this year. The two
of them would have much in common, and they ought to advise
and console one another, and launch the young ladies together.

Now, through that maneuvering, Madam threw Arabelle
together with Corisande Wells, the cousin. Arabelle saw her as soon

as she moved an eye from behind the fringe of the draped curtain to her mother's drawing room. Corisande was a blonde woman of about one-and-twenty, with square shoulders, a high forehead, small glittering eyes, and a prominent, laughing mouth. Her gown was a brown and orange striped *robe a la française,* and she had orange silk flowers and brown ribbons threaded through her high chignon. She sat with a plate of sweetmeats on her lap. She chewed, giggling at someone hidden in the draped book alcove. All Arabelle could see was a man's black shoe with a silver buckle gleaming in a shaft of sun, and a shapely calf in embroidered pale blue hose.

Madam eagerly introduced Arabelle to Lady Chesterfield. She curtseyed to, and kissed, the small dark-haired woman with the shy smile. The Countess's brown eyes were distracted by something behind Arabelle, so she turned to look toward her father's alcove settee. The seat was empty.

Lady Bastwicke shrieked with laughter.

Hands clapped over Arabelle's eyes, and she gasped. She tried to turn, but her pannier hit the someone behind her. The hot fingers removed from her face as someone chuckled. She turned, wondering who in the world would ambush her so.

It was a man in a snowy white wig with three large curls up each side, smiling widely, his teeth looking yellow beside the white powder of his face. He was instantly familiar. Could it be? "Sir Pomeroy Chancet!" she expelled. Here was her showy seat partner from the coach ride to London.

"The Honourable Arabelle Lamar!" his voice quavered joyously. "At last! Did I not promise you we would meet again?" A saucy smile flitted over his rouged lips. Putting forward a pale blue leg, he flourished his handkerchief and bowed deeply. Then he bent eagerly toward her, grasped her by the arms, and kissed her on the mouth.

Appalled by his clinging lips, Arabelle shrank back and strove vainly for an unconcerned look. "This is the way we greet in London," he explained, his eyes droll under heavy eyelids.

Genevieve sat on a large cushion on the floor with a kitten in her lap. She stared at him in amazement.

Arabelle glanced at her high-strung mother. Stung by her failure to recognize a titled bachelor on their ride to London, she could no longer forbid him to ingratiate himself with Arabelle. As she had hinted when she woke Arabelle up this morning, she now found the Baronet a most desirable suitor. What must have clinched the matter was that he appeared well ensconced in the Chesterfield circle. Whether he was rich or not, she was sure Madam would find out.

Sir Pomeroy shot an arch look at Lady Bastwicke. "You and I, Lady Bastwicke, were not exactly introduced before, were we? No matter—for here I am no-ow!" he sang out, wagging his forefinger at her.

Lady Bastwicke simpered, not knowing quite what expression to adopt. She looked at Lady Chesterfield, fanned, and complimented her on her realistic gown rosettes.

Genevieve continued to regard Sir Pomeroy with fascinated assessment. Arabelle could see why, for he had prominent chocolate brown eyes, and his dark, arched eyebrows catapulted upward with every enthusiastic word. His thick wig had a pink satin bow in back, and was so liberally perfumed that, long after he had gone, Arabelle whiffed his spicy-sweet scent every time she passed the room.

"Sir Pomeroy," said Corisande Wells with an edge to her voice, "when are you going to introduce *me?*"

The Baronet did so with aplomb. The ladies made their courtesies to one another.

"Your mother tells me you will soon appear at all the drawing rooms," Sir Pomeroy said to Arabelle, settling elegantly wrong way round on a chair. "That is, at only the *best* ones. Is it not an exciting time for you, arriving in town to take part in all the fashionable parties?"

"It certainly will be, Sir Pomeroy, when the Season starts revolving." Arabelle eyed him sidewise. "So far I am still my own . . ." she foundered, "quiet, normal self."

"Oh, ho!—is that not funny? Her quiet, normal self!" Corisande Wells tinkled with laughter, her eyes squinted sidewise at Sir Pomeroy. "We cannot allow her to continue that sort of a life, can we?" The blonde squared her shoulders and rocked forward and back slightly, as much as her stiff V stomacher allowed her to move.

Arabelle tried not to let Miss Wells's laughter bother her.

Sir Pomeroy smiled and turned to say, "Do not change one whit, Miss Lamar. While you are soon to show yourself to us most *fortunate* gentlemen at balls and routs, she," he flipped his lacy handkerchief toward Corisande, "is about to shut herself up with but one. Is it not tiresome? Will you come to her wedding?"

"I do not know if my mother has received an invitation . . ." Arabelle began.

"All my friends must come," said Miss Wells. "Nobody would miss it, would they, Sir Pomeroy? No private ceremonies for me. I am marrying the late Earl of Ashby's son," she said loftily. "The day is set for this Friday in May Fair Chapel at nine o'clock. Will you be there?"

Lady Bastwicke's beaming nod gave Arabelle her answer, so she replied, "This Friday? We would love to attend. Why, thank you, Miss Wells. What an honour."

Sir Pomeroy, looking glad, gave a click of his fingers. "I shall save a seat for you. I go early to church to tell the organist my choice of music. That is one privilege of a favoured friend. Be sure to look for me in front. I shall save you and your mother each a place. Oh, and Miss Genevieve, was it? You can come if you like, can she not, Corisande?"

Genevieve shot him and Corisande each a level look. Arabelle knew her sister did not care to be tacked on like that, and would not go.

"Of course, if her mother wants her to," returned Corisande, yawning behind a green Spanish fan.

Arabelle gritted her teeth, smiled, and murmured thanks. Poor Genevieve. But the sisters knew that Madam would not be bothered with Genevieve until she was forced to bring her out, and that would be after Arabelle was off her hands.

Arabelle soon realized that Sir Pomeroy must enjoy what he saw of her, for, when he observed her adjusting the bolsters on the blue tapestry sofa and retrieving a white shawl that was crushed behind one of them, he hastened to her side to help. At close range, forehead to forehead, she saw his pupils dilate as his eyes roved over her. When she thanked him for folding the shawl, his gaze was skewered to her bodice. His breath came noticeably quicker. She recalled his similar reaction in their coach ride together. "I shall put that shawl on," she told him, reaching for it, and forcing a cool smile.

"But of course! Allow me," he breathed, and opened it for her.

She turned with a graceful slant of her shoulders to receive the silken shawl. While covering herself, she shared a wondering look with Genevieve, who was still studying Sir Pomeroy Chancet in detail. He was more stunningly dressed than anyone they had ever seen, and his behaviour was much more flamboyant. He sported a coat of French blue silk with multicoloured *passementerie* at the back waist and in flourishes down his pink waistcoat. Long rows of silver buttons gleamed to match the buckles on his black shoes, and his pale French blue stockings featured butterflies cavorting up his calves. Contrasting him with Simon Laurence, Arabelle drew a ragged breath. They were both men, but worlds apart. Yet, according to her mother, the whimsically decorated Sir Pomeroy was the right sort of man to take unto herself as a husband.

Arabelle shuddered. *Dear God help me,* she prayed. *Do not let anyone link me for life to a man like him.* As the visit progressed, she conceded that he was amusing in wit and drollery, but she did not at all like the way his brown eyes devoured her.

"Sir Pomeroy," Lady Bastwicke called, her head tipped invitingly, "come here, you handsome thing. Read to us from this play."

Winking largely at Arabelle, he excused himself and went as bidden.

"It is *The Romantic Ladies.*" Implying herself into that category with batting eyelashes, Lady Bastwicke gave him a book. "At my drawing rooms, we always read the next installment of some play. We have the best time in town." She beamed from him to the Countess. "Would Miss Wells and Arabelle take the parts of Magdalen and Cathos? We only have the one copy of Molière, so you must needs share the book. You see, Sir Pomeroy, I always choose the most gorgeous man in the room to read the men's parts." Notwithstanding that he was the only man in the room, Lady Bastwicke fanned slowly, a look of regret accompanying her fan language to indicate *I am married.*

Arabelle heard a snap at her side. She saw the preening attitude of Miss Corisande Wells, fanning very fast with her own distinct message of *I am engaged.*

Arabelle and Genevieve turned away to hide their merriment. Their mother and this guest were fighting in fan language!

"Ah, Lady Bastwicke," Sir Pomeroy drawled, "how can I refuse you? I find myself transported to unforeseen heights by your flattery."

"And I by such adulation." Lady Bastwicke twisted her torso about and pursed her orange lips as she eyed him up and down.

"Why does Mother always have to flirt around men, especially the young ones?" Genevieve whispered furiously at Arabelle's ear.

It was not only flirtation. At every opportunity, she made Arabelle cringe with her boasting, which had no veil to cover its intent. It grated on Arabelle so painfully that it was with explosive feeling that she presently delivered Magdalen's line, "I *burst* with vexation!"

Sir Pomeroy applauded. "What a fiery actress!" He proficiently read the part of the Marquis de Mascarille, which made Arabelle think long and hard about the lines, *D'ye use a marquis thus? This is the way of the world; the least disgrace makes us be slighted by those that before caressed us. Come along, brother, let's go seek our fortune somewhere else; I see they like nothing here but insignificant outside, and have no regard for naked virtue.*

Yes, indeed. Arabelle would write to Aunt Claracilla that she found her first taste of London society fit the part. Was it possible that no one here cared a whit for *naked virtue?*

Arabelle did not feel herself virtuous that evening. Rather, she felt tightly drawn and rebellious, desperate for shared goodness and light.

She sat down with a single candle at her *escritoire* and began to write. Her mouth went dry, but her heart softened as she penned, *Dear Simon Laurence.* Then she hesitated. How bold did she dare to be? Would he think her presumptive, and even fast, if she addressed him as *Dear?* She sighed, running the soft quill against her lips. Her romantic nature soon got the best of her. She left the word intact, thinking this might be the only true love letter she would ever write. She might as well write it from an honest heart.

> *Please consider the Nine Men's Morris a gift of gratitude. May God richly bless you. I wish you everything good and happy, forever.*
>
> *Arabelle Lamar*

When Simon Laurence read the letter, he sat very still, his heart glowing.

He turned toward the dancing fire in his barracks room, stood up, and lowered his forehead to his fist on the mantelpiece. "Dash it!" he exclaimed, and moaned from the depths of his heart.

He crossed the room and fingered the jet and ivory square of the game she had sent him as a gift, and absently inserted the pegs into the holes. He wanted nothing more than to thank her in person.

He told himself suddenly that his life was like a game itself. He needed to wake up and use a better strategy.

God, show me a way, he prayed. He knew, though, that he faced a great impossibility.

Chapter Eight

Corisande's Wedding

"That must be Chesterfield House," said Lady Bastwicke as their town chariot wheeled her and Arabelle past a high new wall in the wilds near Hyde Park. "Look how close it is for Corisande to come to her wedding. Just across the street."

Arabelle adjusted her *Bergère* hat and looked at the tops of three structures visible above the wall to the west. Rows of windows and stylistic chimneypieces rose against the lowering clouds. On the east side of the road stood May Fair Chapel.

"Corisande Wells is a most fortunate girl to have been taken up by her distant cousin, Lady Chesterfield," remarked Madam, looking wistfully at the stunning new mansion glimpsed through the ornate gate as they passed. "She is amazingly lucky. She has not noble blood, but because of wealth, she has hooked the second son of an Earl."

"Good for her," said Arabelle, wondering why she had to attend the wedding of someone she had just met, and did not really care to know. It was because her mother ordered it. It was a way to wedge their family into the Chesterfield circle.

"Now," said Lady Bastwicke, pressing Arabelle's knee with her tense silver-gloved fingers, "when you see Sir Pomeroy at this wedding, be sure to encourage him. He may be but a Baronet, lower than your father, but he is rich. If you catch him, Arabelle, you can thank your lucky stars." She heaved an exaggerated sigh. "I expect we must leave it to Genevieve to snag someone higher. After all, I was the second oldest, and I walked away with the only title of all my four sisters."

Stung by her mother's darts, Arabelle schooled her face into a bland expression and drew a mirror from her pocket to check her hair. Her loose dark curls were still in place at her nape, and the front and sides swept back under her hat brim, with tendrils curling down her temples in a satisfactory manner.

Their chariot halted. On the hand of their groom, Arabelle stepped out in front of the chapel with its cross on the roof and a porch at its door like a country church.

As promised, Sir Pomeroy Chancet sat near the front. She spotted him half-turned in the pew, watching the arrivals. He was most noticeable with three face patches on his whitened skin, and a black velvet bag containing the queue of his silver-white wig. Rich lace spilled over his crimson coat at the neck and sleeves, and he twiddled his ringed fingers and smiled widely as soon as he saw her.

Music swelled from an organ as Arabelle followed her mother into the church. It would have been more comfortable to sit in the back, away from curious stares. However, Lady Bastwicke made a great parade of advancing her wide golden gown down the aisle, chin aloft, silver hair plumes and gloves waving, nodding to people right and left whether she knew them or not.

Sir Pomeroy's bold eyes paid Arabelle a hungry tribute from her face to her waist and halfway up again. She smiled mechanically at his effusive whisper, "The most beautiful lady in London graces me with her presence!" She felt him kiss her cheek as she sank to the pew. She had turned her face just in time to keep her lips from meeting his eager rouged ones again.

Moving her huge dress over him to his other side, her mother showed no such reserve, but kissed him where he would, and pressed his arm and tittered. Arabelle felt abashed at the way they carried on in church, for she felt it to be tawdry and irreverent.

Sir Pomeroy soon turned back to her and gushed, "Your gown fits you exquisitely! I love your aqua silk brocade with those covered buttons in such an enticing row down the middle." He wiggled his eyebrows up and down.

Arabelle cast him a shocked look. "Sir Pomeroy!" she berated him. "We are in church!"

Nevertheless, he leered above the buttons, where costly French lace showed from her chemise.

With a rise in volume, the organ music heralded the bridesmaids, who glided down the aisle. They were three young women in blonde lace caps and swaying gowns of buttercup yellow, purple orchid, and cerulean blue. Ushers in dark purple livery stood like sentries at the side aisles. The music rose to a crescendo, and everyone looked back.

Corisande stood in the vestibule, smiling. Narcissi and orchids wreathed her forehead, bound by silver ribbons that fluttered over her white gown. With her chin aloft, she smiled and looked immensely proud.

Her bridegroom stepped partially into view behind an entrance column, his head bent toward his bride, the queue of his white wig tied with a black riband and glinting diamond. He was tall and blessed with magnificent shoulders in a deep plum coat embroidered in silver *passementerie* at the back of his waist. He turned and lifted his head. He looked guardedly at the people clambering to their feet.

Arabelle stared, then saw him better, and gasped. Oh *no!* It was he! Her heart jumped with a physical pain. *Her* Simon Laurence was moving down the aisle with Corisande Wells! Oh dear God, was he about to marry *her?*

Of course he was. They were walking forward together, nearer and nearer.

The blood pounded in Arabelle's temples. She stood frozen, unable to rip her gaze from his handsome face. *No, no, no!* she cried silently with all her being. He cannot! *Oh, dearest God in Heaven, do not take him from me!*

As Simon Laurence approached her pew, his downcast eyelids lifted and his blue eyes, by quick magnetism, met hers. His widened sharply.

Oh, Simon, she grieved fervently, her heart in her eyes, *I love you!*

Was it her imagination? She could swear that he looked profoundly affected. A muscle moved in his jaw as he and his widely smiling bride moved by.

Arabelle finally let out her tautly held breath. She knew she had felt a lightning-bolt of emotion from him. Her anguished gaze followed his sleek white head as he and Miss Wells approached the altar. How magnificent a man he was!—far too good and noble to be marrying that vapid Corisande.

Arabelle's corset was suddenly too tight, constricting her. She must get out . . . get air. She could not stay and watch this. She grasped at the pew door, ready to rise. However, a quick, odd movement of Simon's arm at the altar arrested her. Instead of leaving, she watched him closely.

He stood still. The cultured voice of the clergyman began to speak the marriage service, but Arabelle heard no words. She saw Simon's hand reach again, then halt. The third time, though he tried to desist, he grasped for the balustrade in front of him, and missed it, for he was swaying, falling . . . then down he glided. First, there came a clatter of his sword, and then a thump as he landed on the floor.

There were cries of shock all through the church. People stood and pressed forward to stare.

Arabelle had instantly cried, "Oh *no!*" She opened the door of the pew to run to him. Something gold came rolling toward her, and stopped with a clink at her shoe tip. There it glimmered. She scooped it up, and it fitted over her finger. In the confusion of people moving by her toward the front, no one saw what she held on her finger: the ring. The ring Simon Laurence had been about to bestow on Corisande Wells.

At the altar, Corisande let loose a disappointed wail. She rolled her eyes at all and sundry, petulantly pelting questions at Lady Chesterfield who had run forward to grasp her, and worrying her bouquet ribbons as she gazed over her shoulder in dismay at her almost-husband, lying splendid but unmoving at the foot of the rail.

An odd rejoicing began to infiltrate Arabelle's heart as she moved toward him, fingering the smooth ring. She breathed easier. It was almost as if, by holding it, she could prevent Corisande Wells from marrying him. Arabelle wondered if she, herself, was very wicked. She pushed the ring down amongst the fragrant lavender in her corset bodice and hurried toward Simon Laurence.

She would never forget the sight of his noble face lying motionless. Was he safely alive? She bent down and turned his dear, noble face to see if he would open his eyes. He did not, and she saw that he was bleeding from his left temple. "He needs a bandage!" she said to the clergyman towering above her.

He and other men in vestments nudged her away and crowded around him, kneeling, and whispering orders. Two more men strode to the front, and by their conduct, she assumed they were doctors. One quickly knelt at Simon's side and took his pulse while the other called for a cravat from the clergyman. That worthy man fingered his silk tippet, and then told his candle lighter to rush to the vestry and find his own cravat from a cabinet there.

Arabelle was treated as though she were in the way, so she returned shakily to her seat, bowed her head, and prayed fervently, *Please revive him, and cure him, Great Physician, of all his ills.* Her mind could not prevent her ranking his greatest ill of all as Corisande Wells. Maybe that was unfair, but through her intuition, it felt true. When she unclasped her hands and looked up, the clergyman announced the wedding as suspended. They had not revived him.

Arabelle ached to do something to help. A lady triumphantly produced smelling salts as Simon was carried down the aisle of the church on a litter, but Arabelle was unaware if she was allowed to administer them, or if they were effective or not, for the mass of people who pressed after the cavalcade kept her from getting anywhere near.

To approach Corisande to give her the ring or to offer sympathy, Arabelle could not. Lady Bastwicke, however, rushed toward the door in pursuit of her, with Sir Pomeroy following in his clomping red heels. When Arabelle finally approached them, Corisande was gone on Lord Chesterfield's arm, walking toward his home.

Lady Bastwicke grabbed Arabelle and exclaimed, "Imagine! Did you see? Corisande's bridegroom was on that coach with us! Remember? Feature that! You say you knew him from before, Sir Pomeroy?"

"No, but I met his brother, Radford, Lord Ashby, in Paris. I stopped to stay a night with him in Kent on my way to London from Dover. When the blizzard hit, his brother, Simon, hired the

Aynscombe Stage to get himself back to the Academy. Nice of him to take me along. You too, eh, Lady Bastwicke?"

"Well, why did you gentlemen not *tell* me who you were that day? I declare, I go into conniptions when I think of our missed opportunity!" She blamed him with a rap of her fan on his forearm.

Sir Pomeroy smiled wickedly. "You forbade us men to talk to your daughter, did you not?—you naughty, haughty Lady Bastwicke! Do you feel the same today?"

Madam's thin face suffused with colour as she tried to deny her actions, but could not. She hit him saucily on his wig.

Sir Pomeroy caught her fan and held it fast. "I cannot say I blame you, Lady B. A ripe and luscious plum she is." He slid juicy eyes over Arabelle.

She could not endure any more. She moved swiftly past them to the steps outside.

Lady Chesterfield raised her thin voice from behind her, and cried out belatedly to the remains of the departing congregation, "Lieutenant Laurence lost consciousness and hit his head on the font as he went down. Will you all pray for his recovery?"

Arabelle assured her she would; and did so, all the way home, whenever her mother paused in her theorizing.

Lady Bastwicke had several ideas about why he swooned dead away at his own wedding. These included lack of sleep the night before. "No doubt he had roaring parties given him at his clubs, or at Woolwich, and never went to bed at all. Or, he was not sure he wanted to marry her, although I cannot imagine why. She is such a pretty, lively girl." With a poke of the elbow into Arabelle's side, she grinned. "She and I are much the same."

Arabelle trusted herself to say nothing. She wanted to second the opinion that Simon Laurence did not want to marry Corisande, but could not found that hope on anything solid. He had certainly been about to do so. Every uncouth idea her mother uttered on the ride home pierced like a sharp thrust of a thorn into her tender flesh. Her bottled emotions felt about to burst.

"I asked Lady Chesterfield who he is, that Simon Laurence," Lady Bastwicke prosed on, "and she told me he's from the Royal Military Academy. But I thought he was an actor."

Arabelle could no longer tolerate her speaking his name or speculating about him. She grasped the strap as they swerved around the corner of Great Russell Street, and made ready to alight and flee her intolerable prattle as soon as they halted, if not before.

"He is a younger son, and that is why he went into the military, I daresay," Lady Bastwicke informed her. "His brother inherited the title already."

Arabelle rose and paused in the coach's door, holding onto the strap, until the groom unfolded the step. "What title does his brother hold?" she asked reluctantly. "Is it the Earl of Ashby?" Now Arabelle could recall Corisande saying so. Was Radford Laurence the Earl, or did they have another brother?

"I did not get a chance to ask," Lady Bastwicke said. "But I know that Simon Laurence is doomed to be only an *Honourable* on his correspondence and a Mister in life."

"Just like Jerome, Mother. Just like me."

"Not the same at all! Our Honourable Jerome will be a Viscount when your father dies. As for you, we must catch you a titled bachelor or widower as soon as possible. Since your father thinks you are *quite something*, I told him he can prove it in the husband he hooks for you."

On the pavement before their house, Lady Bastwicke proceeded as though she had said absolutely nothing to hurt Arabelle's feelings. "Is it not strange? I would have thought Corisande could find herself some sort of a peer because she is an heiress." She sighed enviously. "I suppose girls like her, in this liberal day and age, can go for men with good looks." Lady Bastwicke caught sight of Arabelle's stricken face and snapped, "Whatever is the matter with *you?*"

Simon Laurence opened one eye. His shoulders and spine felt as if someone had laid him out on a flat plank and now joggled him without mercy over high cobblestones. Daylight shone from both sides of him, but there was a dark roof above. His eye roved to find Radford crouching at his side with one hand on the ceiling. "What the deuce? Radford! Never tell me I'm in my coffin!"

"Simon! Thank God! It took you long enough to revive." Radford gripped his brother's arm in profound relief and said, "Indeed, you are being borne along in a hearse."

"A *hearse?*" Simon shot to a sitting position and hit his forehead on the roof. "Ow! Did you think I was dead? Let me out of here!"

He saw people lining the route, removing their hats with respect. They looked horrified at sight of his face, and a woman grabbed the man next to her in terror when she saw the corpse bolt to an upright position.

Radford laughed hugely and slapped his knee. "You should see your face!"

"It is enough that I can see theirs. You should see yours when I throttle you for giving me up for dead," Simon added, propping himself against the jouncing of the hearse by leaning back on his elbows.

"I did nothing of the sort. Would I ride with a dead stiff? At May Fair Chapel, Simon, there stood this funeral coach, no longer wanted after the burial. The doctors who were guests at your aborted wedding decided that this would be the smoothest way in which to convey you back to bed, it being unwise to prop you sitting up in a carriage."

"The smoothest way? Lack-a-day! Just observe what cock-a-hoop occurrences can transpire when others take control of your life." He shook his head, met Radford's brimming eyes, and laughed reluctantly. "But tell me: what did they think at the wedding? The last I remember was falling over, and a crack of pain about here." Gingerly he touched his left temple and found a bandage there.

"What did they all think?" echoed Radford, his brows raised to their fullest extent. "That you provided them with the most sensational scandal-broth since the last heiress abduction. On the other hand, Miss Arabelle Lamar cried 'Oh *no!*' and rushed to your aid. Do you remember her, Simon? She was the exquisite dark-haired angel who rode with us from Kent to London."

"Yes, *yes!*" Simon banged his head again, sitting upright to query him. "She rushed to my side, you say?"

"She did, but the clergy and doctors shouldered her out. She looked so tenderly at you lying there, and took your face in her hands, that I wished I were you. Ah, you would have revived instantly had you seen her."

Simon flashed a wide smile, gratified beyond words to hear that the exquisite Arabelle had cared what happened to him. "Then it was well worth the risk! I mean, the fall." So Arabelle Lamar had touched him, and cared what happened to him.

Radford grabbed Simon's waistcoat, his eyes pinning him for truth. "Worth it? Do you mean to tell me that you keeled over on purpose? No, Simon! I know you, and you would not do that to your bride on your wedding day."

Simon clobbered impatiently on the window with his knuckles. "Stop this ridiculous vehicle! I cannot lie here incarcerated any longer. Of course I did it on purpose."

Radford continued to stare at him in complete bafflement.

Meeting his eyes, Simon challenged him softly, "Do you think I could go through with the ceremony when a bolt of love seared through me on my way down the aisle? Especially since the love was not for my intended bride?"

Radford gulped visibly. "But Simon, whom do you feel such phenomenal love for?"

Simon's face lit from within. "For the angel who, to my humble joy, cared when I fell. Haven't you just described her to me?"

"Arabelle Lamar!"

Simon's face suffused with emotion. "I could not think ahead when I saw her eyes speak to me. I knew I could not put a vow as insurmountable as marriage between us."

Radford exhaled long and slowly, the whites of his eyes flaring. "I *say!* That was a desperate act. Well-a-day, I do admire your courage!" After a wheel-creaking interval, he stabbed out, "But what are you going to do? You are legally betrothed to Corisande Wells. No matter how heaven-and-earth-shaking your love is for Miss Lamar, you have no way of escape."

"I *know!*" snarled Simon savagely. "My betrothal legally binds me to . . . *her!* Now will you halt this infernal hearse and let me out?"

In the wee dark hours, Arabelle could not sleep. Simon Laurence remained omnipresent. She turned, embraced a pillow, and pretended it was he. She nuzzled her cheek and lips over it, and then stilled herself. She lay and pondered. What had that powerful message in Simon Laurence's eyes meant when he passed by her in the aisle? What had his heart said to her?

As she drew out from under the pillow her glove that he had picked up from the coach floor and kissed before returning to her, she held it to her lips and whispered, "Why, oh, why were you going to marry Corisande Wells?" She wondered if it had been a union arranged by his family. Or, worse yet, had Simon wooed and won her? That possibility made Arabelle feel ill. She took the gold ring from inside the glove and worried it around her finger.

She worried, also, over how he fared, and whether his fall had done him a vital injury. Often during the night, she woke to pray again on his behalf until, as the clock struck three, she fell asleep with her back against Genevieve, who slowly warmed and lulled her into sleep by her slow, rhythmic breathing.

The milkman's bell was ringing in Bloomsbury Square. Wintry dawn illuminated the bedchamber and produced, through Arabelle's closed eyelids, a rosy red pageant of a new wedding before her mind's eye. Simon did not collapse as he had when Corisande stood at his side. Rather, he lifted his dark-haired bride in his arms and thrilled her with slow kisses of love, heedless of the congregation watching. He then whispered how beautiful she was, and kissed her again. Arabelle stretched luxuriously, feeling much better.

Genevieve slept on with a little sigh and a mumble.

Arabelle rolled to face her sister. "Genevieve." She shook her by the shoulder. "Genevieve! I need you to come with me. Can you hear me?" At her ear she enunciated, "Will you keep a secret?"

That made Genevieve turn and blink at her. "Yes, Arabelle, I will gladly keep a secret. Are you finally telling me things?" She sat up, pushing her red-gold curls away from her face and pulled off her nightcap. "Where are we going? *Can* we go somewhere?"

Arabelle hugged her knees and regarded her seriously. "I need you to come, regardless. It's about a man, Genevieve. I cannot pine here doing nothing. I must act, or regret it forever."

"A man?" Genevieve repeated with relish. "I know you are in love with someone, fictional or real. I know this because you were whispering to him in your sleep. Oh, Arabelle, you sobbed a little, and it sounded like you were begging, or praying. Were you? Oh dear, I better not pry."

"Bless you." There was a lump in Arabelle's throat. She left her warm nest, pulled up her loosened stockings against the chill, and yanked the tasseled bell-pull.

"I keep trying to figure out where you could have met someone whom I know nothing about," continued Genevieve, puzzled. "The only time we've been separated was when I came ahead, and you rode to London with Madam. But she was with you, so you could not have met a man or gotten to know one then."

Arabelle gave her a portentous grin. "Well, I did! I will explain everything when my mission today is over. I need you along, for it is extremely vital in order to make Bertha think this is a very legitimate journey. I tremble to do it, but I *will* do it."

"Are you shaking?" asked Genevieve.

"In fact, I am." She spread the fingers of one hand to prove it.

"Oh, Arabelle, it must be important. Of course I am coming with you. Just tell me one thing: who is the man?"

Arabelle could hear Bertha's heavy tread, so she said into Genevieve's ear, "Simon Laurence. The man whom Corisande expected to marry."

Genevieve gaped at her. "The one who fell senseless at his own wedding?"

"Shh! Yes!"

Arabelle drank her aromatic coffee and Genevieve chocolate as they sat in their hipbaths and had warm water poured over their shoulders. Such hurried baths were all they had time for, said Arabelle. When she was dressed, she asked Bertha to remove the rag strips from her hair. She approved the quality of the curls that had formed overnight. She told Madam, who poked her messy head of hair into their chamber, that she and Genevieve could not join her in making social calls because they had to be fitted for shoes.

"Is that today?" their mother queried. "Fie! I wanted you to begin your introductions, Arabelle. But I certainly won't stay and wait for you because I promised droves of people that I would leave cards or visit them today. They are awaiting my arrival," she declared, touching her long green earrings and turning her head from side to side at the looking glass. At Arabelle's reassurance that she and Genevieve could easily order their own shoes, Lady Bastwicke nodded and said, "Well, do not disturb me with any questions because I am having my hair dressed with powder, like the men do."

"Powder?" echoed Genevieve.

"It's a daring new idea I have just seen," said Lady Bastwicke. "Why should I not be one of the first to sport the new mode?"

"It is a good idea, actually," said Genevieve, considering her mother's wayward tresses. "Then the grey hairs won't show up."

Lady Bastwicke walked over to Genevieve and grabbed her ear. "Don't you ever be so impertinent to me again!"

Genevieve winced and backed away.

To Arabelle, Madam snarled, "Teach your sister some manners! Be her example, and curb her wild tongue, for a start!"

"Yes, Madam," said Arabelle, dipping her head and lashes. When she left the room with a snap of the door, Arabelle went to Genevieve and put her arms around her. She kissed the red place on her ear and whispered, "I suspect you were right about the gray hairs, and that's what made her so mad."

They locked eyes and burst out laughing, very softly.

"So I cannot speak the truth, like Aunt Claracilla told us to?" asked Genevieve, blinking her wet eyes.

"Not if it will annoy someone or wound their vanity."

"Madam has cartloads of that."

When Arabelle was arrayed in a white silk corset of a blue-and-violet flower print, and had donned her *robe ronde* with the wide blue petticoat showing where it parted down the front, she tied the blue *échelles* into bows down the front of her corset bodice. She called over her shoulder, "Genevieve, wear extra stockings and your warmest cloak. Bertha, will you have the kitchen maids pack us some bread and fruit and cheese, a jug of cider, and hot potatoes, and bricks for our feet, please? It's snowing a little."

"Melting before it hits the flagstones, though," reported the abigail.

"Good." With a gilt mirror, Arabelle eyed her swept-back coiffure, the rich brown curls falling to her slim waist. It amazed her how the raw-boned Bertha could fashion such feminine styles. "You have a knack with my hair, Bertha."

"It's good hair," Bertha threw back gruffly. "Takes the curl. Are you wearing new stockings? Can't trust those maids not to give you mended ones when you'll be measured for shoes."

Arabelle assured her that she and Genevieve wore good hose. Opening their matching French *armoires*, they assessed their London day and evening ensembles, and made a list of the colours and types of shoes they would need for the coming weeks and months.

The cordwainer arrived. Lady Bastwicke was fond of having tradesmen call, for it showed to other occupants of Bloomsbury Square that she could afford to have tailors, milliners, and merchants come to her.

Bertha sat like a lard barrel on a hassock to supervise the sizing of the young ladies' feet. It was a William Chamberlain of Islington who bowed to them, and then laid his shoe design book and fabric swatch collection upon the table. The sisters chose several styles with curvaceous high heels and pointed toes in brocade, velvet, and kid leather. Some had ornate, round buckles and high tongues, while others dipped lower to show more of the stocking. Arabelle chose a black brocade pair, for her father had given her some rectangular silver buckles for her birthday, dotted with tiny diamonds. Black would set them off stunningly. Mr. Chamberlain took their measurement and returned the buckles to her with a respectful nod, saying what fine workmanship they were, and what a pleasure it would be for him to make the black brocade shoes to feature them.

Gratified, Arabelle ordered more pairs of shoes, with white and silver embroidery on dark backgrounds of blue, red, and purple. Thoughtfully, she fingered the swatch of pink velvet for the dressiest pair she had ordered. She must get going on her mission.

Genevieve settled on Pomona green, aqua, gold, and pale peach as her colours. They asked Mr. Chamberlain to include matching pattens to wear over their new shoes to keep them from touching mud or snow, and he was amenable to all of their requests. He even ventured to commend the young women on their quick decisions—unlike others who kept him for two or three hours as they deliberated over their decisions. He expressed himself thankful for their advance on payment, too.

Arabelle had hurried the proceedings with tactful energy. *How was Simon Laurence by now?* The question kept her moving quickly through her selections. She could not sit longer discussing shoes or their delivery dates when that magnificent man might be suffering on his deathbed.

Chapter Nine

A Daring Expedition

"Bertha, the coach is here," Arabelle called when she had cordially seen Mr. Chamberlain out. "Can you be a dear and fetch my blue cloak with the white fur, and Genevieve's red one?"

When they were settled in the town chariot, Bertha asked forebodingly, "Where are we going now, ladies? Your mother never told me you were to make calls on your own. I find this highly irregular."

"We must call for a doctor," said Arabelle.

Bertha looked askance at her and moved away on the seat. "Be you ill, then?"

To speak the truth, Arabelle could have cried out, *Yes, my heart is ill! I am sick with worry!* But she replied, "We need Dr. Follett to tend to someone." After the first glance, she firmly avoided looking at Bertha's suspicious face. To forestall more of her questions, Arabelle conversed unceasingly with Genevieve until they reached the part of London called Long Acre. She had given her coachman the address she had found on her father's latest bill from Dr. Follett. Now she sent the groom in to the doctor with her note. She could not enter the house of a bachelor herself.

"I doubt you should be doing this," warned Bertha, her jaw set.

Genevieve asked her point-blank, "Don't you believe in humanity?"

Bertha harrumphed, crossed her arms, and ruminated unintelligibly.

Genevieve kept it up. "Because that's what it is when we go out of our way to help someone. But perhaps you never learned that in dour Scotland." She went on in this vein until Arabelle halted her with a touch, amused but fearful that she would rile Bertha into some sort of retaliation.

Dr. Follett emerged with a surgical bag in his grip and a hat under his elbow, willing to go with them as Arabelle had requested. She welcomed the loose-limbed, green-coated serious man, and gestured him to sit next to Bertha Blumm.

Genevieve helped Arabelle keep the doctor in conversation about the smallpox vaccine that the Bastwicke family had received from him last spring. Arabelle said it seemed efficacious since none of them had succumbed, though it had raged through their neighbouring Kentish families, claiming lives and scarring survivors' faces. Dr. Follett was highly gratified to hear of its success.

Shivering, for the potatoes in their muffs had cooled, Genevieve asked the doctor about the likelihood of the Thames freezing over. She wanted to see a real frost fair like the one Arabelle had gone to when she was five. "I want to skate under London Bridge and buy hot cross buns from a tent in the middle of the river."

Dr. Follett shook his horsy face and told her that if she was patient she might get her wish, but perhaps not this year, as it was uncommonly warm for January.

After what seemed like a much longer ride east through the city than Arabelle had envisioned from the map, the coach rolled into a tree-lined lane in Woolwich and came to a stop. There rose before them a majestic mansion with guard towers flanking a three-story entrance. High, arched windows marched in squares along the first floor. Genevieve pointed at a freestanding tower topped by an onion dome powdered with snow. "Look there!" she exclaimed.

On a parade field marched a company of cadets. They looked polished and debonair in the uniform Simon Laurence had worn: dark blue coats, eggshell waistcoats, and light breeches with black tri-cornered hats. Drummers beat a snappy marching rhythm. They heard a partial command that ended in "Right wheel!" The men turned smartly, the ones on the ends marching with long strides while the others took progressively smaller steps to form a moving fan shape. It was riveting to watch the rows of faces—men in their twenties, youths, and even a couple of baby-faced adolescents—marching with sharp precision to the fifes' lively melody supported by the drum tattoos.

Genevieve breathed, hand on her heart, "Are they not grand?"

Arabelle nodded, telling herself she must grasp her courage firmly and do what she came to do. "You and I, Sir, will report to the Commanding Officer," she said to Dr. Follett.

Bertha began her predictable protests, but Arabelle took the doctor's offered hand, descended the coach steps, and hurried away with him. Bertha and Genevieve followed.

They ascended stairs to a central door with a nameplate proclaiming it Tower Place. After Arabelle showed her own name card to the cadet who opened the door, and her father's for good measure, he flourished a white-gloved hand and gestured them in. Genevieve looked impressed.

To the stiffly frowning Bertha, Arabelle said, "Stay here with Genevieve. I must accompany Doctor Follett to attend his patient." To escape Bertha's instant objections, she moved quickly into a reception room, where a superbly painted mural graced a curved ceiling.

Nervousness assailed the pit of her stomach as she approached the office at the far end with Dr. Follett. From within, the aroma of fresh-ground coffee drew them pleasantly. She pushed back her hood and moved into the doorway.

There stood a slender, middle-aged officer in a plain white wig. He frowned at a pile of papers on a desk as he shrugged off a black cape glistening wet with snow, revealing a red coat beneath. Engraved on the brass desk plate she read, *Sir John Ligonier, Captain, Company of Gentleman Cadets.*

"Captain Ligonier?" she asked, stepping into the fire-lit room where swords hung crisscrossed on the wall beside the King's arms and the Royal Military Academy crest.

He looked up. "Yes, Ma'am? May I be of service to you?"

"You may." With a smile, she handed him her calling card.

He read it and bowed. "I am honoured by your call, Miss Lamar. Welcome to The Shop, as we call it."

"Thank you. This is Dr. Follett, doctor to my father, Lord Bastwicke. Because Dr. Follett is so competent, I have brought him to check on the condition of Simon Laurence. Not that I doubt you have your own good doctors, Captain, but to give Mr. Laurence the best attention we have to offer, I—that is, *we* thought—it would be advisable to do this." She found herself blushing under the Captain's interested regard.

"How good of you." He eyed her a bit longer, shook hands with the doctor, and said to her, "Yet you are not his fiancée?"

"No."

"A relative, perhaps?"

Arabelle lifted her chin to combat her waves of guilt. "No, Sir."

"No matter," said he. "However it comes, I thank you for this attention to my most valuable new Lieutenant." He lifted and frowned at a paper. "In my absence, I see that Lieutenant Laurence was confined to quarters. An injury to the head, it says here." Looking concerned, he met her eyes and asked, "Do you know anything about this situation, Miss Lamar?"

"Yes, Captain, I saw his accident. He fell and hit his head on a font, and then landed on the altar floor. An injury to the temple is no light matter, is it?" She looked from him to the doctor, who shook his head.

"I admit I grow uneasy. Ah. Here is a doctor's report that says Lieutenant Laurence was bandaged . . . outcome of wound unknown at this time . . . may be in need of a lift to his morale. Zounds! Pardon me, Miss," he changed his tack hastily, "but this says his wedding was halted when he fell onto a baptismal font and descended to the floor unconscious." He frowned. "I wonder why he fell then and there."

Arabelle still wondered the same thing.

"Come, Miss Lamar, shall we seek him out?"

"Yes, Sir," she responded despite her trepidation. This was madness. She truly had no right to be here.

Back in the reception room, Arabelle saw Bertha fuming, but Genevieve smiling as she watched the uniformed cadets marching by outside the window.

"The cadets just moved into our new barracks," Captain Ligonier explained to Arabelle as he led her across the snow-dusted green to a barrack block at the edge of the regimental park parade. "Before this, our forty-eight inmates had to live in homes in the town. It was a tricky business to find them off-hours. Lieutenant Laurence, while still a cadet, supervised the move into these new quarters, and linked up cadets he thought would suit as comrades to share rooms."

A cadet on guard saluted Captain Ligonier, and flung open the door of a two-story building with rows of gleaming windows. The smell of new wood and paint hung in the air. As they made their way down a corridor, lively violin music grew louder. Oddly enough, it sounded like a familiar country dance tune.

With a double knock and a turn of the lever, the Captain flung open a door, and there was the violinist, sawing away as two men, short and tall, danced away down the room. Arabelle stared in fascination as a small, wizened man in a pink coat and grey pigtail pirouetted beneath the up-raised arm of Simon Laurence.

Arabelle laughed aloud. What an unexpected sight.

Simon spun round at the sound of her voice. In quick succession, his handsome face registered disbelief, monumental pleasure, and sheepishness at being caught dancing.

The music squawked to a halt and his wiry partner froze on his tiptoes. Simon dropped their raised hands.

Out of the side of his mouth, Captain Ligonier said to Arabelle, "We find Lieutenant Laurence at his last gasp."

"A man who needs cheering up," she said, smiling merrily from him to Simon.

A bemused smile flitted across Lieutenant Laurence's face, and she saw his attractive, oddly placed dimple. Oh, the joy of seeing him up and alive! And still free.

"Captain, Sir," said Simon, saluting. His glowing eyes flicked from Arabelle to his Captain and back to her. "Is it truly Miss Lamar?" He bowed low to her. "Here at the Academy?" He looked up at her from under his black eyebrows. He looked flirtatious and rakish with the white linen wound around his forehead.

"Does your head pain you at all?" she inquired gently.

"Not *now*. How incredible—how very gracious of you to come." He grinned at his Captain. "Now I am definitely on the mend, Sir."

"A lovely lady is a sure-fire cure," the Captain corroborated.

"Are you under the care of a good doctor?" Arabelle asked, forcing herself not to look too long into Simon's euphoric eyes.

"I understand that one or two attended me at church, and another here at the Academy."

What did all of this mean from his perspective? Arabelle wondered. *How did he feel about his interrupted wedding?* He looked anything but cast down.

The Captain asked a question she dared not put into words. "Why ever did you keel over at your wedding, Lieutenant?"

"I, ah, locked my knees during the ceremony, Sir."

"Oh? That will do it. It has happened many a time."

"Yes, Sir."

Captain Ligonier gestured the physician forward. and said to Simon, "Dr. Follett is willing to examine you."

Simon asked, "You came here for my sake, doctor?"

The doctor bowed.

Arabelle, smiling, asked Simon, "What were you doing when we interrupted you?"

Wryly, he said, "My dance lesson. All cadets must take a session. Confined to quarters, you see, I had time on my hands, so I thought I would get this over with."

"Good," said the Captain. "I know many who try to skip it. As you are an officer now, it is all the more important that you know the new dances." He eyed Simon meaningfully.

The dancing master piped up excitedly, "Lieutenant Laurence, why not try 'Rufty Tufty' again, but with the honour of this lady's hand? It simply was not working without a second woman. There was no way you or I could lead her away from the set, and I hate dancing with ghosts."

Simon flashed Arabelle a smile of bright invitation. "So do I. Brilliant, Mr. Longwaye. Will you honour me, Miss Lamar?"

Her lashes dipped. "Should not Dr. Follett check you without delay?"

Dr. Follett gave a huff of laughter and voiced his opinion. "A few minutes' dancing can only do him good by the looks of the situation."

What situation? Arabelle wondered as she nervously removed her leather gloves and untied her cloak.

Simon took it from her, and when the violin music began, he bowed to her, looking most anticipatory.

She curtseyed to the one partner in the world with whom she most wanted to dance. She willed her heart to calm just a little as she put her hand in his. Joy replaced trepidation when his warm fingers closed over hers.

"Do you know the 'Rufty Tufty'?" he asked.

With his attention fixed on her, she could not recall whether she knew it or not. "Not anymore," she sighed.

His lips twitched. "Mr. Longwaye, our Academy dancing master, will demonstrate."

She laughed at the way Mr. Longwaye skittered about, trying to show first what Sir should do, what Miss would do, and what he, the other lady, would do through the first half of the dance, but so confused them that Captain Ligonier intervened. He said he would be the woman in the second pair while Mr. Longwaye played the second man. The violinist should play on while Mr. Longwaye called the movements clearly and well in advance as they went.

Moving forward a double and falling back with Simon went smoothly. It involved holding his hand with her left one and moving forward in the same direction, and retreating together. The second time, she felt a liberating buoyancy from the music and their elegant synchrony. She felt self-conscious when they faced and set toward each other, but relieved when she turned away single in a little circle, and could compose her face away from his perusal for an instant.

When Simon had to take her hand and lead her away from the other couple, he said, "My most ardent thanks for coming!"

They turned, switched hands, and danced back toward the two men playing the other couple. Mr. Longwaye led Arabelle away and back again, and they all turned single, and Simon flashed her a smile.

There were moments in the dance when Arabelle and Simon did swooping siding toward each other correctly, and there was a time when Captain Ligonier botched it up and collided with her. Later, not knowing what their caller would say next, Arabelle went the wrong way and walked into Simon, her bosom to his chest. Simon steadied her firmly by the arms and smiled. "I'm sorry!" he breathed. Arabelle looked up, read his thoughts, and he whispered gaily, "But truly, I am not." While laughing with her, he looked irresistible. She would gladly collide with him anytime, anywhere, and in her dreams for nights to come.

She recalled that she had learned this country dance from Aunt Claracilla at one of her house parties at Fawnlake Hall, but she had never performed it in public. How she wanted to perfect it with this most spectacular partner. The moments were stolen from reality, for it felt as if she had landed in another world.

They finally sailed through arming and switches of partners with only one bump into the fiddler, who really got in the way when she and Simon did their last set and turn single. Full of breathless joy, she curtseyed to him as the violin flourished a *finis*. They applauded the fiddler, who bowed his nose to his shoe buckles, and commended them all on their improvement.

Arabelle, elated, smiled freely at Simon Laurence, who twinkled back and lifted her hand to his lips. Was he really going to kiss it? She was not even wearing gloves.

He kissed, and she reveled. She gave him a melting look and curtseyed.

Captain Ligonier, at his shoulder, said, "Will you see Dr. Follett now?"

"Dr. Follett! Is he still waiting? But of course." Turning back to her, Simon said fervently, "Thank you, Miss Lamar." He added for her ears only, "You dance like a desire through my heart," and left on the words.

So do you, her eyes returned before she could stop them. She wondered if he would think of her, as she would of him, when he laid his head on his lonely pillow tonight. Reluctantly, Arabelle left Simon Laurence's magical room on Captain Ligonier's arm.

The Captain ordered a cadet to bring a coffee tray to the visitor's parlour. "Thank you for joining the dance with Lieutenant Laurence, Miss Lamar. Your appearance was providential." He smiled. "It not only helped him learn it, but I stand here, too, very grateful. You brought amazing life to him, Miss Lamar."

She tried to mask her fluttering feelings. "Not too much exertion for one so wounded, I hope?"

"On the contrary; I found him oddly despondent before his wedding. I have been concerned about what his reasons were. I had to leave town, so I could not ask him, or even attend his wedding.

Today I feel much more optimistic about him. You see, he is my most valuable man."

"That is wonderful," breathed Arabelle.

"My cadets, even the unruliest jokesters, look up to him. He is the best example of officer material in this Academy, bar none."

Arabelle heard his praise of Simon Laurence with a bursting heart. Overriding all was the odd implication that he had not been happy over his impending marriage. Could it be true?

Simon in silhouette soon strode into the gleaming hallway, followed by the doctor. When they approached, the Captain said, "Lieutenant, will you see that Miss Lamar is given a cup of coffee? You are at liberty to join her in there." He pointed to the open doorway of a sparsely furnished but inviting new drawing room. "I shall hear what the doctor has to say in my office." The Captain bowed his head at Arabelle over the tray just arriving. It was borne in by a young cadet, crashing pewter and china together as he streaked into the room and lowered it to the table.

With pleasure vibrating his voice, Simon asked invitingly, "Miss Lamar, will you come with me?"

She felt privileged as she accepted his offered arm and walked across the drawing room toward the windows. She took a seat near the coffee service, and arranged her wide blue and white gown, and thought what an extraordinary day of surprises this continued to be.

"You amaze me, Miss Lamar." Simon seated himself in the other chair, and poured coffee into her cup from a silver pot, the long spout emitting a stream of delicious-smelling brew.

"Why ever do I amaze you?" she inquired, accepting the cup and saucer with a shy smile.

He gestured the hovering cadet off to the far end of the long room, and poured steaming coffee into his own cup. "Because you have concerned yourself with my miserable state," he said, casting looks upon her.

"Why ever should I not?" she countered, trying to sound as if her emotions were not involved.

"No one else has."

Appalled, she repeated, "No one?"

"My Captain was gone, so other than Radford, it has been only you."

As she poured in cream and added sugar, she wondered, *What about Corisande?* But nothing could make her ask him that question, for she would not sully this interlude with that one's name.

He said, "Thank you again for this solicitude on my behalf." He reached for and squeezed her wrist. "Do tell me what prompted you to come."

Her heart fluttered. What reason could she give? Her mother had said that one must not blurt out the boring truth. Aunt Claracilla had taught her to be truthful. Suddenly Arabelle felt she should probably not have stolen these moments with this magnificent man, for he was due to marry another woman. Legally he remained linked to Corisande Wells, even if the wedding had not yet taken place.

"Must I forever wonder?" he prompted, head cocked, eyes searching hers.

With a blush, she dipped her lips to her coffee cup, sipped, and said, "I brought my father's doctor to make sure you were all right. I did not hear if you were even revived after they bore you away from church." She looked him earnestly in the eyes. "I am sure everyone who saw what happened feels the same worry over you, Lieutenant Laurence."

"Yet others have not done what you have. And please, call me Simon."

The door plunged open and hit the wall with a bang.

"I must go," Arabelle said breathlessly as another cadet stared at her. This one sauntered toward her with a silver plate of just-baked biscuits. After he set it nervously on the table's edge, he froze to a salute for Lieutenant Laurence.

While Simon dismissed both cadets to attend their engineering class, Arabelle remembered Bertha, Genevieve, and Dr. Follett, all waiting for her. "I'm afraid that I, too, must go."

Simon smiled and handed her the plate. "These smell good. Won't you try some before we rejoin the others?"

Arabelle shot him a playful look, said, "How can I resist?" and enjoyed warm bites of butter shortbread. "Mmmm, thank you. But, will you be all right?" she asked, setting down her cup and saucer and standing, warily studying Simon's bandage.

From beneath its white folds, his eyes twinkled down at her. "Never better."

It delighted Arabelle to see that handsome dimple in an odd spot in his cheek. Truly, he took her breath away. She moved hastily toward the door. "I will pray for you."

"What an honour you do me. To think that I should find a place in the petitions of such a lady. I have done nothing to deserve it." She liked to hear his manly voice almost as much as to listen to what he said. "I will grab my cloak." He entered his room and soon emerged, smiling admiringly at her. "You are truly beautiful," he emphasized with his voice and the look with which he caressed her. He made her heart swell with excitement.

Outside, with a tri-cornered hat shading his eyes from the red sunset, he escorted her across the snow-powdered turf toward the entrance building. She caught him looking at her sidewise. He said, "I wish to thank you again for that package."

"Oh!" He meant the Nine Men's Morris!

He laughed. "Do not be dismayed. I was thrilled to receive it. I treasure it. I would persuade you to play it with me one day in a better world, Miss Lamar. May I have your permission to—" His boots halted their crunching in the snow and he lifted an eyebrow at her.

She peeped at him past the fur of her hood. "Permission to what?"

"To call you Arabelle. You are about to call me Simon, remember?" His lips curved and he looked hopeful.

"It might cause other people's brows to lift if you call me by my first name upon such short acquaintance, don't you think?" she challenged lightly.

"I would not need to do so in front of others for a time."

"What a well-thought-out plan," she teased. Despite her elation that he wanted them to move to first names, she suddenly recalled what she had to do before restrictions forced him back to his barracks confinement. She plunged her hand into her bag pocket. "How could I forget? I came to return something that belongs to you."

"To me?"

The gravity of the task propelled her to add, "I would rather not give this to you where others . . . might see." She glanced back at the windows facing them from many floors and directions.

"We can move." He took her through a hedge at the end of the drilling field to a grove of trees. When they were out of sight of the windows, he guided her forward, his hand on the small of her back. It made her feel precious to him.

In the glorious sunset, with Arabelle Lamar's face bathed golden-rose, Simon feasted his eyes upon her profile. She moved gracefully beside him through the snow. His thoughts were all about *If Only*. He led her toward a spreading willow tree. She would be his for a few stolen moments, and he was not going to waste them.

Lifting the leafless fronds high, he glanced around and gestured her under. "You may give it to me in here," he said when they both stood within the umbrella of branches forming the bower. He gripped the tree trunk and said, "I am so curious, Arabelle. You have a gift for surprising me." He smiled, loving the graceful sweep of her eyebrows over her dark-lashed hazel eyes. "You shivered." He stepped closer to her and pulled the soft fur of her hood around her cheeks. He found the effect so desirable that he could hardly keep from pulling her amorously to him.

"It's just that I left my muff and gloves back . . . there." She sounded breathless.

He removed his gauntlets. Tucking them under his elbow, he gathered her slim, cold hands in his, and began warming them with rubs and puffs of his steaming breath.

Her eyes widened. Then her long lashes dropped, and her bosom rose and fell. Her beautifully shaped lips glimmered in the mottled sunset, and oh, how he wanted to kiss her!

When Simon's warm fingers caressed flowing life into hers, his breath blowing upon them made her afraid her knees and her will would dissolve, and that he would see it. A large bird landed on the top of the willow above them and chirruped loudly, and a breeze stirred the willow fronds against Simon's blue coat.

Arabelle felt Simon's mouth touch her wrist. The contact thrilled her. She held her breath as he turned her hand over and kissed the delicate inside of her wrist. He was telling her something. She feasted her eyes on his straight nose, the texture of his skin, his noble forehead. She wanted to wrap him within her arms, and kiss him, and keep him.

But no, it was wrong! He belonged to another woman. She could not have this magnificent Simon. With a now-or-never burst of will, she pulled her hand away. She groped and found the cold ring in her pocket. "This rolled to my feet in church that day." She placed it onto his bare palm and daringly closed his long fingers over it. She wanted those long-fingered hands to hold her face in them again. Why did she persist in such ideas? Her mind was like flames, flashing up here and there, blazing with longing.

When Simon saw what she had given him, he sounded baffled. "This landed at *your* feet?"

"Yes, mine."

"I find that extraordinary." Without meeting her eyes, he tucked it away inside his coat. Then he lifted her chin and gazed at her face, his countenance a picture of regret. "Thank you for coming all this way to return it to me." His expression was so tender that she sighed, and like another of those unpredictable flames, her tears started. Appalled at her own weakness, she tore herself away from him, desperately lifting layer after layer of fronds to enable her to emerge and run.

He captured her arm and drew her back. He turned her to face him, and held her by the back of her waist, pulling her close to him. One hand moved up to cradle the back of her hair and then moved under her curls to touch her neck. She shivered weakly.

"Arabelle! I know." She heard the timbre of regret in his voice. His hands were paying her glorious tribute. Every wish of hers spoke clearly back to him in the embrace she gave him. When she withdrew her hands from his broad back, she knew that, though she was destined to spend the rest of her days living apart from him, this moment made her life worth living.

He held her so tightly to him that her cheek pressed into his fresh-smelling cravat. His arms kept her close, and she felt his beating heart. "Was there ever such a woman as you? Why did I find you so late?" She felt his lips at her cheek, and because she knew he was hard-pressed to stop there and she so wanted him to continue, she had to stop them. Though her blood raced, she eked out fearfully, "Speaking of late, Simon, do you think we're missed?"

"Yes, I suppose we are."

She lifted the swaying branches and looked back at his illumined face as he ducked under. Streaks of pink and purple painted the orange sunset with bittersweet grandeur, and sparkled on the sweep of snow.

"Arabelle," he said, "Like the beauty of this sky," and he came close and possessed himself of her hands, squeezing them with loving emphasis, "you are, and will always be, the most exquisite thing in my life. I had to tell you this, as I might not find another opportunity." He groaned and sighed, "Ahh! Forgive me if I've said too much."

His words seared through her. The passion in him had set a torch to her kindling, and she felt a euphoria she had never known. She looked at his highlighted eyes and black eyebrows in the glorious pink light and said, "Thank you for that!" Her heart was praying, although she had not words or wit to know what she could even ask God for regarding Simon.

She scarcely knew how they arrived back at Tower Place, but she recalled their footsteps in the snow, crunching underneath, with a soft layer blanketing the top. Her emotions were a-fire, like the sky. What she remembered most was how they touched hands behind her back once as they walked; and it was not by chance, for Simon clung to her fingers before letting them go.

They had to say good-bye in the presence of curious cadets double-timing past them as well as Genevieve, Bertha, and the doctor. But as Simon's eyes caressed her, she had her heart in hers for the man who had shown her his adoration under the fronds. She would never forget what he had said.

Simon must have been swept into duties when he entered Rupert Tower, for a cadet came hurrying out shortly afterward. With a bow, he said, "Here are your muff and gloves, Miss."

The sun's glorious burst had subsided, and now slanted in thin red shafts across the place where it had set. On the parade ground, other cadets gave full attention to the unusual sight of two young women in red and blue cloaks moving out of the shadow of Rupert Tower, followed by their mannish abigail and a lanky man. Against the rules, a young cadet whistled at the ladies, but Arabelle, filled with thoughts of Simon, heeded them not.

Genevieve eyed them with enjoyment, however. Bertha shot them a chilling stare. That produced laughter and another whistle.

"What did you do all that time?" Genevieve asked Arabelle as they approached Josiah, their coachman, who was stamping around the blanketed horses to keep warm. He removed their nosebags, looking relieved that he could finally drive the women home.

Arabelle pressed Genevieve's hand and indicated that she could not talk in front of Bertha.

Bertha hissed point-blank to Dr. Follett as the coach horses trotted out through the gates, "Who, exactly, was it you tended to, Dr. Follett? As these young ladies' chaperone, I insist on knowing what Miss Lamar has taken it upon herself to do." Bertha was the picture of intense disapproval.

Dr. Follett opened his surgical case and reorganized his bottles and instruments. "He was a Lieutenant in His Majesty's Army, Miss Blumm."

Arabelle tried to appear unconcerned even though Bertha's incensed look promised dire repercussions when she reported this. "And how *is* the Lieutenant, then?" Bertha demanded, her arms folded and her jaw jutting.

The doctor said mildly, "Recovering. He has a bruise to the temple and an abrasion on the forehead, but his faculties are normal." Addressing Arabelle, he added, "I assured the Captain that neither of those conditions should keep the man from another try at matrimony."

Genevieve looked at Arabelle, her eyes leaping with questions.

Arabelle's heart sank. Why must all these facts be spilled for Bertha's ears?

After they delivered Dr. Follett to his club, which saved half-an-hour's circuit, Arabelle knew Bertha would strike. "What fool's errand was that?" she pounced. "When I think that I accompanied you chits to doctor an officer in barracks, I am appalled! There is something very foxy going on with you, Arabelle. Does your lady mother know?"

"Bertha! First of all, do not ever call us *chits* again! Secondly, Madam our mother does not yet know because she was not at home when I found I must do this. And Bertha, *I* shall tell her," Arabelle emphasized her words with a stern look which did not waver. "Not you."

When Bertha finally looked away, Genevieve called Arabelle's attention to the lamplighter holding a boy on his shoulders to do the job. She was lamely trying to rescue Arabelle from Bertha's inquisition.

The sight caused Arabelle another reason for unease. "Yes, I know; it's later than I anticipated."

Bertha looked vengeful, no doubt rehearsing an explosive report for Lady Bastwicke.

Genevieve whispered to Arabelle, "Are we in trouble?"

"I certainly am. You shouldn't be, though."

When they rumbled across Bloomsbury Square an hour later, Arabelle wished she could arrive with less bustle. A footman ran out, carrying a lantern to light their way. On the threshold, she asked quietly of Tibbs, the butler, "Is my father at home?" It would be easier to confess to him than to her mother.

"No, Miss Lamar, he has not returned from Kent. Lady Bastwicke awaits you in her dressing room. Rather impatient, she seems." For the tight-lipped butler to offer that much information boded ill.

Arabelle told Bertha to hie herself to the servants' dining hall for a late dinner. Bertha went reluctantly, giving her a look that said *I am still going to tell.*

"Blast that Bertha! Oh, Genevieve!" wailed Arabelle quietly at the first landing. "I want Madam to know as little as possible. I fear a terrible commotion when she hears. If only I could give the impression that Father sent me there; but I cannot."

"What all did you do with that amazingly handsome Lieutenant, Arabelle?"

"Oh, Genevieve, I danced with him!"

Her sister's jaw dropped. "*Danced* with him?"

Arabelle moaned longingly on her sister's shoulder. "I tell you, Genevieve, that he is a man above all others!"

"Arabelle!" rang their mother's sharp voice from above the central staircase. "Come up here right now!"

Genevieve hugged Arabelle in support. They ascended the stairs side by side, while Arabelle wondered how on earth to put her impulsive excursion into words.

Over the railing, Lady Bastwicke, holding a golden comb, demanded, "Where have you two been?"

"On a mission of mercy, Madam," called Genevieve cheerfully.

Arabelle looked up. "To bring Father's doctor to tend someone."

"Someone he feels we ought to help," Genevieve finished without compunction, hurrying ahead of Arabelle to explain things her way. "He left a note for Arabelle to do it."

Arabelle flinched at her outright fib.

"Who was it?" asked Lady Bastwicke, who had moved into her green candlelit chamber, and there held her mirror aloft, checking the back of her coiffure, powdered now from gray-streaked red to a pale orange. When Arabelle followed her sister into the room, their mother was placing a diamond-shaped patch on the side of her beaked nose.

"An officer named Simeon," invented Genevieve. "But Madam," she said suddenly, "Do you think that's the best place for a patch? That emphasizes your nose. I mean, wouldn't it look better on the apple of your cheek, because you have such good high cheekbones, and it's a spot that signifies that you're married, after all?" She broke off as her mother's glare came round. "Well, wouldn't it look better there?" she trailed off quietly.

"You insult my nose, do you? Off to your room, Impudence! Stay there until morning! Arabelle, get back here, I am not through with you. Drat!" she exclaimed as a curl fell from its pin. "Fetch Bertha for me. She is the only one who can fix my hair."

It was a momentary reprieve for Arabelle's explanation, but the last person she wanted in the room was the fuming Bertha.

When the hefty abigail followed Arabelle into the chamber, Lady Bastwicke was ripping all the pins out of her hair. "Bertha, this is impossible! Fix it as I had it for the theatre last week. Arabelle, who *is* that ill man that you should take *my* carriage and traipse off to see him with a doctor in tow? Without asking *me!*"

Bertha said, in sepulchral tones around the pins in her mouth, "He was some military man who that doctor said is free to marry after all."

In the mirror, Lady Bastwicke's eyes protruded at her stock-still daughter. "Free to marry after all? Marry whom? Arabelle?" she said warningly, "what is going on with you? Who is he?" With increasing menace, she rounded on her and demanded, "Did you lie to me?"

Arabelle, with heart skipping and pounding, finally found her voice. "No, I did not. His name is Lieutenant Simon Laurence, Madam. Genevieve did not say his name correctly; she was distracted by your patch."

"Simon Laurence? Isn't that the name of Corisande's fiancé?"

Arabelle's heart sank. "Yes," she confessed.

Lady Bastwicke's attitude changed as she regarded Arabelle intently over her shoulder, the large pleats of her *robe a la française* billowing like a slide to the floor from the nape of her neck as she strode toward her full-length mirror. "Why on earth did you go to him? When is he going to marry Corisande?"

"I do not know. You saw how he fell at the wedding. Genevieve thought it was Father who asked me to go, but she misunderstood. This morning," Arabelle recounted, thinking quickly how to tell the truth, "the task was put upon me to bring a doctor to tend his injuries." *Put upon me by my conscience,* she affirmed inwardly. "I felt I ought to do it, Madam, to show our concern. I could not turn a deaf ear to the prompting of . . . of the one who is dying to marry him." *I am that one,* said her heart.

Lady Bastwicke jumped to conclusions. "Ah! So Corisande Wells asked you to do that! Well, well!"

Arabelle took to coughing, ignoring Bertha's beetling eyes.

Her mother mused, "Now that is gratifying! She has taken a shine to you, has Corisande. I say! This is a welcome turn of events; yes indeed! You and I will call at Chesterfield House tomorrow. I have needed a good reason to visit a second time, and now we have one. Hurrah! You can report to Corisande on the state of her bridegroom. You have not done so yet, have you, girl?"

"Communicated with Corisande about him? No, I came straight home, knowing you would be worried. So you do not disapprove?"

"Not now that I understand what's what," said Lady Bastwicke, darting distractedly back to her vanity table. "On the contrary, I think we shall fare the better for this favour you have done Lady Chesterfield's cousin. From henceforth, I can attend the Countess's drawing rooms as often as I wish." She lifted her pointed chin, and a superior smile played on her thin lips. With a relish, she reddened them for the evening.

Arabelle squirmed inside her corset, trying to loosen it over her ribs, but could find no relief for her constricted lungs. How would she explain all of this to Corisande, the almost-bride, who had *not* sent her on any errand concerning her fiancé?

Chapter Ten

The Coveted Invitation

Simon Laurence banged his fist on the table.

Across from him, Radford jerked back in surprise, dropping his spoon with a clatter. "Now what?" he asked.

"It's an impossible knot!" Simon huffed. "Ho! If I could just go back and undo the idiotic acts of my youth!"

Radford sipped his Turkish coffee and set the cup onto its saucer. The coffee house was full, with men at all the tables, so he leaned toward Simon, who clutched his bandaged forehead. "Which act of idiocy do you particularly long to erase?"

Simon gave him a speaking glare. "My betrothal!"

Radford grunted sympathetically. "That occurred mostly beyond your control. But you were no youth. That happened only last year."

"Believe me, I was only a youth! Never more green in my life. Now that I have emerged through that tunnel of blindness, I shudder to see the wreckage I made of my life while in the dark. How could I have shackled myself to *her?*"

"But she had some attraction, had she not?" Radford pulled his coffee cup out of the way of Simon's doubled fist. "You used to think so, up to a point."

"Not any longer!" Simon set the spoons jumping on the wood table with another smack of his fist. "She was always superficial." Savagely, he broke his pastry into bits and pushed the plate at Radford.

Radford picked up a morsel while he studied his brother soberly. "I know you halted your wedding for a spectacular reason, not just at a moment of uncertainty. You have always been so sure about what you do. Tell me what Miss Wells did to change your mind." Radford's tone conveyed that he would brook no hedging.

Simon clutched the back of his neck and fixed his brother with a grim look. "Corisande began to plague me many weeks ago. As I spent more time with her and discovered just what a vapid female I had promised to cherish until I die, I felt a crisis arising. However," he soldiered on, "I thought I could make a tolerable success of the marriage, as is largely done in our day, if I gave her due benevolence while I continued to discharge my military duties, and those of my estate and yours. I thought optimistically that these duties would give me enough to occupy my time and keep me away. I deluded myself that I could treat her well—but leave her to her own pursuits most of the time."

Radford lifted a finger. "That sounds calamitous. But there is more to it, Simon. You did not just decide you could not handle that plan as you entered the church with Miss Wells on your arm."

"You already know, Rad, what angel obliterated her place in my heart. Whom did I see as I walked to my doom? Whom did I know I loved in an overpowering rush as I beheld her—a gift from God—for the second time? It was a sign, a powerful shaking of my soul. Call it a bright shaft of truth, if you like. I have never been so sure of anything in my life. I need Arabelle Lamar, and no other. Arrrgghh! Tell me what to do before I go mad."

True to her word, Lady Bastwicke, spiffy in her jade *robe ronde*, made Arabelle wear her new white and periwinkle silk, and had them both in the coach at half-past twelve the next day, bowling west.

"I have no idea," remarked Lady Bastwicke, "why the Earl of Chesterfield chose such a remote spot for his new house. Next to the wilds of Hyde Park, of all places."

"For fresh air and blue sky?" Arabelle guessed, her eyes on the white clouds soaring overhead.

"Well, I do not envy him the sounds he will hear on still, summer days."

Arabelle retied the collarette of ribbons and lace encircling her throat and fluffed the lace at her square neckline. "What sounds?"

"From Tyburn Hill. I reckon the screams of men being drawn and quartered will pierce through his open windows at most inconvenient moments. Can you imagine that distraction during a card party?"

Arabelle shuddered. "Madam, please!"

Lady Bastwicke lifted a silver pocket mirror and studied her face this angle and that, saying absently, "I was in the crowd watching once, on a lark."

"A *lark?*"

"A bunch of us went to watch. It was horrific."

Arabelle swallowed hard. She was not used to the brutality of the metropolis. She missed Bastwicke Chase, and the gentle green hills of Kent. These drives through noisy streets clogged with humanity were a far cry from the serenity of her horse rides across verdure-covered chalk hills, where nothing more menacing than a rain cloud or a bracing sea wind ever marred her peace.

When the elegant cross came into view atop May Fair Chapel, Arabelle recalled the face of Simon Laurence when he caught her eye on his way to tie his matrimonial knot. Was it not odd how she had felt the most tremendous rush of love and anguish, and then that cord had remained untied?

Since then, that affianced bridegroom of Corisande's had kissed her wrist and held her close to his heart in the willow bower. That suspended episode of love always uplifted her spirits. She smiled, and her heart swelled with her glorious secret.

Now she had to go tell Corisande, his fiancée, that she had seen Simon Laurence, and brought him a doctor. Praying to God for help in her turmoil, Arabelle adjusted her wide-brimmed *Bergère* hat and retied the periwinkle ribbons at the nape of her neck behind her curls. She joggled off balance as the coach lurched to a halt. Trying to regain her footing, she felt unsettled in more ways than one.

A dog barked savagely from the colonnade in the right wing as the Bastwicke equipage, including outriders, made a clattering, echoing arrival in Lord Chesterfield's courtyard.

Lady Bastwicke peeked out between the pink taffeta drapes of the chariot and said, "I see his need for a fierce-sounding dog. I bet that a parcel of thieves, kidnappers, and murderers lurk in this quarter." Whereupon Lady Bastwicke shook her voluminous green gown free of the coach steps, and crossed the frosty bricks.

Arabelle paused with her gloved hand on a stone balustrade, and looked up. The pale stone house rose for three stories. The balcony above the door traversed the façade and turned at right angles to grace the two wings doubling back on either side of her, supported by columns at intervals. It was a magnificent house, and it felt well enclosed from the city's bustle. A groom led a colt out between two of the columns back toward the gates, and proceeded to exercise him by running beside his tattooing hoofs around the courtyard. Opposite, a laundry-maid hurried out into the chill with a basket of steaming clothes and ducked into another door.

"I heard our Earl got all his ideas for this mansion from France," said Lady Bastwicke.

When admitted to the hall by a servant in light blue livery with silver lace, Arabelle admired the arches of white Corinthian marble that gleamed solidly on either side of her. She instantly thought how lovely it would be to dance with Simon Laurence across the diamond-patterned floor. She ached for him to support her at this moment.

Although the bland-faced old porter told them to wait while he took their cards to the butler, Arabelle, on tenterhooks, walked up the dozen or so steps to a landing bathed in sunlight from windows high above. Overcome by the lofty beauty, she softly exclaimed, "Madam, come and look." In pure white marble, the staircase split and doubled back, rising to higher arches lavished with plaster swags. The balustrade was so adorned with curlicues that it reminded her of the curved scrolling design of *Guipure* lace that covered her bedside table at home. She saw a Duke's coronet and the letter *C* intertwined in the iron. "Lord Chesterfield isn't a Duke, is he?" she whispered.

"Oh, no. He is two rungs lower: an Earl," said her mother too loudly, "but King George did offer him a dukedom. I cannot imagine why he refused it."

At the head of the stairs, a turquoise frock coat emerged through a gilded door and materialized into a white-wigged, black-browed gentleman who stood surveying them from under heavy eyelids.

Arabelle recognized dignity in the handsome man, and curtseyed.

He smiled and bowed to her with courtly grace.

"Arabelle! Who are you talking to?" Her mother looked up sharply. "Oh! I say! Good morning, Lord Chesterfield! There you are!" She twittered her fingers and curtseyed low, her farthingale emitting a long creak.

"Good morning, Ma'am. And whom may I have the honour of welcoming to my home?"

It was a slap in the face for her mother, surely, for Arabelle had heard all about how she had had conversations with him, and how he had admired her excessively.

"The Viscountess of Bastwicke, Your Lordship. Oh, and my daughter, the Honourable Arabelle Lamar."

He took a step down. "I am charmed to meet you." He bowed to each of them. Arabelle noted that his finely curled silvery wig that fell in loose curls to his shoulders was understated, but a costly piece. With a high, noble forehead and an amused mouth, he struck Arabelle as a man of confident dash and worldly wisdom. His eyes held a private sparkle for her, which disappeared completely when he addressed her mother. For her, they spelled boredom with a hint of repugnance.

Lady Bastwicke continued to climb the stairs, hefting her eight-foot-wide skirt.

Arabelle hung back on the landing, waiting to see what he would do.

"Is there some way I can serve you ladies?" he asked genially.

Lady Bastwicke gushed, "Oh, thenk you, Your Grace . . . heh, heh! I mean, Your Lordship. We came to return the Countess's call. We were just waiting for the butler to come back when—" she flipped her fan sticks around, gesturing at the magnificent staircase.

Arabelle detected a ghost of a smile in the Earl's ironic eyes. "We are honoured," he said, putting a halt to her mother's chattering.

She jumped back in, however. "Oh, and even more importantly, my daughter has vital information about your cousin's fiancé, Lieutenant Simon Laurence."

"Does she, indeed? Any tidings you bring of him will be welcome to us all." The Earl descended the stairs with such stateliness that Arabelle had to admire his presence. It made her mother swing her wide skirt out of his way.

She hurried to say, "Oh, yes, we bring new tidings for you, Lord Chesterfield. By-the-by, Lady Chesterfield attended my drawing room before Miss Wells's wedding day, and she invited us to the marriage, which, horror to think on, came to naught with that queer fall." She went on in this vein without pausing, and then recounted their play-readings, David Garrick's last performance, and her husband's quote from the King himself.

Arabelle squirmed inside. Whatever did Lord Chesterfield think? She could see that her mother felt totally out of his league, and revealed it by her blustering boasts and sharp laughs out of nowhere.

The Earl slid cold eyes across her while his lips smiled urbanely. "The Countess is dressing," he said gently. "Do go and tell her your news in the boudoir on the ground floor, Lady Bastwicke." He clicked his fingers.

A footman leapt to life from behind a pillar and escorted her down the stairs and through a door, which, being wider than those in older houses, enabled her to sidle through with only a quick sashay before she and her jade flounces left their sight.

"Now," said the Earl significantly to Arabelle, "I shall take you to my sanctuary." There was a handsome cleft in his cheek. "Would you like to come?" He offered his turquoise brocade sleeve for her hand to rest upon.

"I'd be honoured, My Lord." She smiled at him in delight, and they ascended in state. Arabelle was glad she had worn her swirled silk gown with her best lace chemise, for it put eight inches of *Argentan* lace ruffles upon her forearms. It gave her the confidence she needed in this opulent setting, and with this influential statesman.

Then her mind filled with dread. She feared to confess to His Lordship what she had done. She could offer no story but the truth. She had nosed in and seen Corisande's fiancé on a very slim pretext.

What could she give as a viable reason for her jaunt to the Royal Military Academy? She suspected it would be an unthinkable *faux pas* to confess that it came from the desire of her heart.

Glancing into an anteroom filled with gold-framed paintings, pink and white chairs, and gilded wall panels, she said, "Lord Chesterfield, your house rewards my hunger for beauty. It lifts my spirits to walk through this light and delicate realm."

"Your opinion gratifies me," he said with a genuine smile. "The expense has ruined me, but the house pleases me. I am glad to hear your accolades." He kissed his fingers to the air, French style, twinkled at her, and pressed a door lever. "I wonder if you will like my library."

The first thing she noticed was how cheerful it was, with white walls and plaster work framing large portraits around the room, among whom she recognized Chaucer, Shakespeare, and Pope. On chimneypieces and cabinets stood busts of other famous men interspersed with airy statuettes of nymphs. Marching across his bookcases were hundreds of leather volumes gleaming with gold leaf lettering.

"What an inviting place!" she exclaimed. "I thought all men's libraries had to be dark."

That caused his lips to curve. When he had bowed her to a chair, he went to the white fireplace and poked a log farther into the blaze. "I am eager to hear about Lieutenant Laurence."

Arabelle felt her pulse quicken. "He is under the care of my father's doctor, My Lord, who reports that Lieutenant Laurence suffered bruises and an abrasion. He is now on his feet, but confined to quarters until his Captain gives him a clean bill of health."

"I am glad to hear this report from you, Miss Lamar."

Arabelle looked about, letting a sigh of relief slowly escape. "So this is where you spend your *languid hours?*"

He saw her observation of the letters raised in the white border near the grandiose ceiling. "So you read Latin?" He looked intrigued.

"Ah . . . what does it say exactly?" she parried, recalling that she must be careful not to spew out her knowledge.

"*Nunc veterum libris, nuc somno* . . . Now with old books and sleep and languid hours, to taste the longed-for bliss of private life."

"How nice that sounds, Your Lordship. I would like the same things; especially the private life. I understand that you retired from your post of Secretary of State. Is this what you do now—sleep?" Arabelle grinned impishly at him.

"Miss Lamar, do I look like a man of idleness? Would this house be built if that were true?" His eyes crinkled at the corners. "No, no. Idleness is the refuge of weak minds."

"Which is the opposite of Your Lordship's style, with the book you wrote, and all the weighty positions you have filled . . . so impressively."

"Excuse me, young lady, but what do you know of my career?" He crossed his arms and tipped his head, looking skeptical but rather pleased.

She lifted a new leather-bound book, flipped the pages, and looked at him over the top of it. "That you have distinguished yourself as Lord-Lieutenant of Ireland; and, before that, as Ambassador to The Hague. Twice." Seeing his grateful interest, she added, "My father recounted more than once how brilliantly Your Lordship negotiated the Treaty of Vienna."

The Earl's eyelids lowered though his lips smiled. "You are far more well-informed than I expected any young lady to be." He rose, passed behind her, and touched her shoulder. "I could wager that you are never idle, either. Your efficiency in this matter of Lieutenant Laurence shows me you are not." He sank to a chair and studied her briefly. "Unusual. Highly unusual. You appear to be a woman of worth."

Though she liked his cordiality and his un-looked-for appreciation, she had come to the moment when she must ask a question, or forever hold her tongue. "Thank you for your kind words, Lord Chesterfield. May I have leave to ask you something?"

"I am all yours. Ask."

She blurted out, "How did Miss Wells and Simon Laurence become engaged?"

She knew she was under his intense surveillance then. He replied without reserve, however. "The Countess and I took Miss Wells to Canterbury with us a year ago. We visited various friends along the way. While we stayed at Leeds Castle, the late Earl of Ashby and his sons came to join the house party. That was when he and I discussed the expediency of his second son, Simon, and my wife's distant cousin, Corisande, making a match of it."

Weddings were often arranged this way. Being of a marriageable age herself, the thought made Arabelle cringe. "Did the principals in the betrothal instantly agree?" she asked, wide-eyed.

Lord Chesterfield said, "Put it this way: we told Miss Wells first; and she was enough enamoured by the looks and manners of Simon to give the plan her full cooperation."

Arabelle swallowed. What woman wouldn't breathe "Yes!" if offered Simon Laurence as her husband? "I can imagine," she said, a slight edge to her voice. Having waded in this far, she plunged in up to her neck. "And he?"

"Simon's father approved the generous terms of the marriage settlement. I believe that Simon agreed that the girl his father chose for him had 'possibilities' and was quite . . . 'entertaining.' I believe those were the words."

Arabelle said, "How could a man object? She's . . . pretty."

"Pretty!" His Lordship spat the word. "Whereas you, Miss Lamar, are nothing of the kind."

She lifted an eyebrow at him sidewise.

"You," and his voice took on eloquence as he leaned forward, "are what the French would call *d'une beauté exquise.*" He lifted her hand and kissed her fingers.

"Who is?" It was a sharp feminine query that came from the doorway. "Why, Arabelle Lamar, what are you doing here?" The blonde Corisande advanced, showing her teeth in a smile while her eyes assessed Arabelle and then raked over the Earl with blatant curiosity.

"We are conducting a flirtation," he drawled, and kissed one more of Arabelle's fingers before he let her hand free.

Corisande halted in her progress, looking as if she believed him.

Arabelle smiled at him, then gestured round the room, saying to Corisande, "His French taste in furnishings is but a backdrop to the fine art of the man. His tongue is as gilt-edged as his chairs." He could have his flirtation. She winked at him.

Surprising her, the Earl winked back. "Corisande!" he attacked in mock savagery, "was there a purpose in your storming my sanctuary? You have cut a golden interlude so short that I shall have to contrive a way to keep this lady in the house longer." He cast a bright look at Arabelle. "Even if we do it by devious means."

Corisande sank onto the seat he held for her and pushed down her panniers, which held out her tan silk gown striped in chocolate and crimson. Cocking her head at Arabelle, she said, "You must come and stay with us, by all means. Come for a week or two until I am married. I am dying of *ennui*." She turned to Lord Chesterfield. "I came to ask when I am to begin my sittings. The portrait you promised me as a consolation for my wedding being postponed must begin soon if we are to see it finished in time for the ball."

The Earl waved his hand. "Ask your aunt to invite the artist at once. Sitting for a portrait will keep you out of here, at any rate. But back to that thought, Corisande; how shall we lure Miss Lamar to stay? You need company and more diversion than hours of posing will give you. We will now issue her our invitation, shall we?"

"Oh, yes," returned Corisande, nodding at Arabelle promisingly.

His Lordship looked with mock solemnity at Corisande. "If you are thus occupied with a friend of your own age, will you promise to make less of a nuisance of yourself around my library tables? I built this room for solitude, remember?"

Corisande said behind her hand to Arabelle, "He is a noble fustian, but he has a redeeming quality."

Arabelle, on cue, asked, "Which is?"

"He grants most of my whims. Do ask your mother if you can be my guest."

Seeing Lord Chesterfield's waiting attitude, Arabelle smiled. "Yes, I will ask her. Thank you kindly."

She was very aware of the honour bestowed upon her. To be asked to stay in the finest new house in London at the invitation of Philip Dormer Stanhope, Earl of Chesterfield would be an enormous feather in anyone's cap. But that was not why she wanted to accept. She genuinely liked the man. She could learn so much from him. Moreover, it would be a great relief to get away from her mother.

"The thanks will be all ours if you can stay," said he. "Miss Lamar, tell Corisande what you heard about her bridegroom's state of health."

Arabelle nervously turned to Corisande, whose mouth fell open in surprise.

"My father's doctor has just seen Simon Laurence. Dr. Follett reported that Lieutenant Laurence suffered bruises to the temple and an abrasion on his forehead. He is confined to quarters," she added as though she knew for sure, "and should eventually recover, but he requires rest." *In other words, leave him alone,* she thought.

Corisande picked up on one aspect only, and cried in dismay, "Confined to quarters?"

"Makes it inconvenient to plan another ceremony for the two of you, does it not?" murmured Lord Chesterfield, walking to his desk and flipping through his diary pages.

"But—!" Corisande sat stymied for an instant. She jumped up and followed him. "*You* can have him released, My Lord," she purred, trying to see into his averted face. "If you could bring him here, why, *your* doctor could tend him every day." She adopted a tone of appeal. "I cannot be bereft of my Simon much longer."

"You see what she learns, living in this house?" he put to Arabelle dryly. "That fop of a dancing master has taught her how to charm the feathers off the very peacocks."

"Who's a peacock, then?" Corisande's laugh trilled.

"Corisande . . ." Lord Chesterfield drawled warningly.

"Oops! But I have just charmed you into my idea, have I not?" Corisande, seeing his face, quailed before his forbidding countenance. Backing away, she said quickly, "Come, Miss Lamar, I will show you where I live. Can she have the room that connects to mine?"

Upon his dismissive nod, she paused in the doorway with her skirts in her hands and said, "My Lord, let me know the instant Simon arrives. Oh, and I am sorry." She tapped her lips.

"Apology accepted. You may possibly learn to eliminate those hideous sounds someday. Your servant, Miss Lamar."

"Thank you, Your Lordship. I rejoice at this invitation. You have so much wisdom that I hope some of it will rub off on me." Arabelle curtseyed herself deeply out the door. She left him with a gratified smile glowing from his eyes.

"Isn't it cherry? You are to stay!" Corisande linked arms with her and led her up the marble stairs, their gowns crushing against one another.

"Are you positive he was not just exercising polite drawing-room manners?"

"Oh no. Did you not hear? It is settled. I expect you must inform your mother, but why would she object?"

"Why indeed?" echoed Arabelle wryly. "Why did you say you were sorry to him just now? To what hideous sounds did he refer?"

Corisande said as if it were obvious, "My laughing, of course."

Arabelle really looked at her.

Corisande giggled. "He abhors laughter."

"Why?"

"It is unrefined. He said to me when I first came here, 'In my mind, there is nothing so illiberal and so ill-bred as audible laughter.'"

"But he seems a happy man. He smiled often."

"You did not hear him laugh though, did you?"

"No . . . but what does he have against it?"

"He says it screws up a person's face in grotesque ways and the sounds that emit from people's throats are utterly vulgar." Corisande rolled her eyes.

Arabelle grinned. "It's sort of true. With some people, anyway." She had learned that manners must be perfected in order to live here; but the Earl had left off his forbidding behaviour to her so soon that she already felt at ease with him. But she would remember not to laugh.

The young ladies had ascended one level of stairs, and passed into a feminine domain that overlooked the courtyard and colonnades at the front of the house. "This your chamber?" Arabelle surmised.

"Yes. At this end, it's like a dressing room," said Corisande, gesturing at a large *armoire*, mirror, cloak rack, and tapestry-covered dressing screen. "The water closet is downstairs beside the library. Look here, I have a dressing table from Austria. It was my one-and-twentieth birthday gift from Lord and Lady Chesterfield."

"You are well taken care of," Arabelle remarked. "I like the periwinkle curtains on your bed."

"Yes, and look at this."

Arabelle admired a painted scene of Chesterfield House on Corisande's fan.

"It was done by Robert Agathon; see his signature? Ever heard of him?"

"No."

Corisande giggled and tossed aside the fan. "That is because he is new in London and *he* is a woman: Roberta Agathon. By the way, did you know that the Countess of Chesterfield, my own cousin, is the daughter of King George I? Yes, she is. Illegitimate, mind you," she said, looking droll, "but still the daughter of our late King. If she were legitimate, she would have been a Princess." She curtseyed low, in a mocking manner, and then jumped onto her bed and kicked her feet into the air, showing her blue garters and red quilted under-petticoat. "I doubt that she would have liked being one, though. She is much too bashful for all that."

Arabelle asked, "Where did you live before you came to stay here?"

Corisande said airily, lifting her feet and examining her brass shoe buckles, "Oh, I lived with my cousins in Ipswich after my parents died, but that didn't last long because that family went practically into penury over an investment in India that went sour." She sat up and said emphatically, "I was not going to contribute my money to their pot, so I had the idea to write to Lady Chesterfield. After my fifth letter on the subject, she and the Earl said I could come for a visit. And here I am." She looked proud of her accomplishment. "I shall stay until I am married."

"And they are about to have your portrait painted?"

"Yes, and it had best be soon, or I will be married and they will forget about it. I have a miniature of Simon, but he has nothing of me yet. I think a life-sized portrait of me would thrill him the most."

Arabelle's heart thumped when she spotted an oval frame on the vanity in the corner. "Will you show me the miniature you have of Simon Laurence?"

Corisande went to get it, and presented it with a sidelong look of pride. "What do you think?"

It looked like him! Arabelle said so in warm, appreciative tones while her heart wept. Those eyes! "What talented person painted this?" she managed to ask.

"It was that woman I told you about who did my fan. Miss Agathon is someone my uncle sees as a talent. I, myself, would rather have a man paint me because I could flirt with a man, but it will have to be her because His Lordship wants to patronize her."

"She certainly has a gift." Reluctant to give Simon Laurence's face back to Corisande's fluttering hands, Arabelle turned away and closed her eyes to memorize his image.

She heard his fiancée return his likeness to her tabletop of trinkets.

Chapter Eleven

Thieves and a Self=Styled Romeo

Back in Bloomsbury Square, Arabelle locked the door to the nursery schoolroom behind her, for there she finally found Genevieve. She settled onto the hearthrug to stroke the cat and nuzzle the kittens, and tell her all that had happened. The part that concerned Arabelle as much as her invitation to stay was, as she expressed to Genevieve, that "Corisande as good as *ordered* Lord Chesterfield to have Simon Laurence brought to Chesterfield House to convalesce! I tried to make it sound like he was confined to quarters, but Corisande ignored that entirely."

Genevieve laid down the lacquered box onto which she had been gluing shells. "And you are to be their guest at the same time? My word! You will see him often."

"That will be difficult to bear."

"Because he is to marry Corisande? But Arabelle! I think it must be a sign from God that he fell over senseless at the altar."

"I wish it were. But he is still betrothed to her," mourned Arabelle. "A man of honour cannot cry off from an engagement. The law binds them even now; we all know that."

"True," said Genevieve despairingly. "I suppose she is all a-twitter to marry him," she added with acrimony.

Arabelle absently spun an embroidery hoop on its axis on the table and said, "I must not dwell on that inevitability! Genevieve, come with Madam and me to the Theatre Royal in Drury Lane tonight."

Her sister's eyes grew large. "Will she let me?"

"Just be ready and in the coach before we are, and she will think it too much trouble to send you back. I will tell her that I asked you to come."

Genevieve rarely went out of an evening, for she was not deemed of marriageable age due to Lord Bastwicke's unwillingness to pay two marriage portions in the same year. "I would love to come! I never have any fun without you, Arabelle."

From the doorway came the high voice of Lenora, piping up, "I never have any fun without you, either, Arabelle." Looking adorable in a blue and yellow flowered gown topped by a yellow velvet corset with blue lacings, she ran straight for her with outstretched arms.

Arabelle hugged her. "Yes, you do. You are just a copycat. I am going to miss you the next week or two, you cheeky minx."

Lenora jerked back in frowning alarm. "Miss me? Where are you going, Arabelle?"

"To Chesterfield House."

Lenora stamped her foot. "I do not *want* you to go away. I do not *appreciate* Chest or Field House, or any other house but this one—with you in it, Arabelle."

Her sisters laughed.

Arabelle assured her gently, "I shall be home again soon, Lenora, so do not make yourself wretched." She smoothed her flaxen hair and fixed the stray wisps back into her chignon.

Lenora glanced at Genevieve and said, "I heard all about the handsome soldier who fell down and could not be wed. Can I give him one of our kittens? Can I? Please? It would make him feel better."

Arabelle locked eyes with Genevieve in wonder.

Genevieve smiled secretively as she stowed her shell work in a drawer. She unbuttoned the apron from over her peach-colored gown and said seriously to Lenora, "That would be something special to cuddle in lieu of a wife."

"That is a sweet idea, Lenora," Arabelle commended her. "I shall tell the Lieutenant what you propose, and he will tell us if he can have a kitten at the Royal Military Academy."

Lenora looked a bit deflated, twisting her fingers and thinking. Then she asked, "Will he always live there? Can he have a kitten when he moves? Soldiers go to other places, do they not? Can they take kittens when they go?"

"I shall find out for you," Arabelle promised, and gave her a hug. "You are very thoughtful."

As predicted, Lady Bastwicke accepted Genevieve's presence in the coach with an impatient huff. Arabelle had pointed out that they would all be warmer with more of them huddled together on that frosty night, and Genevieve showed Madam that she had the money to pay for her own ticket.

"I suppose you may as well keep Arabelle company while I talk with my friends," she conceded.

At the theatre, her meaning became clear. As the orchestra played the overture to Vanbrugh's *Provok'd Husband*, Lady Bastwicke chatted to a new friend, a Baroness, whose gown and grandeur rivaled her own. Two male escorts, whom Arabelle had never seen, kept the women shrieking and batting their fans at them with whoops of laughter, even during the performance. Seated at the front of the box, Arabelle and Genevieve tried to ignore their antics. Never would Aunt Claracilla behave anything like Madam did. This was a world far removed.

Arabelle surveyed the crowd below. She nudged Genevieve, who looked up from her program. "Do not glance toward the left now, but is that man in black and grey with a Spencer wig paying me conspicuous attention, or have I caught his eye twice by chance? Watch him for me. He stands next to two tall men in masks."

Genevieve presently breathed, "He is looking at you now."

Arabelle tried not to flinch, but kept her eyes on the cellos. "Still?"

"Yes. Now he is writing something down on paper and looking back at you. Oh, he does admire you, Arabelle."

"Drat!" she said under her breath. She did not like the attitude which he took in ogling her from under straight dark eyebrows that nearly met in the middle.

Genevieve touched her arm. "There are other men admiring you, too. Some are in boxes and some are on the floor, looking up. There are even some in the pit with quizzing glasses aimed at you. Is it not odd that so many wear face masks in London? Why do they?"

Arabelle retreated behind her fan to avoid their leering, and said, "Because some have ruined complexions due to smallpox—and perhaps other sorts of pox as well. I have seen many people in the streets wearing masks, and Madam said they have their various reasons. Often, she said, they want to remain incognito, so that is how they do it. Our neighbours in the country find no need to hide, do they?" Arabelle kept her eyes assiduously fixed on the stage, hoping the gawkers would turn away and watch the new act if she refused to look their way.

When the curtain presently fell on the first act, Arabelle was exclaiming to Genevieve over Carelli's spirit-lifting sonatas when she spied the man again. He was small and lean, with swarthy good looks owing mainly to his distinctive eyebrows. He seemed to be one of a party of rakish men ripe for something to do now that the interval had begun. He caught her eye and smiled up at her with blatant approval.

Arabelle flushed and turned sidewise in her chair. "Genevieve, he caught my attention in the boldest way. Do not look at him!"

"Shall I tell Mother?"

"No! Never!"

"Why not?"

"She will beckon him up here."

Genevieve looked perplexed. "And you do not want that?"

"Absolutely not. Why, look! Father's here!" she cried gladly.

Through the doorway at the back of the box came Viscount Bastwicke, his snowy wig complementing his ruddy face. He blew the girls kisses and tapped his wife on the shoulder.

She turned and jumped guiltily, for her arm lay across a skinny man's shoulder. "Daniel! Where did you come from?" Her gown impeded her from turning anything but her head and shoulders.

"From Kent, my dear," he growled, eyeing the painted men with scorn, his nostrils flaring. "My tenants have all their affairs in order now. When I arrived at home, Tibbs reported where you and my daughters had gone. There was nothing to do since the little ones were asleep, so I came to join your . . . your frolics."

"Well, sit down, then." With confused affectation, she introduced her husband to the Baroness and the men who bore no titles but that of Vainglorious Wit for the one, thought Arabelle, and Catty Coxcomb for the other. What was her mother doing hobnobbing with them, anyway? Arabelle noticed they had cooled considerably since her father put in his robust appearance.

When he settled in the chair next to her, Arabelle thought what a good thing it was to have his solidity nearby to shield her. She told him so in his ear, and indicated the crowd of men below. "How they leer in London!" she whispered scornfully.

He nodded, said, "No manners anymore!" and tweaked her nose.

"I am glad you are here for Madam's sake, too," she whispered as the curtain rose on a new scene.

Lord Bastwicke grunted and eyed the men who were gradually daring to laugh again with Lady Bastwicke at the buffoonery on stage.

When the actors took their final bows to applause and shouts, Genevieve poked Arabelle. "Your admirer is gazing again." Sure enough, he held a quizzing glass to his eye, through which he examined her thoroughly.

Self-consciously Arabelle rose, told her father she could stand it no longer, and could they leave now?

He nodded soberly and cast a dry look at his wife, whose hair plumes waved and earrings swung as she went on chattering with her friends. He must have been upset, Arabelle deduced, because he forgot his hat on the floor.

Arabelle tucked it under her elbow, gathered up her scarlet silk skirts, and followed her father and Genevieve out. She clung close to him on the way down the steps and through the crowded foyer. With Genevieve on his other arm, they passed out of the theatre. He told the girls to wait for their mother near the steps while he walked ahead through the crowd to see if their coachman had pulled into the queue yet.

From the corner of her eye, Arabelle saw a figure in a cocked hat take off running from behind a column and streak through the crowd. As Arabelle blinked, he dodged and crouched past people, and, before her startled eyes, he neatly lifted the white wig off her father's head.

Arabelle's jaw dropped.

Genevieve gasped, and cried, "No! Oh, look what just happened, Arabelle!"

The thief disappeared into the dark between the carriage wheels, and no one could stop him because of the long line of coaches making an effective fence for him.

"Ow! As Oi live! Ye've had your wig nicked!" a raggedy bystander crowed, pointing at Viscount Bastwicke. His fellows, gathered to watch the fine folk leave the opera house, took up with laughter and jeering.

"Father!" cried Arabelle, running and pushing past people to reach him.

With one hand, he covered his grizzled pate in mortification as elegant people flowed by, amused, or in sympathy at his predicament.

"Here, put your hat on!" Arabelle thrust it at him.

He clapped it low onto his brow. "Thank you, Arabelle. Let us depart with haste."

His wife hurried toward them in her grand purple dress and stared, scandalized, at her peculiar-looking husband. "What on earth? You had your wig stolen? Couldn't you do anything about it?" She stood half-laughing, half-censorious as her circle of friends caught up with her and gawped at him.

Arabelle thought it unpardonable and cruel of them all, especially her mother. She hustled her father into the darkness. "Here comes our coach, Father."

She glanced around and saw a sight that made her heart leap. Tallest amongst a circle of military officers and their ladies was the sleek, white head of Simon Laurence. He was doffing his hat and bowing to one of the women. Again out of the crowd, a wily boy of about fifteen streaked, running in his direction. As Simon's hat was still in his hand, the youth reached out to steal Simon Laurence's wig. But it did not come off.

Simon grabbed the fellow and spun him around. Instantly, he was a struggling, writhing victim in Simon's grasp, and though he tried, he could not get away. While Arabelle watched, Simon kept a vice-like hold across the chest of the would-be-thief, talking to him near his ear. A supporting circle of soldiers and other men accompanied Lieutenant Laurence, clearing the way for him as he forced the rascal along and away from the theatre.

When Arabelle crossed in front of them toward the Bastwicke coach, Simon saw her. Though intently clamping the culprit, joy leapt into his eyes at sight of her, and he flashed her a dazzling white smile.

"Who is that?" asked Lord Bastwicke, holding his hat brim low. "I am glad he avoided having *his* wig stolen."

Arabelle ached with the need to speak to Simon, who looked impressive in his dark blue coat, white breeches, and the baldric and smallsword that glinted at his side while he handed the would-be thief off to a group of men. She noticed that on Simon's broad shoulders a pair of silver epaulettes now gleamed.

Looking again at the superb military figure as they wheeled by him in the coach some minutes later, Lord Bastwicke said, "Why, he salutes us."

"He salutes Arabelle," Genevieve corrected.

Lady Bastwicke snapped, "Why would he do that?"

"I see he is an officer. A Lieutenant," observed her husband, still staring back at him with interest. "Well done how he captured that rogue. I wish he would have seen the thief who made off with my wig. He could have captured him, too, I'll warrant."

Arabelle kept her eyes unwaveringly on Simon's white head until they turned a corner and he was lost from view. She sighed from the depths of her heart. She was proud of him for preventing the thief from making him a victim. In her mind, she reviewed what she had seen. "Genevieve," she whispered in dawning delight, "it is his own hair, not a wig!"

Genevieve did not hear her, for she was hugging their father and inquiring sympathetically, "Have you another wig as good as the one stolen, Father?"

"No, he does not!" retorted Lady Bastwicke. "Why he had to wear that one tonight, and come to the opera, is beyond me! Now it's gone."

"I wanted to look my best for you, dear." Lord Bastwicke pressed his wife's hand.

Tight-lipped, she did not respond.

Whereupon Viscount Bastwicke sank back and sighed, "Ah, well. The Bible is true: *Vanity, vanity . . . all is vanity!*"

"Oh, hush!" said Lady Bastwicke.

The next morning's *Spectator* made Arabelle cry out, "Of all the nerve! What insolence!" She was reading, as she often did for amusement, the personal advertisements. "Genevieve!" she stage-whispered, looking round to make sure no one else was near the breakfast room. "Read that!" With an exhalation of renewed rage, she tapped a square of printing. She gestured at the footman clearing trays away to leave the room and shut the door.

Genevieve held the paper up to the long windows and read, *"If the beauteous Fair One, a raven-haired Juliet who sat in a front box at Theatre Royal Drury Lane Tuesday night, dressed in red with but one patch at her temple, so dignified and charming, and a white furred and hooded cloak to halo her as she left, has a soul capable of returning a most sincere and ardent love to one who thinks he had the honour of being taken notice of by her; let her with all frankness send word to Romeo, Lord R, at the Black Bull Coffee House, stating when, how, and where she will give her Romeo a meeting."*

Genevieve's eyes nearly popped. "That's you, Arabelle!"

With something near hysteria rising within her, Arabelle said, "It was the man in black and grey; I know it!"

"Did you not think him well-favoured? I did."

"Fie! If you thought that, then you may have him!" Arabelle dropped her forehead into her hand. "This is awful."

"Why awful? I think it's exciting. He chose you out of all those elegant ladies! Will you write back to this Romeo, Lord R, at the Black Bull Coffee House?"

"No!"

"Why ever not?"

In walked Lady Bastwicke in a loose green morning cartouche and a cap with knotted lace lappets shoved over her mussed hair. "Write back to whom?" she inquired, raising what would have been her eyebrows had they been painted on.

Genevieve jumped up, grabbing the newspaper before Arabelle could stop her. "Just look! A peer wrote an advertisement to Arabelle!"

Lady Bastwicke read the lines swiftly, her mouth twisting. "Well, lack-a-day! What was he like? Quick, describe him."

"He was richly dressed," Genevieve informed her, "in dark grey velvet, and with rings on."

"What was your impression of him, Arabelle?" Lady Bastwicke demanded.

Under her mother's coercion, Arabelle knew she had to contribute some comment. "He seemed to be of some prominence in a group of men quizzing us up in the boxes."

"He stared at Arabelle all through the overture," Genevieve cut in, "and smiled at her when it was over. He was dark and attractive. He could be wealthy because his coat was crushed velvet and he wore silver and gold rings."

"In truth?" Lady Bastwicke looked speculative. "He's a Lord, by his own admission." She told Genevieve to fetch paper, pen, and ink.

Arabelle felt a rising unease.

Her mother took the writing implements from Genevieve and shoved them in front of Arabelle. "Now then, what will you say to this Romeo, Lord R?"

"Say?" repeated Arabelle. "Madam, I am not going to reply."

Lady Bastwicke stared her daughter down. "Not going to reply? Are you a nitwit?"

Arabelle flushed. "No, but I do not want to correspond with that strange man."

"He will no longer be strange when you write and invite him to pay us a visit, will he?"

Arabelle's mouth had gone dry. "Madam, I cannot encourage such a bold stranger to come to this house. I do not want to meet anyone that way, and what is more, I did not like him."

"If that's the way it is, get out of my sight, you stupid girl!" Lady Bastwicke snatched up the quill, thumped into a chair, and picked up the newspaper. As she reread, she drew the feather across her lips, and her eyes took on a cunning look.

Arabelle threw down her napkin in helpless frustration and fled.

Genevieve hurried after her.

Lady Bastwicke shouted, "Pack your best things for Chesterfield House! Tell Bertha to hurry. I promised them you would arrive this afternoon."

As the sisters hastened up the staircase, Genevieve asked, "Why don't you really want to meet him? I thought he looked the most striking of that group of men."

"To answer your question," Arabelle said over her shoulder, marching into their bedchamber and extracting a letter from under her pillows, "read this. It's from Aunt Claracilla."

Genevieve read aloud while Arabelle checked the contents of her trunks standing open about the room. *My Dear Arabelle, You are now, my sweet, removed to London, in which hive of grasping and greed gentlemen are noticing you.*"

"That's certainly true," crowed Genevieve, her face taking on lively interest. *"What I have upon my heart to tell you today is advice to distinguish the true suitor from the false seducer. This will be difficult for you to do without the assistance of your nearest and dearest. Make them your confidantes. Never lend your ear to impertinent go-betweens or infamous match-makers . . ."*

"Like Madam?" Genevieve inserted, and then guiltily continued, *"who are bribed by the sharpers and coxcombs about town to betray ladies of fortune into their hands, as I have seen in my day. Such may attempt to sway you by the words that: some fine man of great merit and fortune is deeply in love with you. Such tricksters may use the following points to influence you in such a suitor's favour: That he has seen you at some public place and is impatient to make to you a declaration of his passion.*"

Genevieve marveled, "How does she know these things?"

"She has lived," said Arabelle, "and she knows the dangers."

"She is always so wise. Let's see what her second point is. *That he would not willingly make any overtures to your father until he knows what reception he shall meet with from yourself. That your father may probably raise such objections to him as may be altogether groundless. That your father may have private views in marrying you to some friend of his own, without consulting your inclination or interest. That it would be improper, therefore, for your father to be entrusted with the secret until you have seen the party proposed.*"

Genevieve looked shocked. "Not tell Father? That is exactly what that man's advertisement infers."

"Precisely."

"That, after all, it lies in your own breast either to admit of, or decline, his offer. My dear Arabelle, discountenance all such officious busy bodies, and boldly assure them: That you are determined to listen to no propositions, how seemingly advantageous soever, without the approbation and consent of your father. For he, you may be assured, is the one who studies in his heart of hearts to further your happiness. Such prudent conduct as this will make your suitors (if they have any sense of shame) desist from their designs upon you. By such response, you will never lose a true lover who is worthy of your encouragement. For, if the man really loves you, he will readily apply to your father. In case he gives up his suit after your rebuff, you may justly conclude that his intentions were to basely betray you.

Then you will have just reason to rejoice that you returned a deaf ear to his artful insinuations. "

"I see!" breathed Genevieve, one hand to her throat. She read on, *"If a fellow should presume to send you letters without first making a regular application to your father, you should get some friend to write him, but be sure you do not write yourself. Your friend can write something in this vein: 'Sir, I am to inform you that the lady you addressed thinks herself obliged to every one who has a good opinion of her, but she begs that you will not give yourself—or her—the trouble of any more letters, for things are so circumstanced that she has neither inclination nor power to encourage your address. '*

Give my love to Genevieve, and write soon to

> *Your ever faithful and affectionate*
> *Aunt Claracilla. "*

When Genevieve looked up at Arabelle, she breathed wondrously, "God bless our aunt!"

"Yes, indeed."

"Has Madam seen this letter?"

"No, and I am afraid that, if I show it to her, she will be highly affronted. Don't ask me why. I just know it. She kept the last letter I received from Aunt Claracilla."

"It is because she does not think like this at all." Genevieve reread silently from the letter. "I shall be that friend if you need one, Arabelle, to write back to that bold man as Aunt Claracilla said to do."

"Thank you, Genevieve, but he does not know my name or where I live, so if I send no reply at all, there should be an effectual end to it."

Arabelle's bath steamed. She drew her knees up and let the wonderful hot water soothe her back and neck, and close in around her jaw as she settled low into its comforting warmth. Her nose received the full effect of the lavender oil from the surface of the water, and she laid her head back on a rolled-up towel to relax and think.

Lady Bastwicke popped her capped head into the bedchamber and reminded her in lecture fashion, "To bathe every day is crucial to Lord Chesterfield, you must recall. Even his servants do it several times a week. He has got all of his friends bathing, for his nose is fastidious."

Arabelle nodded, but was hardly listening, having bathed daily since Madam's same speech influenced the family five months ago. It was an unusual practice, but Arabelle found it so pleasant that she felt she could hardly bear to go through a day without it. She especially liked keeping her hair clean. She and Genevieve had much more luxuriant curls than other women, who coated their hair with powder and brushed it out to try to rid themselves of last week's pomade. Or they added more pomade, and even lacquered their curls into stiff obedience.

When Arabelle tied on her panniers over her chemise and put her arms into the pink silk corset the maid held for her, Lady Bastwicke came in, nearly ready to go, and actually laced her up the back, very tightly. "Remember to take an interest in all that Lord and Lady Chesterfield say," she advised. "Be congenial to Corisande and you will be in the very centre of everything that matters to your present and future life. Since she lives with the Earl, she is a little somebody, whereas she never was before. You are a Viscount's daughter, so you have more of an advantage than she does. Just be sure you do not behave like a wallflower. You must be noticed to catch a husband."

Arabelle could not bring herself to reply. Why would she want men to notice her? There was only one man whose attention she desired. While she pinned silk roses into her chignon, she brightened her thoughts with a will. At least she would enjoy the company of Lord Chesterfield.

Chapter Twelve

The Prude

"I really think," said Lady Bastwicke to Lady Chesterfield the next day as she perched her grand grey gown triumphantly onto a chair in the music room at Chesterfield House, "that we ought to have the two painted together."

Countess Chesterfield, in butter yellow with a fan to match, looked past the harp to the two other occupants of the long room. Arabelle and Corisande made a striking picture seated beyond the marble column against white wall panels graced by gilded *passementerie*. Their spreading gowns in pale gold on Corisande and teal on Arabelle harmonized with the tapestry in the French chairs. "Painted together?" echoed Her Ladyship. "I never would have thought of that."

"An excellent plan, Lady Bastwicke," said Lord Chesterfield from the arched doorway. He actually looked at the woman, not through her this time.

Lady Bastwicke returned his look with smiling hauteur.

"Do you really think so, Philip?" pressed his lady doubtfully.

Crossing one silk-encased leg over the other as he leaned against the shapely chimneypiece, he surveyed the young women and said,

"Arabelle, with her dark beauty, would put colour into an otherwise bland study."

His wife's brown eyes went huge. "Philip!"

With a smile and a bow for Arabelle, Lord Chesterfield left the room.

Lady Bastwicke clearly wanted to preen over this *coup*, but emotions warred on her face as she eyed her strikingly beautiful daughter.

Arabelle, watching her mother make quips to the Countess and silly eyes at the Earl, wished Madam had stayed away today. Having been welcomed to Chesterfield House yesterday afternoon, Arabelle had moved into the chamber of rose and blue next to Corisande's room. Maids and footmen took care of all her settling-in needs, and she had spent a pleasant dinner with Lord and Lady Chesterfield and Corisande. This morning, they had all just risen from the breakfast table when Lady Bastwicke was back, paying a uniquely early morning call. She must have risen at six or seven, Arabelle surmised. It was unprecedented.

Corisande talked on, moving now and then to adjust a tasseled bolster just so beneath her elbow or to lift up puffs of her gold taffeta skirt to her satisfaction. Arabelle had wondered why Corisande almost tripped over her to reach that gilded settee with its pastoral French scenes. It became clear when Arabelle saw the huge mirror opposite.

A footman appeared with cards on a glass salver, and bowed to Lady Chesterfield. "Two gentlemen desire to honour Your Ladyship with a visit," he said.

Hearing that, Corisande left off her description of a supper in Ranelagh Gardens at which she had spoken to a strange man who had paid her a compliment on her mouth. At the news that men were imminent in this very room, she sat up to force her bosom higher out of her beribboned corset. Eyeing her reflection, she settled back onto one elbow, put one foot with plenty of ankle showing onto a footstool, and swayed her fan without covering her bosom. Corisande paid Arabelle no heed, finding it of utmost importance to hold her pose.

Arabelle wondered what Simon Laurence would think of his fiancée's calculated preparations for other men's eyes.

It was Sir Pomeroy Chancet who glided into the far end of the room, wearing a mauve coat and knee breeches, a glittering ivory and silver waistcoat, and an ivory wig with mauve bows down the pigtail. His dark brows lifted in delight when he spotted the young women, but he did his duty by the older ones first.

Arch flirtation punctuated by shrieks of laughter and "Oh, Sir Pomeroy, you *roué!*" emitted from Lady Bastwicke.

Sir Pomeroy looked discreetly around, checking for signs of Lord Chesterfield, who must not hear such inelegant sounds. When the Baronet finally achieved their end of the room, he took Corisande's extended fingers, saying, "Just look at you nymphs, seated here for my eyes to feast upon!" While he kissed Corisande's offered lips, he caught Arabelle's eye and winked.

When he turned with arms outstretched to her, she gave him only her lifted hand with a friendly but challenging look in her eye. She did not like Sir Pomeroy's devouring red mouth. As it was, the kiss he smooched onto her wrist made her want to scrub it off.

His brown eyes were as hungry as his voice. "Fortune favours me! I am so thrilled to see your nubile person here." He finally let go her fingers. "Oh, Corisande," he said in lively sing-song, "you may be interested to see the friend I brought with me. There," he flipped his walking-stick ribbons, "now he comes." He stood still and awaited her reaction.

Corisande slid her eyes toward the figure bowing to her aunt.

He was a thin man in a black Spencer wig, skinny legs in black breeches and hose, and a locust green coat. He turned to smile at Lady Bastwicke. Olive skin, straight brown eyebrows . . . Arabelle realized with dismay that he was the man from Drury Lane who had written the advertisement to "Juliet."

At sight of him, Corisande's eyes flared to their widest extent. "Lord Rutley?" she eked out, her face turning white. Down came her feet from the footstool, and up she leapt. She panicked and grabbed Sir Pomeroy's arm. "How did he get in here?"

Sir Pomeroy detained her by the arm so she could not flee. "Anything for a friend, Corisande," he said in a meaningful tone which Arabelle did not understand.

Lord Rutley walked jerkily toward them, his shoulders slightly stooped, his close-set eyes flicking from Corisande to Arabelle and back with some sort of triumph.

"No need to go primp any more," prevaricated Sir Pomeroy, swinging a desperate Corisande against her will to face the man. "You're lovely enough for him now. Look, here he is. Rutley declares he knows you like the back of his hand," Sir Pomeroy tittered.

Corisande turned to Lord Rutley. She had nailed a smile to her mouth.

He had wily eyes, did Lord Rutley. "Miss Corisande Wells!" he said, snapping them in malicious pleasure. "My, my," he said in a reedy voice while gesturing over her person, "how exciting it is to meet up with you again. Here, of all places," he added in a conspiratorial whisper, gesturing back over the sumptuous room.

Corisande pretended nonchalance, but Arabelle saw how hard her eyes were. In an unorthodox move, Corisande gestured the men's attention away from herself and onto Arabelle. "Here, gracing our society, is the Honourable Arabelle Lamar."

Sir Pomeroy filled the breach with a bow and an elaborate twirl of his handkerchief, paying additional homage to Arabelle. "I know!" he trilled. "We are old friends already."

Lord Rutley's fox-like eyes ran wildly up and down her. "You find me completely staggered—utterly charmed, Miss Lamar." There was eagerness in his manner, but no surprise.

With sinking heart, she realized that somehow he had known she would be here. As her ire rose, he kissed her cheek because she quickly turned her head to prevent his achieving her lips. The man stunk. Obviously, he was not of Lord and Lady Chesterfield's circle. Arabelle instantly smeared off the wetness behind her fan. She hoped Corisande would take back the attention of this unwanted admirer. Two unwanted admirers.

"Shall we take a turn in the gardens?" proposed Sir Pomeroy. "It is uncommonly warm today. It makes me think of spring." He wiggled his eyebrows up and down.

"By all means." Lord Rutley cast a look toward the older women, but offered the wary Corisande his arm. The feeling conveyed was that the men were in a hurry to whisk, in gleeful good fortune, Corisande and herself out of the room. Arabelle did not want to go. She did not think Corisande did, either.

Lady Bastwicke saw their hesitation, and stood up to call out encouragement. "Why don't you young ladies show the men the spacious back gardens?"

Sir Pomeroy smiled invitingly at Arabelle. "Come, that is settled nicely. Let us go enjoy the fresh air, shall we?"

As Arabelle reluctantly rose, her nose filled with his rampant perfume. "I do need air," she said, and followed Corisande and Lord Rutley, but not very closely. Arabelle and Sir Pomeroy passed their reflection in the huge gilt mirror. He touched the clover shaped patch on his cheekbone and turned his head to look at everything else about his person. His hooded brown eyes gleamed in satisfaction.

Arabelle saw her dark teal gown with its lace-edged V down the corset-stomacher. Her waist looked slim and her hair smoothly pulled back from her forehead and temples, her curls loose and abundant along her white neck. Her square bodice had just enough lace tucked in to make her feel confidently covered.

"It is unspeakably wonderful that you are here," Sir Pomeroy purred, moving lithely forward to button her redingote as soon as the footman had her sleeves upon her arms. With Corisande in a short pink cloak and the ladies with pattens over their shoes, the four of them left out the French doors, down the stone stairs, and onto the lawn.

"Yes, isn't it, Sir Pomeroy?" threw Corisande over her shoulder. "Or else you two would have to fight over me. Thank you ever so, Arabelle!" She sounded more like her usual self. What had that rapidly-whispering Lord Rutley said to bring her around? Or was she acting?

Lord Rutley, while supposedly listening to Corisande, turned a wolfish perusal over Arabelle. His manner gave her an uneasy prickle down her spine.

Sir Pomeroy slowed Arabelle's progress deliberately to whisper, "Did you see how His Lordship looked you over?" He pulled her arm close to his side and said near her cheek, "Do you see how I gorge myself on your creamy loveliness?"

"Sir Pomeroy!" Arabelle yanked her hand from his arm and thrust it into her black fur muff.

"You cannot believe my free tongue?" He laughed. "You shall grow to love it. I have a reputation among London drawing rooms for my shocking style. Others are accustomed to it; you are not . . . yet," he emphasized. "You are such a welcome sight in our circle. I am tickled pink that I discovered you first."

Arabelle wished his merry eyes would stop their proprietary ogling. She fastened the topmost silver frog of her redingote so he no longer had anything to see.

Corisande kept up a low dialogue with Lord Rutley as she led the way to two wide swings hung from noble old trees at the bottom of the garden. Lord Rutley seated her on one, and grasped her by the waist to steady her into position. The sun shone, the sky was spacious blue, and Corisande's gown lifted with her first flight aloft.

Sir Pomeroy cleared his throat in a sound of approval, and Arabelle saw, to her shame as a woman, that Corisande's ribbon garters showed, as did all the bare skin above them. What would higher swings reveal to the men when her under-petticoat lifted?

"Have a care, Corisande!" she called, an edge to her voice as she tried to warn her friend of her imminent exposure.

"Your swing, Miss Lamar," Sir Pomeroy hastily intervened, holding the other one for her. "May I do the honours?"

Arabelle eyed him pointedly and said, "Your hat band, please."

He stared at her, uncomprehending.

She gazed at him frostily with her lashes at half-mast.

"Ah, yes," he then replied, and slipped the silver braid off his hat.

Arabelle directed him to wrap it around the hem of her gown.

Corisande glanced at the operation with scorn, which attitude she obviously shared with Lord Rutley. Arabelle watched that one walk around to the front and, with hands on hips, chuckle up at Corisande. She flirted while she swung, her petticoats flaring high. His eyes lit over the sights he beheld, and he stood leering, eyes glued, the next time her skirts billowed.

Arabelle was shocked and dismayed, and felt herself the ultimate prude. She told herself fiercely that never would she expose herself to these men. That Corisande chose to do so made Arabelle feel very tame and out of place. It was obvious that those three were of one mind, and she of quite another. Moreover, what was Corisande, fiancée of Simon Laurence, doing, encouraging Lord Rutley's lewd attentions? And why had she seemed terror-stricken when he first appeared?

Arabelle asked Sir Pomeroy to halt her after only a dozen swings. She did not want to be pushed by men who were so ripe and ready to glimpse whatever they possibly could. Why did Corisande egg them on?

"Oh, but we have scarcely begun this amusement," Sir Pomeroy objected, pushing her again and moving around to her front.

A liveried footman glided toward them from the house and said, "Lord Chesterfield requests your presence in the drawing room, Miss Wells."

Lord Rutley grappled and caught Corisande's swing, and danced about clumsily as he strove to bring her to a stop. She skipped down, and coaxed as she moved backward toward the house, "Come on, all of you, you can't stay out here any longer. A chill breeze came up."

"Up her chemise," quipped Sir Pomeroy to Lord Rutley.

Rutley guffawed and said, "Your turn to escort her, Chancet. I get Miss Lamar."

If it had been in Arabelle's power, she would have streaked after Corisande and away from this self-styled Romeo, but because it took time for him to remove the hatband from her hem, she was imprisoned in his company.

Lord Rutley smiled crookedly up at her, removing her yards of gown slowly from confinement. "I am grateful to you for this *rendezvous*. You were extremely clever." His face lit with intensity. "We can meet so freely in this company. I thank you, fair Juliet."

Arabelle stared at him, frowning. "*Rendezvous?*" She yanked the last of her skirt away, stood up, and moved past him toward the mansion. "You are most mistaken, Lord Rutley," she informed him over her shoulder. "I arranged no *rendezvous* with you."

As he stared after her, the swing banged him in the thigh. "Ow!" He recovered and called condescendingly, "But of course you did not. You are a well-bred young lady, and prudent besides. I shall say no more except that I am the happiest lover in London. You will be here at the Chesterfield Ball, of course. You don't have to return to your *home* before then, do you?" he asked, as if that were the dullest place she could possibly go.

"I stay for awhile to keep Corisande company." Drat! She should not have told him that.

"How providential! I shall dance with you at the ball, without fail," he promised.

Arabelle said coldly, "I may not attend, so do not come on my account."

"I will live for nothing else, O Juliet." He snatched her hand and kissed it before she could stop him. His jaw was dark blue despite close shaving, and she felt repulsed by the texture of his skin and the smell of his unwashed body. Her anger broiled. How dared he make so bold with her? She remembered Aunt Claracilla's letters of warning.

As they entered the house, she met her mother moving with great state down the staircase with the Countess and two other women who had arrived in the meantime. The coy look Lady Bastwicke threw Lord Rutley made Arabelle strongly suspect that this meeting was her doing. Their plot made Arabelle increasingly livid. The more she thought about her mother's answering that vulgar ad with an invitation letter supposedly from Arabelle herself, the more choked she felt. Of course Madam had done it! Struggling with her rage, Arabelle preceded Lord Rutley stiffly into the Earl's drawing room.

By the licking fire stood Simon Laurence. What an unexpected ray of sunshine! Her spirits warmed at once, and it seemed as if all her troubles vanished. He looked divine—manly and vital—and the sight of him slayed Arabelle's heart anew. He wore a thinner bandage angled over his injured temple, which gave him an unusual, rakish look that did not diminish his noble mien at all.

Corisande ran and clasped him by the arm of his blue uniform, and turned up her face for him to kiss.

Arabelle felt like spinning Corisande around and pinching her puckered lips with a clothes peg.

Simon kissed Corisande's hand briefly. "Why, it's Arabelle Lamar!" he called as she moved into the room. He put Corisande aside, bypassed the men with nods, and said socially to Arabelle, "It is a great pleasure to see you . . . here, Miss Lamar."

She squeezed his hand as she curtseyed to him, but she could not speak. She felt weak as a duckling. She stood poised, trying to appear normal. It was a challenge, for she reveled in the fire of feeling that leapt between them. As a log in the white fireplace fell in a shower of sparks, he smiled into her eyes. She acknowledged him for a split-second and lowered her eyelids. Her hardest endeavour was now to hide from everyone her burning love for him.

Corisande sidled up to him. "Oh, Simon," she said pointedly, "we must get married now that you are back."

"I realize," Simon continued, "that I cannot keep myself sequestered at the Academy with this unfinished business to take care of, so I have come to stay here for a time, Corisande. Thank you, Lord Chesterfield, for your invitation."

"You are most welcome," responded the Earl, relaxed in his favourite tufted silk chair, eyeing them all before he turned a page of his book.

"It was my invitation in the first place," Corisande put in.

Staring at Simon, Sir Pomeroy exploded, "You are to stay in this house? Why, that's unfair, you lucky dog!"

Lord Rutley remarked, "That should prove stimulating." He lifted a glass from the footman's tray and drank, frowning.

"Absolutely," Simon agreed. "My Captain said a dip into the world would benefit me at this juncture."

"Yes," said Lord Chesterfield decidedly, "for the knowledge of the world is only acquired in the world—not in a closet."

"Vis-à-vis a barracks room," added Simon. "Although I must confess that I have had the best dreams in that new chamber of mine."

"What kind of dreams?" the Earl inquired.

"Your Lordship, I could not describe all the beauty that has danced into my heart there." He smiled, preventing his eyes from touching Arabelle's, though she gasped at his meaning with a frisson of pleasure.

She picked up a goblet and drank. How audacious he was, conveying secret messages to her so dangerously in front of the others, just as he had done under her mother's nose in the coach.

Corisande straightened her spine, cast a superior look at Lord Rutley, and possessed herself of Simon's arm. Preening, she said to him, "I am glad to hear that you dream of me there."

The secretive look that Arabelle feared—and hoped—to see from Simon now came stealthily from between his double fence of black lashes. Their country dance and his tight embrace beneath the willow tree filled her again, full force. She dared not look at him for more than one appreciative second. She turned to watch the flames.

"So, Laurence," said Lord Chesterfield, "you were graduated early, and Captain Ligonier made of you a Lieutenant. Did you gentlemen know this?"

Sir Pomeroy stepped forward and offered cheery felicitations and a handshake. Lord Rutley merely gave a miniscule bow.

Arabelle turned and said with genuine pride, "Congratulations! You make us all proud of you, Lieutenant Laurence."

Simon smiled at her, looking gratified. How very broad-shouldered and well-made he was, gracing the room with his commanding presence. His intelligent forehead was slightly creased with abashment and pleasure as he received further accolades.

Lord Chesterfield drawled, "Your insistence to return to your precious Academy is a bit tiresome, Lieutenant, but since you must, you must. I am sure that Corisande will join my entreaties to make you convalesce here whenever you can, and for as long as possible. Treat this house as your own."

"Thank you, My Lord."

"I'm glad you're a Lieutenant now," Corisande gushed up at Simon. "What's next?—General?"

Arabelle and Simon locked eyes, and while they did not exactly roll them heavenward, their reaction was the same. Lord Chesterfield's lips twitched and he lifted his book in front of his face and turned a page.

"Oh, Simon, do stay!" Corisande begged, tugging the gilded braid on the pocket of his coat. "I mean, wouldn't it be amusing for us all to be so together? Arabelle is staying with me awhile, but she cannot stay forever, and I need someone."

Sir Pomeroy inserted saucily, "Someone to marry you while the coals are still warm, eh, Corisande?"

She treated them all to one of her tinkling laughs before she caught Lord Chesterfield's eagle eye, and halted mid-tinkle.

Lord Rutley said slowly but pointedly, "What is your rush, Miss Wells?"

She slanted an uneasy, almost fearful look at Lord Rutley, and turned her back upon him. "My fiancé is eager to finish what he began. Are you not, Simon?"

With lips tight, hands clasped behind his back, he gave her a small, wordless bow.

Sir Pomeroy, laughing, observed to Rutley on their settee, "Our Corisande is more than ready, eh?" He grinned at her, but sauntered to take a seat on Arabelle's footstool.

Lord Rutley kept watching Corisande, a speculative light in his eyes. Then he shifted his gaze Arabelle's way. While Sir Pomeroy chatted to her, she felt strange undercurrents between him, Lord Rutley, and Corisande. She did not understand any of it.

Chapter Thirteen

A Model Friendship

"Lower your nose, Miss Wells, or I shall have to paint your long nostrils," said the pert, dark-haired Roberta Agathon who sat at an easel, a white smock covering her blue gown.

Corisande, highly offended, sniffed, and lowered her chin.

The artist turned her attention to Arabelle. "Will you lean your face closer to Miss Wells?" Observing them closely, she moved toward the two young women. "Let me tip your brim up so it does not shadow those graceful eyebrows, Miss Lamar. Now we have it! Can you hold that, ladies?"

"Yes, Miss Agathon," said Arabelle.

Corisande expelled snuff breath onto her. She had been experimenting with the stuff all morning, claiming she excessively enjoyed sniffing it. Arabelle found that hard to believe.

"I imagine you are tired of sitting," murmured Arabelle. She knew Corisande had already posed for her individual miniature that morning. Corisande said she wanted to put the two miniatures side by side on the mantelpiece in their home for all to see when she married Simon. "This modeling is tiresome, but I have to do it for the result. Lord Chesterfield came by and told Miss Agathon to abandon my miniature for now, and get our double portrait done so he can display it at the ball. She will have to paint awfully fast—will you not, Miss Agathon? His Lordship wants to give you exposure as the new talent in town. He expects his friends will be astonished that you are a woman. He likes to create that kind of sensation," Corisande finished to Arabelle.

Arabelle wondered if sensation could be Lord Chesterfield's motive.

Then a movement interrupted her thoughts. Through the arched doorway, Simon Laurence appeared.

The scene he beheld made him halt in great interest. Arabelle and Corisande, arrayed in glorious, wide-brimmed flowered hats, posed, leaning together at a pedestal. Corisande wore a pale pink gown and had one knee on a gilt-legged chair. Arabelle's stance was more of a side view. Her feminine grace showed to exciting advantage as his eyes followed her curving outline. Her dark-haired, romance-eyed beauty made his heart beat rapidly. Since Corisande could not see him, he stood and appreciated Arabelle entirely, from the creamy curves of her lace-decorated bosom to her tiny waist and the outward sweep of her rose pink gown. From the plume of her wide-brimmed hat set at a flirtatious angle, all the way down to her curvy pink shoe, she took his breath away.

Arabelle flushed under Simon's homage, and admired him for a long moment. She thought his manly stance and noble attitude had the same source as real aristocratic bearing. She also knew he had an unselfish confidence that spelled true dignity.

Miss Agathon cried, "Heavenly expression, Miss Lamar! Dear God, let me capture it!" She worked furiously, eyes flicking up to Arabelle and down again to her canvas, her face full of creative impetus.

Corisande yawned without covering her mouth, and suddenly stopped. She jerked around to see what held Arabelle's attention.

Simon relaxed against the doorframe, letting his smile grow.

"Simon!" shrieked Corisande. "When did you sneak in?"

Arabelle felt Corisande's suspicious stare turn upon her again, but she had schooled her expression straight at Miss Agathon in as pleasant a look as she could conjure up without actually smiling.

"Do come here and talk to us, Simon," called Corisande. "This is so tiresome."

"I would love to," he said smoothly, "except the world waits. I have work to do."

"Like what?"

"Duties, and dispatches to write. Having taken in this loveliness, I shall accomplish more with the vision to spur me on."

"Oh Simon," pouted Corisande, her lashes fluttering uncertainly at the compliment not only to herself but also to Arabelle, "I never see you anymore. We must reschedule our wedding."

"I shall speak with the Earl."

The artist smiled and her voice throbbed as she called, "You are looking superb, Simon Laurence. I want to paint you full length next time. May I?"

"Good afternoon, Miss Agathon." He flashed a smile over all three of them and was gone.

"That fiancé of yours is an artist's dream," said Miss Agathon. "I hear he is staying in this house. How divine a situation, but will he sit for me again? Stand, rather? I do not care if anyone pays me, I simply must paint his perfect limbs . . . those shoulders, ah! What lover-like eyes, what sculpted lips!"

"Miss Agathon!" cried Corisande, glaring at her.

"But these men," grumbled Miss Agathon, ignoring her, "always have something more important to do."

Corisande's next icy query was, "Arabelle, what did you look so heavenly about?"

Refusing to be trapped into admitting the truth, Arabelle's mind raced. "It is hard to express, but it is so wonderful to be here, to be invited by you, to have such exciting moments in this grand house"—glimpses of Simon, she thought— "even to having my portrait painted with you. I haven't told you how happy I am to be your guest, Corisande."

"Oh," said Corisande, seeming satisfied. "We'll have more fun than this, I swear. When this portrait is finished, won't all my friends be envious? *Two* pictures!"

"You are fortunate. The Stanhopes indulge you so generously that you must feel very thankful."

"Sometimes," admitted Corisande. "Just think: soon we will have a grand ball here. By the way, I have written to all my friends that you are with me. They are agog that you are my favoured friend. We—you and I—will be *It* at the ball, especially with a portrait of us to be unveiled then, in front of highest London Society. Do you know what that means?"

"Tell me."

"It means power!" trilled Corisande, clasping her hands. "Two such beauties as we are, in this magnificent house, with all His Lordship's influence behind us—why, we can have anything and anyone we want!"

"Please be still, Miss Wells!" snapped Miss Agathon. "I am trying to paint your mouth. Do you want it wide open?"

Corisande huffed, but forced on a beatific smile.

"No teeth," Miss Agathon ordered. "You will never be able to sustain that grin."

Arabelle puzzled over Corisande's effusions. She whispered, "Corisande, who else could you want, with all that power you revel in? You already have Lieutenant Laurence."

"Mm-hm," murmured Corisande, keeping her mouth shut.

As they threw off their wide-brimmed *Bergère* hats and moved out of the painting room, Corisande said, "About the ball, Arabelle. We will want to look our absolute best. I was talking with my friend, Lady Lavinia, about that. A nap is a must for ladies each day before the big event."

Arabelle chuckled. "A nap?"

"We are serious! We must lie down about three o'clock so we will be rested and ravishing for our important night. Will you start with one today, as I shall?" Corisande paused before a mirror on the landing and smoothed back her blonde hair from her forehead. "You have to build up to your best beauty, starting early in the week, or it is not efficacious."

Arabelle, never a day-sleeper, felt at a loss; but Corisande seemed to take her compliance as settled. "We shall be awakened by four, and ready for dinner by half of five each day," she continued. "Keep to the schedule, Arabelle, as I shall. This will be as important to His Lordship as bathing. He will not want us to disappoint his guests with weary faces and no stamina for dancing."

"I see." When Arabelle reached her bedchamber, she spied a letter propped against her pillows in the dimness of her bed curtains. She bounced onto the bed, lay on her stomach, and eagerly cracked the seal. It was from Genevieve.

> *Dearest Arabelle,*
>
> *When are you coming home? Life is so dull without you. Except that Father came in from his club last night, and guess what? He had his wig stolen—again! It was a new one he just bought, too. Poor Father, he had to cram his hat on to get home with some degree of dignity as before, but he didn't look half-odd, just like the first time. He said a huge, rough man went by him, carrying a wood plank on his shoulder. Apparently, a boy was lying on it with his hands ready, hidden under a tarpaulin. The rascal reached out and snatched off Father's wig but threw back his hat, and the man strode away, keeping the board lowered to ward Father off. The scoundrels went into a dark alley, and that was that. How risky it is to have our father going out into vile London streets! Keep yourself safe, Arabelle.*
>
> *Is it worthwhile to stay at Chesterfield House? Are you having a grand time and all that? I probably shouldn't tell you this because it won't do you any good, but Father asked Madam how we are ever supposed to repay all the honour Lord Chesterfield is giving you. He says we are not nearly as extravagant as Lord C is, and what is to happen when it is our turn to entertain the refined Stanhopes? Mother went red, and said Lady C attended her drawing room, and that the vases from Venice were in full view, and that she can certainly give a dinner party some evening for them, and then ask them to share our box at Drury Lane. (Doesn't she think they want to occupy their own?) Anyway, Father just shook his head in a hopeless way.*
>
> *Jerome and Lenora keep hounding me, whining, "Where is Arabelle? I want Arabelle," all the time. I miss you, and remain, as ever,*
>
> *Your devoted sister,*
> *Genevieve*

"Oh, Genevieve!" Arabelle sighed. She went and kneeled on the window seat, wondering why her Father had suffered the same misfortune twice. All she could think of was to tell Simon Laurence, for there he came, strolling toward the front door through the colonnade below. Her heart leaped with gladness. She streaked to the vanity mirror to check her hair and put powder on her nose.

From the landing, she saw the porter open the door to Simon's knock. In he breezed, shedding his caped redingote. What a way he had of brightening up the house. She soaked in the sight of him, splendidly framed in the centre of the three arches held aloft by white marble columns.

When he saw her, his face lit up with a smile. He looked around for onlookers (of which there were none, for the porter had taken his cloak away), and whispered, "Arabelle! What a welcome sight!"

"As are you, Lieutenant," she stage whispered, smiling at him gloriously. Was she too bold? What if Corisande should hear them upstairs via the echoing acoustics?

Simon beckoned her to come with him so they would be hidden from above by one of the flying staircases. She floated down the steps and into the shadows with him. When he took her hand, she whispered, "Simon! I need to lay a perplexity before someone, and I'm hoping you're my man."

He smiled at her from under his dark eyebrows and kissed her hand, sending a shiver of delight through her. "Consider me very willingly your man."

She sighed. "Have you time to listen to the trouble now?"

"By all means."

Leading the way to Lord Chesterfield's anteroom on the ground floor where he received various and sundry callers on business, Arabelle closed the door firmly.

Simon looked at the door in front of them and murmured, "Let me make sure that we're alone."

She did not take a seat on one of the highly polished benches, but fingered an umbrella handle in the grillwork stand while he ascertained that Lord Chesterfield was not in his receiving room.

"Simon, do you find it at all odd that my father should have his wig stolen from his head twice in one week?"

"Yes, I do. Wig thievery is prevalent, but I find it unusual that your father should be a victim twice—unless the thief is someone who knows his movements, and planned it." Simon paced the squares on the marble floor to the end of the room, and about-faced.

"Thank you for listening to this," said Arabelle. "There is likely nothing anyone can do about my father's wigs now that they are gone."

"I would like to do something to find out, Arabelle." How lovely her name sounded when he said it. "I want to know anything that concerns you."

"I am touched. You are so good to me."

He flushed slightly, but looked well pleased. "You may be interested to hear that, outside the Drury Lane Theatre the night you and your family were there, I felt the violence of having my hair pulled."

"Yes, I saw that! I've wanted to ask you about it."

Simon grinned ironically. "He thought I wore a wig, and it was his aim to have it."

"Your hair is your own, then?"

"Oh yes." He shot her a droll look. "It turned white many years ago. I inherit it from my father and grandfather."

"Aren't you fortunate? It looks wonderful. You don't have to powder it, and it's more stunning than any wig."

His dimple appeared. "Thank you."

"What did you do to the scoundrel? I saw you catch him and bear him away. Well done!"

"I demanded to know why he was after my hair. He was a boy of about fifteen who blubbered that his guv'nor had ordered him to lift any good-looking wigs in front of the theatre. We trundled him off to the nearest Magistrate."

"Where is the boy now?"

"In Newgate Prison, awaiting trial. I tell him every time I bring him food that he can get out if he reveals the name of the man for whom he did those foul deeds. So far, he has not told me. I hate to leave him there in gaol, but something has to give. It had better be him. Now I have your father's cases with which to test him. I know he belongs to a band of thieves, so he could give information on the culprit who lifted your father's wig that night, and maybe also in the street. I think he will talk when he feels miserable enough."

Quick footsteps clicked on the marble floor, and the double doors burst open. In breezed Corisande. "Oh-ho, who's in here?" she cried accusingly as she faced Arabelle and Simon.

Behind her hovered a thickset man in an abundant periwig wearing a black and red suit.

Simon said, "As you see, we are waiting to see His Lordship." He gestured to the closed door to Lord Chesterfield's office.

"What for?" inquired Corisande, raking Arabelle with a suspicious look.

Arabelle thought quickly and said, "I need to ask him about going home for a day."

Simon said, "I stop and chat with His Lordship most anytime, but today I shall tell him that my Captain's family has a painting by Goya that they want to sell."

"Oh?" said Corisande, folding her arms. "I know he is absolutely stuck on his *Madonna* by Rubens, but I suppose he might like a painting by a different artist. But right now we have Mr. Colley Cibber here to see His Lordship." She beckoned him in.

Arabelle said, curtseying to the famous actor and author, "I will step aside from the queue so you do not have to wait so long, Mr. Cibber."

Simon gestured Mr. Cibber into the anteroom, and Arabelle whisked herself out of the way of the grateful man, who seemed in a hurry.

Mr. Cibber said to Simon, "I saw you in *A Would-Be Gentleman* with your cadet troupe. If you ever want a role on the public stage, come see me. I don't remember when I laughed so hard. You were stupendous."

Simon grinned, thanked him, and bowed himself out.

Corisande remained fawning over the visitor.

Outside of the half-closed door, Simon, his arm hidden from Corisande's view by a Corinthian column, gave Arabelle's fingers a squeeze. "Let's leave before she discovers that His Lordship is not in his office." He grinned conspiratorially.

Her heart beat fast at his daring ways. This was the sort of adventurous spirit she loved about him. When Corisande's heels sounded on the marble, Arabelle dropped his hand like lightning.

"He is not in his receiving room, so I must go up and find him," she huffed. She skipped forward and took Simon's arm, making Arabelle feel out of place. She did not follow them up the staircase. While Corisande chattered up at him, Simon wore a guarded look.

Arabelle's heart wrenched to see him trapped into marriage with Corisande Wells when he obviously did not love her.

Chapter Fourteen

Caught Napping

When Arabelle laid herself down between the bed curtains, she pulled the blue silk counterpane over her head. She did not generally sleep so covered up, but she found it difficult to take a three o'clock nap as Corisande was doing in the next room. It grew too stifling to breathe, so she threw off the covers, sucked in sweet air, and tried to relax her twitching eyelids.

Where is Simon now? she wondered. Had he rescheduled his wedding to Corisande, as that miss had insisted? Lady Chesterfield had said that May Fair Chapel was booked for three solid weeks.

Though Arabelle dreaded the thought of that final wedding, she felt helpless to do a thing about it. Even if she dared to express her feelings to Simon, what could she say? *I love you? Marry me instead of Corisande?* Aside from the foolhardiness of such a confession, the case was futile. When two people pledged to marry one another, as Simon and Corisande had, the law bound them as tightly as did marriage. No one could legally bow out of a betrothal. The fact was depressing in the extreme.

Sunk into drowsiness at last by such sad thoughts, it was odd, but she felt a touch on her cheek. Was she dreaming? She moved her head. Hands instantly clapped over her eyes and mouth, preventing her from seeing or crying out.

"Arabelle!" In a throbbing whisper, a man's voice said, "I have come to you by stealth, as you bade me."

Who in the world? With violence, Arabelle pushed the hand off her eyes.

Large brown eyes gleamed down on her. Sir Pomeroy Chancet whispered, "I feared you might make a noise. That is the reason I hold your mouth captive, but what a thrilling mouth it is. Now that you know it is I, you will not make a sound, will you? Here I *am!*" His head wobbled in dizzy pleasure, and his teeth looked yellow against his white powdered face and wig.

Arabelle furiously detached his hand from her mouth. "Why on earth have you crept into my bedchamber?" she demanded, incensed.

He looked baffled. "Because I got your message." As his gaze flickered over her form, he said excitedly, "Do move over—ow! Don't jab me! You do not know me yet, my treasure, judging by your skeptical countenance. Do promise not to shriek, my flower, when it is only a suggestion I made!"

"How *dare* you?" Arabelle screeched, sitting bolt upright, yanking the coverlet to her chin.

In his glittering finery, Sir Pomeroy sat eagerly on her bed and said portentously, "What is to dare? I propose that you and I become one."

With barely-concealed rage, she challenged, "What is your meaning, Sir?"

"That we join ourselves, my dear." He took one of her long curls between his fingers and felt its silkiness.

"How?" Arabelle cried, flicking her hair away from him.

He leaned toward her, emitting peppermint breath. "I know a clergyman in Fleet Street."

Arabelle felt so choked that she could barely grind out, "Most Fleet Street marriages are fraudulent! My father knows that to be a fact."

"Some may be, but this man is a true clergyman. He does strictly legal marriages. I would not dishonour you for the world, my lovely Arabelle."

Fuming, she cried, "Even if he were the Archbishop of Canterbury, why do you ask me this when we are barely acquainted?"

"Because I *die* when I am near you!" He tipped his head back, his heavy eyes in slits as he feasted them on her. "And I love that kind of death. But I want to live with you—I *love* you! You are the most pleasing, artistic, and heart-gladdening sight around. Come, give me your lips this time, my voluptuous pudding."

Arabelle tried to scramble out of bed, but he, on top of the covers, trapped her and lunged for her despite her quick reaction to dodge him. It was the wrong move, for, as his pink lips hungrily followed hers, the action put her on her back. With a cry of triumph, he grasped her neck with both hot hands while his eager mouth pursed toward hers.

Arabelle, with difficulty, turned her shoulder, kicked at him fiercely from under the covers, and screamed.

There came a clatter of a lever, and the door to Corisande's room catapulted open. Tall and broad-shouldered, silhouetted in the doorway, stood Simon Laurence.

Wild-eyed, she cried, "*Help* me, Simon!"

Three long strides and Simon had yanked Sir Pomeroy off of her. Before she could draw another breath, the dandy was on the floor, flung to his knees.

As Simon's fist came up, Sir Pomeroy cried, "Please understand, Laurence!—She *invited* me here! No, don't hit my face!" There was a crack to his jaw, and he fell back to the carpet, silenced for an instant before he began to moan.

"Is that true, Arabelle?" asked Simon in a voice like a whiplash.

"No!" she expelled, shuddering.

Sir Pomeroy croaked from the floor, "It *is* true! Despite what the flustered beauty says in front of you, Laurence, she wrote asking me to come to her here at this hour. She *did!*" The whites of his eyes showed over the edge of the bed, punctuating his earnestness.

Arabelle lifted horrified eyes to Simon. "Do you believe that?"

"I do not believe you capable of such behaviour, Miss Lamar. Chancet, take that!" Simon yanked off his gauntlet and whacked it across his face.

Sir Pomeroy reacted, jumping back, his hand splayed over his lace-covered throat. He looked at the glove on the floor. His eyes and nostrils flared so widely that Arabelle thought they would pop. "A *duel?*" he squeaked. "You challenge me to a duel?" He eyed the splendid specimen of manhood towering over him. "About something I did not instigate? Look, I have her note of invitation right here! Read it!" Quavering in voice and groping with shaking fingers, he produced a paper from his enormous purple coat cuff.

Simon frowned deeply as he perused it. He then presented it to Arabelle, who turned it toward the dim light and read:

> *Dear Sir Pomeroy,*
>   *Between three and four o'clock I will lie in my chamber. Will you hie yourself hither and enter without a knock? I find you the most exciting man. Your eyes hold such lively promise. What do they promise?*
>
>   *Yours in great hope,*
>   *Arabelle*

"How utterly disgusting! I did not write that!" Arabelle glared at Sir Pomeroy. "You must have written it yourself!"

"I did no such thing!" His voice rose to a desperate pitch. "Why would I?"

"Perhaps to deceive anyone who came to my rescue after you insinuated yourself into my bedchamber—as you just did?"

Sir Pomeroy gesticulated his arms in a frenzy. "No! A footman delivered this to me as I prepared to enter my coach a half hour ago, so I naturally thought it was from you, and had my coachman reverse direction. I have been in heart-leaps of expectation ever since!" Shielding his head from the wrath on Simon's face, he cried, "Well, wouldn't you be, Laurence, if this had been handed to you?"

Simon advanced on him, his hand moving to his sword. "How dare you intend such harm to this lady? You deserve the worst. There is nothing for it but to meet me at the maze near Lambeth Palace tonight. Seven o'clock. Do not bring a second."

"Tonight? No second? Why not?" he queried fearfully.

"Because the affair can remain quiet that way. Do you understand, Chancet? Do not speak of this to anyone. I will defend the honour of this lady, and her name and the cause will not be noised abroad to anyone but us. Do you understand?"

"I—I understand!" quacked Sir Pomeroy as Simon grabbed him by the coat front.

"Choose your weapon!" he commanded.

Sir Pomeroy blinked, and eventually gobbled, "I—I—I choose a smallsword similar to yours, then." He indicated the triangular bladed, etched silver one that Simon wore. "Is that acceptable?"

Simon thrust him backward, saying, "That will do nicely."

Sir Pomeroy snatched up his hat and made an uncharacteristically clumsy dash from the bedchamber.

Arabelle, with her heart full, turned to Simon and cried, "Oh, Simon, how can I *ever* thank you?"

He said, "I am glad I was nearby."

She looked at him, her courageous defender, and tears started in her eyes. "Now you will fight him."

"Gladly for you," came his soft answer.

Arabelle swiped at her wet cheeks. "You will risk your life's blood—for me?"

"Of course I will." He went quickly to the window, where he leaned in a watchful position over the colonnades.

Arabelle felt a whirl of conflicting emotions. Uppermost was the singing beauty that Simon would to fight for her honour. Though she felt tremours over the dangers of a duel, she knew she must not ask him to desist. "I shall pray that it all goes as you envision it, Simon," she said. "I trust you to conquer him."

"Thank you."

Her eye roved to the connecting door to Corisande's chamber. "How did you happen to be next door when I needed you?"

He approached the foot of her bed. "Please keep this a secret."

"I will," she assured him.

"My Captain gave me a sensitive mission to perform. I was investigating something that may turn out to be totally unrelated while Miss Wells was out of her room."

"Is this a military mission?"

He bent beneath the blue bed curtains to say, very low, "It is not military in nature, so my uniform is my cover."

Feeling breathless, she said, "You may trust me not to give you away."

"I do. I must return to my observations now. There is much I can do in other houses as well."

"Corisande is not in there napping, then?" she asked, needing to ascertain that point.

"In her chamber? Oh, no. I would not have entered it if she were. Ah, dear Arabelle, you look so shaken still," he said with a frown of concern. "Is there any way I can help you further at the moment?"

Feeling about to burst, Arabelle whispered, "Yes!"

"What can I do?"

He should not be in her room any more than Sir Pomeroy should, and she should not long for him because he was betrothed to Corisande Wells, but she whispered, "You can hold my h-hands until I stop sh-shaking." Truly, that was what she needed more than anything: his strong, enveloping touch to reassure her that everything would be all right.

Simon found her trembling hands and held them lovingly. "He gave you a bad scare. He will pay for this."

Ah! Let time stop here, she thought, giving Simon's hands a thankful squeeze.

"I have no doubt that he forced his attentions on you," he growled.

"Yes, but how humiliated *I* feel!" She bit her lip. "If he was telling the truth, who wrote that letter?"

Simon said, "I will find out."

The door opened silently, and Arabelle gasped. Corisande's blonde head appeared and she tiptoed forward, looking at Arabelle in bed. Simon swiveled his head from behind the bed curtain as her shadow fell, and she saw him. He had Arabelle's hands in his.

"Simon! What are *you* doing in here?" With hands on hips, Corisande blinked furiously, looking from him to Arabelle with jealousy writ all over her face.

Simon rose to his feet and recounted that Sir Pomeroy Chancet had entered Arabelle's room by stealth when she was asleep. He had heard her scream, had found him attacking her, and had thrown him out. "She is now trying to recover from the shock. See how she trembles."

Corisande lifted her chin and looked stony. Then, suddenly changing her tack, she said slyly to Arabelle, "Sir Pomeroy came here, into your room?"

Arabelle was so outraged that she was bereft of words.

"Nothing to say, Arabelle?" Corisande waggled her finger at her. "You have dangled your bait in front of him, and he is now on your hook, is he not? Congratulations on your success. She has been so flirtatious with him, Simon."

"That's not true!" cried Arabelle, aghast.

"It is nothing to be ashamed of, for he is a great catch," Corisande continued, possessing Simon's arm and tinkling her laugh. "He inherited his title already, and has plenty of money, so what's to stop you? Even your mother feels he is a most entertaining and eligible gentleman." She added, "Few like him."

"That's right," snapped Simon, "few like him. Arabelle had a terrible experience, fighting him off. She needs your support as well as mine, Corisande. Your matchmaking is not appropriate now. And," he added sternly, "we must all prevent this incident from leaking out. Will you agree to keep strict silence about this?"

"Of course, Simon," returned Corisande fawningly, fingering his silver epaulette fringe.

They left by separate ways, though Corisande would have taken Simon through her room had he followed her beckoning. He did not.

When they were gone, Arabelle sank back to her pillows and let out a shaking sigh. Corisande had not viewed Arabelle's harrowing assault by Sir Pomeroy as a catastrophe. The important thing was that Simon had.

"Who will be the lucky recipient of your letter, Arabelle?" Lord Chesterfield inquired, smiling at her as he set his quill pen onto his gold-edged porcelain inkstand.

Arabelle had just held the tiny brass dipper of wine-red sealing wax beads over the candle flame, dripped the melted wax onto the closure of her letter, pressed her ring with the initial *A* upon it, and risen from one of His Lordship's library tables. After she had left her harrowing "nap" and been redressed by a maid, Arabelle encountered His Lordship in the upper corridor. He invited her into his library, for she told him she would like to write a letter.

She yearned to confide in him about her troubles, but decided not to spill her heart just yet. For one thing, the Earl was busily composing his daily letter of advice to his son, who was traveling in Europe. For another, she was sure Simon's plan of discretion was best.

"I wrote to my father, My Lord. I have asked him to fetch me home until my appearance at Court two days hence."

Lord Chesterfield instantly alerted. "But no, Arabelle! Stay here until then. Your presentation to King George is of the greatest moment, and my lady will know how to present you better than anyone."

"But—"

He turned sideways in his chair and continued earnestly, "I have grown used to your presence in my house—nay, I have grown very fond of you, Arabelle. Why should you flee to your father already, my dear?"

She had promised not to mention Sir Pomeroy's assault because Simon wanted the duel kept strictly in the dark. What could she give His Lordship as a reason? The truth was that she did not dare to stay in the house with the Baronet running tame all over it any day of the week. What if he tried again to persuade her to his wishes when Simon was elsewhere?

"Is the portrait making progress?" the Earl asked, giving her time to formulate a polite excuse.

"Yes. I return for sittings."

"I want it ready to hang at my ball, you know." He watched her with a questioning half-smile.

"Yes, My Lord. I shall come back every other day. If you allow my letter to be delivered by one of your footmen, I will be grateful."

"Consider it done." The Earl looked relieved as he rang the bell. He gave her letter to a footman with the order to run it to Bloomsbury Square at once.

By dinner at four-thirty, she had received a return reply by the same footman, but it was in her mother's hand.

Bloomsbury Square

Daughter!
You must remain where you are, and not even think of coming home! What would Lord and Lady Chesterfield say? It is for all of our good that you move in their circle, so do not, for mercy

sakes, ruin your chances by showing any hint of a wish to leave.
They might not ask you back. Do not disobey me!

I am, as usual,
Your Mother
Lady Bastwicke

PS: Burn this!

Arabelle drew a breath of dismay. She had written to her father, but Madam had opened the letter. Her father, of course, would never see it.

Chapter Fifteen

The Duel

Arabelle kept a vigil at her window seat. Her reward came when she saw Simon leave Chesterfield House at six o'clock that evening, carrying a darkened lantern. He paused and spoke to the coachman at an arched door to the carriage house.

Arabelle flung on her cloak and slipped down the narrow, wooden servants' staircase and out the back, then circled front to the outside of the stable mews through the crisp night air. By avoiding the front hall and the kitchen wing, she hoped that none of the house servants had seen her. As it was, a serving maid had looked a bit askance at her recent request for a hot brick. Was not the fire in her chamber sufficient? she inquired. Arabelle said blithely that she often had cold feet.

I cannot have cold feet now, she told herself as she peeked into the carriage house. She saw a chaise moving out the far door, pulled by grooms, with Simon striding after them. She told herself that, despite her trepidation, she must quickly speak to the ostler with whom she had left her own orders. She managed to catch his eye, and beckoned him. He ambled toward her. "Is my carriage here?" she whispered.

"Yes, Miss. Horses be champing their bits."

"Good. Tell my coachman that he must follow Lieutenant Laurence with all speed without letting him see that we are shadowing him. Let us be off! This is urgent."

"Yes, Miss!"

The Earl, the Countess, and Corisande had left for a rout party an hour ago. Arabelle declined to accompany them, saying she had to go see to a personal matter. Lord Chesterfield assumed she was going home. "You will be back tonight, though?" he asked hopefully.

"Tonight or tomorrow morning, My Lord," she replied, not knowing what the next hours would bring.

As soon as her back hit the squabs, she was wheeled noisily over the paving stones. She prayed that they could stay on Simon's trail all the way to the maze near Lambeth Palace.

It was probably unthinkable for her to be out without a companion, let alone to give chase through London at night, but what kept her moving onward was the knowledge that Simon meant to fight with his sword for her sake. She knew he was a formidable opponent for any man, and much more so for someone like Sir Pomeroy Chancet, but accidents could happen. What if Simon should lose his life fighting for her? She must be there. She could not stay behind.

When the coach finally jounced to a halt, the groom jumped off the back, rocking the coach. He opened the door. "Coachman wants to know what Miss wishes to do now. That chaise we were following? The Lieutenant left it there." He pointed to the empty vehicle.

Scrambling out, Arabelle said to the coachman, "Wonderful work following him!" to which her driver touched his cap and smiled. Of the groom, she asked, "Where did the Lieutenant go?"

"Between there, Miss." Dark green hedges rose to a height of eight feet or more. She peered at the shadowed passage and shivered. It was the entrance to the maze. He added, "I saw another man go in before Lieutenant Laurence did."

Arabelle panicked. "Worse and worse! You must hurry in with me. Will you keep this secret, please? Do you have a weapon?"

"My father's a vicar who taught me to be honest and dependable, Miss. As for a weapon, I, Benjamin, have my fists." He was young and brawny, and he posed his arm with pride. "I can break a branch from that tree as well, Miss. I will protect you."

"Excellent plan. Let us dash into the maze now."

After telling the coachman to wait, they entered the darkness between the towering hedges. Lifting in her panniers, she ran after Benjamin through the dim maze until they came to a solid end. Around they turned, ran into another lane, and finally curved around and raced into a sharp right turning. This they followed until they found themselves with another choice of ways. Before long, they came up against their second solid wall. With time ticking by, it was frustrating in the extreme.

Arabelle heard male voices, muffled but growing closer at times, farther away at others. Feeling desperation at her inability to go straight to them, she retraced her steps. By and by, she heard the men's voices close at hand. The excited groom had found their destination: the centre of the maze. He turned back and mouthed, "This way, Miss," and brandished his stout tree limb with relish.

"Caution!" she admonished him as a glimmer of light appeared. "I do not want to distract them by my presence." Arabelle had never been near a duel in her life. All she knew was that they were illegal, that gentlemen held them as the means by which to uphold their honour, and that principals were often badly wounded and killed. If a man did slay his opponent, he must flee the country or be hanged.

She heard Simon's voice quietly call, "*En garde!*"

Arabelle's heart jumped. Then came a clash of steel against steel. On the circular lawn, she saw the duelists. Two half-covered lanterns on the ground illuminated their faces. Sir Pomeroy pursed his red lips in determination as he forced his slashing way toward Simon, his smallsword gleaming with its blued steel blade and gold decoration. It fit Sir Pomeroy's style: gilded richly not only on the round pommel, but also down the knuckle guard, shell guards, and forte. His red coat edged in gold braid flapped wildly as he danced forward and back with graceful agility. Beneath his curled white wig, his face looked garishly alive.

Simon's white hair in its smooth queue shone in the dark as he lunged with all the freedom that loose shirtsleeves gave him. Tall and fit, he moved like quicksilver, sideways and forward, his black brows drawn together in concentration as he thrust and parried with his etched silver-hilted sword.

Sir Pomeroy sidestepped, but not quickly enough to prevent Simon from ripping his sleeve. With horrified chagrin, he yelled, "Not nice! You sliced my best coat!"

Simon parried, "Why did you wear your best coat?" and gave him an onslaught that made him jump and duck.

"I will not have my"—*clash, clash!*—"fine clothes ripped"—*clish, clash!*—"by you!" Sir Pomeroy snarled.

Arabelle giggled nervously over the dandy's concern, and gripped her cloak tighter around her throat. Intensely, she watched Simon's constant swordplay. He was quick and sure.

Sir Pomeroy lunged at him, lamplight glinting off his long triangular blade. Their swords rasped violently and often, and suddenly, Sir Pomeroy's point flicked up near Simon's face at an evil angle.

Simon leapt back, blinked, and then drove at Sir Pomeroy in a streak of ferocity.

"Stop that!" cried Sir Pomeroy, dancing away, whipping his sword desperately. His finesse had departed.

Simon cut and parried. "Stop what? Striking the face?" He spoke to Sir Pomeroy between their clashing maneuvers. "If you are interested . . . in aiming cuts to the head . . . you should have told me, not just . . . tried it without agreement. But if that's the way . . . you're going to play—" He lightly carved his sword point up Sir Pomeroy's rouged cheek and lifted the wig from his head. It soared far through the air into the black shadows and plummeted onto the grass next to Benjamin.

Grinning in glee, Benjamin picked it up and threw it toward Arabelle. It struck her gown. Grabbing it, she whispered, "You must stay hidden, and not call their attention to us! We could ruin their duel!"

She could not help but stare at Sir Pomeroy's bald head. He looked bizarre with his white powdered face, black patches, and his egg-like head obscenely naked. He was labouring with effort, wielding his elegant sword clumsily, trying to defend himself against Simon's confident and increasingly forceful thrusts.

When Simon forced him to leap around to a new position, Sir Pomeroy caught sight of Arabelle. He instantly cringed, trying to cover his head with one arm.

Poor Sir Pomeroy! she thought. He looked as if he were experiencing the worst moment of his life.

"He's done for," said Benjamin with relish. "Which one are you cheering for?"

Arabelle's heart felt lightened immensely. She watched Simon touch Sir Pomeroy's forehead with a light stroke of his sword point. Surprisingly, it drew blood. It bled rapidly, falling into Sir Pomeroy's eye. He put up his free hand to wipe it away, and when he saw his fingers covered with blood, he screeched, aghast, "You've *killed* me!"

He was so distraught that he froze, and forgot he was dueling with Simon, so it was but the work of an instant for Simon to insert his sword point into the knuckle guard of Sir Pomeroy's sword and wrench it out of his hand. It spiraled through the air and landed on the frosty grass.

Joy seared through Arabelle. She could not suppress a cheer at Simon's victory.

Benjamin was smiling with admiration. "Amazing swordsman!" he exclaimed.

She saw Sir Pomeroy swipe blood out of his fiery eyes, whip out a stiletto, and lunge at Simon.

In an instant, Simon had his sword point leveled under the Baronet's jaw, forcing it up.

Between his teeth, Sir Pomeroy hissed, "All right! I surrender! I'm dying anyway, thanks to you!"

"Shall we consider this affair at an end? First blood, and all that?"

"At an end, yes, for you have killed me! Can't you see that? Where is a doctor? I am wounded in the brain, and am bleeding to death! I can hardly see! *Do* something!"

Simon took Sir Pomeroy's stiletto from him, threw it behind him, and lowered his sword. He pulled out a large handkerchief and said, "Hold still, Chancet." He applied it to Sir Pomeroy's copiously-bleeding forehead, trying to staunch the blood. He wiped it several times, and then examined the wound. "It's only a scratch!" he noted.

"It is *not* only a scratch!" cried Sir Pomeroy, highly incensed. "It keeps bleeding like a waterfall! You are a wicked man, Laurence, to pierce me mortally, and now to tell me a lie!"

Simon seemed unperturbed, and kept wiping the blood away. "Give me your handkerchief."

When he had the two of them soaked red, Arabelle said, "Benjamin, bring him your cravat, hurry!"

Simon heard her. "Who's there?" He looked over his shoulder, peering into the black shadows, and saw her. Astonished, he blinked, and a smile grew on his face, turning into a shining, warm welcome.

In a glad rush, she ran to him, causing Sir Pomeroy to flee into the shadows, covering his head with bloody hands. She slipped on the grass in her haste, and landed against Simon's arm. "You were wonderful!" she said with quiet intensity, hugging him tightly. "I am so *proud* of you!" she exclaimed, trying not to let Sir Pomeroy hear. "I have never seen such impressive swordsmanship, and you won!"

Simon looked mighty pleased, and bathed her in a euphoric white smile. "Thank you. But, Arabelle, how did you get here?" His forehead held a sheen of moisture. He pulled her closer and gripped her tightly to his chest.

She relaxed against him, her mouth in contact with his jaw for such a light brush of her lips that she called it a kiss. "I just had to see you duel for my honour," she confessed, "and I am so glad I did. You were a marvel!"

It was then that she saw the stream of blood trickling down his cheek. She had not glimpsed that side of his face during the fighting. "Simon, I fear your eye is pierced!" She snatched up the nearby lantern to inspect him. "It *is* your eye!" She pulled a handkerchief out of her bosom and dabbed it to his left eyelid.

"Thank you," he said, smiling at her and pulling the lacy hem of her handkerchief to his nose. "Mmmm, it smells . . . like you." He lifted his visible black eyebrow suggestively.

She blushed, and avoided looking into his uncovered eye while he grinned and admired her at close range. She took the handkerchief away to see if she had stopped the flow. Blood appeared again.

"Please keep this pressed right there." She put it back onto the corner of his eye. She nearly stepped on Sir Pomeroy's wig, so she picked it up and turned it around curiously beside the lantern. It was thick and white, and felt very familiar with its three horizontal sausage curls on each side of the face, and a curled queue. It was tied at the nape with a red bow whose centre held a diamond stickpin.

Simon asked, "What do you have there? His wig?" He took it from her, and glanced at Sir Pomeroy who was searching on the ground behind the bench for something. "Shall I give it to him?"

"Wait!" Arabelle took the wig back, opened it up to look inside, and whispered portentously, "Oh, Simon! It's incredible! This wig, that Sir Pomeroy was wearing, belongs to my father!"

He removed the handkerchief from his eye and his brows lifted. "It does?"

"Yes!" she asserted, casting a surreptitious glance Sir Pomeroy's way. He had clapped his hat onto his head, and looked ludicrous without a wig. "It is the first one stolen from my father, at Drury Lane Theatre."

"How can you tell?"

Arabelle hid the wig between her and Simon, and lifted the lantern to give good light. She pointed to a pink thread sewn zigzag inside. "I sewed that myself. There was an itchy part that bothered my father, so I made it soft by sewing across it several times." She set down the lantern and resumed her former stance, adding sidewise to Simon, "All I had with me at the time was pink embroidery floss, but he said he didn't care what color it was; he just wanted the thing not to scratch him, and he was in a hurry to get to Court."

"Fascinating. So Sir Pomeroy wore your father's wig here tonight," Simon reflected, eyeing his opponent across the grass circle, with Benjamin tying his cravat around his head. "Do you have any idea why?" Simon asked her.

"No," returned Arabelle excitedly, "but I'm certainly wondering."

"You have certainly discovered something. I find this vastly interesting, Arabelle. Well done." He gave her shoulder a squeeze. "For now, let me return it to Chancet. Do not tell him that you recognize it." He carried the wig to him, and made a slight bow.

Sir Pomeroy was saying, "Not so tight, you idiot!" as Benjamin knotted his own sacrificed cravat at his right temple. Sir Pomeroy grabbed the wig from Simon and arranged it with injured tenderness upon his head. Then he ordered Benjamin to adjust the knot forward because the wig did not fit over it.

Arabelle watched the Baronet. Simon did, also, when he returned to her side. She said quietly, "I know it was not Sir Pomeroy who ran and snatched it off my father's head that night. It was someone younger and thinner."

"Yes, you're right. I saw it happen from a distance. Another young rogue came to steal mine not a minute later."

Gingerly, Sir Pomeroy pointed at a gold-embroidered black cape and told Benjamin, "Arrange that carefully over my wounded arm."

Arabelle frowned and went quickly to Sir Pomeroy, asking, "Your arm is hurt? May I see it, and bind it for you? I carry extra handkerchiefs in my pocket."

He turned away, rearranged the wig in a mirror he fished from his coat cuff and, placing his foot on the bench, retied one stocking that had loosened from its ribbon garter. Only then did he acknowledge the presence of Arabelle. "Arabelle! Thank you just the same; how kind you are!"

Simon asked him, "Did my sword point do more than rip your coat fabric, then? I did not think so at the time."

"Who knows what damage is done!" Sir Pomeroy returned witheringly. With lowered eyelids, he said to Arabelle, "I honestly *did* receive that note requesting an assignation with you. If you still affirm that you did not write it, I do not understand who did. Or why."

She heard a wan ring of truth in his tone. "Nor do I, Sir Pomeroy." An idea flashed into her mind. Could it have been Madam, her mother? The very idea! She had arranged that Romeo Rutley should meet her in Chesterfield House . . .

"Who gave it to you?" asked Simon.

"One of Lord Chesterfield's footmen. The one with the gap between his teeth."

"Thank you. I shall investigate the matter."

Sir Pomeroy lifted his chin and said to Arabelle, "I would not sully you for the world. I thought I had your encouragement. I believed

I was adhering to your wishes." In an injured tone, he added with a hint of his bantering spirit, "Wholeheartedly, too."

She gave him a little smile. "As you are sorry, I forgive you." She offered her hand.

"Oh no, I cannot touch you; I am bloodied beyond belief." Sorrowfully, he emphasized, "I hope you will remember that, as soon as I saw how upset you were by my proposition, I offered to marry you." His brown eyes replaced the offer with a questioning renewal of hope. "If you ever change your mind . . ."

She dropped her eyelids, shook her head, and gave him a little curtsey.

"Too bad!" he mourned. He bowed himself away with amazing gallantry, and, with his cape swinging, sauntered to the dark exit between the high hedges. There he lifted the bloodied lace handkerchiefs and waved them above his head, saying, "Toodle-oo! See you at the next drawing room."

Arabelle and Simon exchanged wondering looks and as soon as he was gone from sight, broke into quiet laughter.

Arabelle kept ruminating over who had written that letter to make Sir Pomeroy and her look such fools. If he were to be believed, then someone had wanted to throw them together in an almost irrevocable manner. Did her mother see that she resisted Sir Pomeroy's suit, and schemed to force her? Oh, how she wished Aunt Claracilla lived nearby. She needed help and wisdom.

She pulled her cloak closer about her and watched Simon. Each firm word that fell from his lips, the *swish* of his sword returning to his scabbard, his low laugh at the Baronet's parting quip—all made her admire him more and more as each hour with him unfolded.

Benjamin helped him on with a black coat and cloak. Then, with worshipful looks, he offered to carry the Lieutenant's hat as an honour unprecedented in his career. He said he would keep the fine hat from getting bloody from the cut that still flowed from the Lieutenant's eyelid.

At that reminder, Arabelle dug through the slits in the side of her gown and petticoats and opened the dangling pocket attached to her pannier. She withdrew the soft handkerchiefs from there, and gave them to Simon.

Again, he put them first to his nose, smiled appreciatively, and then pressed one to his eyelid and temple. He thanked Benjamin for taking charge of his hat, adjusted his sword in its scabbard, and took Arabelle by the hand. Her bosom rose with her deep breath of well-being.

They left the centre of the maze, their lanterns well shaded. They came up against Sir Pomeroy retracing his steps in frustration. "This maze is such a bore," he drawled.

Simon asked, "Do you, by any chance, have that letter with you, Chancet? I want to figure out who wrote it."

"You may have it, by all means. I never want to see the wretched missive again since it didn't really come from that lovely one." Sir Pomeroy fished it out of his deep red cuff and presented it to Simon between his bloodstained fingers.

"Do we part as friends?" asked Arabelle, putting her hand imploringly on Sir Pomeroy's arm. "I hold no ill will toward you, and hope we can meet henceforth in peace."

"But of course we part friends, since you so graciously forgave me." His voice fluctuated with joy and relief. "I see you are guileless in this, now that my temper has cooled. One day I may even dare to ask you to marry me again. I shall not run or disappear because of this affair of honour. I meant it, you know." He cast a look of longing over her,

"Thank you," she managed to say with a little laugh, but she wished he would not pursue the matter.

They all followed the stout Benjamin, carrying Simon's three-cornered hat and his tree limb like a walking stick. He proved adept at leading them out.

When Sir Pomeroy's turquoise and black town coach rolled out of sight, Simon told Arabelle's coachman that he could give Benjamin a ride back since he had performed a good service for the lady, and because he deserved a reward. To Benjamin's delight, and also the coachman's, Simon filled their palms with coins. He warned them to keep strictly quiet about their journey tonight, and received their grateful assurances.

Simon handed Arabelle into his own conveyance. She asked him to detour to the address of Dr. Follett to have his wound tended. Thankful that he consented after only a token resistance, Arabelle paced up and down the doctor's parlour in the presence of his housekeeper while Simon consulted with him. She prayed that his sight would be preserved.

When Simon emerged, he wore a black patch slanted over one eye. "Dr. Follett declares it too early to tell about my vision."

"Could you see anything from that eye before he covered it up?"

"I could, but it was blurred."

"Oh, no!" When they were bowling west, Arabelle lamented, "All this danger and trouble on my account!"

Simon chided her, "None of this affair is your fault. Remember that."

"But how awful it is that you were cut in the eye! Although you look like a very swashbuckling pirate," she added, grinning at him with admiration.

"Arrrr! This is bad, having an eye covered. I can only see half of what I wish to." He teasingly groped about in her vicinity and patted her face like a blind man, with great liberty.

She laughed and pushed his hands away as he ended by lightly tickling her neck. "Wouldn't it be nice if you could see only the good half of everything?"

"Is there that much good in the world?"

"There is, when you look for it."

"I'm glad to be reminded. Thank you for coming to the duel, even though I never would have taken you there myself."

Arabelle sighed and said, "You, with such courage, took on my oppressor. I am so grateful. If you only knew what my life is like, you would see what a godsend you are. I know that God sent you," she corrected, meeting his eye openly for an instant.

He leaned forward and took her hand as the coach jolted through the foggy streets. "I have seen how your mother treats you and coerces you. I suspect her goals for you. I also see other plans in the people around you." They passed a flickering street lamp, and she saw the earnestness in his face as he said, "I am here to serve you; believe me. You, of all people, need and deserve protection."

"I do?" He made her heart swell. "Thank you. But what about *your* life? Are you not also in a narrow tunnel? It is my impression that you are not free. Is that so, Simon?"

He groaned and admitted, "I am not free. But yet I have much to do. And," he sighed, "my prayers continue."

"Mine, too," she said in a small voice.

Arabelle knew that a decisive change had come over her. She had fought a duel within herself. Her victory was that she knew with all her heart that, instead of striving for her own wishes to come true, nothing must stand in the way of Simon's happiness, whatever that could be. It was sure to be a life without her at his side, but she would continue praying fervently to God on his behalf because it was vital to her that his life be a good one. As she looked at him, and saw him smile at her during their journey, and felt him take her hand and caress it, she lived in warm wonder over all he had done for her. He had willingly fought with dangerous weapons for her, was pierced with a sword point so that his eye was now blurred, and yet, he smiled at her. She had never felt so loved.

The coach drew up to the Chesterfield gates between the flaming torches. Simon pulled down the window shades. "Stay inside with the shades down," he murmured as he made a quiet exit. Inside the coach house, after the horses were removed and the grooms gone to rub them down, he returned to her. "Come," he said, "I will escort you to your room. I hope the house servants are asleep. I want your arrival to cause no raised eyebrows. I've paid the grooms." He flashed her a grin.

"Thank you," she said.

He managed their entry by stealthy forays ahead and whispered reports on the whereabouts of the night porter. After tiptoeing up two flights of the back staircase, they stood in the semi-darkness outside her bedchamber door.

Pushing back her hood, Arabelle lingered after she pressed the lever. "How can I possibly thank you?" she whispered in the echoing gallery.

"Hush! Farewell for now." He stood near, his white hair gleaming in the moon shaft slanting from a fanlight.

She sighed as she eyed his black eye patch. "I shall thank you till I die. Oh, Simon, words aren't telling it!"

His arms closed about her then, and he pulled her near to his pumping heart until she thought she would expire from love.

They heard a sharp gasp.

Arabelle withdrew from Simon's arms.

Corisande was peering at them, having crept on silent feet from somewhere. "My *stars*, Arabelle!" she screeched into the stillness. "What are you doing with *my* fiancé?"

Chapter Sixteen

Courting Trouble

Arabelle hadn't a clue what to say. They were caught.

Corisande stalked toward them in her evening finery, her face screwed up in rage.

Though her heart went erratic and her mouth dry, Arabelle kept her chin level and cast Simon a grateful smile. "I have Lieutenant Laurence to thank to the end of my days for upholding my honour tonight."

Simon gave her a bow of his head and turned to face his flaming fiancée.

Corisande recoiled. "What happened to *you?*" she cried.

His dramatic turn was effective, for the revelation of his eye patch startled her. "A flick of Sir Pomeroy's blade to my eye," he said, watching her closely, as Arabelle did, with the moonlight revealing her expression.

Corisande blinked between stares of incomprehension. "Why did Sir Pomeroy—? Upholding *your* honour?" she shrieked at Arabelle.

Simon interceded. "While Arabelle rested yesterday afternoon, Chancet entered her room and made a vile nuisance of himself, remember?"

"Never tell me *you* challenged him, Simon!" Corisande stared from him to Arabelle in angry disbelief.

"Yes. I called him out because he insulted your friend. It's all over now."

"Over? Is he dead?"

"No," said Arabelle, "but he took the worst of it and had to surrender. Lieutenant Laurence was merciful."

Corisande pinned a desperate smile to her mouth as she looked sidewise up at Simon. "Merciful! Well, aren't you sweet?" She stared at him while undergoing an inner struggle. Then she grabbed his arm and said to Arabelle over her shoulder, "You see what a plummy husband will be *mine?*"

Simon stood unresponsive but met Arabelle's eyes briefly.

With a surge of rage, Corisande grabbed Arabelle tightly by the arm, and pinched hard as she pushed her through her bedchamber door.

The next morning, Arabelle entered the ornately decorated dining room to the sound of wind and fury battering the gold-curtained windows.

Corisande set down a bitten plum tartlet and licked her fingers, ignoring Arabelle completely.

Lady Chesterfield wished her a good morning, and begged for particulars of the duel.

Arabelle's heart sank. So Corisande had blurted it all out.

As Arabelle sat down to soft-baked eggs, toast, and half a kipper, she related a few details as if she had heard them from her champion, not daring to divulge that she had been there. Simon had promised to keep her presence a secret.

Corisande showed signs of extreme irritability, as if she could hardly stand to sit and listen. It was evident by the way she pushed her food around, scowled, and spilled tea onto her sleeve lace.

When Arabelle concluded her sketchy story to the tune of Lady Chesterfield's exclamations, Corisande lifted her chin and said loftily, "Two men dueled for *me* once."

"Is that so?" inquired Lady Chesterfield. "What was it about?"

With a wave of her hand, Corisande said, "Oh, it's a long story."

The Countess surprised Arabelle with a skeptical lift of her dark eyebrows. They both knew Corisande was making it up, seething that Arabelle had been the object of Simon's duel rather than herself, no matter what the reason had been.

Corisande suddenly shouted at Arabelle, "If Simon loses his vision in that eye, we will have *you* to thank!"

Arabelle set down her cup. "Why me?"

"Because you wrote that note to Sir Pomeroy and then denied it! The man I plan to marry put his life in jeopardy because of *you!*"

Arabelle met Corisande's wavering eyes firmly across the table. "I did not write that letter. But perhaps you know who did." Too late, Arabelle realized the words were out, pointing the blame and curdling their friendship.

Corisande looked struck. "Huh! I do *not!*" she cried in high-pitched denial, though Lady Chesterfield tried to hush her. "You have ruined Simon's eye! And if Sir Pomeroy's complexion is ruined even one little bit," Corisande jumped to her feet, raging at Arabelle, "I will be furious! He is my friend!" She swung five candles out of their rococo holder with a raging slap of her hand and ran out of the room. Two footmen leaped forward to douse the flames. In the distance, a housemaid cried out in pain.

The ice hung in the air all day. When Corisande passed Arabelle in the gallery, she swished by with her long nostrils highly visible.

Despite the brittle atmosphere between the young women, their sittings for Miss Agathon continued. Arabelle wondered why they should finish the portrait when they no longer felt the bosom friendship the artist was trying to portray. The relationship was a fallacy, anyway, thought Arabelle, for the double portrait came into existence by her mother's inspiration.

Corisande seemed to switch moods like her clothes, however, for she asked pleasantly enough as they were modeling, "You have never been to Court, I suppose, Arabelle?"

"Not yet."

"Then when are you ever going?"

"Tomorrow."

Corisande jerked to look at her.

Miss Agathon, exasperated, called, "No, no, no! Please do not turn to look at Miss Lamar! Now I must come and set you up again."

She put her palette onto the table and came to lift Corisande's chin toward the light. "Kindly do not move from this position." With a weary huff, Miss Agathon blew some hair up off her forehead, surveyed Arabelle critically, and tugged her gown out at the hem. To Corisande, she said, "I hear this is your last sitting together until Miss Lamar returns, so I must make progress on the shadowing."

Corisande said out of the side of her mouth, "Why didn't you tell me about going to Court?"

Arabelle could have said, *Because you were not speaking to me,* but replied, "I only found out myself last night. My mother wrote that my court dress is ready, so it is time to visit the King. Then," she added to diminish the matter, "I shall legitimately dance at Lord Chesterfield's Ball, or so she says."

"Of course," said Corisande tetchily. "Without a Court appearance, that would be awkward."

"When were you presented at Court?"

Corisande looked at Miss Agathon and pretended that she could not even move her lips for the strictness of her pose, and Arabelle deduced that she had never been to Court.

In a glittering white gown, Arabelle curtseyed to the King.

While her name was trumpeted and her card handed to George II, she studied him. Dressed beautifully, he was quite old—perhaps upper sixties—and smaller than she was. Grandiose amounts of costly lace at his throat and wrists set off his royal blue coat, waistcoat, and breeches. He was shod in white satin shoes with diamond buckles a-blazing, and his throne looked far too big for him.

"The Honourable Arabelle Lamar is the eldest daughter of Viscount and Viscountess Bastwicke, Your Majesty," his advisor informed him.

The King's protuberant blue eyes twinkled as he nodded at her, and his long white curls bobbed. "Ja, ja, I know your fadder," he said. "He is lucky to have a lovely dodder, I see."

She thanked him and smiled at his pink and white face with its proudly tilted chin. She backed out of the audience chamber, his eyes following her kindly. At the door, she curtseyed low, and that was that.

She found herself in a room full of relieved young ladies and their mothers, friends, and relatives. Her lace choker scratched her neck and her corset-stomacher felt too tight. It pushed her bosom up too high in the low neck of this fabulous gown, and her posture was rigid. She could not relax.

Lady Bastwicke, like a broad-beamed frigate, sailed to Arabelle's side. "The King actually spoke to you, Arabelle! I watched through the peephole! Whatever did he say?"

"That he knows my father." She smiled meaningfully at her mother.

"Oh? Well, well!" Lady Bastwicke bristled with self-importance, looking about to see if their neighbours had heard.

"See, Mother?" whispered Arabelle, "Father is well known to His Majesty already. He does not need his own levées to cultivate the King or his courtiers."

Lady Bastwicke did not respond. After her first frown of irritation, she spread her vermilion smiles round the room. She pulled Arabelle along as she accosted first this elegant woman and then another, and promised many that she would bring her card and her daughters to their drawing rooms one day soon.

When Arabelle and Madam descended a staircase to a gleaming parquet corridor that would lead them to their carriage, Arabelle caught her breath. Coming toward them, against the light of the long palace doors, was a figure that moved just like Simon Laurence.

It *was* Simon Laurence.

"What is that Army officer doing here?" murmured Lady Bastwicke.

Arabelle smiled at him, her heart swelling with joy.

Looking dazzling in a dress uniform of deep blue with the silver baldric and sword and white satin slash ribbons, he made her sigh. He bowed to them with athletic grace, his hat under his arm and white gloves on his shapely hands.

Before her mother could ruin the moment with a negative remark, Arabelle said, "Lieutenant Laurence, how nice it is to see you here."

"The pleasure is all mine. Are you ready to leave, ladies?"

Lady Bastwicke's headdress feathers swung as she checked to see if anyone else watched them. "Are you here to escort us to our coach?"

"Yes, Your Ladyship; and I shall precede you all the way home."

Arabelle asked, "You came here just to perform this service for us?"

He bowed his handsome head, and she saw that charming dimple in his cheek. "Yes, Miss Lamar."

Lady Bastwicke preened, eyeing the gaggle of white-gowned young women and their mothers pressing by. She accosted one with whom she had just spoken, reporting the escort service the King had provided for her and her offspring on this grand occasion. She threw in nonchalantly that the King had told her daughter he knew Lord Bastwicke well.

"How you beautify this palace," said Simon to Arabelle while her mother was occupied. "You are so stunning that you have to pardon me. I don't know where to look for fear I shall miss all your other bewitching angles."

She laughed with genuine joy. "Why, thank you." She gave a self-conscious twitch to her glistening skirt, and could not feel any offense in his honesty.

He walked with her a few steps away from the buzzing women. They were all watching him except for Lady Bastwicke, the talker.

Arabelle turned and accidentally caught her gown lace on the end of his sword scabbard. Connected in that way to such a man gave her a frisson of pleasure. While he was releasing her lace, she said, "Tell me: are you here for any other reason than the one you gave my mother?"

"I have just met with some of the King's courtiers on a matter of grave importance."

"I see." She touched her white lace fan to her lips. "I shall keep mum. Oh dear, she looks about to return."

Simon smiled and took Arabelle's closed fan from her. "Alas, you used the wrong end." He turned the handle up and touched it to her lips before Lady Bastwicke swung her huge grey and silver dress around. Arabelle heard nothing her mother said for she was smiling tremulously over Simon's action. She flipped the handle of her fan downward quickly to cover from her mother's eye the signal Simon had suggested with such a bold, fun-filled look: *Kiss me.*

Lady Bastwicke did not see the folded paper Simon Laurence slipped inside Arabelle's glove when he took her hand to help her into the coach. Alight with curiosity, Arabelle rode in state all the way home without knowing what his note said, but she was euphorically happy because she had it.

Simon rode before their coach on a stunning dappled horse, parting the way in grand style, the silver on his three-cornered cocked hat glittering in the winter sun. In Bloomsbury Square, he saluted Lady Bastwicke as soon as she alighted from her coach. She stood smiling and blinking and shading her eyes against the sun, and prolonged the moments of their parting longer than necessary. Arabelle knew she was trying to make sure that anyone looking out of the windows round the Square should understand where she and her daughter had been, and that they had this handsome, impressive escort from the Palace besides.

Arabelle smiled at Simon, whose eyes were glimmering upon her in the most exciting way. He lifted a hand and blew her a kiss off the tips of his gloves. This was the best part of her magical day at Court.

"Why did you do that?" demanded Lady Bastwicke, her eyes sharply pinned on him, his broad shoulders and black three-cornered hat high above them as he sat astride his horse.

"Do what, Your Ladyship?" inquired Lieutenant Laurence genially.

"Dare to throw a kiss to my daughter!"

He sat his horse very dignified, and blinked his dark eyelashes. "It is the traditional salute from His Majesty's officers to ladies presented to the King. Long live the King!"

Arabelle giggled inside, and turned it into a flashing smile at Simon for such cleverness.

If Lady Bastwicke had any doubts, he had allayed them by use of his grand military voice.

"Oh," she said, changing her attitude and simpering profusely. "Well, thenk you, indeed!"

He saluted them snappily, and turned his horse and cantered smartly away down the Square.

Arabelle smiled with such winging joy that Genevieve, waiting on the steps above, watched her with wonder. Then her eyes followed the attractive sight of Simon Laurence on horseback.

Together the sisters had to eat dinner with Madam their mother, who had a gaggle of silly women and questionable men assembled for their homecoming. They talked of parties in Bath, Devonshire, Paris, Liege, and Venice, and the more they ate and drank, the louder they laughed, and the more they interrupted each other's stories.

It was after all the good wishes and posies had been offered her that Arabelle escaped upstairs and clicked shut her bedchamber door. Dashing to hide behind a long curtain, she opened the paper from Simon that she had transferred from her glove to her bosom.

> *Dear Arabelle,*
>
> *As I write this, I plan to offer you and your mother my escort in order to see you on this day of days.*
>
> *Thank you for your solicitude and your handkerchief, which I enclose. I appreciated your being there, ministering to me like an angel after the affair.*
>
> *We spoke about the dilemmas that have us trapped. We did not voice our wishes, however. If you were to ask me what I do wish, I would take you into my arms and you would understand.*
>
> *If only . . . Yours*

Arabelle sank back, all a-glow. *If only . . . Yours!* Had he truly written that?

She put the laundered handkerchief to her nose. There was a vague stain of blood left upon it. She was glad there was a reminder of the duel left on it, for it was now a treasure.

Genevieve breathed, "I can *see* why you love him! Oh, isn't it obvious that he wants you, Arabelle? It is disastrous that he cannot have you! I have never heard any man say anything so marvelous in my whole life! Have you?"

Arabelle rolled her eyes dreamily. "Never. Only him." She did not even mind that Genevieve had read over her shoulder.

Arabelle stretched her arms over her head, feeling blessed luxury. "It is the most gratifying ecstasy to be with him, and to read the words he writes. But, oh Genevieve," she moaned, "I don't know what it is all leading up to, for I cannot belong to him."

Chapter Seventeen

One Serenade after Another

The next afternoon, Lord Rutley was among the crowd of men and women who thronged Lord and Lady Chesterfield's levée. Arabelle hoped she had seen the last of the wiry, dark-complexioned peer who had sent her the newspaper advertisement—he who then appeared in this house at the *rendezvous* set up by her mother.

To Arabelle's chagrin, Lord Rutley brought her a cup of coffee. He shoved the Persian cat off the settee and lowered his spare frame next to her. "Good morrow, fair Juliet," he said, his close-set eyes prowling from her fichu-crossed bodice to her shapely aqua shoe.

She pulled a bolster away from her back and moved away from him. "That is not my name." She deliberately laid the bolster between them.

"It is a lover's alias," he corrected, eyeing the barrier she had erected. "You look marvelous in that colour, but why cover up your neck with all that fluff?" He gestured to the ruffle-edged fichu that surrounded her shoulders and formed a V where it tied at the low neck of her gown.

To keep unwelcome eyes like yours from gawping, she felt like snapping. Instead, she excused herself and rose to leave.

He grabbed her forearm, squeezing the lace ruffles into her skin. "Do not leave me!" He smiled and drew her down, slopping coffee from her cup onto the saucer. "I brought a missive for you," he effused, as though that would make her skip and cheer. "Will you read it while I sip this tantalizing brew and breathe your aphrodisiac perfume?" He motioned at the atmosphere around her.

She eyed him icily. She saw that a letter he dug out from within his waistcoat had *Juliet* sprawled erratically across it.

Because people seated at Lady Chesterfield's card table glanced curiously at them, Arabelle took the note as politely as she could. She held it out openly as though it were something innocuous and public, but groaned as her eyes roved unwillingly over his words:

> *Dearest Juliet,*
>   *Are your affections engaged? Do you belong to any man? Let us discuss this vital question.*
>   *I want to be*
>
>   *Yours in Heart, Mind, and Body,*
>   *Romeo*

It was too much to endure! She felt low and cheapened just by reading it.

"Well?" Lord Rutley's black eyes skewered into her. She knew he would not let her escape without an answer.

"I belong to no man, and I will certainly not belong to you," she said quietly but distinctly. She rose and went to where Lord Chesterfield stood visiting with Colley Cibber. Lord Chesterfield was her safe haven.

She greeted the men with smiles and a few words, and then excused herself, leaving them both looking after her, the Earl slightly puzzled, the actor assessing her with a smile on his face. She also felt Lord Rutley's eyes beetling into her until she rounded the stairs up to her room.

Where was Simon? If he had been in that drawing room, he would have put a halt to Lord Rutley's lewd actions; of that, she was certain. It seemed, more and more, that an hour was not worth living without Simon's presence.

Arabelle suffered a pounding headache two hours later. When the guests left, she and Corisande posed for Miss Agathon, during which time Arabelle pondered, with mental shudders, Lord Rutley's relentless pursuit. Despite the fact that he was that mother's dream, a bachelor peer endowed with a country estate, it was pure horror to imagine him as her husband. Anyone's husband.

Corisande ignored her during their posing despite their close proximity. Arabelle could hardly endure her rose-milk fragrance. Miss Agathon tussled with their poses, made many sounds of exasperation, and dismissed them early because nothing seemed to go well.

Hearing their exit cue, Corisande threw her hat on the floor, which spilled Miss Agathon's brush-cleaning solution. Corisande just flounced out of the room without a word of apology.

Arabelle apologized to the long-suffering artist, saying, "This is partly my fault. I have not contributed to Corisande's happiness of late."

"No one can do that with such a spoiled chit," declared Miss Agathon.

Parting with a look of mutual understanding, Arabelle returned to her chamber and wrote to Aunt Claracilla. She thanked her for her letters, recounted her bewildering circumstances, and begged for advice. She did not mention Simon by name, but divulged the condition of her heart to her dear aunt.

Music suddenly wafted up outside her window, which seemed distinctly odd. She pulled back the blue curtain to look into the courtyard. Below her stood about twenty men playing instruments. The conductor, wrapped to his ears in a muffler, looked gratified at sight of her, and immediately the music took on buoyancy. She wondered what it was all about.

A singer stepped forward, and with hand swinging to his heart, sang in a rich tenor, "It was a lover and his lass, with a hey, with a ho, with a hey, nonny no . . ."

She heard a rap on her door, so she called "Enter."

It was a footman with a letter. "Please to open this at once, Miss. That is the message sent with this billet, Miss."

"Thank you."

She snapped it open and read it at the window, while the musicians played on.

> *Dear Juliet,*
> > *I want to be that lover!*
> > > *With a hey, with a ho,*
> > > > *I want you, don't you know?*

> > > > > > > *Your*
> > > > > > > *Romeo*

Repulsed to the core, she crushed the paper and threw it at the window. Outside, the orchestra and soloist extolled,

> *Between the acres of the rye,*
> *With a hey, with a ho, with a hey nonny no, and a hey, nonny nonny no!*
> *These pretty country folks would lie,*
> *In springtime . . .*

Arabelle fumed, and covered her ears with her hands. Lord Rutley had hired musicians to serenade her with such words?

The music ended to applause from servants clustered on the front steps, the courtyard, and peering from the stable and coach house arches.

Arabelle's chamber door burst open, and Corisande breezed in. "Arabelle!" she cried gaily. "Did you hear that song?"

"How could I help it?"

"I think it was for you. I bet I know who it was from," she added, eyeing her saucily.

"Do you?"

"I guess: Lord Rutley. Am I right?"

A movement below caught Arabelle's notice. Her heart skipped as she saw Simon Laurence's white head and broad shoulders approach the orchestra. She completely forgot Corisande's question.

Corisande pushed next to her and looked down.

Simon pressed something into the hand of the conductor, who listened and bowed. Simon walked back in through the front door.

After speaking to his soloist, the conductor raised his baton and his musicians struck up the song,

> *Drink to me only with thine eyes,*
> *And I will pledge with mine,*
> *Or leave a kiss within the cup,*
> *And I'll not ask for wine.*

The tenor continued singing straight at Arabelle.

> *The thirst that from the soul doth rise*
> *Doth ask a drink divine;*
> *But might I of Jove's nectar sip,*
> *I would not change for thine.*

She felt Corisande stiffen furiously next to her. She struggled with her breath before she found her voice. "I told Simon I would run up here to see your reaction to Rutley's serenade. So what does my Simon do?" her voice rose to a false pitch. "He paid them to play a love song to *me!*" With that, Corisande shot a resentful look at Arabelle and hurried off, calling defiantly, "I shall go thank him with a kiss."

Arabelle began to worry, for she knew that Corisande was about as irate as she could be.

"The way you move is so fluid, Juliet," effused Lord Rutley that evening as she moved toward the edge of the ballroom hand-in-hand with Corisande, and led back toward their dance partners. The weasel was still in the house. He had followed her into the music room, and stood lounging against the elegant chimneypiece, studying her every turn and sway with unswerving tactlessness. Lady Chesterfield had arranged for dancing lessons for Corisande and Arabelle as a last-minute brush-up before the ball.

Arabelle did not deign to look again at the unwelcome Rutley. She still sizzled with outrage at his lewd serenade. She must speak to Lord Chesterfield and ask if his porter could please turn Lord Rutley and his ilk away at the door from now on.

Arabelle, Corisande, and two male assistants to the dancing-master practiced not only country dances but also the new square dance called the Quadrille, even though they were missing two couples. Lord Chesterfield had said at breakfast that he wanted a set of quadrilles played and danced at his ball, for his son wrote that they were popular in France. Corisande and Arabelle moved to the melodies of the harpsichord played by a music-master, for Lord Chesterfield deemed it low and vulgar to play musical instruments oneself.

When they finished the first three dances, and a goblet of lime cordial was served to them all by a maidservant, Rutley came near, holding a newspaper. He said, "You are dainty of foot and turning, Arabelle Lamar. But," he said, lifting a finger, "you lack what is most important to a man."

Irritated, she flickered a bored look past him over her glass rim.

Corisande stared agog, eager for what Lord Rutley would say next.

The dancing master objected. "What can Miss Lamar possibly lack but the opportunity to learn more dances, Your Lordship?"

Tapping his issue of the *Spectator*, Lord Rutley smirked. "She, like Cleomira here," and he read: *"dances with all the elegance of motion imaginable, but whose eyes are so chastised with the simplicity and innocence of her thoughts that she raises in her beholders admiration and goodwill, but no loose hope or wild imagination."*

Corisande, laughing loudly against the rule of the house, went and tapped her fan sticks on Rutley's arm. "Oh, you rascal! But how true! That is exactly Arabelle."

Rutley's narrowed, glinting eyes sent Arabelle a challenge. "Would you like to study how to change that?"

Arabelle turned away and refused to look at him more. Then, to her joy, she saw Simon move out from behind the tall topiary beside the harpsichord. When had he entered the room?

"You catechize Miss Lamar with such borrowed epithets?" he asked Rutley, an edge to his voice.

Rutley started, and then masked his guilt with a crooked smile. "Miss Lamar knows that I admire her excessively, so Lieutenant Laurence, why cannot you be quiet? Besides, you must own that

I am one foot in the truth. Have you ever seen such freshness or such innocence as Arabelle Lamar's?"

It was mortifying to be the centre of everyone's attention, as though she were a French fashion doll on the coffee table, open to criticism from all angles. Rutley's was intolerable.

Simon towered over him. "I agree entirely. Freshness and innocence are virtues beyond value, and impossible to contrive. Or, to regain if lost."

Corisande, who had moved toward Simon, halted as he looked levelly at her.

"You, Lord Rutley," he added with a glint of steel in his eyes, "with your wish for 'wild imaginings,' can go imagine in your accustomed ways, but do it out of the presence of these ladies." He indicated the open doorway.

Rutley's smile fell off. "Do you presume to order me out?"

Unflinching, Simon looked down his nose and said, "Certainly, if you will not govern your tongue in their presence. I will not tolerate your one-man campaign against such freshness and innocence as you find in our midst."

Lord Chesterfield stood observing. He nodded at Simon.

Rutley suddenly said, "Miss Lamar, I—I—I apologize. I beg to kiss your hand as a token thereof." With quick steps, he reached for her.

She whipped her hand behind her back and turned away. "That is not called for," she said with finality.

He followed her and leaned his head over her shoulder, eyeing her décolletage and whispering, "Remember, my dear, you must promise us men—namely *me*—a little more. You will not regret the outcome." He smiled in a ravenous way that left her wanting to scratch his eyes out.

That evening, Arabelle accompanied Lord and Lady Chesterfield and Simon and Corisande to a salon at Elizabeth Montagu's house. They rode together to Hill Street near Berkeley Square. Arabelle felt pleased, jittery, and jealous all at once as she sat next to Simon, feeling the vital warmth of his arm next to hers. Across from them sat Lord and Lady Chesterfield, looking very fine in the gold-tasseled interior of their town coach. The four white horses clip-clopped at a smart trot. Corisande made a show of leaning against Simon's epaulette on his other side and mentioning more than once how it tickled. The others ignored her.

Lord Chesterfield explained to Arabelle that Madam Montagu's home was a meeting place for wits and intellectuals. "Others insinuate themselves through her portals, or sneak in on the coattails of invited guests because it is so fashionable to be seen there."

Simon said pleasantly, "As I do tonight, being neither a wit nor an intellectual."

Corisande, sounding affronted, declared, "You and I have a right to be there."

Glancing sidewise at him, Arabelle saw the glint in Simon's eye. Corisande had become accustomed to putting herself on a plane with members of the established high society without knowing much about it. He cleared his throat. "What credentials have we?"

"We are engaged!" she gushed. "Everybody wants to see us! We are, as Lady Bastwicke told me, 'an excessively good-looking couple!'"

Arabelle glanced at his handsome profile in the dimness, and sighed. She detected a movement in his jaw, as though he clenched it to fight back words. He adjusted the position of his sword, which made Corisande let go of his arm. He said, "I meant to mention, Lord Chesterfield, that it would behoove us to be extra vigilant over these young ladies tonight."

"Oh? Ah yes, you are absolutely right."

"What? Why? Is there a reason? Why did you say that?" fussed Corisande.

"Do you remember those three young ladies who were abducted from London drawing rooms?" Simon asked. "Do you, Miss Lamar?" he turned to Arabelle.

"Yes, and how terrible that was!" she returned, knowing he referred to his brother's reading the news to them on the ride to London. "Tragically, they ended up on the Continent," she said, "delivered to foreign princes, or sheiks, as the papers have since reported."

Lady Chesterfield said, "It gives me the shakes to think of such things actually happening. Please, no more of that horrendous subject." She spread a gloved hand over her mouth.

"We shall respect your wishes, My Lady," intoned Simon. "I am sorry to have disturbed you. But let us all be careful and aware, shall we?"

The Earl said, "By all means. We will keep an eye on our damsels."

"Those two," said Lady Chesterfield, indicating Corisande and Simon, "will be glad to have your advice about when to affix a new date for their wedding. My friends inundate me with queries, and I hardly know what to say."

"My dear," said the Earl, "in matters of matrimony and religion, I never give advice."

"Why not?" asked Corisande.

"I will not have anybody's torments in this world, or the next, laid to my charge."

They all evoked some show of merriment without laughing outright. All except Corisande, who had thought through his words, and looked vexed. "Torments! Well, my matrimony will not be tormented." She looked smug. "I have news for you. I have rescheduled our wedding."

"You have?" asked Simon. Arabelle felt his arm go rigid.

"Yes, I have. It is for three weeks hence, as that is the earliest date I was able to secure May Fair Chapel. Only three more weeks of freedom!" she sang out.

They all looked at her, but no one smiled.

Arabelle felt a pang of despair. It would be their real wedding this time, and Simon would be lost to her forever. What was even more tragic was that he did not appear happy about it.

The coach rolled to a stop. After the others had made their exit, Simon reached back to give her his hand. His face was golden and shadowed by the torchlight, and he conveyed tenderness to her as they touched. He always made her spirits soar.

Lord Rutley perched on a stone balcony in the cold, a keen eye on her arrival. Arabelle saw him and panicked. How could she ever avoid him all evening? How she wished she had not come.

He planted himself at the top of the stairs to greet her even before she entered the drawing room. He wore a snowy wig with two sausage curls above each ear and a black silk bag at his nape. Lace spilled from his russet coat sleeves embroidered in bronze. Simon frowned when Rutley joined their party.

What, Arabelle wondered, did that kind of a man want out of life? Certainly not to serve others, she deduced, contrasting him to Simon. Any hapless wife of Lord Rutley's would live under his fist, and be pestered constantly by his determined attentions. Arabelle was forced to make a public reply to his bow and greeting, but her eyes strayed to the tall splendour of Simon escorting Corisande into the gathering just ahead of them.

Rutley appropriated Arabelle with an irritating grip on her elbow when she moved into the salon. It was all pale, shimmering green walls and chandeliers, and chatting people who turned to look the newcomers up and down. Lord Rutley placed a chair for her, and she sank hesitantly upon it, not knowing where else to go. Lord and Lady Chesterfield were already engaged in a circle of conversation with people she did not know.

Corisande waved at a young woman, and soon the two were giggling and posing for a corner full of intellectual men in deep discussion who paid them no more than a cursory glance.

Arabelle felt Simon's eye upon her, discreet but often, as he conversed with another officer in a red coat.

As a flautist trilled an introduction, and the chamber trio struck up a Handel piece, Lord Rutley said, scraping another chair across the wood floor to the carpet next to her. "Miss Lamar, since you admitted to me that your affections are not engaged upon any man, I take this opportunity to ask—"

"Please stop!" She rose quickly.

He pulled her back down. "I am offering you marriage! I am not a fool. I won't bungle this, like Chancet did." He smiled in beguilement as she tried to pull her hand away. "Now," he said, gripping her arm tyrannically, "will you marry me?"

Afforded a whiff of his unpleasant breath and an excruciating crush of her delicate skin, it was too much to bear. She gave him an offended stare and yanked herself away with successful force. She lifted her fan to cover her mouth and whispered angrily behind it, "How can you possibly presume to ask me such a thing?"

"You are the most beautiful woman in London at the moment."

Anger inflamed Arabelle.

"I want you!" Rutley pressed urgently, groping for her hand, which she had hidden beneath her wide skirt.

She made a sound of fury and flicked off his hand. "Stop it!"

Simon was talking across the room, and since he seemed to be watching her proceedings with Rutley, she was relieved to catch and hold his eye. Down by her gown on the opposite side of her tormentor, where Rutley could not see it, but Simon could, Arabelle snapped her fan shut in the signal, *I wish to speak to you.*

Simon gave her an infinitesimal wink, and concluded his conversation with the officer.

Meanwhile, the hot breath of Lord Rutley came nearer to her temple as he put a sugared sweetmeat in a small plate upon her lap.

She passed a hand over her brow and tried to keep her voice calm. "Lord Rutley, I cannot, and will not, entertain your suit!" She put the plate on the floor.

"Why not?"

Since people were passing in front of them, she waited, then flicked open her fan and said to him behind it, "My father knows nothing of this, and I am so circumstanced that I cannot and will not encourage your addresses." Wasn't that how Aunt Claracilla said to put it?

"You can!" Rutley whipped out. "You told me your affections were not engaged."

"That is correct. But do be quiet, someone might hear you."

He spread his hands incredulously. "Then why do you refuse to entertain *my* suit?"

"Must I explain it even more clearly?" she asked incredulously. "Then here it is: I do not love you or even esteem you!"

He stared at her, disbelief crinkling his short, straight brows. "What?" he ejaculated. "You do not *love* me, you say? That is the most *ludicrous* reason for not marrying me! Come, Arabelle, *I* love *you,* and that is more than enough! You will see."

You love my money, and you're made of lust, she corrected him silently.

Simon was suddenly there, a glass in each hand. What a relief.

Oblivious to his approach, Rutley continued in a fierce whisper, grasping her wrist tightly. "Why do you think love matters? You are a Viscount's daughter. You should be sophisticated enough to know that such *bourgeois* ideas of love do not apply to ladies of your status." Though she gave a tug, he would not let go of her wrist.

Simon, holding the two full goblets, swung wide to call a greeting to a woman walking away, and slopped liquid neatly onto Lord Rutley's lap.

"What the deuce?" He jumped up, dropping her hand. He cursed at Simon and snarled, "Thank you very much!"

"Oh, did you want one of these?" Simon asked innocently, handing Rutley a glass. "Arabelle, I promised to introduce you to the lady of the house. Come, Madame Montagu is waiting."

Arabelle put her trembling fingers on Simon's arm. "You came just in time," she said in utter relief as they moved in state across the room. "I almost choked with glee at your 'accident' just now. How well it served him! If you only knew what he was saying to me! I needed rescuing."

"I could see that. Care to drink the rest?" His lips curved as he handed her the glass.

"Yes! I will drink to you for your brilliant intervention." Their eyes touched, and she felt she must not look at him long lest the occupants of the room should see how very much she loved him.

They greeted Madam Montagu, a dark-haired wit with a large nose and a knowing smile, wearing a cap tied under her chin with a black velvet ribbon. After they had chatted amicably awhile, she asked them to come again next week. "I never invite idiots to my house," she declared with a curl of her lips, "although a few slip in somehow. Lord Chesterfield wrote to me that you, Miss Lamar, are so well educated that you read Latin; and you, Lieutenant Laurence, are the sharpest officer at the Academy. So, come see me often." She turned to her next guest, having given them no opportunity to utter anything but thanks.

Lord Rutley sat seething at Arabelle from across the room. As soon as she glanced his way, he snatched a woman's fan from her, opened and shut it several times, and then dropped it back into the astonished woman's lap. With fire in his eyes for Arabelle, he stalked out of the room.

Simon shook his head and remarked, "He tells you that you are cruel."

Though it had looked childish and silly, she felt shaken by the livid hatred she had seen in Rutley's eyes.

Chapter Eighteen

Sneaking Suspicions

At Chesterfield House the next afternoon, Simon descended the grand staircase and paused at the bedchamber level, listening. At the top of the house, in a room smelling of oil paint, Arabelle and Corisande still modeled for their portrait. They would likely remain there for another hour.

He watched until all the footmen and maidservants were out of sight in the marble hall below. Then Lady Chesterfield disappeared into her boudoir with a woman caller, talking in soft voices, and the porter closed the front door.

Simon moved silently across the landing and into Corisande's room. In a few minutes, he ducked out again, and saw Lord Chesterfield perusing, with a magnifying glass, a picture by Titian on the landing gallery. His eyebrows rose. "Good day to you, Laurence."

"Good afternoon, Your Lordship. I must look a bit suspect coming out of that room, but the young ladies are sitting for Miss Agathon. Perhaps I can alleviate their boredom by reading to them." He tapped a book in his coat pocket.

"Oh? I would be interested to see what reading material you have chosen."

Simon fished out a small blue volume and handed it over.

The Earl ran his glass over the title page. "What is this? *Rules and Orders for the Royal Academy at Woolwich—Directions for Teaching the Theory and Practice?* Never tell me that Corisande wants you to read her that!"

Simon chuckled. "Actually, it is Arabelle who is curious to hear it; and as soon as she said so, Corisande wanted the book, and has kept it in her room ever since. I promised to fill the ladies in on what I do at the Academy by reading a few of our rules to them and expounding on how they translate to my daily life at The Shop."

"Ah," said the Earl. "I suppose stranger things have women done when in the race of courtship."

"Race, My Lord?" Simon grinned, took back his book, and left Lord Chesterfield with eyebrows still aloft.

In his own guest chamber, Simon looked at the paper he had found deep in Corisande's pillowslip. He unfolded it and read:

> *Dear Miss Enterprising,*
> *   If you want a sizable chunk, do one more important thing:*
> *Wrap the goods in black.*
>
>   *Fox*

Delivery carts rumbled into the Chesterfield courtyard in a chaotic stream, day after day. Finally, the ball was only two days away.

A letter arrived from Aunt Claracilla saying she was truly appalled at Arabelle's lack of chaperonage. She would come to London herself, and try to alleviate her dear niece's troubles. Grateful for her aunt's plan, Arabelle felt that she could use Claracilla's support at home, but did not see how she could incorporate herself into Chesterfield House.

In the early afternoon, morning callers filled Lord and Lady Chesterfield's music room. Lady Lavinia, the friend with whom she had giggled at Madam Montagu's salon, played cards with Sir Pomeroy and another man. Arabelle caught Sir Pomeroy's eye as she rose from the gossip circle surrounding Lady Chesterfield. He gave her a merry twiddle of his fingers, and slapped down a card. She wondered how he felt toward her after the duel. Despite his *gaffes* and overt pursuit of her, there was something about him that smacked of a good heart deep beneath his costly lace and affectation.

She wove through the bowing, smiling men and the haughty women who gave her a look once-over from her hair to her brocade shoes. She smiled at them all, and slowed behind Sir Pomeroy to touch his shoulder as she went by. He turned instantly and grasped her wrist, dropping his cards on the floor.

"I'm sorry!" she said, and stooped to pick them up for him.

He had bent toward them, also, and met her eyes with great interest after ogling her neck with more subtlety than ever before. "Thank you, Arabelle! I delight in seeing you again . . . so close! Will you dance with me at the Ball?"

She noticed a faint red scar up his cheek, camouflaged with powder. "Yes, thank you," she replied. With a slight curtsey and a smile for Corisande, Lady Lavinia, and Colley Cibber, whom she had not recognized from the back, she made her way out of the room and up the central staircase.

In the clock-ticking emptiness of Corisande's room, Arabelle passed the lowboy and the bed festooned with lavender curtains. The sun glinted through perfume bottles on the chest of drawers in the corner, and slanted onto Simon's miniature. The realism of his face drew her. This was the reason she had come. Sitting amongst all those people, hearing all the Court news that scarcely interested her, she felt lonely for Simon.

She cradled the frame with both hands and gazed at his likeness. An overwhelming longing drained her heart as she saw the kind expression in his speaking eyes. *Dear God,* she prayed. She let her heart and soul plead the rest, for words were not sufficient. She did not even know what she could pray for regarding him. As her eyes blurred with moisture, she kissed Simon's image.

She felt, rather than heard, a presence behind her. Stunned by the shame of being caught, she lowered the portrait and slowly turned, her heart thumping.

Simon's torso was half in the room. When he saw her, he closed the door with a soft click. "Thank God it's you in here, Arabelle."

Though she was thrilled to see him, a blush warmed her cheeks; she could see it in the mirror. She wondered why he was glad it was she and not Corisande in her room.

He touched his lips for caution, and approached her.

She tried to hide his miniature by standing in front of it, but he was so tall that when he flicked his glance over her shoulder, her pulses pounded. How embarrassing to realize that he may have seen her kissing his picture! Trying to smile at his real face, she asked, "Are you still investigating something?"

He wore a knowing look as he studied her pretty confusion. "Yes, I thought I would take these moments, while these upper floors are deserted, to look for more material."

"So you spy on . . . Corisande?"

Simon went to the bed and felt inside his fiancée's pillowslip. "She has intriguing correspondents."

Arabelle said, "Isn't that most irregular?"

"Very."

"Do you know who they are?"

"I will soon ascertain whether my suspicions are right. Will you please guard the door so that if she comes, I can beat a hasty exit through your room? If she catches you in here, can you, ah, pretend to be borrowing something?"

Arabelle smiled. "I *am* borrowing a gown for the ball—one she offered me. I can start searching for it now."

"Good. That serves our purpose well."

As she watched his broad shoulders in a dark blue coat bending between the lavender bed curtains, he extracted a folded paper from another one of Corisande's pillows. He turned and whispered, "She doesn't suspect me, or it would not be so easy for me to find these missives. I just keep returning the ones I have already read. It's a lot like a circulating library."

Arabelle put her hand over her mouth and giggled. "Can you share with me what is happening?"

Striding toward her and planting his shoulders against the door next to hers, he unfolded the page and held it so they could read together.

> *Dear Miss Enterprising,*
> *No point in assigning blame. You say you should be Mrs. Enterprising as of some time ago, but your groom ducked you. Let me say that he is back and willing, as you have seen and heard.*

Simon murmured, "Words to pique the curiosity, eh?"

Regarding my next venture, if you do not cooperate fully, I will spill the beans in front of Chesterfield and everybody. Think on't.

Fox

They locked eyes.

"Who is Fox?" No sooner had the whisper left Arabelle's lips than the lever turned in the small of her back. She eyed Simon in fright, pointing to the door behind her. "She's trying to get in!" Digging her feet into the carpet, Arabelle kept her shoulder blades firmly against the door and pointed him urgently toward her chamber.

Simon touched her cheek and streaked across the room and through the connecting door. Arabelle made a silent sprint to Corisande's tall wardrobe, turned the key, and managed to put her hand on a garment before the door behind her opened.

In flounced Corisande, frowning back at the door lever. She turned and saw Arabelle half inside her wardrobe. "What are you doing digging in there?"

"Oh, Corisande, I didn't know most of those people in the drawing room, and I did not feel like staying. I remember you said you have a gown you want me to wear to the ball. I thought it would be nice to try it on and see how it fits. But I do not know which gown it is, so I'm glad you came." She smiled and motioned helplessly at the array hanging before her.

Corisande's face lit up. "Oh, oh, just wait until you see it, and hear my brilliant plan!" She ran back to tell Lady Lavinia, who poked her red head in, not to come in yet.

"Why not?" whined Lady Lavinia, her orange eyelashes blinking with resentment.

"Because I am occupied with something that does not concern you. Go back and entertain those poor men with a song. They are probably wilting with *ennui.* You can come up here later." After shutting the door firmly in Lady Lavinia's face, she turned to Arabelle. "I don't want anyone else to be in on this. It will be our splendid and stunning appearance."

Arabelle's mind was distracted, wondering where Simon was now. "I shall be right back," she told Corisande, who was pushing gowns and petticoats aside. "I must take this ribbon off my neck; it itches." Arabelle slipped into her room and shut the door behind her.

"Simon?" she whispered, keeping her back against the door. She could not see him in the shadows beside the carved French *armoire* or behind the long curtained windows, for there his boots would have shown beneath.

With a rattle of the lever, Corisande said, "Here's the gown."

"I am coming, Corisande," said Arabelle, fumbling at her neck ribbon and keeping her foot against the door.

"Let me in. You might as well keep this in your room."

For lack of an excuse, Arabelle admitted her.

Corisande looked animated. "I want us to be noticed—*really* noticed—at the Ball; so guess what I thought of doing?"

"What?"

"You and I will wear white and black gowns. I have a new white silk sprinkled with silver brilliants—my wedding gown, you know—and look, this is my mourning banquet gown that you can wear. I got it after my parents died, but only wore it once. Don't you like it?"

Surprised, Arabelle took the black silk petticoat, *robe ronde*, and matching corset from her. The latter had black *échelles* in a ladder from the low squared neckline to the pointed waist. "How elegant," she remarked, fingering the abundant ebony lace on the sleeves and admiring the ruching that decorated the draped sides of the overskirt. "I have never worn black before."

"Is it not dramatic? It was very expensive, and these are jet beads sewn over the bodice. No one in ordinary colours will be as striking as you and I will be. Here, we might as well hang this up."

Arabelle hastily took all the pieces of the costume before Corisande could touch her *armoire* door. What if Simon hid in there? It was certainly large enough to hold him.

"I can call a maid now, and try this on; no need to hang it up. Thank you, Corisande; you are so generous. I do have gowns, you know, but this—!" Arabelle gasped. Someone had touched, oh-so-lightly, the back of her ankle. So Simon lay under her bed!

"Yes, doesn't it take your breath away?" Corisande fingered the rich lace and beads, and finished Arabelle's sentence. "You should look quite good in it."

Arabelle smiled. "How nice of you to think so." Self-consciously, because she knew Simon Laurence was listening inches from her ankle, she asked, "Is that Lady Lavinia knocking on your door again?"

"I suppose!" huffed Corisande. "But you and I must plan our jewels and hair ornaments and fans and everything tonight. I must entertain Lavinia until her father leaves, and I swear, he never stops talking to Lord Chesterfield." She bounded back into her own chamber, calling, "Oh Lavinia, has anyone new arrived? We need more men to liven us up. I do not know where Simon went. He is always so tiresomely occupied with Army business. Where are you, Lavinia? Fie, she must have gone away again."

Arabelle closed the door that had no lock, and smoothed out the dress ensemble upon the bed. "Is there a shameless eavesdropper in this room?" she whispered.

"Guilty as charged," came Simon's voice from under her bed.

With a little laugh, Arabelle eyed the edge of the burgundy and blue Persian rug upon which his white hair, forehead, and black eye patch appeared. He lay on his back, relaxing in great good humour, and fixed her with one sparkling eye. "I do declare!"

"What?"

"What a sight of pure pulchritude you are, even from this perspective. Even from one eye." He captured her hem and held it.

She tried to pull away, and said in laughing rebuke, "You are a rascal, and you must leave."

He swung his long legs out and dusted off his close-fitting breeches. "The amazing things one hears in a lady's chamber."

"What amazed you?" Arabelle inquired, giving him a hand to rise.

He maneuvered himself onto one knee. He did not answer, but pressed his face into her gown and embraced her about the petticoats.

Much moved, she touched his thick white hair. Her heart swelled with tenderness for him. Then she heard Lavinia's sharp laugh in the next room. She panicked. "Simon! Hie yourself away! The ladies may pop in at any moment, and then where would you be?"

"I would be caught with you again. I do wish we could cease to care about the consequences."

"That's madness! We both know that. Hurry, please!" Arabelle shot a stressed look over her shoulder.

Corisande's voice uttered some exclamation as her knuckles groped against the door for something on her door hook. "I need to give this to Arabelle," her muffled voice said.

Arabelle knew that the door would plummet open. The distance was too great across the open floor to the landing door. Simon knew it, too, and pulled her quickly by the hand. He opened the door of the immense carved *armoire* and removed the key. When the mirrored door swung outward, he pushed aside the few garments on the sliding hooks inside, shot Arabelle an inviting look that gave her a delicious shiver, and pushed her in. With wildly beating heart, she stepped up onto the solid floor while Simon compressed her pannier and, to her great astonishment, stepped in after her. The last thing she saw was his white grin and shining eye before he inserted the key from their side, pulled it closed, and turned it with a click, which locked them in.

"Oh, Simon!" she whispered, amused. They were so close together in the dark amongst her gowns. "You are such an innovative spy! What am I going to do with you?"

He laughed low. "What would you like to do with me?" She felt his lace cravat tickle her cheek.

Sounds of a door opening and footsteps clunking across the wood floor and stopping on the carpet outside the *armoire* did not stop Simon from touching Arabelle's forearm. She held her breath, quivering.

When Corisande yelled, "Arabelle!" she jumped. Simon's fingers stopped her lips.

Corisande huffed petulantly. "Where did she go?"

They heard sounds of quick walking to the outer door, a pause, and "Oh, the deuce!" and a slam. Arabelle's heart beat rapid-fire in her breast. It was after more footsteps and Corisande's door slamming that Simon's breath moved closer . . . closer to Arabelle's cheek. Oh, how she wanted to kiss him. They must part, and quickly.

"Forbidden Arabelle," he whispered. "Dear God, what a tragedy this is."

Arabelle fumbled for the key. It was heavenly, incarcerated with Simon Laurence, her arm held by him and her side pressed to his vital strength. She knew that if she stayed another minute, she would deepen the danger of moving on to very tempting indiscretions. She wanted nothing more than to wrap her arms around him, kiss him, and . . .

Corisande's door to the landing slammed, making her jump. The sound of two pairs of heels receded down the corridor as Corisande shouted at a maid, "Find Miss Lamar!"

"I have found her!" said Simon in a warm tone, holding her tenderly around her ribcage.

Arabelle, fearing what would happen if she perpetuated such lovely sensations, scrabbled to turn the key. Breathing fresh air, she stepped down out of their hiding place.

Simon, smiling as he emerged, put a paper into her hand and closed her fingers round it. She loved the feel of his hands on hers. "Will you put this back into Corisande's pillow for me?"

"Yes."

"Thank you, Arabelle. I must away."

"Yes."

He winked and said, "That interlude was wonderful beyond belief. I shall dream of it." He leaned toward her and breathed in beside her temple curls. "Mmmm . . . I shall remember your scent." Then he was gone.

With a full heart, Arabelle returned the letter to Corisande's pillow. Then she dashed back to her room and ascended the steps to her bed. Throwing herself upon it, she laid her cheek on the silken bolster. It was truly amazing what could happen in this house.

Shortly after, Corisande and Lavinia sauntered into her chamber, asking where she had been and not waiting for an answer, for Corisande could hardly wait to show her a Meissen pitcher that had just arrived, another gift for her wedding. She threw a jet necklace onto the vanity table and said it went with the ball gown.

Arabelle was so relieved that Simon had escaped, and that he and she had eluded detection, that she nodded and admired effusively without knowing what she said.

Chapter Nineteen

Lord Chesterfield's Ball

"You have the complexion for it, Miss." The maid hovering behind her looked over her shoulder into the looking glass.

Arabelle stood before it, arrayed in the ebony gown. Her skin looked very white, from the scoop of her beaded bodice to the widow's peak of her hairline. A natural blush tinted her cheekbones and her dark-fringed hazel eyes looked lustrous with anticipation. Her wide-eyed serenity did not reveal the alarming feeling that hummingbirds flitted wildly in her stomach. *Calm yourself,* she admonished her reflection. She rearranged her long curls from the back to fall over one shoulder. She wore a cluster of black ribbons with short peacock feathers at her crown, gleaming in iridescent lapis lazuli. They were the only colour accent to her black gown, and they looked very pleasing.

Chesterfield House swirled with a cacophony of excitement and much rushing about. The maids, including Arabelle's dresser, had fussed over their matching pale blue gowns, and they all had silver ribbons fluttering from their tiny lace caps. Servants streaked to place last-minute pink bouquets and silver punch bowls, and to light chandeliers to blazing brilliance. From the ballroom came the sound of musicians warming up their instruments in discordant squeaks and scales. A footman left behind a faint cloud of powder from his wig as he dashed by Arabelle and Corisande on the stairs. Wiping off shaving soap with a handkerchief as he clattered down the marble steps, another footman yelled, "Why isn't the porter at the door yet? A carriage is rolling through the gate! Ye gods! Where is he? Will I have to open the door?"

Lady Chesterfield, in her perfumed and gilded boudoir, looked baffled when the young ladies arrived for inspection. While they revolved for her in their black and white gowns, Her Ladyship said, "I just wonder if those might not be too stark . . . pastels would have been more the thing . . . that is what all young ladies wear. But it is too late to change, I suppose?" She herself wore pale green silk with a pink and ivory lace petticoat.

The Earl knocked on the open door, and strolled in, looking pleased. "The Duke of Hamilton is here already. I gave him a brandy, and teased him not to look too eager. Could it be that he has heard about our Arabelle? Corisande, you look pale in white. Try for some colour, will you? The sky blue fichu we gave you would do it. Put that around your neck."

"Your Lordship, I am *tired* of looking like other women!" cried Corisande scornfully. "Tonight it is Arabelle and my aim to stun everyone!" Her nose rose. "Besides, I am soon to be married, and I want everyone to remember it." She looked pointedly at Arabelle.

Lady Chesterfield said, "Oh, is that your wedding gown? You just removed the silver stars and added the white *échelles;* I see."

Lord Chesterfield stepped up onto a French chair and viewed in the mirror above the mantle his dark magenta coat with pink and silver *passementerie* gracing the stand-up collar and the back of his waist. Satisfied, he jumped down, adjusted his knee breeches above his snow-white hose, and said, "The new coat is perfection. It is good to be well dressed." He lifted an index finger. "But not too well dressed. Never be ostentatious."

Arabelle smiled and said, "You look marvelous, My Lord."

Thanking her, he approached Corisande. "Since you want to be known as the bride-to-be, why do you wear that patch in the 'coquette' spot, hmm?"

Corisande fingered the black heart near her mouth and tried to look naïve. "Is . . . is that what it means?"

"You know very well that it does!" chided the Earl. He turned to Arabelle. "Whatever possessed you to wear black, my dear?"

"I am the black sheep." She smiled and tacked on, "Just ask my mother."

"I do not believe it. However, you two will certainly be noticed." Speaking low, he said, "You look beautiful, Arabelle—absolutely breathtaking. Remember," he rubbed his hands together and glanced at Corisande, "be ready when I announce the portrait. It is done, and I call it a triumph." Smiling mysteriously, he strolled toward the door. Pausing there, he shook his head in playful futility, eyeing them under his heavy lids. "Ah, ladies, ladies! I believe you have but two passions."

"We do? Only two? What are they, then?" asked Corisande.

"Vanity and love. You, Corisande, seem to overflow with the former, and I fear that yon fiancé will not be able to cure you of it."

"I need no cure!" she threw back. "He loves me the way I am."

The Earl paused on his way out. "He *loves* you, you say? You astonish me." He came back into the room and fixed her with an intent look. "Do you think to convince me that *you* love *him?*"

Corisande recoiled as if struck. "But of course! How could I not love him? He is the handsomest man in England!"

"Handsomest. Ah! It is just as I perceived." He pointed at his wife. "This is what comes from a steady diet of romantic novels." He said to Arabelle, "She sends a maid out many times a week to change her piles of romances for more of the drivel. You don't read those fantastical accounts of courtship, love, and marriage between terrified maidens and dastardly heroes, do you?"

Arabelle's lips curved merrily. "Yes, My Lord, I sometimes do. My Aunt Claracilla took turns reading them aloud with my sister and me. But we often read serious books, too."

His twinkling look belied his teasing. He left, calling expansively, "The cream of London is arriving. The house looks magnificent, the women will stun, my wine is superb, and the portrait is done. What more could even a Duke ask for?"

Arabelle was relieved that the Earl of Chesterfield had not expounded about love. All seeing, as he often seemed to be, she wondered if he saw the burning love within her. If so, it was but a short jump, she feared, for him to detect the man for whom she felt such flaming adoration.

Hurrying up to her chamber, Arabelle tussled with her emotions. Sorting through her patch box, she picked out a tiny circle. It fit, because her mind cartwheeled round and round. Where should she put it? She studied her face and decided to cover the tiny mole at the outer corner of one eye. She consulted the French list next to the drawing of a woman's face in the box cover. Worn at the corner of the eye meant *La Passionnée.*

Very fitting, she thought. *I am full of passion tonight.* It was futile passion, but passion nonetheless.

From her window seat, she observed the long line of carriage lanterns snaking as far into London as her eye could see. She tightened her fingers over her fan and descended the staircase in the ebony gown with the skirts fluffed and held up by bows to show the silk petticoat. Soft ruching round the low square neck framed her white curving breasts, the necklace fell daintily just above them, and the black beads sewn in designs over the V bodice glistened as she passed the *girandole* of candles at the mirror. There, on the second landing, she paused.

Quartet music played as chattering people arrived. As they entered the house, footmen whisked away their cloaks and hats. The butler announced their names when they entered the ballroom, and the hard-working serving-maids and footmen put warm mead cups into the cold hands of the guests. It was a chilly night, and it was obvious how grateful the guests were to be welcomed into the warm, opulent rooms of Chesterfield House.

Arabelle and Corisande ended up chatting for a quarter of an hour on the landing that led to the ballroom, sometimes sitting on the gilt chairs, sometimes leaning to peer through the dense black iron railing at the people milling below. Corisande was awaiting the appropriate moment to make their appearance. She had carefully planned her part in this ball, and looked to be in buoyant spirits. She could scarcely keep her tongue, hands, or feet still. She explained, while primping her hair in her fan mirror, that they must not show themselves until the latecomers were there to see their grand entrance.

"This is your coming-out ball in a way," she said to Arabelle, "since your father has not given one for you. Your mother said this might just serve. Look, there's my Simon! Does he not look utterly military in that red dress coat?" They could see his broad shoulders and back, with epaulettes adding distinction to his nip-waisted *justacorps.*

Arabelle, trying to hide her admiration, observed, "He has a glittering new scabbard with a great deal of etching."

Corisande's voice turned petulant as Simon turned and they saw his face. "Why, oh why does he have to wear that black eye patch? To this ball, of all things! It makes him look for all the world like a pirate."

Arabelle's eyes shone. She loved him looking like a pirate. Her heart sighed, *Please pirate me away.*

Corisande thought she had not heard, and insisted, "Well, don't you think that spoils him? I shall tell him to take it off."

"Not at all, Corisande. I wouldn't ask that because he obviously needs to wear it. People will assume it's the injury he got when he fainted at your wedding."

"Oh, well good, then. It will remind them of me—that he is betrothed to me."

Simon by-passed a bevy of open-mouthed, fan-fluttering women. They all turned to watch him stroll onto the ballroom floor, and moved to follow him thither.

Corisande said in a brittle tone, "It is time to make our entrance!"

"Yes," agreed Arabelle. Corisande was very jealous about Simon.

The butler saw Corisande's fan signal when she moved down the steps. He shouted to the company assembled, "Miss Corisande . . . Wells!"

As prearranged, Arabelle gave Corisande her moment to preen as she descended first, her smile flashing at no one and everyone. She had not observed precedence, for she did not allow the Honourable Arabelle to go first. "I am established in this society, and I live here with Lord and Lady Chesterfield," had been her excuse, "so I should go first. Besides, I'm engaged."

Arabelle did not buy into her brand of logic, but neither did she mind having her go first. Giving her the whole staircase, Arabelle followed, eyes bright but lips composed, for she did not know anyone she happened to glance upon, and her smile would not come by force.

"The Honourable Arabelle Lamar!" the butler trumpeted.

Halfway down the steps, she saw Aunt Claracilla, of all people. Arabelle's spirits leapt, she smiled widely, and hurried straight into her aunt's outstretched arms. "You came, you came! Thank you!"

Lady Shepley beamed, her pretty eyes expressing her gladness at their reunion. She pointed to herself and motioned as if writing, then at Arabelle's hand.

"You came in response to my letter," said Arabelle. She hugged her again. "Come to my chamber with me after the ball, and we shall talk. You look so lovely." Lady Shepley wore her light brown hair pulled back with tiny braids looped intricately round her chignon. Her slender figure carried off a pale blue flowered gown with pearls and Chantilly lace in ruffles upon her forearms. She smiled her delighted thanks for the compliment.

A trumpet flourished with clear, cheerful notes. The butler called, "Lord Chesterfield will now unveil a portrait executed by the artist, Robert Agathon."

Lord Chesterfield took the smiling Miss Agathon upon his arm up the steps to the landing. Surprised murmurs circulated at sight of the creature at his side, gowned in lemon yellow with her dark braid festooned with matching roses down the back. "Robert Agathon is a woman?" was the question buzzing around the room.

The Earl bowed to his guests. "It may surprise some of you that our artist is a lady. Yes, her Christian name is, in fact, Roberta. I have told her that, hereafter, she should go around with her paintbrush, adding an *A* to all of her paintings. She has no need to hide any longer behind a male alias because she has quickly become a stellar portrait painter. You shall now see the most recent of her works, a double portrait of Viscount Bastwicke's eldest daughter, The Honourable Arabelle Lamar, and Lady Chesterfield's second cousin, Miss Corisande Wells. You see them in the flesh here first." He gestured to the two of them, his eyes twinkling.

Arabelle felt herself the object of hundreds of curious stares.

Aunt Claracilla squeezed Arabelle's arm. Her face showed surprise and excitement.

Lord Chesterfield stood for an instant with his hand upon the yellow silk that covered the painting. Then he whisked it down and threw it around Miss Agathon's shoulders, where it matched her gown exactly.

To Arabelle's amazement, upon the large canvas, there she stood with Corisande! The likenesses were lifelike and striking. A chorus of approval and thundering applause rose from the sea of guests. Miss Agathon curtseyed with gratified smiles to them all,

In the picture, Arabelle's dark hair was pulled back under the fetching *Bergère* hat, but the curls slipping down the curve of her neck and spilling over her shoulder to her dark pink gown made her look very seductive. Her eyes were large and luminous, and she looked as though she were gladdened by a heavenly sight. *Did I truly look like that?* she asked herself. That sight had been Simon Laurence.

She flushed as people turned again to look from her face to the portrait and back. Comments grew like a wave as people compared her and Corisande favourably to their full-length renditions. Corisande's pink-gowned likeness showed a tip-nosed nonchalance that was typical of her. She leaned with one knee on a chair and looked as if she felt superior to everyone. Miss Agathon was, indeed, a skilled artist.

Applause filled the house, and the triumphant Lord Chesterfield bowed to them all. "Come, Arabelle," he motioned. Corisande was already mounting the stairs. He reached for Arabelle's hand, and they bowed to the sea of guests, like actors following a performance.

When she descended again, Corisande's set of friends squeezed toward them with their giddy exclamations. Arabelle tried to feel—or at least look—at ease. She apparently succeeded, for they were both paid much court by awestruck women eyeing their portrait and then their gowns.

In addition to the praise and exclamations, the women were caught off guard by their bold new fashion of black and white. Corisande, in her pristine ensemble, wore black ribbons in her puffed blonde chignon, and fluttered a fan of black and white feathers. Men who gathered around them wore transparent admiration when Arabelle met their eyes over her black lace fan.

A bright turquoise coat embroidered in black moved into view. In a cloud of perfume, and with a hand on his pale pink wig, Sir Pomeroy Chancet was the picture of smitten wonder as he regarded Arabelle. "What alluring beauty! What a stunning picture it is! I could look at it all evening if you were not here yourself. How delectable you are—both here and there!"

Everybody in their circle laughed.

He came close to Arabelle and, looking at her black patch, said sidewise, "Passion, eh?" Since she kept her chin raised and refused to look at him, he gave up baiting her.

He perused Corisande's costume next. "I see, Corisande," he called, "that you have learned the value of contrast in throwing your charms into relief. So, tell me, are you portrayed as Good? And Evil?" He gestured his frothy handkerchief over her and then Arabelle.

"Yes, what else?" Corisande laughingly declared, "I am the white angel."

Her friends nodded knowingly, and guffawed, and twitted her.

Arabelle tipped her eyelids and said, "I am the black one."

"Oh-ho!" said Lady Lavinia. "We didn't know that!"

Men moved closer.

Lord Rutley materialized like a flash and groped for her fingers. "You are most fascinating this way!" he whispered excitedly. Aloud, he urged, "Say you'll eat your supper with me, Miss Lamar."

Arabelle had not yet formulated her negative response when a strangely familiar man moved toward her. He said a smiling word to Corisande.

"Arabelle," said Corisande, "the Earl of Ashby wants to be presented to you."

"I remember you!" cried Arabelle, pleased. It was the nice-looking man with chestnut hair from the carriage ride in the blizzard—Simon's brother, in fact. He stood tall and lithe in a suit of dark blue trimmed with silver.

Arabelle curtseyed and asked, "Lord Ashby, are you also Radford Laurence?"

"Yes, I am. I'm enchanted to meet you again." He reached out and removed Lord Rutley's hand from her arm, to Rutley's scowling chagrin. "Excuse me, Rutley; you owe me a debt, remember?" he threw genially over his shoulder. "I claim your payment now."

Lord Rutley looked awash with "but's."

"I only meant that I heard your invitation to Miss Lamar. However, if you give over to me the honour of watching her sup, there's an end to that paltry sum."

"Ah!" Lord Rutley concurred, recovering his colour. "If this is how you wish to be paid, what can I say but that you have a calculating head on your shoulders, Ashby. *Adieu* for now, Miss Lamar. Remember my original question." His black eyes pinned her until she could not stand his encroaching face any longer. She looked away, repressing a shudder of revulsion.

She found Lord Ashby frankly studying her.

"Good evening, Arabelle," said Simon's warm voice from behind them.

She turned.

He stood there twinkling at her from the eye not slashed across by a black patch. "How exquisite and mysterious you look."

Arabelle smiled.

"I see you've met up with my brother. Keep her safely in your sight," he said quietly to Lord Ashby.

"Right."

Arabelle was touched to hear herself so cared-for by Simon.

"Yonder is Chancet, whom I warned to stay away tonight," added Simon. "As you can see, he is here, so keep him away from her if I am occupied."

"*He* is the joker you dueled?" asked Lord Ashby, perusing the dandy in the pink wig and face patches.

"The same."

Sir Pomeroy had powdered his face very white, and consequently, his teeth appeared yellow when, while teasing Corisande, he smiled at her outbursts.

Arabelle's eyes followed Simon when he led Corisande out for the first dance. With his red coat, shining epaulettes, and his piratical good looks, she knew hers was not the only female gaze that lingered on him, longing to be his partner.

Lord Ashby asked, "Shall we follow Lord and Lady Chesterfield into the set? It's appropriate for you to dance at the top, as you are the coming-out girl and guest of the house."

"Thank you! I would be very pleased to dance with you, Lord Ashby. Do you live here in London?" she asked, moving hand-in-hand with him across the marble floor, vaguely aware of the crowd of faces on all sides.

"I seldom venture into London. I like my peace. So does Simon. I cannot imagine how he stands life at the Academy. Too chaotic for my bookish ways." His manner was charming, and belied his words in some measure. "I visited him there after my tour abroad. You remember . . . the day after we shared the stage coach."

"Yes. What did you think of his situation?" she asked as couples whisked next to them and behind them, forming a second line of dancers.

"I could not help but admire the discipline he keeps. One cadet told me he is an influence for good in that wild place. I only hope they appreciate him."

"Doesn't Captain Ligonier acknowledge his merits?"

Radford stepped close and replied, "Certainly he does. He graduated him to officer status and put him on assignment. But I've said too much already."

"I already know that, and will say nothing to anyone," Arabelle quietly assured him, "but his uniform proclaims his rank."

With her hand in the Earl's, she moved amidst a dipping, swaying sea of pale brocade gowns and embroidered coats as soon as the caller began to teach the movements of the country dance. Her inky gown made her starkly noticeable in the long mirrors. Perhaps she ought not to have worn it. People eyed her and Lord Ashby with great interest.

Unsettled by doubts, she promenaded with him. So Simon Laurence's brother was this polite and refined Earl. It came as a pleasant jolt that the man she loved—yes, loved!—came from a noble family. But what good did that knowledge do her? Her parents would bestow smiles upon Simon now, if they knew; but still, he was a younger son, not the heir. Moreover, he was Corisande's man and entirely out of the picture for Arabelle.

She and Lord Ashby linked arms and revolved. "Your Lordship is not a total recluse, surely? Do you have a wife, perhaps, who keeps you happy in the country?"

"No, I have no wife as yet," he admitted as they armed the other way. "Do you think it would help?"

She enjoyed the droll expression on his face and threw back, "Do you?"

"I would enjoy the right woman immensely." With a bright-eyed grin, he quipped, "Are your affections engaged, Miss Lamar?"

At that moment, when taken aback by this teasing but possibly serious line of questioning, Arabelle gave him an amused smile, then chanced to meet Simon's eye. The first sequence was finished, and he was their new neighbour in the dance. She dropped her lashes, and when she met Lord Ashby's quizzical regard after a half-figure-eight, she knew he had seen the interchange of looks between her and Simon. Radford looked gravely at Simon over her and Corisande's heads as they all linked hands and moved up a double and back.

Arabelle felt chagrined at her inability to manifest the fact that her affections were engaged. She wondered if Radford, who surely guessed her secret, would condemn her for coveting his unattainable brother.

The violins, harpsichord, flutes, and cellos played buoyantly on, and Arabelle and Radford danced with many more couples down the line. Arabelle saw Corisande's white gown and Simon's red coat at the end of the set as the dance concluded, and so did Radford. He led her straight to them, thanked Arabelle with a kiss upon her hand, and asked Corisande to dance.

As Arabelle turned from Radford to Simon, her heart thumped in her breast. He was looking down his nose at her with a gleam in his eye.

Radford said, "Simon, are we not fortunate to partner the spice of this ball? Pepper and salt."

Corisande crowed giddily, "Arabelle, he called you pepper! Will you let him get away with that? Whereas, without me, where would the world get its savour?"

"Where indeed?" asked Radford, smiling and drawing her away. Corisande looked displeased to see Simon reaching for Arabelle's hand.

Simon possessed her fingers with such a tender caress that she wanted to turn into his arms and hold him. "This is a dance I learned in this house recently," she said to him.

"Yes. The *Confesse*," he returned. "But since we cannot properly confess anything here, let me say that you are exquisitely beautiful."

She glowed up at him.

"And I like your portrait immensely," he added.

She flickered eyes with him and thanked him. Her heart was full. "It *is* immense, isn't it?"

The exuberant caller and the lilting music soon had them revolving in a right-hand turn. Arabelle turned left hands with the smiling Lord Chesterfield, and then returned to Simon, who said decidedly, "I will ask His Lordship if I can buy it."

"Buy it?" Her heart skipped. "But don't you get to keep a miniature of Corisande already?" she asked before she revolved in a back-to-back with Lord Chesterfield.

When she clasped Simon's arm again, he said, "I want that one," and flicked the long lashes of his uncovered eye toward the new portrait.

"Do you think His Lordship will give it up?"

They circled, honoured their neighbouring partners, and, when reunited, Simon said, "I wish to speak with you, Arabelle. Will you meet me inside the French doors at twelve o'clock?"

What a heavenly thought. "I shall . . . try," she said, giving him a quick smile. He and she were again parted by the dance, and had to turn with their new neighbours.

Through the noisy, perfumed throng skipped a little blonde girl. Clad in a pink and blue gown, she dodged around the dancers until she stood behind Arabelle. She reached out and tapped her back, and then stood respectfully against the wall so that she would not spoil the dance figure.

Arabelle turned hand-in-hand with Simon to the music and said, smiling at her, "That is my sister, Lenora."

"Charming," he said, flashing the little one a smile. When the dance ended with curtseys and bows, Lenora ran to them.

Simon bowed low to the little girl whose thick lashes lowered as she curtseyed to him. "Your servant, Sir," she said, shyly fluttering an interested look from him to Arabelle. Snatching Arabelle's hand, she pulled her away, and said happily, "I am glad I got to meet the pirate. Oh, Sir," she said back to Simon, "here comes our other sister, Genevieve."

"Yes, I met Genevieve once," said Simon, and greeted her with a bow and a smile.

Genevieve curtsied in her Pomona green gown, and looked him over from his white head to his silver-buckled shoes. Her apricot-gold hair was a smooth sheen pulled back, and she looked very pretty. Arabelle told her, "I wish you were already out. Young men are looking at you, and shall soon pester you for dances. You will have to be strong tonight to decline them all."

Genevieve flushed with pleasure.

While Lenora chatted on to Simon, Genevieve whispered to Arabelle, "And *you* got to dance with *him!* Was it wonderful?"

Arabelle gripped her hand and cast a euphoric look upward.

"You looked the most beautiful of your life when you danced with him."

It was Arabelle's turn to blush. They admired Simon, the most striking Army officer present, with the eye-patch that rendered him so swashbuckling.

Lenora was asking him, "Would you like one?"

"At my home in Kent, I would love one." He smiled and patted Lenora tenderly on the head. She jumped for joy, and squealed. She skipped to Arabelle and Genevieve and said, "He wants one! I'll give him the one Jerome and I picked out for him."

They heard the butler announce, "Lord Bastwicke!"

Arabelle left her sisters with Simon Laurence, and made her way to her father. Men stopped her along the way, asking her to dance. She smiled and thanked them, declining one after another.

Lady Bastwicke reached his side first. Arabelle had spotted her earlier, bedecked in a grandiose orange and rust gown. A parure of gold and topaz glittered from her head, neck, ear lobes, and wrists. Tonight, her gown spread ten feet wide, and her lace and petticoat were of blonde ruffles cascading from each elbow. She wore three face patches. She pinned snapping stares of speculation on Arabelle as she approached, and uttered a string of words to Lord Bastwicke behind her huge fan.

He left his wife, and hurried toward Arabelle. He looked distinguished in a chocolate brown brocade suit with gold buttons and braid embellishing the wide cuffs. His cadogan wig was powdered white, and his grand nose gave him an air of distinction.

"Father! I have missed you."

He assessed her with pride. "Arabelle, you have grown up since you left home. You are lovely indeed. Alas! Am I to lose you now that we are of a size to dance together?"

"You shall never lose me, Father. There isn't a man here whom you need fear will carry my heart away from you. Come, let us dance together. All these men will see what a big, strong father I have, and quake lest they have any wrongful designs upon me."

Lord Bastwicke barked out a laugh, then drew her into the line
and glared about him as though to tell such bucks that they had
better watch their thoughts.

Lady Bastwicke eyed them in consternation. She snapped her
fan shut for *I wish to speak to you.* Her eyes spat, *That's no way to snare
a husband, dancing father and daughter together!*

He appeared to ignore her, but took Arabelle's hand and said,
very low, "Your mother thinks I ought to toss you into the arms of
Sir Pomeroy Chancet or Lord Rutley, whoever proves more loaded
with estates and guineas. She has been investigating their assets."

"Oh, *no!* Father, please convince her that I must marry a man
with whom I *want* to spend my life—and most definitely not with
men I have been striving to avoid! If you only knew! Oh, promise
me, Father, that I will not have to marry against my will!"

"If I say you may choose whom you like," Lord Bastwicke
predicted balefully, "your mother will be furious. She will make
our lives a living hell."

Arabelle said desperately, "Please impress upon her that I must
marry not only for the gain of the family but also for a chance at
happiness. Will you uphold me, Father?"

He bent his head and said, "You are a dutiful daughter, and I
trust you to remember what is important. Do not attach yourself
to anyone unsuitable. No cloak-and-dagger courting on the sly, as
I am sure your Aunt Claracilla has warned you. Now that you are
in London," he said, glancing unwittingly at his wife, "you will have
your head filled with all kinds of rubbish. Arabelle," he said firmly,
"*you* are too intelligent to let silly passions rule you. Keep your head
clear. I will do what I can for you."

While she nodded, her breath came shallow. Her eye strayed
to the clock. An hour until midnight. She could hardly wait
for her *tête-à-tête* with Simon Laurence. Was that considered
cloak-and-dagger? She felt a modicum of guilt. Yet she thought of
little else as she and her father danced the first sequence together,
and moved on. It was a circle dance and a mixer, so she did not
have time to make conversation with her kaleidoscope of partners,
and for that, she was grateful.

At the end of it, Lord Ashby came to collect her. She ate her
supper with him looking on, as men always did, not eating a bite
themselves until the ladies had supped. He provided her with all

sorts of tiny meats and savoury tarts and iced cakes, and made himself her agreeable servant. She enjoyed his kindness very much.

"Were you at your brother's wedding?" she asked him.

"The aborted ceremony, yes. Too bad, was it not, the way he keeled over and knocked himself out?"

"Yes, terrible. Are you going to be at . . . the next one?"

"I shall stay in town until his future is secure, yes. We always stand by each other."

"How nice," said Arabelle from the heart. "I have a very close sister myself. That is Genevieve in the Pomona green gown, holding our youngest sister, Lenora's, hand. Genevieve is better than any other friend."

He looked suddenly very fascinated with Genevieve. "I am sure I have seen her before . . . somewhere!" he exclaimed softly. His eyes sparkled, and Arabelle took pleased notice of it.

With a signal of her fan, she beckoned Genevieve over. "She and my aunt, who is following them, are my closest confidantes. I would like you to meet Lady Shepley. Aunt Claracilla, this is Lord Ashby." Arabelle explained to Radford, "My aunt cannot speak, but she hears perfectly."

Aunt Claracilla admired him up and down in her subtle way, and Arabelle saw that approval shone in her smile for him. Did she think this was the man Arabelle loved? Later tonight, she would confide her futile longing for Simon, and ask Aunt Claracilla what she could possibly do. She must ask how she could go through life without him.

Lenora was sweetly graceful in their meeting with Lord Ashby, but Genevieve, oddly enough, looked abashed and white as she curtseyed to him. Arabelle would have liked to see what would transpire between them, but Sir Pomeroy cut in and asked Arabelle to dance. Saying she was still having supper, she left him nearly sputtering with astonishment, to which she added that she would be glad to dance with him later. He grabbed the hand of a passing woman to prevent himself being left with no partner.

Arabelle wanted to know the cause of Genevieve's behaviour with Radford Laurence, Lord Ashby. "Have you met him before?" she asked Genevieve while adjusting the gold locket catch to the back of her sister's neck.

Genevieve's wide eyes bored into her with huge significance. "Oh Arabelle! *He* was the man waiting for me to finish having my corset measurements taken that day!"

Incredulously, Arabelle gripped her wrist. "The man who came out of hiding and saw you in only your chemise?"

"Yes, the same! Without a doubt! Oh, I could die!"

Arabelle wiggled her arm to draw her subtle attention to Lenora. Lord Ashby was bowing to their little sister, asking if she would do him the honour of dancing with him.

"Thank you, Your Lordship," said Lenora with sparkling eyes, "but I and Genevieve cannot dance. We are not out yet," she informed him, twisting a curl round her finger.

He laughed, and looked straight over at Genevieve with an interested gleam in his eye. "Then come with me, and let us sit over there. Let me bring you each an ice."

Lenora accepted with a joyful skip. Radford quirked a questioning eyebrow at Genevieve, who looked radiant despite her hesitation.

"Go!" Arabelle, smiling, prodded the small of her back. Genevieve therefore stepped toward him with a becoming, blushing sweetness, and Radford looked pleased.

Arabelle soon received a gold-rimmed china dish of lemon ice from Lord Ashby, and saw him take two more from the servant's tray for her sisters. As soon as Radford handed them the confections, Lenora pulled his hand to make him sit next to her. She vaulted onto his lap, half facing him, where she claimed her dish from his hand and began to eat daintily with a golden spoon.

Arabelle and Genevieve looked at each other in astonishment. They had not known the social propensities of their infant sister. By then, the four of them were snug in their little circle of chairs. Radford shot a smile at Arabelle, and then turned it to Genevieve.

Lord Bastwicke strolled by with curiosity burning in his eyes. Arabelle beckoned their father over and introduced him to Lord Ashby. She saw the grace of good manners her father could so naturally employ toward his fellow man. As he left them, she saw him ask his sister, Claracilla, to dance.

When Arabelle rose, she saw Lord Rutley with her mother on his arm, so to speak. He actually paced at her starboard stern, for her broad skirt kept anyone from invading her elbow space. As her cloud of honeysuckle perfume reached them, Lady Bastwicke fanned coyly at Lord Ashby. "I am thrilled to the gills to see you again," she declared, smiling down her thin nose at him, her golden earrings swinging, and her close-set eyes snapping.

"Come dance with me, Miss Lamar," Lord Rutley said to Arabelle.

"Thank you, but I will not dance just now," returned Arabelle, trying to hide her loathing. "I am tired, and am eating an ice."

"Oh, *go* with him, Arabelle!" cried Lady Bastwicke, giving him a playful shove in her direction. "I'll take that," and she grabbed Arabelle's dish. "Now you are free."

Lord Rutley had catapulted toward Arabelle, off balance, and caught himself on the back of her chair. He then arranged his shoulders and chin to offended dignity. "I understand, judging by your phenomenal popularity, why you are exhausted, Miss Lamar. You should hear what the men are saying about you. Come. I will not tire you with another dance."

"No?"

"Instead, let me show you the remarkable copy of Titian's portrait of somebody-or-other in that little salon. It's done by none other than Rubens, if you can believe that. Perhaps you will know if it is true."

Arabelle found she could not refuse Rutley's escort since they had been literally thrown together by her mother for many to see. She shot Lord Ashby a long-suffering glance.

He set Lenora gently onto her chair, and stood to honour and watch her leave.

Informing Rutley coolly about some of the pictures in the corridor that he asked about, Arabelle felt increasing impatience. She feared what Madam was saying to Lord Ashby, the Earl whom she would now find such a good-looking bachelor. He was another man on the coach ride whom she had snubbed when she was unaware of his title. Arabelle wondered just how her mother would inquire into *his* financial condition.

"Let me take this moment to say that the picture of you and Corisande is delicious beyond belief!" gushed Lord Rutley, expelling snuff breath onto her. "Such expression in your eyes, and in your attitude. Why, it's enough to make a man lose control."

You lose control anyway, she thought with disgust. "Please do not speak so to me."

"That artist, too! What a surprise that she is such an attractive woman. What is this world coming to, with female artists and titillating women dancing in every direction a man looks? This is indeed the finest party I have ever been to. As for Miss Agathon, Lord Chesterfield will garner her plenty of commissions after tonight. Especially from men." He gave a jocular snort.

Arabelle shuddered. She must warn Miss Agathon not to take any commissions from the likes of Lord Rutley.

In the east salon, whose door entered onto the garden and swings, he pointed out the copy of a Titian supposedly done by Rubens.

"What a strange undertaking to copy someone else's masterpiece. Why would he do it," she asked, "when he has his own talent?"

"For money, of course. Not many can afford a Titian. It makes sense to me. I, myself, would copy the greats if I had the talent."

"Oh, you would, would you?" That infuriated her. "Is that what motivates you? Money?"

"It is the reason of reasons for most everything I know. *Almost* everything." He moved close and ogled her up and down. She smelled the snuff again and saw his eyelids lowered.

She felt like shouting, *Look at my face while we're talking!* She demanded, "Is there not a higher calling than the love of filthy lucre?"

"Oh, yes!" His eyebrows jumped in his excitement. "The love of women."

Arabelle's breast rose with her revulsion for him.

He announced, "I have spoken with your mother, who has arranged for me to meet your father in the morning."

Arabelle narrowed her eyes on his self-satisfied face. "Why ever should you meet my father?"

He touched her bare forearm before she could yank it away, "Everything can be settled soon in the way you want, Miss Lamar. May I call you Arabelle? No, don't speak for a moment; just listen to what I have to say." Despite her obvious revulsion, he splayed his bony hand over the white ruffles above his black coat and waistcoat. "I have all that a woman could want to make her happy: a title, ancestry, a country estate, a town house, and of course, my loving self. I will ecstatically share them all with you." He bowed, grabbing her hand in his clammy one.

Arabelle drew an incensed breath and yanked her hand away. How had he come so far with his spiel?

"Will you now give your consent to take me as your husband?" He moved her into the shadows and gripped her fervidly to him by the waist.

In the face of his intensity, she flung his hands off and cried, "Are you insane?"

It encouraged her to see Lenora hovering in the doorway, a sweet little silhouette against the colourful dancers. God keep her from such menacing suitors as this!

Lord Rutley's eyes were now diabolical pinpoints. "Arabelle! Your mother said—"

"Excuse me!" snapped Arabelle, grappling to get away. "My mother may have said a lot of things. She may have written an assignation note in reply to your advertisement in the paper and signed it from me, but I had no part in it. I knew nothing about it!"

He looked baffled, but hung onto her arm, causing her pain. "You didn't?"

Arabelle could not stand to hear another word of his and her mother's plans for her life. She yanked her arm away. "Knowing I have my father's support for my happiness, I say again, *no*, Lord Rutley. Do not bring this up again!"

His eyes sparked malevolently as he bit back words because Corisande and several of her friends hurried into the room. They headed straight for the long windows. Corisande did not approach Arabelle, but discreetly kept her distance, chattering with the young ladies.

Arabelle, wishing they had all barged right into this brangle, diverted Rutley by pointing. "Look! It's the Earl's fireworks." She hurried away from him to press her nose to a cold window. She watched the arcs of light crackle and burst into spheres of pink and gold sizzly stars. She welcomed this diversion, and she felt better, and safer, with Corisande in the room. Little Lenora was gone.

Rutley had gained control of himself to some degree. "All right, then," he said low to Arabelle, gripping her other arm with his two clammy hands, "you will not marry me."

Detaching herself with a vengeance, she glared at him askance; glad he had gotten that through his head. She saw how tensely his jaw muscles worked. She only hoped that Corisande had not heard any of their dialogue.

"How expensive this party must be," Arabelle murmured, moving around him and closer to Corisande, feeling uncomfortable under his intense regard.

"Oh yes," agreed Corisande enthusiastically, turning toward them, "it has taken pots and pots of money to bring off this huge of a success. But it's worth it," she said, beaming. She nodded to Lord Rutley, who bowed his head at her. He flicked out his large handkerchief and proceeded to polish his quizzing glass, and Arabelle wondered what was causing his eyes to flicker here and there with odd expressions.

Corisande waved at them and left the room, her chattering friends following. Corisande's white wedding gown sparkled under the *girandole* of flickering candles as she turned and called, "Aren't you going to wish me well, Lord Rutley and Arabelle? Simon and I are going to announce our new wedding date when the clock chimes midnight." She lifted her chin, smiled smugly at them, and rustled away.

Oddly enough, a flash of anger forked over Lord Rutley's countenance, but he said in a half-laughing tone, "She takes such morbid delight in that Lieutenant of hers. But, getting back to your complaint, Arabelle, I suppose you are one of these people who think money is the root of all evil," he taunted.

"You are very near the truth, but—"

"Listen, you innocent!" he stabbed out. "Does not even your father give money to charities such as foundling hospitals? Doesn't money do some good?"

"Of course it does, but I was about to beg you not to take that verse out of context. It is written: The *love* of money is the root of all evil."

"What a wit you are."

Her breast rose with anger. "That is not wit! It's truth!"

"Whatever you say. Shall we look at the fireworks from the steps? I cannot see the star bursts anymore; they are too high. Hmm, I see that Lieutenant Laurence out there has the same idea." He lifted a black cloak off a hook by the door and put it over her shoulders, then snatched another and clasped it over the lace at his throat.

Arabelle hesitated, but hearing that Simon stood outside, she went. She said, as she stepped out into the darkness, "I am afraid that, if I continued to be a part of this high life, it could grow easy to love money, for it seems to pour like water into any project or whim that strikes us here in Chesterfield House. I am in danger of the rest of the verse, you see, and I fear—"

Out on the step, she watched a green and gold thistle of light shoot off with a whistle and burst with a bang above the treetops. She looked for Simon's white head, but it was dark again, so she saw no one.

"I am in suspense," said Lord Rutley. "What is the rest of the verse that you are in danger of, O learned lady? I confess to some ignorance of the Holy Writ."

"About money, it goes on to say that, 'which while some coveted after, they have erred from the faith, and pierced themselves through with many sorrows.'" She quoted on to herself, "'But thou, O man of God, flee these things; and follow after righteousness, godliness, faith, love, patience, meekness.'"

She heard a new country dance melody begin in the ballroom. "I'm going in." She wanted to see Simon, and she did not see him outside. Only a few giggling young ladies and their swains rushed up the other stairs to the ballroom, for it was too cold to linger outside. When she turned and paused for Lord Rutley to open the salon door for her, he pulled off his white wig with a quick motion and tucked it into his waistcoat.

She stared at his closely-cropped dark head, uncomprehending. Why on earth did he expose himself like that? He was difficult to see in the dark, except for the whites of his eyes. She did not like what they said. In a stab of fright, she groped for the doorknob.

She did not reach it because Rutley made a quick grab at her shoulders. Next, she felt herself spun around violently and her mouth attacked by his. She struggled and pushed at him, trying to scream, but he was indomitable. Clinging to her lips with his, he whisked her down the steps by a hard clamp around her waist, her feet hardly touching the ground.

His hurtful mouth and the whistles and loud bangs of many skyrockets in succession muffled her screams. Her back bumped into something high and hard: a carriage wheel.

As soon as Lord Rutley cut his hateful contact with her lips, Arabelle screamed. Another hand slapped instantly over her mouth and held on tightly, giving her pain. The second person, shrouded in a black hood, shoved her into a vehicle with great energy. They pushed her mercilessly, and Arabelle sensed an air of triumph between them. The coach door slammed as another loud rocket burst beyond the trees with a glittering crack.

Grabbing the door lever in panic, she rattled it. It was locked. She was alone in the dark interior. There was no other door. "Somebody help me!" she shrieked. The coach rocked as someone jumped onto the driver's seat. She shrieked as loudly as she could, and pounded at the door. The horses leapt forward and the wheels clattered her away from Chesterfield House. In panic, she watched the long, lighted windows and the dancing guests recede. She could not even hear the music any more. All she saw was another skyrocket streak upward and explode in sizzling stars.

She tried to draw attention to herself by knocking on the glass and waving wildly, but she only raised a dog to vicious barking after the service gate clanked shut behind them. She cranked a window the few inches it would open. She shrieked, "*Help* me!" and stretched her fingers out, pleading for anyone in the street to notice. The few wanderers and ragamuffins who may have seen or heard her pass through the winter darkness would do nothing to aid a frantically waving lady in a coach cantering with all speed up Tyburn Hill.

She sank back in futility. It was quite apparent she could do nothing at this moment. She sat back, trembling. What did this abduction mean?

How appalling that Lord Rutley had so easily taken her! The blackguard had done it while she quoted Scripture at him.

Had anyone seen it happen? She doubted it, for everyone else seemed to be watching the fireworks from the other rooms, and the group of young men and women had probably not even looked their way. Lord Rutley himself had been all dark but for his face after he removed his wig. Of course! That was why he removed it.

Arabelle realized that her black gown, too, had equally hidden her in the night. He had thrown dark capes over both of them.

She sat bolt upright, fingering the jet beads on her borrowed gown. Corisande had given her the oh-so-dramatic black frock to wear tonight; in fact, she had insisted on it. Arabelle gripped the seat and wondered if her reason had been far more than a wish to stun her friends by their dramatic gowns.

As the wheels churned Arabelle into the unknown, her mind whirled with the question: *Why have they done this to me?*

Chapter Twenty

For the Love of Money

Lord Rutley was determined to have her. That, Arabelle deduced, was why he took her off by force. She expected they would soon veer into Fleet Street, where the marriage peddlers did a rip-roaring trade in wedding people for profit. The words in Aunt Claracilla's letter seared through her mind: *they put into practice every stratagem and deceit they can conjure up to corrupt the innocent and betray the unwary.*

Since he had abducted her by force, did he think he would *marry* her by force? If he thought so, she would fight him to her dying breath.

The coach jounced through a cloud of acrid smoke, and she saw a house wild with flaring fire. What a terrifying night this was! She wondered if she could somehow escape Rutley if they stopped in this press of running, frantic people. As she pushed hard at the window to see if she could push it out, the driver swerved down an alternative street, and her hopes dissolved. The windows were too well fixed, and too thick to break.

She heard the loud gong of a clock as they jounced through a sparsely lit street. It kept striking. It was midnight. She had promised to meet Simon now. What would he think when she did not appear at the French doors? Would he search for her? Even if he did, he would never find her, for here she was, miles east, hurtling down streets she had never traversed.

Her throat went dry from desperation. Simon would have no inkling that this abomination had happened to her. No one at the ball would dream of such a bizarre occurrence as this taking place at such a glittering ball. Her heart sank even further. Perhaps Simon was not even looking for her now because Corisande had declared they would announce their new wedding date to all the guests after the clock finished its midnight chimes. Since Chesterfield House had many floors of rooms, Arabelle would not be missed in the throng. She pounded the unyielding window and rattled the stiff door lever, frustrated to the core.

The coach halted and swayed, and the lead horse reared and whinnied on the cobbles. A weight left the driver's box.

Arabelle tensed, her hand on the lever, ready to plunge and run. They had stopped before a fine brick house with light high up in the first and second-story windows, draped expensively with fringed edges. Was this Lord Rutley's town house?

She saw a coffee house opposite, lit with yellow candlelight, full of people. Could she dash in there and beg for help?

It was a large coachman wearing a hat and greatcoat who opened the door and said ominously, "This is the end, Miss."

"It is not!" she retorted. Her hope to make her escape died when he swung another cape heavily onto her head so she couldn't see or be seen, apparently. As she fought and struggled, he pinioned her arms at her sides and carried her, writhing and screeching, into the house and up two flights of stairs. During this ascent, she wriggled her arms free and threw the cape off her angry, hot face. "You horrible man! How can you use me this way? Don't *you* have a conscience either?" she railed at him.

He gave no response, and his arms remained unyielding in their tight hold of her.

The place looked to be a house of luxurious apartments. People slept behind those ivory doors with the gilt edging. She thought of screaming as loudly as she could. She tried, but sound would not move from her throat in the clock-ticking stillness of the landing.

She heard muffled thumps below them on the blood-red carpeted stairs, and saw that it was Lord Rutley skulking up after them.

"Rutley!" she cried, startling him in the quiet.

"Shhh!" he warned her, frowning darkly.

"How dared you abduct me?" she raged at him, hoping people behind doors would hear. "What are you doing? Do you think I'll *marry you* if you force me? If you compromise me? Well, I won't! And *you* won't!"

He looked cunning. "Now there's an idea: marry you, or compromise you by force." He rubbed his gloved hands together with relish, but as soon as he saw her expression, he raised his hands up between them, warding her off. "My, what malevolent sparks! I get the message. Let me tell you that since you would not agree to marry me, you will live a life of another sort entirely. You will, no doubt, long for the golden days when you had your chance to be Lady Rutley."

Arabelle's breath came shallow with prickling fear. "Why? What tyranny do you plan next?"

He pulled off a glove and touched her collar bone. "You are just what he wants."

Arabelle slapped his hand hard, making him yelp.

He soon recovered and licked his purplish lips with relish. "I am delivering you."

"Delivering me to . . . whom?" *Dear God, help me!*

"A foreign Count has his heart set on an exquisite, high-born English virgin," he said, counting off the specifics on his fingers.

Arabelle stared at his gleeful face, and gasped. The truth sank like a lead weight upon her.

Pausing before a door near the stair rail, he said softly, "Unattainable, he was told. I, however, have brought him the moon. I will be rich beyond belief, all due to your lovely face and pure, unsullied form."

She cried, "You will *not gain* by this wicked plan!" and kicked her stout bearer, who yowled but would not let her go.

Rutley's eyes danced with smiling evil. "Why won't I? My plans have often proven successful." He tapped his whip four times on the elegant door.

The portal fell away. There stood a man in a dark grey embroidered mask that covered his face. Arabelle cringed and stared. His hair fell in silver-gray curls to his broad shoulders. He was clad in a dark purple domino as if he had just returned from a masquerade. "Ah-ho!" he said in what sounded like a foreign accent, "*Le Comte* will be gratified that you have come, and with the goods?" he finished with hopeful excitement.

"With the goods," replied Rutley, triumphantly gesturing to the wildly resisting Arabelle.

Outraged, she fought the coachman's vise-like arms. "*No!*"

He carried her in anyway, and the door shut behind them. The room was lit with low wall sconces full of candles, and the silk settees and chairs of the drawing room looked curvy, carved, and expensive. She sniffed a faint scent of peaches.

"Yes, the new Princess of Society, that is who I have brought you," declared Rutley, preening.

"In truth?" responded the masked man.

Lord Rutley strutted and said, "Nothing less than Viscount Bastwicke's breathtaking daughter, the one I wrote you to observe at Drury Lane Theatre *and* her Court presentation. I saw you at the theatre, but were you in the anteroom of the Palace as instructed?"

"*Naturellement!*" said the man, who turned to regard her with eyes glimmering within the mask's eyeholes.

Arabelle struggled for breath, she felt so furious and betrayed. This was monumental!

Out of an arched, draped doorway, another broad-shouldered, tall man appeared, wearing a full-face black mask with silver designs curving around its edges and eye slits. "Indeed," he said in a quiet French voice. "You managed to get me the Bastwicke beauty? I cannot believe it, I."

Rutley said with a bow, "She is yours."

Arabelle stared, horror-struck, at the second man. In a black wig curling loosely and abundantly to his shoulders for all the world like King Charles II, he was tall and broad, and had shapely legs in white silk stockings. He wore a brocade wine-coloured suit buttoned and embroidered down the coat front and waistcoat in silver, and his breeches were gathered below his knees with black silk ribbons. When he flicked back his wrist lace, she saw the sparkle of a solitaire on one long finger. He exuded the essence of opulent life in some grandiose French *chateau*.

Those horrifying reports of heiresses kidnapped and sold to foreign princes jumped again to Arabelle's white-hot mind. So! The crime was manifesting itself again—in this very room! The magnitude of the knowledge that she, Arabelle Lamar, was the newest victim frightened her as nothing had ever frightened her before.

"Dear Count," said Rutley, smarming all over the tall foreigner, "for introduction's sake, I remember from your instructions that you must remain nameless to us all; but this is the Honourable Arabelle Lamar whom I have brought you."

"My heart overflows at this meeting," came the smooth, chilling voice. Rising from a graceful bow, the Count altered his attitude and said sternly to Rutley, "Please to let go of her." He took Arabelle's forearm out of Rutley's fevered grip, shook his head over the marks on her skin, and soothed her arm and wrist with his bare fingers.

At his touches, tremors went through Arabelle. She was manhandled by a frightening, diabolical French Count. She stared at the almond-shaped eye slits of his mask. She tried to see the Count's eyes, but the light was behind him, giving them no glimmer. However, there was a human being in there—a man with at least a grain of compassion for her sore arm.

"*Help* me!" She knew the words were futile, and they sounded daft in the circumstances, but she wailed them from her heart before she could stop herself.

She felt a startled silence behind the mask. He reached again for her hand and held it in his warm fingers. Yet she did not want him to affect her in his favour, so she pulled her hand away.

With an oily chuckle, Rutley said, "You will help her a great deal; will not you, noble Count? To become a woman, for instance?"

Arabelle could not bear the sound of Rutley's hiccupping laughter.

"I intend to do it," replied the Count in his careful, foreign way of speaking English, "but do not be so *gauche*—so crass, I beg of you, Lord Rutley."

What now? Was she truly to be "sold" to this pair of powerful men?

"Is she not breathtaking?" pressed Rutley, unhooking the cloak and throwing it onto a chair to reveal her white bosom in the ebony dress.

Arabelle stamped fiercely on his foot with her heel. His hiss of pain gratified her greatly. "Lord Rutley," she railed in rage as she covered herself up, "why did I wear this black gown tonight?"

"To look irresistible to men?" he guessed.

"Tell me the truth!"

As he touched the side of his nose and opened his mouth to tell her some sort of lie, she cried, "Say: because I wrote Miss Wells to 'wrap the goods in black!'" His terminology in this house had confirmed it. She and Simon had read his note to Corisande. And Arabelle knew that it was Corisande's scent she had whiffed when she and the malodorous Rutley forced her into the coach. She had worn the same sickening rose cream during their portrait sittings. Arabelle skewered Rutley with her eyes. "Was this all planned by the two of you?"

He obviously wanted to avoid her inquisition, but the Count gestured and said, "Go on. Satisfy this lady's curiosities so she can be peaceful here with me, Lord Rutley."

Rutley's voice trembled, and spit flew from between his teeth. "When you refused *all* my proposals, I enlisted Corisande's aid in case you refused me again tonight. If you would not marry me, you stupid girl—"

The Count intervened with a snap of his fingers. "Rutley! You will not talk so to this enchanting creature!"

Lord Rutley's spare chest heaved as he fought to control his ire over her rejection of him. "You see? I warned you!" he pointed at her with a shaking finger. "I am not a man you can cross! You were terribly cruel to me. Now the cruelty is turned back upon you."

Arabelle fumed. "My so-called friend, Corisande, helped you to do this to me? Why?"

"Ho, she is mad at you, all right. I bet you can guess the reason."

"No, I cannot!"

"She wants to enjoy her marriage—without *you* in London. She wants you out of Chesterfield House, and out of Simon Laurence's sight." In a silkier tone, he said, "And you will be. Our noble Count has not revealed where he lives, but it is very far away, is it not, *Monsieur le Comte?*"

"It certainly is," said the Count, his arms crossed and his chin at a tilt. "Now, are you through with your angry stories, Rutley?"

"Of course." Rutley put his hands together in an attitude of reverence to him and inquired tentatively, "Is . . . is there somewhere you can put her while we make our transaction?"

"Certainment." The Count gestured to his purple-clad cohort. "Please to take our beauty through there." He indicated a black velvet-draped archway with golden fringe.

He, himself, had come from a room of shell pink walls. Flanked by flaming candelabra within stood a narrow Tudor box bed. The sight of it made Arabelle's heart lurch. How would they subject her to their will?

She glanced back and saw the burly coachman planted in front of the drawing room door. She must forget any plan to dash. It was pointless to reason with these men, or try to make them release her. If she observed carefully, she might possibly find a way to escape.

The root of all evil had grown and borne fruit in Rutley, for she could see the spark in his eyes as he and the Count seated themselves at a carved desk for business.

Fringe brushed her nose as she followed the purple-coated man with the silver curled wig into a dark-paneled sitting room.

He gestured her to a George I armchair with clawed feet and gargoyles. "Would you like something to drink?" He unstopped an etched crystal decanter on a black Persian sideboard near the crackling fireplace.

"Heavens, no!" Arabelle threw back. "Is it your plan to drug me?"

He paused. "Why no, *Mademoiselle.* Forgive me if I gave to you a start of that kind." She stared, sensing that he smiled behind his mask.

Suddenly, he proposed, "Can I interest you, perhaps, in a little music?"

"Music? At a time like this? Are you lunatic?"

"Not that I know of. Do lunatics know if they are?"

Biting back a giggle in spite of her stress, she lifted her hands in a futile, helpless gesture.

He opened a cream and black *Chinoiserie* music stand and took out a page, set it on the perch, and produced a violin. "If *Mademoiselle* will pardon me, I am not so good," and he sawed a bar of high notes.

Arabelle winced.

If the man noticed, he kept it to himself. He adjusted the instrument under his chin and played *A Lady Faire, O Men Beware.* During his squeaky performance, Arabelle sat in head-shaking exasperation, one ear strained for the murmur of men's voices in the other room. It was impossible to hear what they said. Likely, that was the idea.

At the *finis*, her serenader bowed.

Arabelle clapped ironically.

"Thank you. *Mademoiselle* is not overly discriminating. Kindness it is, I think."

"What is your name, O Musician?"

"François." He cocked his head apologetically. "That is enough for our purposes tonight, if you will forgive."

"Why not rip off your mask and let us get to know each other?" she threw back.

His chest convulsed as if he were laughing. When he must have felt sure of his voice, he said, "Please, not to probe too deeply, dear lady. We, the Count and I, are here but for a short while and we intend to remain incognito. For reasons obvious."

"Yes, of course," she responded dryly.

He went to observe the other men from between the velvet drapes. Then he shot out of the room, and the violin, which he threw back toward a chair, hit her gown as she jumped up. As it struck her knee and fell, she accidentally stepped on it and heard it crunch. "Oh dear, it's broken!" she said with sardonic regret. She hurried to see what chaos had erupted, by the sound of it, in the outer room.

Before her startled eyes, men scuffled, strained, and lunged at each another with oaths and thuds and toppling furniture. When she saw the Count overpower the grimacing Rutley, she found herself rejoicing.

As none of the men wore weapons, they fought physically, grappling until Lord Rutley flipped and landed on his back with a sickening bang. He yelped, "Ow, ow, *ow!*" with increasing volume and pitch as the Count wrenched his arms behind his back.

The Count ordered the large coachman to bring cords from a cabinet. Fearfully, the man brought a coil of rope, which Rutley berated him loudly for doing. François helped the Count and the coachman to tie the peer tightly around his wrists and ankles.

Arabelle saw this unlooked-for altercation as her sudden hope. She ducked back into the music room, looked with quickly growing determination at a long, thin triangle-bladed rapier crisscrossed with a medieval broad sword above the mantel. She stood on a chair and drew out the ancient cup hilted sword. With her hand firmly holding the brass grip, she got carefully down, hid the weapon behind her wide skirt, and took a deep breath for courage. This sword was long and much lighter than the broadsword could be, so it was why she chose it. It had a sharp-looking point on it, too.

Back at the scene of battle, she waited for her moment, gripping the sword with grim resolve behind her back. When the Count turned, half-crouched from checking Rutley's bonds, she swung it dramatically in an arc until, with fortuitous timing, she connected its point to his lace cravat.

The Count froze when he saw the long length of blade leading from his neck to the hilt in her tightly gripping fists.

"Do not move!" cried she, lifting the sharp tip firmly under his jaw. She kept an eye on his hands. Daringly, she added, "Put your wrists together behind your back! Now!"

He did so, which astonished her with a frisson of victory. With her blade pushed into his throat, he stood so, and said nothing for many moments. Long eyelashes blinked within his mask holes. Finally, he asked, "For how long shall I not move, *Ma'amselle?*"

The sword grew a bit heavy. With a firm will, she renewed her grip and kept the sword point trained on his neck. "For as long as it takes me to get away from this street." Her arms shook slightly.

"But *no, Ma'amselle* —" His arms moved.

She gave the sword a warning shove, which thrust it through his throat lace.

He appeared to wince, and then stood motionless, regarding her through those disturbing thin slits in the mask, which moulded over his high cheekbones. She was stunned to see the lace turning red, and the red spot widening.

Panic knifed through her. *What have I done?*

Nevertheless, she lifted her chin. Maybe now she had the advantage, and they would take her seriously. Backing toward the door, she kept the sword pointed with every muscle in her two arms, even though it wobbled.

"*Ma'amselle?* I have been honoured by your sword. You have won. I stand amazed. We shall grant you two minutes' grace."

"You will grant me a *lifetime's* grace!" She shot him a smouldering glare, fought behind her for the door lever, and swiveled the key until she backed herself out.

The scene before her would forever remain in her memory: the men still as statues, regarding her with disbelief. Lord Rutley, trussed up on the Turkey carpet, eyed her furiously from his humiliating position. The big, docile coachman and François guarded him with their legs. The Count stood erect, looking most forbidding in his black mask, clamping his lace *jabot* over the bleeding wound that she had put there. She must run before they moved.

With a dramatic swing, she slammed the door shut. It echoed grandly throughout the house. With giddy amazement, she hefted the sword blade onto her shoulder, and with her other hand, yanked up her pannier and black rustling petticoats, and scurried down the stairway. At the street door, she came nose to chest with a man. When he saw her weapon, he jumped aside and let her streak past him. Joyful at her escape, she dashed across the street cobbles, her throat wheezing. She burst into the coffee house.

The air was warm and aromatic with freshly ground coffee. Men sat eating, drinking, and talking at all the tables.

Now what do I do? she wondered.

Men swiftly looked again when they saw her bosom-revealing black ball gown, mussed-up hair, and an ancient cup hilt rapier with a three-foot blade as her accessory. In seconds, all noise hushed.

Arabelle stood like a wild-woman, surveying them. "Please!" she entreated, not knowing how to begin, "I need help!"

From behind a counter, a man set down a cream pitcher, and approached her cautiously. "That you do, I am sure. Ma'am, please put down that wicked blade. I'll have no trouble in my house."

"I do not mean harm to anyone, Sir. I am the one in danger! I have two minutes to flee from men of evil intent. They are across the street." She pointed. "You must hide me!"

"Indeed?" He crossed his arms over his apron and looked her over dubiously, then peered, squinting, through a window. "I see no one."

"It's true!" She swung the sword down off her shoulder.

The men at the nearest table jerked back, and a chair fell over.

A man pointed. "There's blood on her sword point!"

There was a collective gasp. People strained to see.

Arabelle's mouth went dry. "That's because . . . because I had to defend myself. I did not realize a slight poke would draw blood."

A cup hit a table and a huge, brown-wigged man stood up. Exchanging significant looks with the proprietor, he moved toward Arabelle with a purposeful stride. "I'll have that weapon, Ma'am." Her eyes widened as he whipped from within his own scabbard a parrying dagger. "Give it to me now, young lady. What are you doing with your great-grandfather's rapier? That blade still looks sharp enough to kill. Was that your intent?" he asked ominously.

Her heart pounded. This was not going at all the way she planned. "Sir, I did not plan to wound anyone, but they *abducted* me! A foreign Count and his minion will be after me in minutes! Please believe me! *Save* me from them, *please!*"

With a flick of his dagger, Arabelle's sword was gone from her hand with a painful jerk. It clattered loudly to the uneven wood floor, and rocked back and forth on its half-circle cup hilt.

"It's bloody, all right," snapped the man. "I'm a Magistrate, and I'm taking you in."

"No! You do not understand!"

The door crashed open against the sword's hilt.

The grand Count swooped up Arabelle's rapier.

"Lawk-a-day! Who's this masked cavalier?" a man near Arabelle exclaimed.

"He looks mighty formidable," said another.

The Count's long black curls swung as he looked around the room until he spotted Arabelle. Moving backward with panic in her throat, she stopped with hands on the table behind her, facing him, unable to back any farther away.

"Good evening," he said into the tense silence, nodding his head at the large Magistrate. "I am here to retrieve my ward."

The proprietor in the apron called, "Your ward, or your sword?"

Men laughed.

"Both," he replied.

One man asked, "Why are you wearing the mask, Sir?"

The Count leaned toward him and said, "Smallpox."

To that, the man nodded and dropped his gaze to the table. The Count seemed to have gained sympathy from the crowd.

To Arabelle, he said kindly, arm outstretched in his brocade coat, "You must come home now, dear one. We are worried about you." He turned to the Magistrate as he passed, and gave a wry tap to his temple.

The Magistrate's eyes dawned with intelligence.

Arabelle, beside herself, shouted, "That is one big lie!"

Everyone roared with laughter. She knew why. She had used the King's famous phrase.

Frowning, the Magistrate examined the red point of the blade. "Someone used this recently. Was it this ward of yours?"

"Ah, yes." The Count gave a short laugh behind his mask. "We were involved in a little dispute, and she nicked me playfully here, in the throat." He lifted his bloodied *jabot* carelessly to reveal a crude bandage, and then strode quickly to Arabelle and reached for her hand.

In terror, she dodged away from him.

"Come this time without my carrying you." He gestured her charmingly toward the door.

Arabelle could not believe what was happening. "I am *not* his ward!" she shouted to the room full of onlookers. "I did *not* do it playfully! He is *abducting* me!"

The people laughed. The men looked vastly interested, as though watching a comedy play.

It infuriated her to such a degree that she glared almost cross-eyed at the Count's mask eyeholes, trying to see in. She realized later that she thereby confirmed everyone's belief that she was seriously unhinged. None of them took her seriously, for she made so many mistakes, and the Count was a consummate player, sounding so plausible and superior.

He took her by the waist. "Come peacefully this time, my pet, and I will forgive you for the little sword play."

When she yanked her elbow away, saying she was not his pet, he chuckled indulgently and used gentle force on her. Notwithstanding her panniers flaring her gown to new heights, he set down the sword for a moment and hefted her onto his shoulder. She was assured, by the male cheers that rose behind them, that all eyes were treated to a sight of the flesh above her garters as the Count made off with her into the night.

Chapter Twenty-One

Held without Consent

Although she screamed, "Let me go!" in the stairwell of the Count's house, only one door opened. A footman popped his white-wigged head out. At sight of the resplendent masked man hefting her on his shoulder and carrying a three-foot blade unsheathed, the servant slammed his door and shot the bolt. Therefore, the Count had a simple task to bear her back into the rooms where François awaited them.

Inside, a grey-gowned maidservant hovered in the corridor, looking round-eyed at Arabelle's unceremonious arrival.

The masked François greeted Arabelle pleasantly as he turned from throwing bits of paper into the crackling fire. "It is now cinders," he said to the Count.

"*Merci.*" The Count sounded gratified. He handed her infamous borrowed sword to François, and set her down on her feet. "Clean it," he said.

Arabelle glanced around and asked, "What became of my considerate escort, Lord Rutley?"

"He is taken care of," replied François. "Not to worry, his room is far from yours, and well locked. You will be guarded from him, of that I assure you."

She shivered, and raised her eyebrows. "I am very curious, gentlemen. Why did you make a *deal* with him—and then bind him up?"

The Count replied, "Because he was less than gentle with you, *Ma'amselle*. A swine like that does not deserve the staggering sum of the cheque I wrote him."

"Which is now but a vapour," added François, gesturing at the flames.

"Your actions surprise me," she said. "I suppose it should comfort me that he will not profit for his misdeeds." *Now*, she wondered, *is there any way to ensure that these men will not profit from theirs?*

She felt a touch on her shoulder, and the Count guided her into the antechamber with pink silk-covered walls. He lifted her quickly upon the Tudor bed, with her feet up and her back supported by a large tapestry cushion.

Arabelle's heart began to thump at this further physical handling of her after her collection in the coffee house. She cried warningly, "You must return me to my father!" She fixed the shadowy eyes with intensity, trying to make her logic penetrate through that uncompromising mask.

François entered the room and crossed his arms, eyeing her through his mask holes as well.

"Will you explain to us what happened to you on your way here tonight?" asked the Count, motioning the maidservant to her duties in the next room. As she passed by with her candlestick and then touched it to other candles within, Arabelle saw the room light up gradually. There stood a bed of immense grandeur, hung with red velvet curtains. Arabelle shivered and returned her attention to the Count's question.

François closed both doors. "We are interested in how Lord Rutley got you to come here."

The Count added, "Surely you did not come willingly, so what did he do?"

Arabelle let out a ragged sigh. This whole affair was so degrading. She told them the sequence of events.

The Count leaned forward. "Who was that second person who put his hand over your mouth and pushed you into the coach?"

"I never saw a face. But I smelled her perfume."

"*Her* perfume?"

"Yes!" Arabelle asserted fiercely.

The Count tipped his head. "Please to tell us who she was, if you know."

Arabelle gave a stressful sigh. "Her name is Corisande Wells, and she stays in Chesterfield House, where I, too, have been a guest of His Lordship. Corisande and I, we began as friends. Or, so I thought." Arabelle's throat constricted. She would not cry before these men.

Oh, Simon! she thought longingly. Corisande had caught him and her in two near-embraces, and she would stand for none of it. *I am punished,* thought Arabelle, *for I am guilty of loving him. I am guilty because I have responded to him with my whole heart.*

The Count pressed her hand in an odd attempt to soothe her. "It is too bad. Bitter it must taste to you, and very shocking, yes?"

Arabelle nodded and dropped her lashes.

"Does this upset you as it does me, François?" he asked, with an ominous edge to his voice.

"It does. This was not our way; it is not our style."

The Count said, "Be so good as to leave me now with my," he gestured tenderly over Arabelle, "my precious acquisition."

"No!" Arabelle drew her feet up beneath her petticoat and backed to the headboard.

François left with a bow.

"I want to say that, while I deplore the ethics of Lord Rutley and this Miss Wheels," said the Count, "I am overjoyed to have you, for I see you are a woman of strength, and a character most admirable."

"Do you think I want your compliments?"

She heard him chuckle. "So a little word about your beauty—which I would like to say—is not what you would enjoy?"

Arabelle, wondering how she would ever leave this nightmare, made a sound of exasperation.

"Sheila," called the Count, decisively flinging wide the door to the red bedchamber. He gave the maid whispered instructions.

She curtseyed to Arabelle. "This way, Miss."

Arabelle shot a look of distrust at her masked captor, but followed Sheila, for she felt too exhausted from fighting, both physically and emotionally, to do anything else. When she and the maidservant were alone, Sheila drew off Arabelle's buckled shoes and said she would unlace her corset.

"But what will I wear?"

"You can wear a night chemise if you want, but if you prefer to sleep with nothin' on, well, that's your affair, Miss."

"Give me the chemise!" snapped Arabelle, alarmed. "But why must I stay the night?" A rhetorical question, that.

The brisk maid took it as such. "You must eat something and go to bed, Miss. It's past two-thirty. Are you not weary, Miss?"

That was how Arabelle came to have her sudden appetite satisfied by hot milk, a potato and fish soup, a plate of shrimps, and a hot cross bun followed by a peach, sliced and juicy. After she cleaned her teeth, she wanted to relax, but she felt jumpy and increasingly nervous. What would come next? Ill-at-ease in her plush surroundings, she laid her body slowly onto the immense bed and turned to look at the high, carved headboard. It seemed to be full of gargoyle faces grinning from the centres of flowers and trees, shifting in the flickering candlelight.

When Sheila was gone, only a bedside candle remained alight, and the flickering ceased. Arabelle grasped a handful of the gauzy lace bed curtains inside the velvet ones and prayed, "Oh God, save me!" Her eyes raised in fright to the fluted tester spread above her. It looked like the inside of a casket.

A door closing made her jerk up and stare into the dark corner. Opening there was a concealed door that looked like a tall wardrobe set into the wall. She heard it click shut. The Count asked, "So you think that to bed with me would be such punishment that you cry out to God to save you?"

Arabelle gulped. He stood tall and commanding, with his hands outspread, holding onto the bedposts.

Would a firm stand help her? She would try. "I will not bed with a man until I am married to him! You would do well to understand that right now."

"Ah! A woman of virtue."

"Why wouldn't I be?" she challenged.

"Indeed. Then marry me, *Ma'amselle*." There was a softness in his French voice that gave her an odd quiver.

Her words came out choked. "Now you are dreaming!"

"It is a dream most enchanting." He mounted the two steps to the bed, flipped up his flared coat, and seated himself.

Arabelle tensed as his weight settled on her toes. She retracted them from under his thigh, and tried to retain her dignity as she pulled the covers up to her neck. Assiduously overlooking his unorthodox presence not only in a lady's bedchamber but also upon her bed, she declared, "I was raised by people of integrity, *Monsieur le Comte.* Furthermore, I will have you know that I must marry the man of my choice."

"My, my! Am I in the presence of a modern English lady? One who does not accept the arranged marriage by her family, but marries where she finds . . . love?"

"That is correct. You are in the presence of such a one."

He smiled; she could tell by the way that his jaw moved the mask.

With vigour, she attacked. "You have no right to smile! My father's heart will fail when he hears what happened to me."

"If we marry, he will be pleased, no?"

"Absolutely not! Why would he be?"

The Count raised his chin and eyed her sidewise. "I am rich beyond any father's hope, I do believe."

"Money! I do not care for that. The obvious matter is, I do not know you," she said with desperation in her voice.

"Ah. But many marriages are made on less acquaintance than you and I have, Arabelle."

She knew it was true. She stamped her fist on the bed. "Do not call me by my name now that you have besmirched it!" she said for a diversion, but she betrayed herself by a sob. She struggled with herself and threw up her chin. "All of a sudden, my life is catapulted from hopeless dreams to a living nightmare! Do you not care a whit for a woman's feelings? For her hopes and dreams?" Her voice broke as she tacked on, "Her need for *love* in marriage?" She turned and buried her face in the coverlet. Why had she said so much to a brazen virgin-buyer? Her shoulders heaved and her hands shook.

She felt the bed move. She started. One of his hands touched her shoulder. With the other, he pulled her covers off. She gave a gasp and opened her eyes. He had plunged the room into darkness. She smelled the snuffed wick, and could see nothing.

She jerked when his fingers touched her temple. Then they moved down her cheek. There was no mask between them, and he was leaning over her. He huskily whispered, "I am sorry for you, dear lady. You have endured too much. I wish to comfort you."

What was he proposing? Her heart beat a thunderous tattoo in her breast. His voice sounded so genuinely caring, but his morals were not. Could such a man possibly have a good streak in him? She felt he could, but his manner was so polished. Surely that was the way he acquired what he wanted.

His warm, moist lips touched her cheek, and she actually tingled. She felt one of his long curls graze her bosom. It made her shiver to her toes. His scent was nice, like the peaches she had smelled upon arrival. His arms around her made her want to melt in trust against him. Why did he feel so strong and protective? As he held her and hummed a little tune under his breath, her stiffness melted away. She wanted to believe only good of him, even if she was foolishly, disastrously deceiving herself.

"Do not be afraid," he whispered, his breath touching her cheek.

A daring thought forked through her. Since she could not have Simon, the only man she loved, would an experimental kiss with this powerful but tender man hurt anything? As his lips moved to kiss her ear lobe and the soft skin behind her ear, she felt a dizzying attraction to him. Her mind reeled with the confused thought, *I must know if I will feel anything like the joy I knew when Simon held me in the armoire and the leafy bower.* After all, since this Count had bought her and would take her away with him, she would have much more of this intimacy to come. Still, her mind warred against it. With her senses involved to a pitch of longing that was dangerously overriding her good sense, she felt helplessly divided.

As soon as she lifted her face to tell him he must leave her, the Count kissed her closer to her mouth, then closer, until his lips touched the corner of it. Arabelle could no longer resist the magnetic pull of him. He was kissing her with a sweetness that beguiled her, shot through her, and begged her to trust him. With her responsiveness, she pleaded with him to console her woes. She beseeched him to remove her from the evils of the world.

Common sense hovered a long way off, asking, *Why am I letting a villain give me love and consolation?*

"Stop!" she gasped. "This is not right!"

"To kiss you is not a crime, is it?" His French accent, so low and charming, made it hard for her to think.

"You removed your mask," she breathed, unable to answer his question. She reached up through the pitch-blackness and touched his face, trying to decipher what he looked like. A straight nose, smooth skin over the cheekbones. She found his soft, full lips. He hungrily kissed her fingertips. That made her weaken further, which he sensed instantly. Next, his fingertips grazed her neck, moved up and curled round her ear and down the back of her sensitive neck to her shoulder. "You are irresistible, *Ma'amselle.*" He groaned softly.

Her body felt like melting fire. "I must go home! I cannot stay, for you will . . . *ah!* . . . seduce me." There was an edge of panic to her voice.

"*I* seduce *you?* Ah no, Arabelle, you have seduced me!" He kissed her again, thoroughly on the mouth, until she groped for breath and the ability to think of anything but the splendour of sensation and the beauty of his manly power over her. She was shocked at how she loved his tenderness. She absolutely had to put a stop to it before it went too far to turn back. "Take me home, *please!*" she said. "You cannot be a wicked man, bent upon the ruin of an inexperienced girl . . . can you? Will you kindly, in the name of all that's good and right, return me to my family and friends? Please, Count?"

There was a long pause.

Then he astonished her. "Is there any man who will challenge me if I do not?"

"Yes!" she cried, heartened by the idea. "My father! And Lord Chesterfield."

He laughed softly. "I do not fight elderly men."

He was incredible. She strained to see him through the darkness, but could not. "Do you mean to say that you will let a young man fight for me?"

"Tell me," he said, tracing a pattern up her bare arm as he spoke, "is there any younger man who would prove my adversary?"

Was this hope? She knew she must be cautious and respectful. "There is someone I want to summon if you will grant me the privilege of doing so."

"Do it then." He sighed deeply. "As much as I want you, my honour as a gentleman says I must be fair to you in order to win you. I *want* to be fair to you. I want your respect."

"I am . . . overjoyed to hear you say that!"

"That I want you?" He grasped her shoulders and kissed one, for her chemise no longer covered it.

Her heart thundered as her body melted toward him again. "No. That you'll . . . *ah!*—don't do that, please!—that you'll be fair. But why are you suddenly seized with a sense of honour?"

She heard his wry chuckle. "Because I can see that, to live a life of bliss with you, I must prove myself the victor; not just the stranger who bought you and took you against your will. I want you to admire me, not despise me all our days."

Goodness! thought Arabelle, *keep talking in this manner and you'll have me plunging into your open arms.* Wrestling with herself, she managed to ask, "Do you mean to tell me, Count, that if a man fights you for my sake and he wins, I am free?"

"Alas, yes. But if I win, do you agree to be mine?"

Arabelle swallowed. *Do I?* She bowed her head and gripped her knees tightly. Tortured that she felt drawn to a man other than Simon, she tried to look reality in the face: *Simon is not mine and never can be. I am ruined before all English society, including my family. My life stretches before me, with no good outcome in sight.* This Count, by his words and kisses and odd kindness, had made her see that there was something undeniably warm and exciting about him. He treated her as though she was desirable and precious, and made it abundantly clear that he wanted her. These were the words and actions one read about in love stories, at which her father and Lord Chesterfield scoffed, but which she and Genevieve longed for in their own lives.

Arabelle answered him at last. "If we are legally married, then . . . yes." As she whispered the last word, she felt like a liar because she had faith that Simon would win. He was quick and sure with his sword. She had seen his prowess when he dueled Sir Pomeroy. She felt sure that Simon would prove himself even deadlier given a worthier opponent.

"Ah, Arabelle!" the Count whispered joyfully, and he drew her close to him.

The attraction of their lips proved so magnetic in that moment that no power within her could have made her resist. She not only kissed him, but also moved her hands over his buttons, braid, and throat lace to embrace the strength of his shoulders, arms, and chest. She tipped her head back and sighed for air. She felt his lips burn down her neck. He was excruciatingly magnetic!

Suddenly she stopped his progress and took his face in her hands. She liked the feel of his high cheekbones, his silky eyebrows, the lashes that flickered around her fingers.

"I must not touch you more," he said, setting her hands decisively, and with the sound of agonized regret, on the bed.

"No," she agreed breathlessly, wanting his arms around her still. She moved away until she lay propped against the pillows, all her nerves throbbing. With a light challenge in her tone, she asked, "Will you promise to let me lie in peace until my champion settles the score?"

"Until *he* settles the score? Ho, I can hardly wait to see this knight who holds your confidence to such a degree. I shall skewer him, I!"

"The sooner I dispatch my message to him, the quicker he will dash here for you to do it, then."

He gave a low laugh, and she felt the bed move with his departure. When he opened the antechamber door and lit a candle from the sconce there and carried it back into her room, she was disappointed to see his mask back in place.

"*Voilà*," he said, gesturing as he set down the candlestick and rattled open a drawer at the *escritoire*. "Your writing materials."

"I am to write at this moment?" she asked, pushing back her tumbled hair.

"Why not?" He looked her over thoroughly with admiration, quite obviously holding himself back from touching her. His voice was low and thrilling as he admitted, "I am more than impatient to have you for my own. I have never seen such beauty, ever."

Feeling her cheeks flame, Arabelle snatched up the flowered silk *robe de chambre* that Sheila had given her, whirled it on, and seated herself at the carved writing desk. She forced herself to breathe calmly as she chose a quill pen. Faced with a stark page on which to write the reality of her dilemma, she sat back. It was too monumental to think through in all its ramifications, but it was clear that, if this abduction episode leaked out to the world, her reputation would hang in tatters for all to jeer at for the rest of her days. She reminded herself that it would matter only if she ever saw her friends or family again.

How could this abduction account not spread far and wide? She had disappeared from Lord Chesterfield's ball after all the glory and honour bestowed upon her by the portrait's unveiling. Why, oh, why had she consented to any of it, especially to wearing that wicked black gown of Corisande's? *Vanity!* she thought. *I succumbed to it by the cartloads.*

She did not want to contemplate the misery of being outcast from friends and family after this Count made sordid history of her chastity. That was why she had made marriage her stipulation if he won her. But would he abide by it? He had not honoured his bargain with Lord Rutley.

She sat up and gasped at what she had done. *I just made a verbal espousal. What I promised the Count is as legally binding as a signed document!*

It must never come to that! she told herself fiercely. Simon would deliver her.

"The ink bottle—I will open it for you, no?" came the Count's smooth voice.

Arabelle eyed him askance. The embroidery glittered, looping around the eye slits of his black mask. "If you wish," she said, her apprehension rising to a high pitch at what she had done. He removed the silver stopper. She eyed the way his long fingers moved around the ornate bottle, making her think of how lovingly they had moved over her skin.

"*Comte?*"

"How may I serve you, *Ma'amselle?*"

"Will you remove your mask for me, please?"

"Ah, no! But why?"

"So I can see what sort of a visage my gaoler has."

"You have seen it with your fingers, *ma petite.*" He slid the bottle across the desk to her hand. "No one must be able to identify the man who whisked you out of London. In another place, when the time is right, you shall see my face."

Do I want to? she wondered, and shivered. Some very gross-looking men sometimes had nice voices and attractive hands. She had seen that phenomenon in the theatre.

"So your criminal activities make you uneasy?" she inquired.

She knew he smiled as he tweaked her chin. She fought to keep herself thinking positively about the chance that Simon would come to save her. She would *not* be carried away to a far place, there to view the Count's face. After she dipped the plumed pen, she waited. He had not moved away. He could view her paper from where he stood. "Excuse me, but may I compose my missive alone, O noble Count?"

"Certainment." He took a seat in the far corner by the curtained doorway in the dark.

It began to bother her that he sat there contemplating her cry for deliverance from him. *Take hold of your good sense,* she told herself. *Face reality! Look your predicament straight in the eye, and save yourself. Miraculously, he is giving you a chance.*

She could not afford to be distracted by misplaced feelings of guilt, especially about hurting *his* feelings, no matter how euphoric she felt in his arms. She wrote:

February 12, 1752

> *Dear Lieutenant Laurence,*
>
>   *I have dire need of you. Will you please come quickly to the address at the top of this page? Please come prepared to fight. A foreign Count holds me prisoner! I was sold to him—yes, sold!—by Lord Rutley, who abducted me from Lord Chesterfield's ball.*
>
>   *This Count has not harmed me—yet. It amazes me that, after a serious discussion, he has agreed to let you duel for my release. How I pray this reaches you soon, Simon! Yours is the face that came to mind when he asked if I have a champion.*
>
>   *The bargain I have made is that, should you win, I shall be free. If the Count wins, I must be his.*
>
>   *God speed you!*
>
>   *With my undying thanks and confidence in you,*
>   *Arabelle*

"Finished?" the Count asked, moving to her side.

She blew on the ink, wanting to fold her missive and seal it before he saw what she had written. But, how daft that was. He had all power over her, and could easily break the seal and read to his heart's content. He did not even have to dispatch her letter. She would simply have to trust that he would.

"Will you tell me this address so that he will know where to come?" she asked.

"Number 3, Black Walnut Lane, Chamber 22."

She wrote it at the top and folded it before he could read her plea for rescue. She penned, under his watchful eye: *Lieutenant Simon Laurence, Chesterfield House, May Fair, London.*

He pointed with an adamant thrust of his finger at the name. "So this Lieutenant is my adversary?"

"Yes, if that is how you wish to term him."

He crossed his arms. "Will he come in your defense?"

Arabelle bowed her head. "I hope that he will."

The Count moved closer, lifted a long curl from the back of her head, and breathed in its scent. "Ah. Is he your lover?"

She did not answer. The curl dropped.

"Do you love him?" he persisted.

She still said nothing, but her pulses pounded in her temples.

"I take it you do not want me to kill him?" he pressed.

She whirled to look up at his black mask. "Kill him? Heavens, no! Do not, I beg of you, duel to the death! Only to first blood, if you must. I think it might be best not to duel at all."

The Count folded his arms over the letter and regarded her. "You would call this off and submit to my will, in order to save this," he flipped up her letter scornfully and read, "Lieutenant Simon Laurence?" He gave his name the French pronunciation.

Arabelle, angered at the tone he used in reading that beloved name, stood up and cried, "He does not need me to save him from anything! He rescued me from an improper advance, dueled, and took an injury to his eye because of it! I know he will race here and fight you!—*if* he receives my letter," she emphasized, her eyes very bright.

"Ah, *oui!*" With that ironic response, the Count strode out, saying, "I am a man of my word!" and she heard the key turn abruptly in the lock.

As Arabelle lay in the bed, clad in only the scoop-necked chemise, a kaleidoscope of thoughts wracked her peace. She felt the Count's kisses all over again. *Oh, this is traitorous!* she cried to herself. She pulled the covers over her shameful head and tried to think clearly. *I cannot have Simon this side of Heaven, for he is a betrothed man. He and Corisande have their new wedding date set.* It was likely announced at the ball, as Corisande planned. *So Simon will be hers. Since I cannot have him, perhaps this is what is meant for me: life married to this French or Swiss or Belgian Count.* Why did he attract her at all? She did not know, but he most definitely drew her when he held her in his embrace. Could it be because she, so new to a man's touch, could not resist the power therein? She had read of the magic between a man and a woman. Did it happen with most any man when he kissed and touched a woman?

She shuddered. It could not be so, because when Sir Pomeroy Chancet tried such things with her, she had felt a strong revulsion. To think of Lord Rutley, who hotly begged to be her husband, having his way, why, it made her gag. She wanted to screech, "*Eeuuuw!*"

The door opened, startling her. "*Ma'amselle?*" the Count whispered as he moved toward her, carrying one candlestick before him. The smoking light highlighted the glittering silver borders of his mask.

"Yes?" she responded, wondering what was next on his agenda.

"A footman is running across London with your letter." He found her hand with his free one. "This will be good-night." He stood by her bed without his coat, his white linen sleeves long and loose, and his shoulders powerful looking where they stuck out of his waistcoat.

"Good night," she returned, lying back regarding him.

He blew out her bedside candle, blackening the room. "You are unbelievably beautiful," he said, his voice husky. The warm grip of his hands lifted her close to his beating heart.

A sudden shriek came from Sheila in the corridor. "He's loose! Master, come quickly!"

Dropping Arabelle, he moved, the antechamber door opened, and by the light beyond, she saw him stride through and turn left in the corridor. She heard a scuffle beyond. He shouted, "François! Block his escape!"

Arabelle scrabbled around on the bed for the *robe de chambre*, whipped it on, and followed. From the entry foyer came a thump, a crash of heavy porcelain, and the Count's cry of "*Trés bien!* Hold him!"

Arabelle reached the scene of the altercation and stared. There, beneath the flickering wall sconces, François held Lord Rutley fast, one of his arms twisted behind his back. The small peer was looking wildly desperate, breathing hard, unable to move. The Count produced a length of curtain cord with which he deftly tied Lord Rutley's kicking legs, and then, with superior strength, contained his arms. "François," he said, "another cord!"

There seemed to be nothing at hand. Arabelle, adjusting the dressing gown she had pulled on in such haste, felt the twisted silk belt, and looked at it. "Here!" she said, "I have something. Use this!" and she pulled it quickly out of its loops and handed the tasseled cord to the Count.

"Wonderful!" he said, and whipped it around Rutley's knees, then, when those were together, he slid it down over his black silk stockings and gave a tight pull at his ankles, and Rutley yelped. He clearly wanted to berate her for helping, but what could he say? She saw his impotent struggle.

Arabelle heard the coachman's voice outside the door rumbling in response to a woman's high voice. The door opened, a black-hooded, cloaked figure slipped in, and the door locked behind her. Arabelle quickly hid herself in the shadow of the corridor to observe. It seemed impossible, but she heard what sounded like Corisande's voice accusing, "Rutley! You diabolical *sneak!* You *promised!*"

"Get me free of these blackguards, and I will!" Lord Rutley snarled as the Count tied a complicated knot to secure his ankles. "Think that'll hold me?" he taunted up at the Count with all the belligerence possible from his demeaning position.

The feminine voice from under the caleche hood demanded, "I want my money *now!*"

"Miss Enterprising, I do not have your money!" spat Rutley in trembling fury. "Why the deuce did you follow me here?"

"To make sure you paid up, you thieving fox!" It *was* Corisande. She pushed back the hoops of her caleche hood, which caused her cloak to part and reveal the white dress. She wielded a black mask on a stick. She pointed it at Rutley and cried, "You owe me! Do not think that because you're tied up that you're not going to pay me what I have coming!"

Rutley writhed in renewed vigour in the combined grip of François and the Count. Rutley spat out with rabid force in the face of Corisande's advance, "I cannot cash the Count's bank note because he took it away again! Didn't you, Count? *Tell* this stupid woman that I haven't a hapenny for my pains!" To Corisande, he said through clenched teeth, "You were likely seen and probably followed, you idiot!"

The Count interjected haughtily, "Please to tell me who is this woman."

"Never mind!" snapped Corisande, her eyes fiery, "except that I set the stage for that virgin's abduction, and Rutley promised me thirty percent. I had a feeling, after he left with her, that he would skip off and leave me with nothing. When he didn't return in an hour *as he promised*," she threw with rancour at Rutley, "I knew the scoundrel never meant to share the money with me *at . . . all!*" She hit him twice with furious emphasis on the head with her mask stick.

Lord Rutley yelled out in pain. "*Ow! Ow!* I *planned* to pay you—I *did!* They held me here against my will! I just now got free of the blasted cords, but now they have tied me up again. I've been robbed of my due!" His colour changed as his snapping eyes swiveled and he saw Arabelle. "Even she helped them!" he said, as if that were the last straw.

Corisande turned toward Arabelle, wondering why his countenance changed. At sight of Arabelle, her face went ashen.

The Count said, "Your argument will now cease. Come with me, *Mademoiselle.*" He grasped the guilty-eyed Corisande firmly by the arm. "François, send that vermin off with Roger now."

When François opened the door and beckoned, the coachman entered. "Roger," he directed, "please hail your troops from the coffee house. Cart this Rutley you-know-where. A Magistrate named Degan awaits him."

Rutley gaped. "What? A magistrate? Me? But I'm a peer! You can't do that!" One moment he stared at the Count with eyes bulging in outrage, and the next moment his open mouth received a balled-up handkerchief and a cravat whipped around his face by François, who deftly tied it around Rutley's head to keep the gag in. As he choked and bellowed in ferocity against his mouth full of cloth, Roger clapped a hood over Lord Rutley's head.

Arabelle watched, impressed, as François and Roger contained her abductor. The ignominious peer kicked his bound legs like a maniac, and made desperate but futile jerks, but they bore him out the door just the same.

The Count whisked Corisande in the opposite direction into the corridor, where she gave him rebellious resistance. "Stop touching me!" she cried.

"No weapons," he drawled, and tossed her mask on a stick toward Arabelle, who caught it.

Arabelle pinned Corisande with a deeply questioning look.

Corisande returned only evasive blinking. "What do you think you're doing, pushing me by force? Where are we going?" she demanded of the Count as he forced her before him. "And why are you wearing that mask? Are you hideously ugly? Did you have the smallpox?"

He did not reply, but shoved her into the chamber where François had serenaded Arabelle on the violin. The Count was busy containing the vociferous chit, so Arabelle took her chance. She tiptoed to the outer door to try to escape *incognita*, holding Corisande's mask on a stick over her face. But there was no key in the lock this time, and the handle would not turn. "Drat!" she expelled from the depth of her heart. Arabelle struck the door handle with the mask, which broke off the stick.

Sighing, she went to peek beneath the gold-fringed door drapery of the room where she had broken the violin, which now lay in a corner. There was no sign of the Count or Corisande. She strained to hear where they might be. By moving down the corridor, she finally heard the timbre of the Count's deep voice through the wall. There must be a camouflaged door from that music room to another one beyond, for she saw no other door by which to enter.

Corisande's voice rose in a shriek, and Arabelle caught the words, "not a virgin!"

Had she heard aright? Arabelle put her ear to the flowered silk wall covering.

"You *aren't?*" the Count queried in monumental censure. "But, Miss! You tell me that you are a spinster, living in the house of Lord

Chesterfield, and you are ready to marry a respectable man. Does
he know that you are not a bride of purity?"

"He doesn't *need* to know!" she shouted. "What does it matter
to *you,* anyway?"

There came a silence. Arabelle's heart thumped hard in her
breast. Imagine that! She could hardly believe what Corisande
had just confessed. Her next words sounded belligerent, but also
fearful. "Do you plan to take . . . *me,* too?"

"Why not?" the Count snapped. "You could be made to look
pretty enough, provided you can smile. You are probably lying to
me about not being qualified because you think I will sell you in
Persia or Morocco."

"No!" she screamed in terror. "You cannot sell me
anywhere!"

"Why should I not? You stand here before me. You know that
it takes a deal of planning and a lot of risk to abduct fashionable
young ladies, *n'est ce pas?*"

There was a pause.

"But you wouldn't want *me!*" cried Corisande viciously. "I told
you I am not . . . what you wish!"

His voice was hard. "Where is your proof?"

"P-proof? What do you mean?"

"We shall have to have someone ascertain the truth of what you
said."

"How? Who?" shrieked Corisande in disbelief. "You?"

In a freezing tone, the Count said, "No, thank you!"

Arabelle could just imagine how offended Corisande looked
to hear that.

Close to the wall where her ear lay, the Count proposed to
Corisande, "If you will have the man in question verify in writing
that you gave away what you ought still to retain as bride-to-be to an
honourable man, I may release you. But I must have a signed paper."

"Then get Lord Rutley back here, and I'll make him sign it!"
yelled Corisande.

"Lord Rutley, was it?" queried the Count, his voice dripping
with disgust.

Behind Arabelle, a woman's voice said, "What are you doing
there, Miss?"

Arabelle whirled. The maidservant, Sheila, stood there with a steaming water basin and towels over her arm. Arabelle was fairly caught, listening blatantly through the wall.

Sheila looked amused, but hastily gave a *tut-tut* of disapproval. "Orders are, you must come back into your room, Miss. I thought you could use some hot water to bathe your face, Miss. It might relax you to sleep." She escorted Arabelle back to the bedchamber, where she knew the irritation of being held prisoner again.

But my, oh my! What revelations she had heard this night! It was almost too much to take in. Now, it sounded like the Count was keeping Corisande in this house until he received that signed statement. Would Rutley write it?

As Arabelle submitted to Sheila's removal of the *robe de chambre* minus the silk belt, her mind returned to her friends and family. Would there be an uproar at Chesterfield House now, with both of the portrait girls missing? What was everyone thinking? Surely no one knew what had become of her, or of Corisande. No one could possibly imagine what an iniquitous abduction had transpired during Lord Chesterfield's Ball. Everyone there trusted Corisande and Lord Rutley, or they would not have been there.

What were Arabelle's family and Lord and Lady Chesterfield doing now? Most of all, what did Simon believe had happened to her? He would certainly have plenty to say about this. What would he do when he heard that she was the latest victim?

It was the vilest fact that all of this was perpetrated by the machinations of that depraved viper, Lord Rutley—with Corisande as his conspiratress! What baffled as well as cheered Arabelle was that the Count and François had reportedly carted Lord Rutley straight to a Magistrate. Could that really be happening? Or was that a ruse for her ears, while they did something else with him? Would he, a peer, actually suffer for his crimes? Such things transpired so rarely. She devoutly hoped they would clap him into gaol so he could not get out, and that the House of Lords would try him, and convict him.

Had Lord Rutley been the one who abducted the other three daughters of peers from fashionable drawing rooms?

She shook her head, and poured hot water onto a cotton towel in the bowl and leaned over and pressed it to her eyes. Drops fell into the water as she breathed in and out, in and out. They reminded her of tears. She was too numb to cry.

As she loosened her ribbon garters over her stockings for comfort, Arabelle mulled over the fact that the Count and François had revoked the cheque they had written to Rutley. Such polished and unscrupulous men, as these masked Frenchmen were, could act with duplicity and without twinges of conscience, it seemed. While she approved their action toward that villain, it made her uneasy over her own quandary. Would the Count be true to his word to her? Why should he be? He held all power over her.

As she brushed her hair, it shocked her anew to think that Corisande had lain with that insidious sensualist, Lord Rutley, of all greasy men. And she confessed to the act now to save herself.

But the thought that made Arabelle hot with searing anger was that Corisande planned to marry Simon Laurence . . . without telling him!

He arrived in her dream as the first rays of dawn sparkled through the diamond windowpanes of Arabelle's prison bedchamber in Black Walnut Lane.

Arabelle felt someone shaking her. "He's here, Miss!"

Blinking webs of sleep and visions of Simon winking at her in a dim coach from her brain, she opened her eyes a fraction. "*Who's* here?" She saw Sheila's excited face between the ruffles of her white cap coming into focus above her. She was tottering on the top of the bed steps waving something white.

"Here is his card, Miss."

Seeing the sweeps of lace and the scarlet velvet drapes around her, Arabelle remembered in what bed she lay. She sat up and grabbed the card. "Who did you say sent up his card?"

She dropped the card onto the salver and presented it to Arabelle.

When she had groped it off the smooth silver, she felt a flood of joy to read *Lieutenant Simon Laurence, Royal Military Academy, Woolwich* printed on it. "Lieutenant Laurence is . . . here? Truly?" When Sheila nodded encouragingly, Arabelle threw off the blankets and jumped down from the high bed, her bare feet landing on the Turkey carpet. "I am so relieved! Dress me, Sheila, quickly!"

As she aimed her toes into the stockings Sheila found with some difficulty in the bedclothes, Arabelle's elation gave way to sudden dread. Had he come to fight the Count? Undoubtedly so. Oh, how dangerous it would be! The Count was no squeamish dandy like Sir Pomeroy. He gave the impression that he knew his swordsmanship.

Sheila dressed her in Corisande's black gown, for it was all Arabelle had. While Sheila laced her snugly down the back, Arabelle looked at her lips in the mirror, red and full. She wondered if they were swollen from kissing the Count, or if she had bitten her lips with worry all night.

What would Simon think if he knew that she had kissed the French Count who had bought her? This morning, it was difficult to find a rational explanation for her susceptibility of the night. Could she call it the Count's uncanny magnetism? She chastised herself for being a wayward, fickle romantic. She did not even understand herself. She went to meet Simon with her eyelids lowered.

Her heart gloried at sight of him. His pirate's patch made her heart skip with the aura of mystery it gave him. While it slashed dramatically across one eye, his other one gleamed at her with ecstatic relief. "Arabelle!" his voice resonated across the room. He sounded monumentally relieved. He opened his arms and strode to her.

"*Simon!*" She clung round his chest while his arms crushed her to his thumping heart. "Thank God you've come!" she cried against his fine wool coat.

While thus held, she saw that, in the drawing room, the silver-masked François was locking the door and adding his tricorne to the iron rack. He appeared to be watching her and Simon menacingly through his mask slits. The Count had, oddly, allowed Simon to call, but François was keeping an eye on them. She could see his hand on his flintlock pistol. He stationed himself where he could see every move they made.

"What have they done to you, Arabelle?" Simon whispered, searching her face.

She trembled with the relief of his nearness. "I will try to tell you."

He kept an arm tightly about her, his long fingers holding her ribcage as they sank together onto the silk settee. She spilled out everything that had occurred since Rutley and Corisande pushed her into the carriage. She omitted only her heated embraces with the Count.

Each detail she recounted made Simon more livid. "Rutley!" he spat. "I knew he was capable of evil, but this heinous abduction of you is the outer limit! I have been on his trail, Arabelle. I rejoice that you wrote to me and confirmed all my suspicions. The part of this abominable horror that relieves me is that you are here, unharmed as you say, and that I am with you now." He pulled her close, conveying his immense relief. "I'll tell the King who kidnapped you immediately!"

When Arabelle told her account, ending with the carting off of Rutley, and the closeting of Corisande in the back regions of this very house by the Count, Simon's hand went to his sword. "I will meet this foreign blackguard and run him through!" With dark lashes squinted and eyebrows nearly meeting, he looked fierce.

François cleared his throat and called, "At four o'clock, Lieutenant, you can try to run him through. Until then, no! You must now depart. Do not think you will win him," he finished with a pose of grim confidence.

Simon began to rise, aiming a threatening gaze at François. "I will draw his blood for what he did, buying this lady from that unspeakable Rutley!"

Arabelle sat bolt upright and stared at Simon.

He lifted a black eyebrow at her quizzically and let the etched sword clink loudly back into its scabbard. "Why not? You wrote asking me to come defeat your villain, did you not? I can start with this one, and get them both out of our way."

Words warred on her tongue. "Please, Simon! I asked nothing so violent as *killing!* It could even happen in these rooms today," she whispered, flicking a scared glance toward their guard and his ready pistol. "If anyone died, I could not live with myself hereafter." Unwilling to explain further, she let it go at that. She could not confess to him that she had found momentary joy with another man—a man with perverse intentions interwoven with heated tenderness toward her.

Suddenly it hit her: Aunt Claracilla's warning that a man who *made love* to a lady could do it most ardently through a motivator called *lust.* That described, surely, the Count's motivation toward her. At last, she was learning about men . . . but by a very dangerous method.

Simon regarded François, his eye gleaming with the light of battle. "In the ancient maze behind Lambeth Palace at four o'clock, I shall skewer him on this lady's behalf," he promised. "Why do you look so horrified, Arabelle? I am more than willing! I ardently *wish* to rescue you."

"Thank you, oh, thank you! If I look horrified, it is because I cringe to imagine anyone hurt. And you have a very sharp and dangerous sword."

"I do." Simon removed his black patch, blinked a few times, rubbed his eyelid, and roved his gaze tenderly over her. "It is my chance to win you back from him. That blackguard has harmed you, and he deserves severe punishment."

She eyed the red scar that began under Simon's eyebrow and continued down onto his cheekbone. She gripped his arm, her fingers feeling the strength of his flexed muscles under the dark blue wool. "He hasn't exactly . . . *harmed* me, Simon."

"How can you say so? The villain bought you! He incarcerates you here, and plans to take you for his own! Why do you look so terrified over my dueling him, Arabelle?"

She blurted out, "I cannot say!"

He gripped her shoulders. "Are those tears? Ah, Arabelle!" Taking out his handkerchief, he wiped the streak of tears off her cheek. "You have such a tender heart. Please don't fret; especially not about me. Why do you cry?"

Hiding her concern for both the men, she could only say breathlessly, "You are splendid, and you are . . . you!" She wanted to say, *You are the man I love.* She did not dare to say that he might be run through, because he clearly believed he would win. She must encourage him to know it, and therefore do it. "You will win for me," she said, glowing at him as she wiped her eyes, "and I will thank you with all my heart."

Simon looked pleased. He took her chin between his warm fingers. "Thank you for your confidence, Arabelle. I will not let you down. But we must also face the remote possibility that the worst can happen."

Arabelle eyed him askance. "What worst?"

"What will you do," he asked seriously, making her lose concentration by rubbing his thumb tenderly over her hand, "if the Count comes out best in our encounter? He won't, but—"

Arabelle gasped, "He cannot, Simon! He simply cannot!"

"He will not. However, let me mention it, just for speculation's sake. What did he say would happen then?"

Arabelle confessed slowly, with pounding heart, "It's not what *he* said, but what *I* said!" With a hand to her forehead, she moaned. "I promised him that, if he wins the duel, I will . . . marry him!" She shuddered at all she had done in that candlelit room in the wee hours.

Simon stiffened. "Marry him? You promised him *that* if he wins?"

She squeezed her hands over her face. "Yes!" she wailed. "It's tantamount to a verbal espousal, is it not?"

Through her fingers, she saw him give her one abrupt nod.

"Oh, Simon!" she entreated him with a frightened edge to her voice, "please understand! I had to agree to both sides of the arrangement, or he would not let me summon you to fight for my release! He would simply have whisked me out of the country! I had to agree to his terms, don't you see? It's a miracle that he let me write to you, and that he let you enter this place to see me."

"It is. I understand. What a risk you took, Arabelle! How courageous you are." Simon's caress down her arm communicated his deep admiration for her. "I am honoured to be here for you, but may I ask: Why did you choose me?"

This was no time for coyness. "Because, even though you are affianced to Corisande, you have a special place in my heart." Seeing his face soften as he looked upon her, she added, blushing, "I knew you would come."

"Lieutenant Laurence!" called François in a crisp tone. "You must leave now. The Count granted you a quarter hour, and it is over."

"Take heart," said Simon to Arabelle as he lifted her hands to his lips, kissed each one while his eyes reassured her, and rose. He looked so fine, his sculpted cheekbone and eyelid marred just a little by the red scar.

"I will, Simon," she returned, marveling at her monumental blessing—that she had this broad-shouldered, caring man to defend her.

Arabelle bade Simon a quick good-bye, urging him to disappear before the Count emerged from the back of the house. After all, the cunning foreigner could be plotting to trick Simon and trap him here by the clever tactics he and François had used to capture Rutley and Corisande. With the pistol François held, they could achieve it. Ironically, Arabelle deemed it safer for them to meet on the dueling ground.

After Simon left, she hurried to the writing desk in her dim chamber, where she lit a pair of candles. Her fingers were nervously damp as she tried to open the bottle of ink. Running the end of the feather back and forth over her lips, she worried for many minutes, and then wrote:

February 13, 1752
3, Black Walnut Lane, Chamber 22

My Lord Chesterfield,
You are, no doubt, wondering why I left your ball. Please keep the following a strict secret. Lord Rutley abducted me from your back door during the fireworks, and delivered me to a foreign Count, to whom he sold me. I am now held at the above address. I summoned Lieutenant Laurence to champion me, and he arrived this morning. He was not allowed to take me away, as they guard me with weapons at the ready. However, the Count has agreed to duel with Simon for my release. Yes! He is willing to fight for me.
I write to you because you have great diplomatic powers, My Lord. While Lieutenant Laurence is a formidable swordsman, I do not want either party maimed or killed. The foreign Count who bought me is powerfully adamant. He asserts that he will end up keeping me by winning this duel. Simon Laurence is just as determined to win me away from him.
Do you know the maze near Lambeth Palace? They will fight in the centre of it today at four o'clock. I have only time to write this one letter.

Your frantic
Arabelle

She heard the maid come in so she whispered, "Sheila! Will you post this letter at the coffee house for me right away? Surely they keep footmen there to perform such services?"

The maid looked skeptical. "I don't rightly know, Miss. Are you allowed to send messages, I wonder?"

"The Count dispatched the letter to the Lieutenant for me last night, did he not? Will you go now and see this one off? It is very, very important." She put the folded page into Sheila's hand and gripped her forearm, pleading earnestly.

"I don't know if I can do this for you. I doubt my masters will allow it."

"Do not let them know!"

The maid eyed the letter, sealed in warm red wax. "The delivery is bound to cost, Miss."

Arabelle had no money. She carried not so much as a reticule with a comb or handkerchief in it. "If you will pay the cost from your own coin, Sheila, I will give you my shoe buckles. They are silver with small diamonds sprinkled through, as you see." She stuck out a toe of her shapely black brocade shoe with the glittering buckles.

Sheila's eyes flashed wide, but she tucked her dusting rag under her elbow and took the letter. "In that case, Miss, I might just try for you."

"Good! Thank you. I shall write you a promissory note that the buckles are yours if you see the letter off with a footman. Bring me his receipt."

"Yes, Miss." She curtseyed respectfully.

Arabelle sighed in giddy relief as Sheila left with the letter tucked inside her grey wool corset bodice.

When she returned a quarter hour later, she discreetly closed the door behind her, curtseyed to Arabelle who had been gazing out the window at a stone wall with shuttered windows, and presented a scrap of paper. "He's done it, Miss. Went runnin' off, sayin' he'd take his horse out of mews to speed him along, seen's how this is a rush job all the way to May Fair. I paid him, but I told him he'll get his other half when he gets back."

"That was shrewd of you," said Arabelle approvingly. "Thank you ever so much."

"Says he knows right fine where Chesterfield House is, for it's nigh Tyburn Hill, where his uncle was hanged."

"He is right, that's where it is. Here, these buckles belong to you. With them comes my undying gratitude, Sheila."

"Glad to help you, Miss."

Arabelle prayed that Lord Chesterfield would be at home, that he would come quickly, and most of all, that he would somehow prevent the duel by some brilliant diplomacy.

Chapter Twenty-Two

A = Mazing

Arabelle heard the chip of brick hit the glass of her prison window. She saw and heard another one flung up from below, so she dashed to look out between the wavery diamond-shaped panes. Simon Laurence stood down in the street with sunlight gleaming on the white band of his three-cornered hat. His face lit up when he saw her. He motioned for her to open the window. After loosening the long metal bar, she managed to push the top lever to swing the window out about six inches.

"Good morrow, fair maiden!" he said, bowing and holding his hat to his heart. How wonderful a sight he was, with his black brows rising in pleasure. It made her more cheerful just to see that dimple in his cheek. "I am soon on my way to my *rendezvous*." He looked over both shoulders, then moved closer, speaking confidentially up to her. "I came to ask if there is anything I can do for you."

"Take me to the duel!" she responded instantly, gripping the leaded window. "I'll go frantic in this room, not knowing what is happening. He cannot keep me sequestered here!"

"Why not ask him to take you along?"

Arabelle considered this with surprise. "Just ask him? Oh, I doubt if he will even consider it. I might escape, you see." She lifted an eyebrow.

"Then I will tell him that the lady in question must be present. We need a witness, do we not?"

"You are not going to meet him face to face *now*, are you?"

Simon flung his cape back, and the sunlight glanced brightly off his ornate sword hilt. "I imagine he will speak to me if I await him outside his front door. I came to exchange a word about our choice of swords."

Tensely, she asked, "Who will act as your second, Simon?"

"I will tell this Count that we will bring no extra individuals in the way of seconds into our affair. Not even that cohort of his with the pistol. I hope to impress upon him that it's far too risky. The quieter we keep this, the better for us all, as you know from our experience with Sir Pomeroy. I will see you by and by. Take heart." His dark eyes glistened on hers, and he blew her a solemn kiss. He strode out of sight.

How his appearance had warmed her!

Then the clock in the distant drawing room dropped an ominous gong, striking her heart with dread. Only an hour and a half until the duel. She picked up her abandoned coffee cup and drank, though it had gone cold.

A floorboard creaked. She heard light footsteps as someone entered the antechamber and shut the door. Soon her chamber door opened, and she saw small eyes peering at her from the shadows.

Arabelle crashed her cup to its saucer. "Corisande!"

Corisande gasped, and made a wild-eyed retreat.

Arabelle streaked after her, grabbing the back of her wool cloak and swinging her aside. Whirling around, she threw her shoulder blades against the door, and Corisande plummeted into her. "What are you doing?" Arabelle asked her intensely. She shoved her away, unwilling to smell her sickening rose cream again.

The shifty-eyed, terrified Corisande looked as if she were calculating by what move to shove Arabelle out of her way. "Trying to get out of here! What do you expect? Hop aside!"

Digging in her heels and blocking the doorknob, Arabelle ground out, "You are not allowed to leave, and you will not get past me!"

"Won't I?" Corisande moved closer, her eyes narrowed, her last night's coiffure in tatters. "I came here to try to save you from these monsters."

Arabelle scoffed, "Would you expect *anyone* to believe that?"

Corisande tried to jerk Arabelle aside by the arms, but Arabelle was stronger. Corisande cried out, her skin pinched between the fury in Arabelle's fingers. "You betrayed me, my *friend!*"

Corisande tried to look blank. "What can you mean?" She suddenly lowered her head and bit Arabelle's arm.

Furious with pain and outrage, Arabelle kicked her in the shin.

"*Ow!*"

While Corisande hopped and wailed, Arabelle continued to clench one of her arms. "You came here to collect thirty percent of the money Rutley expected to get for *me!* I heard it all. I even heard about the letter you will write so that you won't endure the submission and slavery into which you sold me. Or, was your claim to impurity another lie?"

Flames flushed up Corisande's cheeks as she tried to yank away. "It's . . . true!"

"Well? Did you write the letter?" asked Arabelle, shaking her. "Will an answer come to free you?"

"Yes!"

The door pushed behind her back. She moved aside, shoving Corisande into the corner so she couldn't get out.

"Please to tell me who is in here with you, Arabelle." The Count's head and shoulders appeared. With eyes glinting between his mask slits, he took in the two women who had been fighting so fiercely.

Arabelle let go of Corisande, but continued to block her way of escape.

"That witch hurt me!" Corisande showed him the red marks. "She's almost drawn blood! She *did* draw blood! Look!"

"Is it not a pathetic sight," the Count commented dryly. "Miss Lamar drew blood from my throat, Miss Wells, which is a deadly place for her to pierce me." He lifted his lace to reveal the bandage around his neck. He looked intimidating with his long, black curls against a dark green coat and waistcoat buttoned down the length in black pearls. "It is a wonder I still live."

Corisande stared at him. "Not for long, you won't," she eked out, "because Simon is going to kill you!"

The Count remarked, "What a pleasant woman." To Arabelle, he said aside, "Your request is granted."

"To go?"

"Yes."

Her heart flooded with gratitude. "Thank you!" Simon had succeeded. She could go to the duel!

"What request?" sneered Corisande.

Arabelle said to the Count, "Miss Wells was looking for a way to escape; however, I believe she expects a letter before she can go?"

He took Corisande's arm and said to Arabelle, "Excuse us. This virago is my prisoner until that letter arrives."

Corisande tried to fight, but the Count dragged her away. "Help me!" she screamed at Arabelle. "Arabelle! *Save* me! For pity sakes, I am your friend—remember?"

Her sharp yaps ceased when the portal at the end of the corridor shut with finality.

Sheila entered, casting Arabelle a wide-eyed look.

"Can you guess what he will do to her?" asked Arabelle.

"He will retain her until the required paper arrives, Miss."

They heard a loud knocking. Sheila hurried out to the drawing room, so Arabelle promptly followed.

"This is addressed to *Miss C. Wells*," said a perspiring footman, fresh from the cold. Behind him on the landing stood Roger, guarding the proceedings with a hand on his sword pommel.

Sheila took it with thanks. "Will you follow me?" she said to Arabelle after she eyed the writing on the folded paper and noted the sealing wax.

"Can it be the letter Corisande is waiting for?" Arabelle looked over Sheila's shoulder and noted Rutley's erratic handwriting, slanting left and right.

"I think so, Miss." Sheila waddled down the corridor and rapped on a door panel.

It was not long before the Count emerged. He took the missive and read it, one hand on his hip, the other holding the opened page before him. He announced in a hard voice, "This Lord Rutley writes that he did, in fact, compromise Miss Wells. Therefore, I do not want her. Bah! What a worthless baggage!"

A volatile shriek issued from the room he had left. "I don't want you, either! But why you had to broadcast this in front of other ears is pure devilishness on your part! I hope you feel a demon's reward forevermore!"

"Merci, merci," he intoned under his breath, fed up. He walked back to wherever he had incarcerated Corisande, and Arabelle hovered just behind him, curious to know what would happen next.

Addressing Corisande, the Count said icily, "Now please to remove out of my sight. Get back into that dressing room. In my country, women like you would be put on public display, and all sorts of unpleasant things done to them."

Corisande yelled, "I *hate* you!" There came sounds of her being bustled against her will into the dressing room, where Arabelle glimpsed a narrow bed. Corisande flounced to the window, and suddenly, she was scrabbling at the crank, opening the leaded window as far as it would go, which was only about six inches, as in Arabelle's room. "Oh, *Simon!*" she screeched desperately, "take me home!"

Arabelle and the Count simultaneously darted after her, and saw what she saw: Lieutenant Simon Laurence standing below.

Corisande kept hollering at him, saying she was kept prisoner. "Get me away from these persecuting *fiends!*" she insisted.

Simon asked after Arabelle. "Is she not there, too? How do you expect me to sneak two of you out?

"Forget that one!" cried Corisande with grand dismissal. "She is not worth it, for mercy sakes! Tell that diabolical Count to drop this whole affair, Simon. I insist!"

He shook his head and rolled his eyes. "It will not help to insist. A duel is an affair of honour. I have something of the utmost importance to settle."

"I don't *care* for gentlemen's honour! It is daft in the extreme! Besides, *I* need you! I want you to take me home *now!*"

"I don't think you would enjoy the conversation which would ensue if we were to take a coach back to Chesterfield House together, Miss Wells."

"Miss Wells?" she shrieked incredulously. "Simon, I am your Corisande!"

The Count quickly locked the door behind the three of them, and shouldered her aside at the window. He dropped the letter from Rutley down to Simon. As it fell and Simon sprinted and caught it, Corisande made fists and jumped in fury. "What did you throw that to *him* for? You black, vile *demon!*" She hit the Count, but he swung her around and held her fast with her hands bent behind her back.

Arabelle, staying out of their way, but watching Simon reading below, saw his ashen face as he finished.

Corisande strained to yell out of the window, for she had seen his reaction, too. "Simon! My love! Please get me out of here, and I'll explain!"

When he looked up at her with narrowed eyes of stony coldness, her manner switched from demands to artificial sweetness. "You are upset about the letter, aren't you?" She tried to mouth something at him so that the Count, behind her, would not know what she said. It appeared to Arabelle as though she conveyed the words, "It was made up! Not true!" She turned back and said belligerently to the Count, "Will you step out and let me have a private word with my own fiancé?"

The Count heaved a sigh and said, "Fine. But Miss Lamar will stay with you."

"No!" Corisande objected, her close-set eyes blazing with hatred at Arabelle.

Adamant, though, the Count remained. He shut the door, saying aside to Arabelle, "Stand against this. I shall be on the other side." He left her with the ferocious Corisande.

"Simon!" she called downward, for Simon's back was turned to her. He turned only his head and looked askance at her.

"Rutley owes me a debt, so I got him to write exactly what that Count required. Don't you see? It worked!"

Arabelle wondered what kind of a look Simon gave her in the awful pause.

Corisande hurriedly followed with, "We must find a way to get Arabelle out of here, too. I know! Let's have Sir Pomeroy write the same kind of letter about her. That he and she—you know—that afternoon."

Arabelle gasped.

Corisande spat, "Simon, don't glare at me! Wake up and face facts. They probably were going to, anyway, when you barged in and supposedly *saved* her."

Arabelle stiffened in every vein, and let out a furious huff. She fought her urge to reach out and strangle the vile-tongued creature until she lay blue and gasping.

Simon's voice roared, "For your own safety, Miss Wells, I must pretend you never spoke those words. If you were a man, you would now feel the slap of my gauntlets on your face, and you would have to choose your weapon. Apologize to her at once!"

Corisande's face blanched with shock, then flushed with rage.

The Count opened the door and drew Arabelle out of the room, pausing only long enough for Corisande to apologize, if she would. He had listened to every word.

Corisande threw up her chin, and remained fuming and mute.

After the Count drew Arabelle tenderly away from her, he paused, listening. Simon was still speaking from the street to Corisande, saying, "I have held a certain suspicion for some time. Answer me, Corisande: did you write the note that invited Sir Pomeroy to Arabelle's chamber that day? Well? Did you? Answer me!"

They heard Corisande's squeak of fear, then nothing more, for the Count pulled the door shut and locked Corisande in.

Arabelle shivered as she hurried through the dank maze. With the setting of the sun, fog had rolled over London and swirled above the square-topped green hedges, curling grey fingers down to obliterate her vision. Beneath her gloved fingers, the Count's arm felt tight and muscular. She wished it did not feel so muscular.

They had been careful upon their arrival not to be seen leaving the coach on their skulking dash toward the maze. Someone had erected a makeshift gate to the entrance of it that said *Maze Closed—Extreme Danger.* Had that been Simon's work to keep out wanderers?

The Count picked her up and lifted her over the sign. As she adjusted her panniers, he stepped over with his long legs in black leather boots. In a dark cape and a full black mask, with his hat pulled low, he looked powerful, confident, and frightening. A long, flashing scabbard held his choice of weapons for the assignation: a jewel-hilted Pappenheim rapier, as he informed her when she asked him what sort of sword it was.

"I thought you would fight with smallswords," she said, remembering Simon's duel with Sir Pomeroy. After all, that was the style of sword that aristocratic gentlemen trained with and carried for dress these days.

With relish, the Count said, "Ah, but I chose rapiers. I am well-versed in the old school of fencing and dueling with these beautiful, long blades." As he swung his long, dark curls, she could tell that he smiled while he patted his magnificent sword hilt.

She looked at him askance. Her heart jumped and fluttered. She certainly hoped Simon was skilled with them as well.

They reached the circular centre of the maze, where three lanterns threw shadows high and low. The Count said, "I am impressed. You knew your way without a wrong turning. You have been here before, I believe."

"I have. I hope never to come again."

"At last I can fight you!" called the Count when he saw Simon moving about in black breeches and coat, shrugging the latter off his broad shoulders to gain the comfort of shirtsleeves. Drawing his sword from its scabbard, the Count said to Arabelle with the suggestion of a sneer, "Your champion is practicing, I see."

Arabelle's heart skipped in chagrin as she saw that Simon still wore his black eye patch. How would he see well enough to duel for her? He had just lifted a four-foot-long swept-hilt rapier from a special case, and was brandishing it in the air, ignoring the Count. *Good,* thought Arabelle. He must know how to use a long, old-fashioned sword since he had one.

"You will be sorry that you came so eagerly," taunted the Count. Then he wickedly whipped through the air with his own naked blade, going through the fencing phases: "*Prime, seconde, tierce, quart, quinte, sixte, septime, octave!*" Arabelle watched his rapidly-changing sword positions with unwilling admiration and dark foreboding. It made such evil sounds, flicking through the cold air in that razor-sharp way.

She hurried to Simon. "Do not pay him any heed," she said, feasting her eyes on his noble face.

"Why should I? Don't you see?" he asked, shooting her an ironic smile. "He is going through his defensive repertoire." He lifted his eye patch off and gave it to her. "I shall use both my eyes for this."

"You shall? Can you see clearly now?"

He twinkled at her. "Yes, I can see clearly now."

Clutching the patch, she kissed it and breathed, "I am so glad."

"And what a sight I see," Simon added, looking at her face wreathed in the fur-lined hood of a purple velvet cloak. The Count presented it to her before they left.

She blushed, for Simon must have seen her kiss his eye patch.

He lifted his free hand and blew her a kiss.

It made her heart lift. "God be with you, Simon," she said, dropping him a curtsey of respect.

"He is." Her champion sent her a confident look before he strode back to his trampled spot in the grass.

She shot an apprehensive glance at the Count. She had kissed that man and been whirled into passions she should never have felt for such a stranger. With the black mask over his face, he was certainly a mysterious opponent for the man she loved. *What on earth does he look like?* she wondered for the fiftieth time.

Simon whipped his sword back and forth in the air, making his own wicked-sounding flicks. He had doffed his waistcoat, which now lay on the grass.

With mounting trepidation, Arabelle ran and gathered up his clothing. She did not look at the Count, whom she felt watching her as she cradled Simon's garments to her bosom.

They heard a slight commotion, and then came what sounded like Lord Chesterfield's voice calling, "Will you guide me in by your voices, please?"

Simon shot Arabelle a startled look.

She dropped her eyelids in guilt. Perhaps she should not have written to His Lordship.

Simon responded quietly, for fear of eavesdroppers, "We're here. The party is this way."

He ran lightly to meet Lord Chesterfield, who emerged from the dark lane with a half-covered lamp, saying, "Ye gods! It's true, then, Laurence? Where's Arabelle?"

Simon gestured to her.

Lord Chesterfield, in three-cornered hat and greatcoat, strode toward her. "I am infinitely grateful to see you! What an unthinkable tragedy befell you, my innocent girl! How *are* you?"

he demanded, enveloping her in a warm, tight hug, his long grey curls tickling her cheek.

She clung to him, then smiled tremulously into his searching eyes. "As you see."

"I have suffered such anguish over you, my dear. How wretchedly responsible I feel!"

"You, My Lord?"

"I held a ball in my house, from which safe haven my dear young lady disappeared from under my nose. We, in the House of Lords, were all warned by what happened to the three heiresses before you. Thank God you are not on a ship bound for Morocco or Istanbul as we speak. If you were, it would surely be the end of me."

"Oh, My Lord," she exclaimed softly, tucking her gloved hand into the crook of his arm, "none of it is your fault, but someone else's, as Simon Laurence discovered. For now," she hurried on, "my fate hangs in the balance here today."

"Tell me what I can do."

"You can try your diplomatic skills to dissuade them from fighting. Neither one is taking our advice, for they are bent on skewering each other."

He studied the masked Count, who, with a victorious cry, lunged and pierced the point of his sword into the hedge.

Lord Chesterfield took a deep breath of resolve, put a pleasant look on his face, and strolled toward the Count. He approached him conversationally. Arabelle did not hear what words ensued.

The Count soon leaped away from the persuasive efforts of Lord Chesterfield, faced Simon, and yelled, *"En garde!"*

Simon strode to the middle of the grass circle and squinted ominously at the Count. Presenting his four-foot-long rapier, he flashed it up, fist to his face, in salute.

The Count did likewise, the jewels on his wire knuckle guard glinting red and yellow in the dim light.

Arabelle held her breath at the sight of the two arresting figures in fencing form. *Dear God, save them both,* she prayed. Acrimoniously, she said to herself, *This is happening because of me.*

The opponents, in mirrored symmetry, posed with bodies sidewise, one foot forward, knees bent, and swords in level suspension. As each man's arm curved up behind his head, Simon's voice rang out with a cloud of chilly vapor, *"En garde!"*

It was immediately thrust and parry and sidestepping by both men until blade clashed with blade. Back and forth, rush and retreat, Simon lunged with muscle-rippling energy, his white shirt loosening from his breeches. Then the Count, in white sleeves and long green waistcoat, viciously jabbed his weapon through the biting winter air, making the steel ring, over and over.

They both slipped on the frosty grass. The Count hit a bench with the back of his leg when Simon pushed him back half-a-dozen paces with clanking vigour. Their swords connected and held, then one of their blades slid, and they jumped back and surveyed each other again, breathing heavily, striving for openings.

From Arabelle's peripheral vision, she saw a figure move. She was astonished, as she turned, to see Lord Rutley! She gasped in horror. What was he doing here? How did he get free? He bore a hostile aspect, sneaking sideways, his close-set eyes avidly following the duel. Alarm sliced through her. He could go straight to a Magistrate and report this duel. Then the law would be after Simon.

Lord Rutley crouched.

Clish, clash! went the swords. She dared not scream, for she might distract Simon and ruin his swordplay.

Rutley, his face contorted with bitterness, flung something at the Count's feet. It was a black croquet ball rolling rapidly through the grass.

Horrified, Arabelle screamed a warning to Simon anyway. "Watch out!"

Her outcry alerted the Count, but because of the duelists' lightning movements, the ball missed him and kept rolling, making confusion under Simon's feet. He tripped and went down, forward, and onto the Count's quick-thrusting sword.

Arabelle screamed. 'No!"

The Count yanked his weapon back, out of Simon's side.

Simon's white shirt turned red under his arm before he hit the ground.

"No!" shouted Arabelle, running toward him, "No, no, *no!*"

The black exit to the maze swallowed the intruder like a ghost.

Chapter Twenty-Three

The Victor

All her life, Arabelle would remember the jeweled rapier, covered with blood, as the Count stared through his mask holes at Simon, fallen at his feet.

The Count wiped his blade down its crimson length with a handkerchief and returned it with a rasp into his scabbard.

Arabelle prayed desperately as she lifted Simon's bloodied shirt up from his chest. He was pierced in his left side, bleeding above the waist of his breeches. His eyelids lay closed and still. She felt panic about to overwhelm her, but his breath upon her cheek when she bent to his face galvanized her. She hastily moved on his behalf, giving orders.

With Lord Chesterfield, she staunched Simon's blood the best she could. Lord Chesterfield lifted Simon's back off the ground so they could wrap him round with the bandages she had brought. She helped Lord Chesterfield deftly wind his torso round and round and tie it tightly.

Near his ear, Arabelle asked, "Simon, can you hear me?" His handsome face remained unresponsive. She smoothed back strands of hair from his face. He did not move, and hot tears rolled across her eyes.

Blinking furiously, she looked up and saw the Count's gaze upon her through those almond-shaped holes.

She laid her hand flat on Simon's chest inside his damp shirt, reassuring herself of his heartbeat. "How can we revive him?" she queried. There was no water in the maze.

The Count administered a slap to his cheek, but it did not help.

"Stop that!" said Arabelle. "Haven't you hurt him enough?" She enlisted the men's help to put his wool coat and cape on him. "Lift him with care," she directed.

Lord Chesterfield stooped and gripped Simon by the legs and nodded his readiness to the Count, who held Simon firmly under the arms.

About to burst with emotion, Arabelle picked up Simon's long sword, wondering, *How could my magnificent Simon be downed by Lord Rutley's treachery? How diabolical is that devil?* How evil he was to throw that vengeful ball into the fray. She felt almost sure that it had been meant for the Count's destruction, but look what it had done. *Simon* was hurt!

Arabelle said urgently, "Follow me. I will carry my light ahead. Lord Chesterfield, when we get out, please speed Simon to Dr. Follett."

"Doctor Follett it is," agreed Lord Chesterfield. He and the Count carried Simon through the maze.

Arabelle moved past them, gripping Simon's swept sword hilt with its graceful curves to her breast. It was difficult to walk so, and she felt the cold mist of the fog down her neck as she also carried a lantern to light the path for their cavalcade. She waited to light the men at the next switchback of the labyrinth.

The Count's back muscles strained against his coat as he carried her beloved Simon by. Lord Chesterfield fought to keep a tight grip on his booted legs. As the Count maneuvered Simon around the switchback, he asked Arabelle gruffly, "You saw what happened?"

"Of course I did. Did you see, also, that Rutley aimed to wreak revenge on *you?*"

"What a coward!" he spat. "All because I foiled his dreams of wealth in exchange for you. Now I have you for good, thanks to his black ball. But remember, sweet lady: this was not my way." There was a deadly gravity to his accent that she had not heard before.

Lord Chesterfield's coach, with Simon on the floor, his unconscious head on the seat, was ready to go when Arabelle put her foot on the step.

A black shadow fell across her, and the Count touched her shoulder.

She suddenly felt frightened by the proprietary look in his eyes behind the mask. "Let me go!" she said under her breath. "Surely you cannot keep me to your bargain *now!*"

His hand tightened on her shoulder. "I can, and I will."

Arabelle whispered to his hidden face, "Where is your heart? The man I love is wounded! What if he dies? How can I go off with you at a time like this?"

After a pause, he replied, "It is not my intent to marry instantly, my beauty. Even I am not that inhuman. I will come for you tomorrow. Where will you be tomorrow if I should be so trusting as to let you go now?"

Lord Chesterfield, who had moved close behind him, asked her, "Would you like to come to my house tonight, or go to your home, Arabelle?"

So Lord Chesterfield would rescue her from the Count in this conversational method. "You are taking Simon with you?" she inquired.

"I am. The Count can see you at his pleasure, I should think," Lord Chesterfield explained carefully to Arabelle. "As winner of this duel, it is his . . . right to marry you, by the contingent verbal espousal you made with him. I am sorry," he said as he shot a futile look at her, "but that is how things stand. There is nothing any of us can do to change it."

"That is true," said the Count. "I won, and I trust you are a man of your word, Lord Chesterfield, so I will leave Miss Lamar in your house until we marry. That will be very soon."

Arabelle said numbly to the Count, "There went my mother's dream to choose for me a rich and titled catch."

"I *am* titled," declared the Count in an affronted tone, "and who says I am not rich? I believe I have always been considered a catch, as you say," he added reproachfully. "Arabelle Lamar, what do you know about me?"

"Nothing!" she sobbed. "Except that you have no heart!"

Back at Chesterfield House, the Countess overcame her reserve and hugged Arabelle tightly upon her arrival. "I have fretted over you, my dear! Have you survived your horrendous ordeal?"

"Yes, Your Ladyship. Both of them, but barely."

After the lady's fidgets were soothed somewhat, Arabelle mounted the beautiful, familiar staircase. Her emotions pulled her hither and yon until she felt weak, and battered with worry over Simon. Lord Chesterfield had rushed him to Dr. Follett, and, between them, they decided that Dr. Follett would convey Simon Laurence to the Royal Military Academy, into the jurisdiction of Captain Ligonier, who must be informed of what had happened to his Lieutenant. Arabelle heard, to her joyful relief, that Simon had revived. Would they care for him well enough?

As her mind went round and round over all the events, Corisande came up against her in the hall outside their rooms.

Arabelle looked at her with utter disbelief. "Why are *you* here?"

"I live here!" snapped Corisande, angrily flicking her brown striped skirt as she turned away.

Lady Chesterfield, coming up behind them, still in her voluminous mint green *robe de chambre,* said, "Lord Chesterfield retrieved you, you *vile procuress,*" she hissed, "but you must stay in this house on pain of imprisonment." She glared at Corisande, her fists tight, then floated down the stairs to her boudoir. Strong footmen, armed with smallswords, stood lined up like sentries at all three doors below.

"Think you're something, don't you?" Corisande whispered furiously at Arabelle. She pinched her arm as hard as she could, then dashed away and slammed her chamber door.

"Ow!" Blinking tears, Arabelle bit her lip to endure the pain, rubbed her arm, and took a deep breath, praying for endurance.

After she wept on her window seat for awhile, she washed her face and made her way to Lord Chesterfield's library, where she gave him a silent curtsey and seated herself to stare into the fire.

Lord Chesterfield left his writing, took Arabelle by the hands, and looked down into her face. Between his long, grey curls, his thick eyelids looked a little wrinkled, and his blue eyes were earnest beneath his distinguished black eyebrows. "You are one valiant lady! You have endured too much, my dear. I have heard how bravely you are holding up. If I could have a daughter, I would want her to be exactly like you." He hugged her close.

Arabelle's tears rolled down her cheeks. "Thank you, My Lord. Thank you for coming to the duel. I don't know how else I would have gotten Simon to the doctor after his terrible sword wound."

After supper at nine o'clock, she accompanied Lord Chesterfield back to his library while he consulted books on marriage law. He kept shaking his head, for he could find no instances whereby she could be released of her promise to marry the Count.

She pressed, "Not even if he is a foreigner?"

"I am afraid not, Arabelle. You are English, and you gave him your word here."

The gap-toothed footman approached Arabelle with a folded note propped on his salver. Alerted by the sight of him, she said, "You are the footman who delivered a letter to Sir Pomeroy Chancet one day as he entered his coach, are you not?"

"Yes, Miss."

"Who gave you that note for him?" She fumed again over that *billet-doux*, signed in her name, which had bidden the Baronet to her bedchamber.

"Beg pardon, Miss, but I am under orders not to say."

Lord Chesterfield said sternly, "Tell her at once!"

"Yes, My Lord. The lady who gave me the message for Sir Pomeroy Chancet was Miss Wells, My Lord."

Arabelle's heart beat a rapid tattoo. She threw a wild glance at Lord Chesterfield. So it was not her mother, but Corisande! How could the chit have pretended friendship with her, and simultaneously carried out scheme after scheme to ruin her?

Lord Chesterfield dismissed the servant, and began pacing the room. He asked Arabelle to tell him all the details of that episode, which she did.

Arabelle opened the note the footman had just given her. *Dear Arabelle,* it said in Simon Laurence's handwriting, *My love for you tonight is beyond expression.*

She laid a hand on her heart.

"Bad news?" asked Lord Chesterfield quickly.

She shook her head and turned delicately away.

I kiss you a thousand times for the woman you are. As I have dashed around love's labyrinth, I have run up against many obstacles. With you at the centre, I have striven to correct my mistakes and find a new path to you. Now I have another wall before me. I vow to find a way out of this predicament.

God knows I have much to be sorry for and I pray you will forgive me. In my endeavours to save you, I have plunged you into misery, hour-by-hour, worse and worse. It is not what I would have done to you, for all the world.

I hope I will be granted life and grace to (the phrase left off)

I planned to save you by the duel, but

Arabelle saw, with sudden dread, that Simon's writing ended again. It was obvious that someone else had taken up the pen. In a totally different slant, the words continued: *everything went wrong. From Lieutenant Laurence*

"What can this mean?" She stared at the change of writing. "He didn't finish writing this himself!" Could his soul have left this earth as he wrote it?

The footman knocked and entered with another letter for Lord Chesterfield.

"Here's news," he said to her presently. "A messenger from the Royal Military Academy just brought me a note from Captain Ligonier. He writes, and I quote: 'Lieutenant Laurence is awake and sitting in bed, telling jokes. Though he passed out earlier while writing a letter, he is now revived.'"

That was the letter to me, Arabelle thought. She wondered who had written the addendum, *Everything went wrong.* It must be someone who knew how badly Simon felt about the outcome of the duel.

She gave the letter to Lord Chesterfield. He read it and said, "He cares deeply for you, does Simon." They looked at each other. They both knew what a futile situation it was.

He said, "Go up to sleep now. You will need to be strong for the . . . ah, event that lies ahead. I spoke with your father, and he concurs that marriage to the Count must be your next step," he finished softly. He turned away to poke at the fire.

A tremour shook Arabelle. "Oh no, my Lord! But I know it is the law. I suppose there is nothing for me to do now but retire."

She returned to her bedchamber, quaking over the hopeless look in Lord Chesterfield's eyes. All her friends were mightily affected by her irreversible promise, but no one could do a thing about it.

As she curled into a pillow-hugging ball for the night, the foremost thought thrumming through her heart was, *Simon is alive! He is sitting up and joking.* Thank God he had not died from Rutley's perfidy or the Count's sword.

When she lay against her pillows, she felt a lump rise in her throat. Though Simon had written her this letter of longing that she clasped to her heart, he was just as dead to her as if the Count's sword had slain him. Even though he now despised Corisande for her liaison with Rutley, he was legally betrothed to the tart, and had to go through with it. Moreover, even if he were somehow free (if Corisande choked on a fish bone and died tonight), Arabelle was still forbidden to Simon, for her parents deemed him unacceptable as a husband.

I, myself, have a ruined name, she acknowledged, *so what does it matter if the Count, with all his desire for me, claims me as his own?* She had no life left in England.

The darkness of the night brought back that other, pitch-black bedchamber too vividly. Was it because she had not seen the Count's face that she had allowed herself to respond to him? Life with the Frenchman might not be so detestable after all, her logical side tried to point out. That is, unless he had a disfigured face she could not bear to look upon. Even if he proved ugly, would it matter so much? There were men with tolerable features—handsome, even, by some women's standards (such as Lord Rutley)—who would make hellish husbands. She would much rather take the Count, no matter what he looked like, than a demon like Rutley.

But you don't know anything about the Count, she reminded herself. He had told her nothing, not even his name. He could be a slave-owner on some French-speaking island with concubines galore. Perhaps he treated them like mud under his boots. Perhaps he used them and threw them out when he found younger, prettier faces. Was she, herself, replacing cast-offs? Why, she wondered, would the Count be here in London, taking her away in such a well-oiled fashion if he had not made a practice of this sort of shopping?

It bothered her that he had watched her from somewhere at her Court appearance. He undoubtedly bought women with a nod, as he bought furniture or ships or art.

Arabelle faced her present reality. She had to take her only option and live with it. Could he possibly, in time, make an endurable substitute for the man she loved? Could she, by looking for his good qualities, like him eventually? She had glimpsed tenderness, and an ironic but gentlemanly honour, in him.

When Lord Ashby walked into his brother's room at the Academy, Simon sat propped up in his bed, frowning at a paper.

"Radford! Glad to see you. Take this rat's statement and safeguard it, will you?" He tossed the page across the bedclothes.

"Can you believe this?" Lord Ashby read aloud, "*I testify that I have taken the spinster, Corisande Wells, from maidenhood to womanhood. Signed, Rutley.*" Radford snapped the paper with scorn. "He is the lowest scum imaginable! Magistrate Degan better catch him, and secure him against all bail this time."

"He will." Simon sighed and laid back his head. "I don't understand why Miss Wells wastes her money on bail for him. I am quite sure she did it, but when did she have the opportunity?"

"I don't know. But Degan will not let it happen again. Are you feeling any better?"

Simon sighed heavily. "It is said we are judged by the company we keep. So what does that say for me regarding Miss Wells?"

"That she has come up in the world? From Rutley to you?"

"Don't make me groan," Simon clutched his tender, painful side. "I wish there was some way to dissolve an engagement. I would rather remain single all my life than tie the knot with her."

"I wish it, too," said Radford, running a hand back over his brown hair. "You don't deserve a life sentence like this."

Arabelle tossed her pillows this way and that, never comfortable, and wondered how satisfied Corisande felt now. She had not appeared at supper with the rest of them, but had a tray brought to her room as ordered by Lord Chesterfield. Lady Chesterfield intimated that Court officials would soon arrive and take Corisande into custody for Arabelle's abduction.

Arabelle thought of the double portrait, and wondered what Lord Chesterfield would think whenever he looked at it in future. The girls, thrown together as friends, had quickly turned enemies. How sad that jealousy and the love of money should have motivated Corisande to betray someone she had called "friend."

Aunt Claracilla arrived just before bedtime, and was given a guest chamber. As the clock on the landing struck half-past eleven, Arabelle heard a scratch on her door. In swished Aunt Claracilla, candlestick in hand and a pale yellow *robe de chambre* and cap making her look like an ethereal ghost. She held out a page on which she had written, *Marry him without delay.*

"I *know* I must marry him!" Arabelle reacted in sharp dismay, "but why do *you* advise this? You, my aunt who loves me! You, who have told me I must wait for the man God has prepared for me!"

Aunt Claracilla gave her a sad look and snatched her page back. She sat on Arabelle's bed and wrote for some time with her pencil. Arabelle next read, *God has heard our prayers, and always knows best, dearest. The Count cares for you, which is an amazing relief to me.*

"Amazing relief?" repeated Arabelle, casting a baffled look upon her aunt.

Claracilla took the paper back and hastily wrote on its reverse side, *You have this one chance to be wed honourably after what happened. Take it with grace, and trust in God. I shall continue to pray about this to the last minute. I want your happiness, Arabelle!*

As Arabelle read over her shoulder in growing apprehension, in walked the Countess of Chesterfield, her cap lappets flapping, also frocked in a dressing gown, which made Arabelle realize that the two women had been discussing her plight in the boudoir. Arabelle saw their eyes scanning her with concern. Her spirits fell, and she dropped her forehead into her hands.

She heard the pencil scratch and felt her aunt touch her shoulder. She had added, *One thing worries me, Arabelle. Do you truly hate the man?*

Before she could formulate an answer, Lady Chesterfield asserted, "That's probably it. Look what he did to her. He bought her from Lord Rutley, who abducted her for him. That would be enough to make her feel like chattel."

"Lady Chesterfield, I *should* feel like that toward the Count, but oddly, I do not. This will sound strange, but he was kind to me . . . in his extraordinary way." Arabelle's thoughts strayed to their kisses. "I am afraid to marry him, a stranger, but I have no choice. I promised, and now I am legally bound."

"Your aunt and I have come to tell you," said Lady Chesterfield, "that we have paid the clergyman at the May Fair Chapel triple his fee to give your wedding the priority the day after tomorrow, early in the morning."

Arabelle gasped. "Why so soon?"

"My dear, we cannot have you let loose in this town, bait for every gossip-monger and lecherous trout, without the protection of a husband. Otherwise, you would find out what true misery is." The Countess looked regretful but wise. "Society would ostracize you, even though none of this was your fault or doing. They would all assume that the worst had happened to you, which it has not, and would treat you accordingly."

Aunt Claracilla had been writing, and handed Arabelle her addendum. *Why did you make such a bargain with the Count?*

"I stipulated that if he won the duel, I would be his, as his wife only. I struck the deal so that Simon Laurence could try to win me away from his clutches. I did *not* expect the Count to win! And he probably wouldn't have if Rutley hadn't interfered!" Arabelle broke down in tears on her aunt's shoulder, regretting again how her worst fear had come true.

Both ladies kissed and patted her while she let her tears flow.

"I understand," said Lady Chesterfield soothingly, "that you did not want to be anything other than the man's lawful wife, and that was extremely well done of you. Lord Chesterfield and I find it remarkable that you got the Count, who held all power over you, to agree to fight instead of just taking you to his lair, wherever that may be. Was it not incredible?"

"Yes," Arabelle admitted, wiping her eyes and nodding.

"How did you do it?"

Arabelle blushed. "He wanted me to respect him," she said. She could not confess that she had softened him by experimental kisses.

Chapter Twenty-Four

Sir Pomeroy's Tittle = Tattle

The apartments Sir Pomeroy Chancet kept on St. James's Street were on the first and second floors, and overlooked fashionable tailor's shops, snuff merchants, and a gentleman's club. Simon Laurence paused in the doorway of his yellow and purple salon. As he called, "Good morning, Chancet," the whites of the Baronet's lazy eyes flashed wide, and he grabbed the arms of his chair.

Simon glanced back at his brother, Radford, who had dressed as a servant and had a listening trumpet ready to place on Sir Pomeroy's door after Simon went in.

He shut the door, and strolled across the expensive plum and buttercup carpet, smiling, until he stood towering above his former dueling opponent. "No need to go into paralysis, Chancet."

"But you're on your deathbed! That's what I heard!" cried Sir Pomeroy, handkerchief to his horror-stricken mouth. "Did you not duel again and nearly die?"

"It's only a flesh wound," returned Simon. "Although I cannot bow properly, I do expect to live."

"How fortunate you are!" Sir Pomeroy pointed at a yellow velvet chair. "Please sit there, Lieutenant Laurence."

"You have furnished your rooms with artistry, and surprisingly good taste." While Sir Pomeroy was taken aback by his last words, Simon looked about him, appreciating the air and space left amongst the gilt-framed pictures and fine Italian consoles, music stands, and bolstered sofas. The lace curtains let in plenty of light, and set mirrors and glass vases and golden boxes glimmering.

Sir Pomeroy seemed less than his perfectly turned out self, however. He wore a tourniquet around his forehead. He got up, went to a mirror, and poked at his messy pink-powdered wig that matched his pink waistcoat and contrasted with his dark purple coat and breeches. He looked as if he wanted to renew his blood-red lip rouge, which had worn off in the middle, but he wet his lips with his tongue instead. His crescent moon patch drooped at the corner of his eye so he ripped it off with a wince. Meeting Simon's eyes in the mirror, he asked, "Is there something I can do for you, Lieutenant Laurence?"

Simon carefully lowered himself to the yellow silk settee instead of the chair, the better to see Sir Pomeroy's face. "Sir Pomeroy, I believe you can give me a clue to a puzzle."

Sir Pomeroy sank elegantly to a lavender chair opposite Simon, and gave him full attention over a table of inlaid wood flowers. "Oh good, I love puzzles." The slice that Simon had cut up his cheek in their duel was healing but still visible under the white powder.

Simon fingered the tight, silver wire around his sword grip as he said, "I have a fifteen-year-old youth named Harry Boggs in custody in Newgate Gaol." He eyed Sir Pomeroy's reaction.

Sir Pomeroy reacted. He paused in crossing his legs, which left one red-heeled shoe aloft as he stared fearfully at Simon.

"He tried to lift my wig," stated Simon. *I have gripped him by the throat,* he noted.

Sir Pomeroy asked in an unnaturally high pitch, "He tried to lift your wig? But he did not succeed?"

"Of course not. He did not succeed because I don't wear a wig," Simon explained as if to someone of poor understanding.

"No," breathed Sir Pomeroy, and set his foot down. "I mean . . . so I heard. You are the most fortunate man in London to have such magnificent white hair that you never even have to powder. No itching scalp under the wig, either. And I'll be you never get broiling hot in summer, either. Life is not fair," he finished, perusing Simon's head longingly.

"I think you will sympathize with my efforts to uncover a certain wig thief," said Simon, "since you have an interest in fine hairpieces. I have never known anyone to possess such . . . variety." Simon gestured at his present coiffure, a shell pink, fluffy affair.

Sir Pomeroy looked at a loss and sputtered, "Yes, I . . . well, thank you. I . . . what will you do about this . . . this wig thief?"

"Harry Boggs? He wants to tell me who the head of his wig-stealing ring is, but he is afraid. I was wondering, do you have any inkling who that kingpin might be? If so, I could save Harry another interrogation."

Sir Pomeroy looked whiter than ever. "N-no, I cannot say anything about any kingpin, as you call him."

Simon rose. "Then I shall bid you good day, Sir Pomeroy. Thank you for your time. The Magistrate will soon set the poor lad free, and then clap his leader in irons. You see, today I am prepared to offer Harry Boggs bags of money for the information. I will even help the lad leave the country after he confesses. And he will." He bowed his sleek head to put on his hat, and headed for the door.

"Lieutenant Laurence!" Sir Pomeroy's voice sounded urgent.

Simon turned. "Ye-es?"

"I have nothing else to do. Care if I accompany you?"

"To that stinking Newgate?"

"Well, why not? I was dying of *ennui* when you walked in. Didn't make it to bed all night."

Simon looked interested. "Why didn't you make it to bed all night?"

"Rutley was here, filling my ears by ragging against that Count who cheated him of his money. Can you believe that? I'm sure he's insane. I kicked him out an hour ago so I could eat my breakfast in peace."

"I know. The Magistrate and his men and I caught him leaving. He should be stewing in a cell by now."

"You did?" Sir Pomeroy stared hard. "I say! That's excellent," he expelled thoughtfully. "Well done!"

Simon beckoned. "By all means, come along with me, if you like."

He winked at Radford outside on the landing, who hid his listening trumpet in his pocket and plunged down the stairs. Lowering his head, Radford held the door for the pair of gentlemen so disparate in appearance.

As they swerved around a corner, Sir Pomeroy gripped the coach strap. He was thinking deeply, wavering about something. It was obvious to Simon, so he grabbed his chance and asked, "Why did you bail out Lord Rutley before my duel with the Count?"

Sir Pomeroy began to prevaricate, then thought better of it. "How did you know it was I?"

"You or Miss Wells, at any rate." Simon's tone turned stern. "Before that, we had Rutley deservedly under lock and key for abducting Arabelle Lamar. He should never have been released for such a heinous crime!"

Sir Pomeroy's nose twitched like a trapped rabbit. "I know! But I had no choice but to help Corisande with the bail money."

"No choice!" Simon exploded. "How could that be?"

"Lord Rutley sent me a message." Sir Pomeroy's chin came up and his lids lowered in remembered scorn. "A threatening kind of scrawl it was, too."

"On what grounds could Rutley threaten you?"

"By declaring that unless I bailed him out so he could attend your duel with the Count, he would disclose a secret he discovered through Corisande. A secret about . . . me."

Simon lifted an eyebrow. "What was that?"

Sir Pomeroy cringed down into the lace at his neck. "First let me ask you something, Laurence. Are you a man to make a . . . bargain?"

Simon folded his arms. "That depends. What is it?"

Twisting a button covered in embroidered flowers, Sir Pomeroy said, "Dash it!" He sat thinking desperately. "I'll have to high-tail it to France as soon as I tell you. And I did want to stay here." He dropped his forehead to his white hand and said in a strangled voice, "I suppose there's nothing for it but to confess to you."

Simon eyed him shrewdly but kindly. "That's right, Chancet. What hold does Lord Rutley have over you?"

"Only he and Corisande know what I am about to tell you." Preparatory to his tale, Sir Pomeroy flipped open his oval snuff box and inhaled a needed sniff from the back of his hand. He moaned as he shut it, and leaned back against the leather squabs of the coach. "A few months ago, I needed money. I lost fifty pounds to Lord Rutley at the gaming table when he came over to Paris. I already owed a hundred and thirty to various gentlemen here in London, which was horrendously deep for me. My quarterly rents were already paid me, with three months to wait until the next. I had no way to bring in the ready, and you simply cannot keep a gaming debt in abeyance."

"True," agreed Simon as the coach rumbled over high cobblestones, making Sir Pomeroy's cheeks vibrate. "So what did you do?"

"Promise you won't prosecute me . . . if I tell you something to your startling advantage?"

Simon's eyes twinkled wryly. "If the advantage is valuable enough, perhaps."

"Oh, but it is!" Sir Pomeroy assured him grandly. "I put myself entirely in your hands with what I am about to tell you."

"Fascinating. Go on."

"Well, I almost had my wig stolen by that same chap, Harry Boggs, on Christmas Eve. However," Sir Pomeroy looked smug, "I grabbed him with the hook of my walking stick and snatched my property back. The fellow was terrified of me." He arched a supercilious brow at Simon, who began to laugh, then clutched his injured side with a wince and a groan.

Sir Pomeroy paused, and they heard a street vendor crying, "Hot bricks! Hot bricks!" as they passed. "The next evening," Sir Pomeroy went on, "I stationed my groom and two footmen outside the haberdasher's doorstep where the theft attempt took place. Sure enough, there came Boggs from behind me, trying to steal a silver-blue wig from my head as I stooped, looking in the window. My men had Boggs as soon as I gave my signal. The signal I have for them is a neat whistle and three loud knocks of my walking stick. They've caught two pickpockets for me, and driven away women of the street since then." Sir Pomeroy's hooded eyelids revealed his pride.

"A useful tool, your signal," said Simon, his lips twitching. "What did you do with Boggs?"

"I took him into conference." Sir Pomeroy sighed. "The depths of my depravity surfaced on that occasion." He leaned forward and confessed, "I gave him commissions of my own."

Simon's black brows skyrocketed. "You sent him to steal wigs from other men?"

"Got it in one, Laurence. I found that, since I paid such astronomical sums for my own superior wigs, I could collect good money for each one Harry lifted." His voice was remote as he added, "I have seven expert thieves working for me now. Harry is the first I lost, thanks to you. I am, however, sick of the business and the problems that arise in splitting the money, with increasing greed on their part. I wish I had never dipped in."

He is tormented, noted Simon. He said, "We all make misjudgments."

"Yes; and I was desperate! But my bills are actually paid now, imagine that." His change to a cool tone did not fool Simon.

"I am relieved to hear you regret it," said Simon. "Is it because Harry is caught, and about to tell me and all the world, that you're sorry now?"

"Of course not! It is a terrible sort of relief to realize I may be exposed now. I have wanted and wanted to quit this, but each time I tried, here would come another prime trophy or two, and the money the wig shop poured into my pockets made them bulge so nicely. I want out, but I am faced with the problem of how to quit." He spread his hands helplessly. "Any of the boys could turn against me and divulge my activities, or blackmail me—at any hour. This ruins my joy in living."

"Yes, it would. Why did they work for you in the first place and not on their own?" inquired Simon as Radford opened the coach door. Simon gave him a private thumbs-up.

Sir Pomeroy whispered, "The young thieves needed me because I had the contacts they could not get, being of such lowly estate. I sold the wigs when I went in for my own fittings, saying I had tired of the bag of coiffures I brought in. A fine wigmaker will not usually deal with ruffians from the street," he explained. "Too risky for his business should it ever leak out."

"Ah. You had a respectable entrée."

Sir Pomeroy looked wan as he followed Simon. In the shadow of the grandiose Newgate Prison, they looked at the frost-covered statue of Richard Whittington and his cat.

Sir Pomeroy stated, "Now my fate is in your hands. Unless you like the news I give you, I shall make a run for the Continent in the next few hours. Better than being incarcerated in this place," he motioned to the sumptuous façade of the building, "where I would have to sleep on a stone floor, smell that vile stench, and spend all my money on food and water at exorbitant prices. I do not, after one visit here, find it to my taste." He shuddered violently.

Simon looked steadily at him. "I can hardly wait to hear your news, but I would like to know why you wanted to come here with me since you know what it's like in that bastion of hell."

"I must talk to Harry Boggs, that's why. He is not a bad chap; just misguided. I am responsible for his most recent misguidance," Sir Pomeroy said. "I need to bail him out, tell him to mend the error of his ways. I will make him promise to give it up for good, and spread the word to the others in the ring. I will say I am through forever, and don't mind whom they tell because I have already told you. Big mistake and all that. Harry Boggs should feel the same since he's been housed within those reeking walls."

"Who knows? Your forthrightness may keep them quiet," offered Simon reasonably. "You are now clear with me, but muddled in conscience and with the law. Take care of your soul," he added softly, touching his shoulder.

Sir Pomeroy nodded, head bent. Suddenly he brightened, looked down toward Newgate Market, and drew Simon toward a coffee house. "Come; let us talk a while longer before we are faced with the horrors of that place. I know something that a certain someone would kill me for if I told you." His brown eyes bulged with great portent. "You, of all people, must hear it."

The two men occupied an alcove table on the first-floor gallery of the Gilded Gauntlets coffee house. Simon sat carefully upright in the carved wood and upholstered booth, watching Sir Pomeroy lift his walking stick to the waiter in a haughty summons.

Simon saw that Radford successfully appropriated a table within easy earshot, his back turned to Sir Pomeroy. Good. A witness would be invaluable regarding whatever the Baronet might reveal.

He did reveal. "This is about your fiancée," began Sir Pomeroy.

"Oh?" Simon blinked in surprise.

Relishing his power to rivet Simon's attention, Sir Pomeroy assumed a story-telling pose, one finger raised. "Something momentous happened more than a year ago, in Harrowgate. It has to do with a man. A man whom Corisande was not happy to see enter Chesterfield House after she was affianced to you, Lieutenant."

Simon stared coldly into space.

"You will not look so remote or disinterested after you hear the reason she was afraid to see that man."

"What is the reason, and who is the man?" growled Simon, shoving his hat aside.

"Your Corisande," Sir Pomeroy said portentously, "is espoused! She is espoused to someone else besides you."

The statement sent a jolt through Simon. He gaped at the knowing eyes boring into his. "What? Is that true?" Simon whipped out as a waiter set steaming coffee cups between them.

"True as that's hot coffee," Sir Pomeroy said airily before the waiter, who was conveying cream, sugar, and tarts from his tray onto the table.

Simon had not removed his gaze from Chancet's face. "Is it *you?*" he demanded.

Sir Pomeroy jerked, and looked affronted. "Heavens, the thought! No! It is not I!"

"Who is it, then?" Simon demanded, nearly leaping from his seat to grab the Baronet round the throat.

The young waiter fled.

Sir Pomeroy put up his palms. "I will tell you! Please, sit back down; people are staring." He straightened his throat lace and leaned toward Simon. "She promised, at age eighteen, to marry Lord Rutley!"

Simon's black brows remained aloft for many ticks of the old clock. "You don't say!" he expelled.

"I do!" Sir Pomeroy twitched excitedly in his seat as he watched Simon's electrified reaction. "Lord Rutley and Corisande," he said, deriving pleasure from his revelation, "made a verbal espousal to each other, sure as night follows day."

"Were there any witnesses?" Simon demanded, his eyes piercing Chancet's with a strange light.

"Myself and another."

"Who was that?"

"Corisande's father."

Simon slapped his palms together in triumph. "Hurrah!" he shouted so loudly that the entire house heard. Simon's eyes were a-flame with leaping joy as he let the glorious news sink in. It was all he could do not to collar his brother, Radford, and ask to be congratulated on his release from Miss Counterfeit Wells.

Radford looked over his shoulder and they locked eyes in astounded elation.

"Why didn't they marry?" asked Simon of Sir Pomeroy, lowering his jubilant voice with difficulty.

Sir Pomeroy waved his hand airily. "They were in the midst of their sizzling romance when her father, and soon afterwards her mother, died. Then they read the Will. That's when Rutley heard the awful truth."

"Which was?"

"She has very little money. Don't you know that, Lieutenant?"

"I do now. When we were betrothed, she quoted her portion as being very large, calling herself a considerable heiress. However, Lord Chesterfield discovered that her portion is, in fact, quite small."

Sir Pomeroy rolled his eyes. "How despicable she is! But it's true. Rutley could not stomach such a pittance. He is very fond of money."

"I know," Simon ground out. "He stoops to the lowest crimes to get it!"

"So do a lot of people," confessed Sir Pomeroy mournfully.

"So that's why Rutley sheered off and left her!"

"*Touché.* He is greatly in debt. He didn't turn up in Corisande's sight until he spotted Arabelle Lamar in a theatre, wrote an advertisement to her, and met Corisande again by chance at Chesterfield House. I arrived at the same time as he did. I saw Corisande go into panicked conniptions before my very eyes when she saw her real fiancé before her, storming her haven."

Simon sat, one booted leg out straight, leaning back in delighted contemplation. "Go on," he urged.

"I am the only living witness to their lawful link. But I have proof."

"Proof? You do? What proof?"

Sir Pomeroy produced a folded paper with a burnt edge. He handed it with a smile to Simon.

Simon opened it and read,

Darling Rutley, you foxy fox,
>   *I am giving this to Sir Pom to pass on because I do not want*
> *everyone to know we are betrothed. Can you hurry the wedding?*
> *I am nervous about putting it off because of what we did.*

>   *Your lover, Corisande*

Simon asked incredulously, "How did you get a hold of such a letter?"

Sir Pomeroy looked rather proud. "I walked into my drawing room one day, where she had been waiting to see me. She jumped in guilt and threw that into my fireplace. But it didn't burn, and I picked it out after she left."

Simon said, his voice reverberating gratitude, "Thank you for giving this to me. I applaud your wisdom in retrieving and keeping this. This will make a great difference in my life. You have done me the greatest service, Sir Pomeroy."

"We will help each other," he replied humbly. "Do you know," he gestured with his sugar spoon, "regarding that Rutley cad, Lady Bastwicke told me that Arabelle would not answer his advertisement, so she herself answered it, and arranged for Rutley to meet Arabelle without her knowledge."

Simon's eyes narrowed. "That's execrable!"

"That woman!" ejaculated Sir Pomeroy with a shudder. "But look what it has finally brought about, Laurence: My telling you all of this."

"Thank you! Thank you!" Simon shook his hand heartily. "I am infinitely grateful to you." He continued to ponder the weighty stone that had just fallen from his back. "I am incredulous. All this time, those two, Lord Rutley and Corisande, have been lawfully promised to one another? And she dared to enter into another espousal with me?"

"She did! Moreover, I am deeply sorry I was a party to the knowledge. Lord and Lady Chesterfield do not know. There were times when I almost—"

Simon cut in, leaning intensely on the table, "To think that, if I had not seen Arabelle Lamar for the second time at my wedding, I might be married to that sneaking Corisande? When she belongs, by body and promise, to the rutting Rutley?"

"Now, Lieutenant Laurence, count your blessings," Sir Pomeroy reminded him as they stepped out into a light snowfall. "I will support you in any way I can so you can get out of Corisande's clutches. I have observed for some time that she is not the woman of your dreams."

"Thank you," said Simon warmly, his eyes lustrous as they walked toward Newgate Gaol. "I will always be grateful to you for telling me this."

"How generous of you to say so."

"One thing you can do," said Simon, "is to return Lord Bastwicke's wigs. Or the equivalent."

Sir Pomeroy bowed his head. "I will. I felt badly for Arabelle's sake after I saw what a pure angel she is. We should never have harmed her father. It's just that it was so easy to station my boys in the after-theatre crowds. He wears the highest quality wigs. The boys noticed them right away." Suddenly Sir Pomeroy grasped Simon's arm, almost pulling him off balance on the icy pavement. "Does Arabelle need to know that I am the cad?" he asked with fearful dismay in his brown eyes.

Simon smiled. "Not if you supply your written and verbal statements to expose Rutley and Corisande."

The Baronet's face lit with joy.

"Just return the wigs with an anonymous note of deepest apology," said Simon reasonably. "Have we an agreement?"

"Most definitely. Thanks forever, Laurence!"

Simon shook the spongy hand in his strong grip and said, "By the way, I found out something that should relieve your mind on another front, Chancet. The note that Arabelle supposedly wrote to invite you to her bedchamber? The reason we dueled?"

Sir Pomeroy looked unhappy to be reminded of the event, for his hand went with abashment to the scar on his cheek. "Yes?"

"It was written by Corisande. To ruin Arabelle."

Sir Pomeroy's jaw dropped as he thought about it, and the whole scenario sunk in. "And me, too! Why, that hypocritical sneak! Wait until I get my hooks on her!"

Sir Pomeroy walked into Lady Chesterfield's music room full of people, bowed near Her Ladyship's ear, and said, "Will you kindly rid yourself of all these guests in time for a private dinner this afternoon? Just leave the following persons, please: yourself and Lord Chesterfield, Lady Shepley, Arabelle, Corisande, and myself. What do you say?" He smiled, his red lips curling and his eyes promising a treat.

Lady Chesterfield smiled faintly before she told him behind her fan, "Yes, I suppose I can. But His Lordship, until he decides what to do with Corisande, has confined that impossible girl to her room, with footmen guarding her door in shifts."

"Yes, for her vile misdeeds against Arabelle. But please ask him to let the footmen escort her here this once, for I have something of monumental import to say. Corisande, of all people, must hear it. His Lordship can tell her the dinner is to be her Valentine's Day treat." Sir Pomeroy chuckled, and Lady Chesterfield promised.

When the Valentine's Day diners finished their savoury courses, the servants glided out to fetch dessert plates. Sir Pomeroy nipped off two pink icing hearts from the quiver of the spun sugar cupid. He gave them to Corisande, saying, "When is your new wedding date? Am I to choose different music for better luck this time?" He observed her as she bit into a pink heart.

"It is to be the second Friday in March," Corisande replied, tossing a defiant look at Arabelle. "Yes, pick new music, Sir Pomeroy. Make sure it's really grand." She placed the other heart on her tongue and stuck it out at him.

He asked nonchalantly, aware of his listening audience, "Have you made sure that the second Friday in March is good for Lord Rutley? Will he be free of chains and bonds, do you think? Or will he ever be?"

Corisande blanched, and nearly choked on the heart. "Why should I care about *him?*"

"It is of the utmost importance, I would think," returned Sir Pomeroy conversationally, "that your bridegroom be present at your wedding. But you may have to have your ceremony and honeymoon in Newgate."

Corisande stared at him as if her blazing eyes would pop out.

The Valentine dessert was over, and Arabelle was still stunned.

Sir Pomeroy had explained to them all, after Corisande's ear splitting screams, that Lord Rutley was Corisande's real, lawful fiancé.

Corisande hit Sir Pomeroy with her fork. She battered him with dire, unspeakable threats until Lord Chesterfield jumped up and pulled her off of him. With aid of three large footmen, His Lordship hustled Corisande toward the stairs to the tune of Sir Pomeroy's parting shot: "Don't worry, Corisande, my business is confessed, so I'm not afraid of you or Rutley any longer."

"But *Simon* is my fiancé! I *will* marry him! I will!"

Sir Pomeroy glanced at Arabelle, then folded his arms, and said to Corisande's spitting eyes, "He is not your fiancé. You deceived him all along. You had already promised yourself to Rutley. *I* know. I was there—remember? You will not marry Simon Laurence, for I told him all about your prior betrothal."

"You—you—you vile *beast!* You are the most despicable scum!" She snatched a statuette to throw at him.

"Cease that at once, Corisande!" shouted Lord Chesterfield, signaling the footman, who grabbed the figurine and forcibly conveyed her, red-faced and screeching, up the stairs.

Though clamped by the footman, she shrieked on about losing Simon because of Sir Pomeroy's perfidious lies. She screeched, "I *detest* Rutley!"

Arabelle echoed the feeling as she locked eyes with the raging Corisande over the banister. She recalled Corisande's terror when she had first seen Lord Rutley enter this house. So that was why. The two had been betrothed, and they had pre-anticipated the marriage bed, and after that, Corisande feared him, and therefore did what he asked.

Lord Rutley, thinking he could defy the law because of his lofty position, had left Corisande because of her less-than-grandiose dowry, Sir Pomeroy explained. He came back to pester her again when she landed in the home of Lord and Lady Chesterfield. Corisande had been jumpy with apprehension that Lord Rutley would spoil her second, illegal betrothal to Simon Laurence.

Sir Pomeroy told Lord Chesterfield and the ladies all about the subsequent cover-up to which he was privy. Before he went to France, Corisande had demanded Sir Pomeroy's silence so she could marry Simon Laurence without any opposition. In return, she would not tell the world a secret that she knew about him.

And here Sir Pomeroy begged their forbearance, for he did not plan to divulge what that was, but he did state with lowered eyelids that a certain Lieutenant knew, and that was all that mattered.

When Lord Chesterfield asked how Corisande had kept Lord Rutley from reasserting his rights to her when she landed in his house, Sir Pomeroy replied, "The power Corisande wielded over Lord Rutley *not* to press his rights to her came from her knowledge of his virgin-stealing activities."

The others gasped. Lady Chesterfield cried out, "It was he who abducted the three before Arabelle?"

Sir Pomeroy further revealed that once, when a pretty heiress spurned Rutley before he met Corisande, he had been so angry to see the lady at a *fête* in Harrowgate that Corisande had noticed his scowls and asked him what he held against that lady. He had spat that he wanted to waylay her and sell her to some brutal foreigner to pay her back for spurning him. Furthermore, he had said he could probably get rich doing it, for he knew that fair English women were highly prized in far-flung countries.

Corisande, after hearing the shocking tidings that such abductions had really taken place, decided to find out if Lord Rutley had done those deeds. She discovered, through wiles only known to herself and Rutley, that he was doing a brisk trade in lovely virgins, and getting away with it. He was becoming extremely plump in the pocket through each transaction.

Corisande wanted money. Lord Rutley offered to marry her again since she now had Lord Chesterfield supporting her, but she said, "Nothing doing," for she was marrying the handsome Simon Laurence, who had money of his own. She dictated that if Rutley kept forever quiet about their verbal espousal, she would not expose his crimes. If he did reveal that they were betrothed to each other, she would tell that he was the infamous abductor, and he would hang.

When it came to Rutley's making a new "sale," she herself suggested Arabelle. The reason? Corisande could see that Simon Laurence found Arabelle far too desirable. Corisande wanted the woman he admired out of London, and out of his life.

All this Sir Pomeroy told them after they had formed a shocked circle of chairs in the music room. He knew it all. Corisande had whispered freely to him because they knew each other's secrets. They were all three tied to silence about one another.

Though the revelation was astounding in itself, the song singing through Arabelle's mind was, *Simon is free of Corisande!*

Then her heart sank like a stone in a well. Joy and misery tangled in her breast as she thought, *Simon is released. Corisande cannot marry the "handsomest man in England."*

"But neither can I!" wailed Arabelle. "I am betrothed to the Count."

Chapter Twenty-Five

Tracks in the Snow

In a dark, pre-dawn hour on the awful day, Arabelle rang for a maid.

With her eyes watering from a yawn as she appeared in less than perfect order, the young Chesterfield maid stared in bafflement at Arabelle when she asked to be bathed and dressed in her Court gown.

"So early, Miss Lamar?"

"Yes, please." By candlelight, Arabelle made her toilette and had the exquisite white lace gown with three velvet bows laddered down the middle of the bodice on before breakfast.

The maid had a tray brought up, including coffee and warm scones with marmalade. Arabelle ate, trying not to think. Soon she asked for her black velvet cloak lined in the white fur.

"Be you going out of doors *now*, Miss?" The maid looked askance at the clock. Orange streaks painted the eastern sky, visible through the filmy curtains, but the sun was not yet risen.

"I am," asserted Arabelle. She paused on the verandah steps to look at the brightening sky. The day dawned tragically beautiful. Rays of pink slashed through orange clouds and cast a shimmering sparkle onto the snow.

At the back of the mansion, no one else stirred. Arabelle needed to walk, think, and breathe the chill air. She had hardly slept all night. These steps in the white expanse beneath the ancient, spreading branches would be her last of maiden freedom.

With a will, she tucked the rest of the world away while she kicked sugary snow in front of her pink, shapely galoshes, watching the snow clumps land and make small indentations. The white, powdery blanket was marked only by a mouse's footprints where it had jumped and landed, its tail dragging before it disappeared into a dark hole in the snow. There were no human tracks anywhere. She came across some delicate bird tracks.

My future is like this clean snow, she thought. *All my hopes, dreams, and nightmares that went before are covered. I have a new life ahead of me, with very little imprint on it.* She stood looking at the brightening heavens in cathedral silence outside the garden wall. Where would she be tomorrow?

There came a far-off bark of a dog, *Yap, yap, yap!* One in the Chesterfield stable answered, *Woof!* She walked around the perimeter of the gardens and through the trees, realizing that she could go to no person for help, but she could still pray.

As she veered down the hill toward the swings, she was alarmed to see a set of man's boot tracks circling round them. What were they doing here so early in the morning? Whoever he was, she felt it unwise to encounter a man alone. He had gone up the brow of the slope. Perhaps he had just missed her. She decided to step into each of his tracks, but in the opposite direction. By so doing, she hoped to hide the fact that she had been there.

Her gown and cloak grew heavy with her exertions up the rise in the widely spaced footprints. Below the stone balustrade, she stopped to catch her breath. She heard a squeaking sound of steps in snow.

Whoever it was, he was coming back. He might have seen her steps inside his, after all, discerning that a woman came this way. Her close proximity to Chesterfield House was no guarantee of safety. She had learned that lesson all too clearly the night of the ball.

Stealthily, she picked her way past shrubs until she rounded the corner of the verandah staircase so she could hide behind a bush and watch the man go by. As her foot touched the snow in the corner, it made a loud *crack* in the morning stillness. She jerked off-balance into a puddle of ice. She jumped back. Jagged pieces stuck up like shards of glass.

"Who's there?" a male voice rang over the crisp morning air.

Arabelle edged out of the shadow. "Who are you?" Her breath came out in a cloud.

"Arabelle!" It was Simon Laurence, flashing her a fabulous white smile.

Her heart gave a lurch of joy. He was cloaked in dark burgundy, and his black tricorne on his white hair glittered in silver around the edges, rivaling the whites of his deep blue eyes.

"What are you doing striding about here so early, Lieutenant Laurence?" She must be formal, and tamp down her euphoria at seeing him, for this was the morning she must wed another man.

"I came to see you, alone, on this day of days. How amazing it is to find you out of doors. How do you feel? How beautiful you look in that black cloak with the white fur around your rose-tinted cheeks." He reached for her, and pulled her to him with a bittersweet air.

Her heart pounded. "Don't, Simon! I cannot bear it."

He slayed her anew with the love gleaming from his eyes. "Bear what?"

"You!" she admitted daringly. "Your being here, touching me, when I must go and . . ."

His breathless, waiting attitude encouraged her to go on and finish what was burning in her heart.

"You see, I must marry the Count this morning."

With a pained glance at Simon's troubled profile, she turned away in response to the call of her name from the French windows above. It was Lord Chesterfield.

"I must hie myself to church now," she said in a broken voice, not meeting Simon's sad eyes for more than an instant.

With a tortured look, he said, "Arabelle, do you want me to do anything?"

"Don't! It cannot be undone!" she cried over her shoulder as she hurried up the icy stone steps to the elegantly coated Earl who waited, hat under his arm. Arabelle could not bear to look long at the fine figure of the man she loved as he bowed good morning to Lord Chesterfield and good-bye to her.

She would have liked to share her state of mind with Lord Chesterfield, but because of Simon's presence, she could not. She accompanied him to join Aunt Claracilla, Lady Chesterfield, and Corisande in the entry. The older women exclaimed and fussed over her, and called the maids to remove her snowy galoshes.

Corisande flounced around the entry hall, hanging on the column and watching the proceedings with a cocky attitude. The only remark she addressed to Arabelle was, "So where will you live with that Count, anyway?"

"You hush!" snapped Lady Chesterfield in uncharacteristic savagery. "Not one more word out of you." To Arabelle, she explained that Corisande had to come with them so they could keep an eye on her, with footmen seated in the pews around them. Otherwise, if she were left in the house, who knew what could happen? They had to keep her for the King and his Magistrates to deal with. They would collect her this afternoon.

The wedding was set for eight o'clock, for it was the only time the clergyman could squeeze them in, his next marriage beginning at nine. In quiet groups, the Chesterfield party filed out the door and into carriages and sedan chairs. Arabelle heard a rooster crow as the sun rose in a blazing red ball.

The impending event suddenly seemed very real to her when she was carried by sedan chair to the May Fair Chapel across the road. As soon as the chair door was opened for her, Aunt Claracilla was there, patting Arabelle's face and hugging her, trying to get her to cheer up and smile.

The bride could not smile.

There stood her family coach, with four steaming horses, and outriders turning their mounts in circles. Lady Bastwicke was already chattering away on the pavement in a glittering gold cloak and headdress. Lord Bastwicke carried Lenora and little Jerome, who was yawning. The sight of the little ones made Arabelle blink back her tears with fierce resolve.

Though she knew she had made a verbal espousal and must stick to it, her emotions screamed, *How could Father let this happen to me? He knew I needed to marry for love and happiness!*

Must this kind of thing happen to her sisters, too? Was it only in plays and novels where love and romance lived and flourished?

Lord Bastwicke, wearing his stolen but returned wig with the pink thread inside, kissed Arabelle and murmured, "Count Mascarille has agreed to a very generous settlement, my pet. We will sign it after the ceremony, at the wedding breakfast."

Arabelle stood amazed. Count *Mascarille* was his name?

Lord Bastwicke looked triumphantly down at her. "Smile, my dear. You have done extremely well for the family. Even your mother is impressed." He flipped his blue cape back and lifted his chin with pride, moving on to greet someone.

"But, *Father!*" Arabelle cried, incredulous at his lack of sensitivity to her turmoil on this day of all days. But he was already bowing to Lord Chesterfield.

Done extremely well? What about her life with this Count Mascarille in the far-off unknown? And that name, Mascarille. She had read it somewhere before.

Arabelle scooped up Jerome and squeezed him, and hugged Lenora next, answering her big-eyed query with, "Yes, I am to be married this morning, Love."

"Is it to a beautiful man, Arabelle?"

Arabelle touched her rosy cheek and whispered, "He wears a mask. I do not know. Pray for me!"

Lenora promptly put her hands together and squeezed her eyes. "Dear God, please let him be a very beautiful man for Arabelle. In Jesus' name, amen." Then she added, "Please let him take his mask off soon so Arabelle and I can see him. Amen."

Aunt Claracilla, who had been inside the church, rushed out, looking full of bottled-up exclamations. She grabbed Arabelle by the arm and gesticulated in such a way over her face—making a mask with eyeholes with her fingers—that Arabelle knew she was talking about the Count. There was great portent in her eyes.

"Yes, yes, I am sure he looks impressive," Arabelle sighed. Dread of the finality of this step began to pervade her so mightily that her hands shook.

Aunt Claracilla made a *No* with her lips, shook her head, and tried to make out the motions of a sword she admired in a scabbard.

"Is he wearing the jeweled sword? That deadly Pappenheim rapier? No doubt he expects he may have to protect himself during our departure," she said, "or coerce me into marrying him." Moving past her aunt, she said dismissively, "I am sick of swords and duels!" She had expected that Aunt Claracilla would have tried her utmost to get Arabelle's father to oppose this marriage by finding some legal loopholes. But that was a moot question now, for her father sounded very pleased.

Aunt Claracilla caught Arabelle's arm and tried to impress something upon her about the sword, and who knew what else, with confusing motions. Whatever it was, Arabelle did not want to discuss the Count with her, especially not in this public scene, with wedding guests spilling out of carriages and sedan chairs all around her.

"Genevieve," she said, turning away from her frustrated aunt, "are you ready to be my bridesmaid?"

She received a sweet-smelling hug from her sister, whose eyes were intently watching her to read her feelings. Arabelle felt a lump in her throat at the love and concern she sensed from Genevieve.

"I brought flowers for us both, Arabelle. Here are yours." She handed her a generous pink and white bouquet of roses. They smelled sweet. "Are you all right?"

"No, I am not." Arabelle gave a little sob of frustration.

Genevieve grabbed her tightly and said in her ear, "Is there any way we can possibly stop this?"

"If I knew a way, I would not go through with it, but there is absolutely no alternative. I am trapped. But, Genevieve," she whispered, "I would rather marry this Count Mascarille than Lord Rutley or Sir Pomeroy, so take that as a small consolation. But how I wish I could wake up from this nightmare and find myself free."

"If only you could marry Simon Laurence, right?" Genevieve asked.

"Yes, but don't make me cry! I'll look horrible when I walk down the aisle."

"Arabelle!" called Lady Bastwicke shrilly. "Hurry-scurry! Come in right after your father and I promenade down to the front where the bride's parents sit."

Up on the cross of the chapel, a little bird twittered down at her. Why, she thought, did he sing so cheerfully? He was, of course, free.

But she had prayed, and she would go forward. She must have faith.

"Are you ready, my love?" Just inside the church was a little room where she had been instructed to await her bridegroom. It was there that Arabelle heard the Count's French voice.

She whirled to find herself face to face with his black velvet frock coat, a gold and black patterned waistcoat, and throat lace of the costliest *Point d' Alençon*. The Count, her husband-to-be, grasped her in his arms, and his abundant black curls tickled her cheek. She looked up at the eerie gold mask that covered his face today. Of course, he had to wear it, or he could be recognized and taken. She saw very little inside the eyeholes; only the long eyelashes.

"Ready for what, exactly?" she returned with a hitch in her voice. Her heart thudded against her corset.

He pulled her close to him with ardour. "To marry me," he said. "I can hardly believe my heaven-sent fortune."

Am I mad? Arabelle asked herself, pulling back. *Or is this a fantastical dream? Will I soon awaken to reality and lie gasping in relief that none of this is true?*

His hands were warm as he removed his gauntlets and then her gloves. "I will want your fingers free when I put the ring upon you."

She knew what she must do. She dropped her rose bouquet and the white fur muff that had graced her arm. To distract him, she adjusted the bodice of her gown with both hands in a way that might interest him, and when he was gazing upon her, she reached up with both hands and yanked the mask off his face.

She gasped.

Chapter Twenty-Six

The Wrong Bridegroom

Arabelle stared at his startled face. She was stymied.

With a laugh and a "Ho, she's caught me now!" he jerked the ribbon to free the mask from around his neck, threw off the long wig, and pulled his white queue out of his collar.

"What game are you playing this morning, Simon?" she stage-whispered, glaring at the transformation from Count Mascarille to her beloved Simon.

"I have come to marry you, Arabelle."

His startling words and manly voice were heaven to her ears. But it did not make sense.

"*You* have? How on earth can *you* marry me? True, you are rid of Corisande, but there is still my espousal to the Count!"

He just looked at her. She could not read his expression. Her heart began to thud and her mouth went dry. The only thing that she could think of that would clear their path struck her with fear. She grasped his arms and whispered, "Have you killed the Count, and come to save me in this madcap way by impersonating him?"

"Yes to all your questions. I killed the Count."

"You did, Simon?" Her heart jolted painfully. "Then we must flee to the Continent! Oh, *Simon!* I didn't think you could ever do something so wrong!"

Into their sanctuary burst Aunt Claracilla. She gesticulated over Simon with a look that said clearly, *I told you so!*

"How did you know?" cried Arabelle, looking with amazement at her aunt's glowing face.

Simon said, "Lady Shepley discovered the truth by a look at the sword I carry. It has the insignia of the Royal Military Academy. She wanted to study it more closely. When Lady Shepley ran out to tell you her suspicion, I watched her try to convey it to you. But, without paper for her to write upon, the truth proved too preposterous for her to explain."

Aunt Claracilla was nodding and laughing triumphantly.

"Arabelle," said Simon, "I had terrible pangs of conscience. How wretchedly used you must feel, having to marry the Count because I failed to win the duel."

Arabelle, tingling with racing blood from head to toe, grasped Simon's outstretched fingers and returned to her concern. "But you killed him, Simon?"

He leaned toward her and whispered, "Are you not glad?"

"No!" Flushing, she realized she didn't know what she was saying, but the law would now be after Simon. "I am not. You will end up hanging on Tyburn Hill!"

They heard footsteps. Simon cautiously lifted the curtain. "Ah, here's Radford."

Very fine in dark green and ivory, Lord Ashby slipped in. Genevieve ducked in after him.

"Arabelle," said Simon, gathering her close by the waist despite his brother and Lady Shepley and Genevieve's presence, "the time has come for me to marry you. Will you? Marry me, my Love?"

"How can this be?" she breathed, thrilling as he held her and looked into her very soul.

He touched her under the chin. "Just listen to me."

She gloried in his power to love her with a touch. She glanced at his strong, well-shaped fingers and pressed a kiss onto them. Her heart thumped. "I am listening," she said in a stifled voice, "with every fibre of my being."

"Do you know how distraught I was when you were taken off by Lord Rutley from the Chesterfield Ball?"

"You were?"

"I must explain something to you. Radford, signal the organist to play on. Darling Arabelle, I started out with a plan to save you. After I discovered the schemes against you, I wrote a letter to Lord Rutley from Count Mascarille." Behind his hand, he said, "I offered Rutley twice the amount of money a Turkish prince had promised to pay for you. The Turk viewed you at Drury Lane Theatre and bid a very high sum for your delivery to his ship on the Thames."

"No! Really?"

"Oh yes, it really happened. I heard him; I stood next to him. That's when I decided to bid higher."

"But how did you ever know that I was their targeted victim?"

"Among other methods," said Simon, "I found note after note in Corisande's room."

When Radford lifted the curtain to signal the organist, they could see Corisande's blonde head at the front of the church.

"Rutley wrote her instructions and signed them *Fox*, remember? He wrote to Corisande that if she wanted a share in the proceeds, she should *wrap the goods in black*. When I saw you in the black gown at the ball, I took Radford aside and pointed it out."

Radford added, "We were ready for what would happen, but that dastardly foreshadowing on your innocent form made us so incensed that we could hardly keep ourselves from choking Rutley and Corisande at the ball."

"But we couldn't do that," said Simon, and kissed her hand fervently. "We needed to catch them in the act and report them to the King. I'm sorry that I couldn't spare you that ordeal."

Arabelle remembered Corisande's deceitful, smiling enthusiasm when she had declared that the two of them would be so dramatic as opposites in black and white. "Rutley and Corisande did a clever job of preparing me for the abduction."

"But their scheme did not prosper," inserted Radford, "thanks to Simon's imaginative, clear-headed plans."

"What plans? You were at the ball," Arabelle pointed out.

"So we were," Simon agreed, tracing a sweet path up her cheek with the back of his finger. "We had fast horses saddled and ready.

When Rutley took you away to look at paintings, as reported by your little sister, Lenora, we knew he was preparing to make his move. When Genevieve said he was taking you out to look at fireworks, Radford and I slipped out of the house and rode hell-for-leather across London to the house we had prepared for your delivery, praying he would not harm you while you were out of our sight. For that, we had to trust in God, and in the vigilance of the coachman."

"The coachman?" Arabelle stood stock still, baffled. She asked Genevieve, "Even you and Lenora were involved?"

"Oh, Arabelle," said Genevieve, squeezing her, "we knew nothing that was going on, only that Lieutenant Laurence and Lord Ashby needed us to take turns keeping an eye on you and reporting to them your movements through Chesterfield House."

Simon said, "We had just made ourselves ready in that house when you arrived, Arabelle, carried by our planted coachman, Roger. I was furious because Rutley had really done it: delivered you to foreigners for money. I felt like heaving him head first out the window."

"You can imagine how *I* felt!" Arabelle stage-whispered at a pause in the music.

When a new organ piece began, Arabelle parted the curtain and peeked at her parents. They were craning their necks to locate her and the cause of the delay. Lady Bastwicke shot a pasted smile across at Lord and Lady Chesterfield, then spotted Arabelle and made a quick widening of her eyes as if to say, *Get on with it!*

Arabelle, who felt empowered to ignore her, said, "I thought Lord Rutley was going to force me into marriage with *him!*" She shivered.

"I imagine," said Simon.

Curiosity prompted her to ask, "From where did you watch all this, Simon?"

His lips curved. "My brother, Radford, opened the door and invited you in with his French accent, perfected in Paris on his travels. He wore a mask, wig, and gaudy purple raiment."

Arabelle, riveted by Lord Ashby's wide grin, cried, "*You* were François? He who played me the violin?"

"Yes, I was," he admitted laughingly. "Too bad I quit lessons at age nine."

Arabelle shook in amazed laughter.

Simon bowed his head and fingered his lip. He glanced covertly at Arabelle, and said in an unsteady voice, "I am sorry to have deceived you, Arabelle, but you see, in order to protect you, I had to play the Count who received you. I couldn't let you out of my sight."

Arabelle, with head suddenly whirling, grasped the curtain for support. She bored her eyes into him. "*You* were the Count, Simon? No!" As implications of this sank in, she saw his lips twitching. She cried, "Simon Laurence! Are you telling me that you have been the Count all along?"

He got down on one knee and kissed her hand with rapture. "I have. Most of the time."

She groaned. Remembering the kisses she had given the Count, she wondered what Simon's perception of her behaviour must be. Her voice reached a pitch of frenzy. "Oh *no!*" she wailed, and could have expired from embarrassment.

As the loud chords of "Love Divine, All Loves Excelling" began, Radford smiled at Arabelle and said, "Simon, your wedding begins."

"Simon Laurence!" Arabelle exclaimed under her breath. "You are the most . . ." She could not find words, but stared down into the bold, loving eyes of the man she adored, for he was still down on one knee before her.

"I love you, Arabelle. Will you please marry me?" His intense feelings seared into her from the most hopeful and happy look she had ever seen light his handsome, flirtatious face.

"Yes!" she said joyfully, her heart full to bursting, "I will marry you! We made a verbal espousal, did we not, dear Count? Oh, Simon, you terrible deceiver, I love you so much!"

Tears squeezed out of her eyes as he embraced her. She hugged his warm cheek to hers, and the faces of their witnesses beamed with joy.

As she turned to face the music, Arabelle knew this was the happiest, most scandalous moment of her life.

Lord and Lady Bastwicke, Lenora, Jerome, and Aunt Claracilla were looking back from the front of the church, as were Lord and Lady Chesterfield with Corisande.

Sir Pomeroy, rising to his feet first, stood dazzling in pink, black, and silver braid, smiling proudly upon the bride and groom, for he had done much to make this wedding possible.

Genevieve kissed Arabelle and whispered, "I cannot *believe* all this, Arabelle! What fabulous romance! Do you truly get to marry Simon Laurence?"

"I do!" Arabelle stood in a glow as her sister retied a white silk *échelle* on her bodice, then dabbed perfume onto Arabelle's neck from a bottle she produced from her bag pocket. It was the scent of lilacs. How appropriate, for there was spring in her heart.

"Thank you, Genevieve." She kissed her sister's smooth cheek and said, "You go down the aisle first, remember? You look exquisite. Oh, this has turned out to be such a blessèd day! I never could have imagined this, even a quarter hour ago! God is *so good* to me! Why did I ever doubt?"

Simon heard her words and kissed her tenderly on her lips. It thrilled her with promise.

They watched Genevieve sway gracefully toward the waiting clergyman, her red-gold curls falling from her simple, backswept coiffure. Ivory roses were tucked in, and echoed in the aqua gown with ivory brocade roses embroidered over her sacque back. Arabelle's heart kept thumping erratically with joy. She kept her eyes on Genevieve's heels moving beneath the lace of her hem until she reached the railing where Lord Ashby stood. They smiled at one another.

Arabelle took a breath that lifted her sparkling, square-necked bodice. Trepidation warred with exultation in her breast. She fingered her rich court gown and knew she was ready. She looked up at Simon.

He winked his long lashes at her. He was devastatingly handsome, incredibly exciting. Was he truly to be her man for life? Yes, those were the lashes she had glimpsed through the mask slits, and which she had felt against her fingertips in the pitch-black bedchamber. Her heart fluttered just as it had when she had sat across from him in the coach the day he so nobly gave her and her mother passage.

"Arabelle, I have so much to apologize for," he said low as he moved out of hiding and they began their walk down the aisle, "but for now, let us savour our wedding, shall we? Look at them stare!" He smiled in delight.

Arabelle, on the arm of "the handsomest man in England," saw Corisande's eyes start from their sockets. She saw her large mouth form, "Simon!" in utter disbelief.

Though Lord and Lady Chesterfield also looked stunned, the Countess had enough presence of mind to pull Corisande back after she jumped to her feet in outrage. A struggle ensued, with footmen rising and clamping her back down. Lord Chesterfield said something to the red-faced Corisande that instantly halted her.

When Arabelle turned her radiant eyes to her parents, what she saw on their faces was profound shock. Lady Bastwicke's mouth began to move and her hand came up imperiously as if to prevent what was happening.

But no one could prevent it now.

With her hand on Simon's arm, Arabelle felt strong. What she was doing, marrying Lieutenant Simon Laurence, felt beautiful and blessed. She was ecstatically in love with him, and he with her. She could hardly believe that she would be his, to have and to hold . . .

As she looked at the kind-eyed clergyman and heard him read the Word of God and the marriage service, Arabelle felt the blessing of the Almighty upon their union. When the clergyman said to Simon, "You may now please kiss your bride," she saw the seriousness in Simon's eyes turn to shining happiness.

She trembled, for she felt the same. As their lips met, Arabelle felt the strength of their love, and knew that life would be glorious.

In the oddest, most mysterious and persistent ways, this recent stranger, Lieutenant Laurence, had fought for her. He had defied all the evil odds thrown before him by diabolical members of London high society. And he had won.

So had she. Thank God, so had she!

When Lord and Lady Bastwicke fully understood what all had taken place due to the espionage and clever acting of Simon Laurence and his brother, the Earl of Ashby, they were bereft of words. Arabelle saw Madam, her mother, sitting twiddling a silk bow on her gown and staring into space, her lips working.

It was Genevieve, sitting next to Arabelle and Simon at their festive wedding table in Bloomsbury Square who said, "It is the most wonderful, most *mysterious* courting ever! Better than any of our books or plays." Her eyes glowed as she turned to their mother. "Arabelle is the most blessed girl in London to be so loved, is she not, Madam?"

Lady Bastwicke's mouth could not find a satisfactory position. She cast a narrow-eyed glance Arabelle's way, but it must have been too much for her. Her eyes were so full of envy that they could not bear to touch on her happy daughter on the most beautiful day of her life.

Lord Bastwicke filled the breach by booming, "She *is*, our Arabelle! Welcome to the family, Lieutenant Laurence. I am proud to have you as my son-in-law, and that's a fact."

Lord and Lady Chesterfield were also seated at the table, as were Lord Ashby, Sir Pomeroy Chancet, Aunt Claracilla, the children, and even Captain Ligonier and several of Simon's fellow officers and cadets. Simon glowed with pride in Arabelle as he introduced her to them one by one. She could see that they respected her husband immensely. She watched them now and then with interest. It would be fun to invite them to visit. They seemed such upright and genial young men.

Genevieve had noticed them, too.

Arabelle saw her mother's back stiffen when one of the cadets leaned to talk to her next marriageable daughter, a breathless smile on his face. Lady Bastwicke immediately asked Genevieve to pass the sugar.

So their mother's prejudice against "common" men had not been squelched by Arabelle and Simon's wedding. It was likely stronger than ever, reflected Arabelle, since she had failed to produce a peer as a husband.

Simon had mirthfully dropped the word in her ear during the carriage ride from May Fair Chapel that he had plenty of money, and that the marriage settlement he had proposed to Lord Bastwicke when he was Count Mascarille still stood. The amount had been the decisive factor in Lord Bastwicke's willingness to see his daughter wed the Count. Arabelle had not let the subject of money ruin her glorious wedding day.

Aunt Claracilla, braving Lady Bastwicke's haughty, disapproving stare, rose from her chair and walked around the long table to touch Arabelle on the shoulder. Her eyes blinked with glad tears.

"Thank you for all your love and your wonderful counsel," Arabelle said, squeezing her. "See? Your prayers, and mine, are answered."

Her aunt nodded, and she turned to hug Simon. He set down his goblet and stood to kiss Lady Shepley on the cheek.

Arabelle moved past Simon and Aunt Claracilla to her mother's side as soon as the footmen pulled back their chairs. "Thank you for that sumptuous wedding breakfast, Madam. May I . . . may I tell you something that is on my heart?"

Lady Bastwicke's eyes slid over Arabelle's slim waist in her white and silver spangled gown. "What is it?" She kept avoiding her eyes.

Arabelle gave her the bouquet of pink and white roses, saying, "This is for you." Arabelle gripped her chair for support. "There is a passage I read in the Bible last night which fits the way I have felt for most of my life," she began bravely. "It goes, *Remove me far from vanity and lies: give me neither poverty nor riches; feed me with food convenient for me.* It is from Proverb 30, the eighth verse."

Her mother lifted her nose and snapped her fingers down the bouquet ribbons. She looked about to move away, her lips tight.

"Mother," said Arabelle quietly, moving closer to her huge golden gown, "I realize that you value titles and wealth. I know that being with people who possess them is what you like best. However, I have found that there is too high a price to pay for much of that. I have joy in Simon Laurence. What I quoted just now will remain my prayer all my life. I just wanted you to know that I appreciate what you and Father have tried to achieve for me, as I'm sure you meant it all for the best." She touched her mother's lace-covered forearm. "Be assured that I now have what is best for me." She smiled at her.

Her mother sniffed, but did not respond, so Arabelle turned and smiled helplessly at her Father, who had heard the whole discourse.

He cleared his throat. His eyes were wet. "Yes, Arabelle," he said in a voice husky with emotion, "go with your Laurence and be happy. Deservedly happy. He is an exceptional man. You would not be here safely if he had not intrigued so wisely to save you. I still marvel. The King is ecstatic at what Simon achieved: the catching and conviction of Lord Rutley is now complete. And, Arabelle," he said, hugging her with his gentle strength, "you are a wonderful daughter."

"Thank you, Father. I love you." She gulped back tears, hugged him, and then moved behind her quiet mother to take Simon's outstretched hand.

He was looking at her in a way that made her breathless with anticipation for the hours that lay ahead.

Chapter Twenty-Seven

The Wedding Night

Arabelle gazed with heart-thumping awe at the man she loved. From her vantage point, his white head gleamed in a smooth curve and his braided cuffs glistened in the moonlight that bathed him at the window. They had traveled in easy stages from Bloomsbury Square to this white, graceful mansion in the countryside near Maidstone, Kent.

It was Simon's own house, he said, granted to him by his brother, Lord Ashby, for acting as steward for the Ashby estates. Simon had willingly performed that service for him while Radford enjoyed himself in Europe, taking the Grand Tour after their father died.

But Simon, Arabelle learned through questioning, had wanted more out of life than stewardship of his own and his brother's estates, for that did not take all of his time or mental capacity. He had applied for admittance to the Royal Military Academy, stating his academic history at Eton and Cambridge, and his interest in serving England as an officer in His Majesty's Army. He had been awarded the high honour of entry to the Academy, conferred by the Master-General, in whose hands alone lay all appointments to that prestigious institution. There, he became a Lieutenant in record time.

Arabelle felt very proud of Simon. He had acquitted himself nobly in his mission for the King in the matter of the abductions. She, herself, owed everything to his intelligent handling of the situation, as her father had acknowledged that morning.

Now she felt as though she had been transported into another life. She and Simon had their own home. It was an easy drive of seven miles from Uncle Trent and Aunt Claracilla's Fawnlake Hall. This lovely mansion of white stone and curved walls, towers, bow windows, and iron balconies was named Merryview.

Before they arrived, Simon pulled out of a leather case beneath the seat the long, ebony wig and the mask, which he held in front of his face. In a suggestive French accent, he asked, "Will you come stay with me tonight?"

Arabelle grabbed the mask off of him, laughing. "Oh, Simon, don't!"

"I will save these for the first costume ball we are invited to in London, shall I? To prolong the scandal, and all that?" His derring-do ended in a slight scuffle, which resulted in a heated embrace.

"Why did you name the Count after a character from *The Romantic Ladies*?" she inquired.

"Because my father was a *devotée* of Molière's comedies. He saw them all, and especially liked the character of Marquis de Mascarille. It just popped into mind when I had to suddenly give your father my name as the Count."

"Ah yes, I remember the Marquis. He was the one who said, 'Let's go seek our fortune somewhere else; I see they like nothing here but insignificant outside, and have no regard for naked virtue.'"

She and Simon looked at each other. "Sounds like us," he said to her.

"Thank you for taking me far away from all that," she said, and kissed his eager lips.

With the newlyweds' welcoming supper concluded in the tower dining room at Merryview, the maidservants had smilingly accompanied Arabelle to her new dressing room. When she was undressed, bathed, and her long hair brushed, the maids retired, leaving Arabelle feeling warm and pampered. The servants had catered to her with great reverence. How nice it felt to belong to Simon, the master of these three hundred tidy acres, and to be tended by such willing servants.

She grew joyful and somewhat breathless at the sight of her handsome husband by the window. She had to talk to calm her emotions. "There is something that still puzzles me, my husband," she said, lying in the blue and white curtained bed in his oval chamber with its carved furniture and curvy-legged tables. He had held her close to him in the carriage nearly all the way from London, and she felt ready to melt into his arms again. Soon he would come closer.

"Ask away," he said, setting his officer's coat onto the wood valet at the bow window, which overlooked the snow-covered garden, white in moonlight. His face lit as he eyed her in her half-reclined position against the pillows, lit by candlelight. "Don't you look beautiful there! You look good enough to—Sorry! What did you want to ask me?"

Feeling very happy, Arabelle had to blink herself back to the question she had for him. "Ah yes; why did you faint at your first wedding?"

He cocked a black eyebrow and eyed her sidewise. "I am so glad you asked." He gave her a slow smile, his eyes glistening near the *girandole* of candles on the dressing table. He removed his lace jabot. "I aborted my wedding to Miss Wells deliberately, Arabelle."

"You fell on purpose?" She sat up to attention. "Why?"

"Because of *you*. You had hovered in my mind every day, every hour since we parted at the George Inn. How I longed to come and find you so I could look at you again, and hear your mellifluous voice . . ." His smile turned to a sigh. "But I was espoused. What a wretched prospect that was! Torture! As I walked down that church aisle with the wrong woman on my arm, I debated what to do. I begged God to help me, quickly. When I saw your eyes in the crowd, present at my wedding, of all places, a bolt of clarity hit me. It was the love I felt for you—and from you." He gave her an intimate smile. "In that moment, I knew, come what may, that you were the one and only woman for me. If I could not have you to love, I wanted no other woman."

Arabelle trembled with the impact of his revelation. She recalled vividly the jolt of awareness between them as they had locked eyes during his wedding march. He was right. It was love.

Her eyes played luminously over him. She said tenderly, "But we couldn't have each other then. There was no hope."

"True. Even if we could not marry, I could admire you from afar. Or, somehow become your friend," he said in remembered remorse.

Arabelle could only marvel.

His shoulders were very broad in his waistcoat and sleeves. He shrugged off the waistcoat.

"What about Corisande?" she asked.

"I chose to put off my marriage indefinitely by one tactic or another." He gave a mirthless laugh. "In my schemes, I thought of staging my own death and burying myself in this house for as long as I could get away with it." He lifted his snowy shirt over his head. "Not a sound idea. But I could not marry Corisande when you had set my heart on fire."

Her breath caught as she saw his wide, bare chest. This splendid man was her husband! His linen hit the valet with his impatient toss.

He turned to face her, his arm muscles moving as he pulled off his boots. "It was far more than your beautiful surface, Arabelle, that drew me. It was more than your intelligence and learning, which I profoundly admire. Your faithfulness to your convictions in the face of overwhelming temptations; that was something I did not expect to find in a high-born young woman of your position." He shook his head. "When I saw how courageously you behaved when I posed as the Count who bought you, I fell deeper than ever in love with you." His eyebrows lifted as he eyed her in the bed.

Before she would allow herself to melt into his coming embrace, she said ominously, "It boggles me to think it was *you* behind the mask when I asked the Count if I could call for a champion! And that it was *you* who let me summon Simon Laurence to fight for me!"

He laughed. "That bothers you, does it?"

"Enormously! How could you do that to me?"

"You see," he took her hand, "after I had intercepted Rutley's plan to sell you to the Turkish Sheik, I meant to restore you to your family."

"Why didn't you?"

"I had to continue to make the Count act. Although," he said, lifting one of her curls and inhaling its scent rapturously, "being delighted with my 'delivery' took no acting at all. As you know, I am mightily drawn to you, Arabelle, no matter who I am."

His dark blue eyes glinted between his black lashes. He put a hand over her lips to detain her outburst. "When you begged to call a man to save you, I had to know who that man could be. Was I in the running, I wondered? Would you think of the man who would do anything to spend his life serving you?"

Arabelle sighed at his words. "You had already been hurt in the eye by Sir Pomeroy while you dueled for me."

His eyes sparkled upon her as he threw off the velvet ribbon that held his hair in its queue. "Imagine my joy when I saw the note to your champion with my name on it. Arabelle, that was the hope I needed to whet my appetite for life."

"But that was unfair, finding out my secret like that! What an inside look you had on my foolish heart!" she moaned, covering her face. She realized that Simon had acted out of pure motives even then, wanting to discover the state of her feelings toward him.

He lifted the lace-edged sheet and she felt his warm body slide in next to hers. "Foolish heart?" he echoed. His warm lips touched hers briefly, making her tingle. "Your trust kept me alive through my most painful moments, believe me. Please don't regret it, Arabelle."

She exclaimed faintly, "So that explains it!" She drew her fingers through his long, loose hair and found that its texture pleased her.

"What explains what?" he murmured, tracing her eyebrow with a tender touch.

She couldn't make excuses for the heated kisses she had reveled in with the nefarious, alluring Count, for his lips had been Simon's. It was still astounding to think that he and the Count were one and the same. "Never mind," she said, blushing, for she was craving those kisses again.

Simon said, "Hmm!" in a knowing tone.

Her eyes sparkled in the candlelight as she sat up. She pounced upon another vital question. "What did you think when I wrote, begging Simon Laurence to save me from *you*—you dastardly Count!—and you realized you had to duel yourself?"

"Ho, you had me there!" He tipped back his head and laughed. "My brother, Radford, howled his head off!"

"I'll bet *you* weren't laughing."

"I was . . . and I wasn't." He tickled the back of her neck while his lips showed the ghost of a smile. "Ho, what challenges you threw my way!"

"Tell me: I am so curious; how did you show up as Simon, my champion, and still fight for me so fiercely as Count Mascarille?"

"I was the Count until the duel." He switched to the Count's French intonation. "Mine was the fair *Ma'amselle* no matter which of me won."

His voice brought it all back, and Arabelle laughed weakly. "Yes, but you went through a great deal to insure that. However did you keep your roles straight? You could not be two people at once!"

His muscles flexed as he took her into his arms, thrilling her with elation, cradling her against his chest. "At the duel," he said, "and in one episode when the Count and I had to appear in the same room, Radford donned my guise and became the Count. Temporarily."

"Radford did? But he's so serious and sensible," Arabelle objected, remembering what Genevieve had said about him.

Simon grinned. "No, he's not. He only appears that way in public. He's the Earl of Ashby, and takes on a certain reserved dignity in front of people. But he's good at acting, and we've had a lot of rollicking good times growing up."

"I'm glad to hear that."

"He's a great brother. During this charade, he was good at detail, even to the bloody bandage around his neck." Simon shifted her on his shoulder so he could look into her face. "My, but you were a woman formidable in resourcefulness! We will never forget the sword you wielded, which caught me unawares, which pierced me in the throat, and which got you across the street to the coffee house while we four men watched like statues. *Touché!*" With the arm not cuddling her, he made her an imaginary sword salute. He kissed her forehead and laughed softly into her hair. "I had to do a vast amount of jockeying to pull myself through the logistics of my plans because they went awry, thanks to you."

Arabelle smiled. "Where did you get your convincing backdrop?—the fashionable house, the furniture, the wigs, and those ostentatious clothes?"

Simon laughed and ran a hand down her bare shoulder. "All my diamond buttons, you mean? Paste! I fitted Radford and myself with the most opulent costumes from the Drury Lane Theatre costume room. It was the Charles II rig that I wore as Count Mascarille. I borrowed things quite often for our Academy productions, so it was easy to acquire stage furniture and everything else we needed to furnish that place realistically."

"You did a wonderful job of it. You were so magnificent yourself that you terrified me into visions of a grand *chateau* full of jewel-draped mistresses as your home."

Simon looked at her in silent awe and laid her back against the pillows. "I am sorry you had to go through those kinds of fears. I must confess further how despicable I have been." He watched her face seriously for several ticks of the clock, tracing down her profile with his finger, over her lips, down her neck . . .

Arabelle's breath became shallow.

"When you felt distress, my darling, I wanted to halt the charade, but I could not. We had Lord Rutley in the house, believing I was a foreigner. We used that ruse—my outbidding the Turk—to trap him in his abduction activity. Then, with the duel upon us, we had Corisande under lock and key. We needed to interrogate her, and she would not have revealed what she did to me about Rutley and her had she known I was Simon."

"Oh, no," agreed Arabelle, "that she would never have done. Don't apologize for the role you so brilliantly played. I rejoiced when the Count took her well in hand and did not let her get away with her wiles. You were masterful and tough, and it brought you rewards of information."

"Yes. She confessed to her liaison with Rutley." He shook his head as if to banish those thoughts from his head. "But let's talk about you, my Love. You made a very honourable marriage bargain with the Count. That was me," he said proudly, his eyes gleaming slits between his black lashes. "For the duel, Radford and I had our tactics all planned so that I, Simon, would win. I would restore you to your family, and that would be the last of the Count."

"That would have been a neat ending."

"However, because of Rutley's croquet ball, I tripped and fell onto Radford's sword point. Was he ever upset about that! I was, too, when I came to my senses. We had a devastating mess on our hands. He, the Count, was the obvious victor. Though we knew it would tear you apart, Radford absolutely had to maintain that he won the prize of your hand in marriage."

"Yes, but he wasn't the same person to whom I made my promise, was he? And the person to whom I did promise, in my ignorance, was you, a betrothed man."

"How would it have looked if the Count did not take what he had fought to win? I am really sorry it had to be that way. One thing led to another, winding us all tighter. I would gladly have taken you aside and told you the truth after the duel, but I was unconscious and transported far away from you. Then I realized it would be best to keep you to your bargain to marry the Count, or your parents would prevent me, as myself, from seeing you again."

"That's true. They accepted you as my bridegroom when you were the Count."

Simon gave a chuckle of remembrance. "At my bedside, when I was recovering, Radford offered to marry you himself; that is, play the Count to the bitter end. Then, in some future situation, he would tell your parents it was all a subterfuge. I said 'Absolutely not!'"

Slyly, she queried, "You did? Why not, when it would have been a good solution? My parents stipulated that I should marry wealth and a title."

He grasped her tightly and growled, "I wouldn't let my *brother* marry you! It would stick." He kissed her neck until she giggled and told him to stop; he was tickling her.

In a more serious voice, he explained, "The worst part of all my subterfuge was that you suffered such terrible agonies of mind, thinking you had to marry an unscrupulous Count, who paid Rutley for you. How I wish I could have spared you that."

She thought it through as she lifted her arms around his neck. She acknowledged something else. During and after the duel, she had not felt her earlier attraction for the Count. "It was all true," she said as Simon's hand moved the chemise off her shoulder. She had responded passionately to the Count when he was Simon, even as she reveled in his touch now. When she had hurried to the duel with Radford as the Count, she had felt nothing for him, even when he lifted her over the barricade. She felt contempt for that Count, so eager to fight her Simon. She explained this to her husband, who grinned and eyed her predatorily. "What an act you brothers put on!" she concluded. "And how consistently I felt drawn to *you*, my love. In disguise or out, it didn't matter. You were the same man, compelling me."

In a French accent, he murmured, "That is good to hear." Cringing deliciously, she felt his lips on her temple as he added fiercely, "I was madly jealous of the Count!"

She stared up at him in surprise. "When?"

"In those moments in the bedchamber."

"Do explain," she urged, her heart pounding against his.

"Those kisses you gave that Count! Ahh! I die! I still want to run him through!"

Someday soon, she would explain to him why she kissed the Count, but now she had no more will to speak.

It was hours later, and the moon shone a shaft through the window. Arabelle lay with Simon, wide-awake, pondering the miracle of love. A low fire crackled across the room in the white marble fireplace. And fire glowed within her.

She took soft, shallow breaths, for Simon's head lay upon her, his hair tickling her neck. She sniffed his luxuriant head and ran fingers through his long hair with wonder. He slept peacefully on. She recalled a verse in the Song of Solomon. *"A bundle of myrrh is my well beloved unto me; he shall lie all night betwixt my breasts".*

No sooner had she whispered the words than Simon's lips moved against her skin. "That is beautiful, my Love. This is where I have wanted to be since I first beheld you." He raised his head to meet her shining eyes. "I want to take care of you all my days."

She hugged him close and felt wonder over the fact that he cherished her. "You say the most perfect things, Simon. I love you. And there is something I want you to know without a doubt."

"Ye-es?" The challenging cadence of his voice gave her a shiver up her spine.

She touched his straight nose and traced her finger up and over his eyebrows. She blurted out, "I am not fickle."

His eyes twinkled. "I know. It was dark, you enchanted me, and I tempted you unfairly as the lustful Count."

Arabelle's heart thumped. "Yes, you did, pretending to be a wicked foreigner bent on seducing me."

"I could see you were a woman of virtue. I heard it stridently from your lips. That convinced me you were nothing like Corisande. But let us continue to be truthful. *You* seduced *me*, remember?"

"How?" she cried.

"By lying there in that flimsy garment with your hair flowing in such gorgeous abandon—ah!—Arabelle! I could go on. It was extremely hard to be a gentleman." Smiling, he said, "I have longed for such a situation again. Now, my beauty, we have it. The night is young, for yonder clock says but half past three." He pulled her to him and kissed her until she could scarcely think or breathe.

But she had more to ask him. "That convincing French voice," she gasped. "You told me how Lord Ashby acquired his, but how did you manage yours?"

"Oh, I have been an actor through most of my boyhood days in one dramatic scheme or another," he said as he smoothed tendrils of hair from her face. "I acted at Cambridge, and once a month in the cadet productions at the Academy."

She cupped her hands over his well-formed shoulders and asked, "Were you studying lines on our coach ride to London?"

"All I remember about that ride is you." He flashed a smile at her. "Yet if I tickle my memory, I believe I was memorizing for *A Would-Be Gentleman.*"

Arabelle laughed. "Would you be a gentleman?"

"My Arabelle does not want gentlemanly behaviour at a time like this, does she?"

When she felt his lips sear into her neck, she gasped, "No! No more gentlemanly forbearance, please!"

Chapter Twenty-Eight

A Picture of Bliss

It was a thick letter that their footman presented one sunny morning less than a month later, while she and Simon sipped coffee and played Nine Men's Morris. Arabelle gave a glad cry at the sight of *Mrs. Arabelle Laurence* penned in Genevieve's hand. She settled down to let Simon read with her as she lay against his chest on a cherry red settee. She heard icicles fall and crash with tinkles from the eaves, and melting snow dripping to the paved verandah below the drawing room bow window.

"Will this be news or chit-chat?" Simon asked, fingering the three folded pages that came apart when Arabelle cracked the Bastwicke seal.

Arabelle smiled. "Genevieve's chit-chat is always full of news."

Bloomsbury Square
March 13, 1752

My Dear Arabelle,
I miss you already! So does Father, and Lenora keeps asking when she can come to your house again. Jerome doesn't understand, but wants you to rock him, and tells me to find you.

I think he's getting used to my filling in, however. Poor baby has no choice. Despite all these complaints, Arabelle, I am so glad you're so happy with Simon! You went through so terribly much that you deserve everything sweet and good now.

Sir Pomeroy was just here, calling on Madam and me. He says he misses the sight of you in all the drawing rooms, and that even Chesterfield House has lost its sparkle since you aren't there. What a compliment.

He told us that Corisande, who is in gaol now, begged him to take her to see Lord Rutley, who is housed in a better cell in Newgate. While there, the horrid couple discussed marriage. Lord and Lady Chesterfield want Corisande out of their lives as soon as can be done, so it sounds like she may link up with Rutley after all. Can you imagine that? I pity her with all my heart. However, she may live her life as a wife in name only because he is up for trial by the House of Lords. Who knows what will happen to him if he is convicted of those crimes against you and the other, unfortunate heiresses? Father is rubbing his hands, waiting for Rutley's trial to begin.

Father and I both thank you for a lovely time last week. It was so wonderful to visit you and Simon, and see you so much in love. You have a beautiful place to live with the handsomest and best man in England, Arabelle. Aunt Claracilla and I say in our letters to each other that we can thank God for letting you both squeak through those awful traps and come out married to each other.

I can hardly wait to come to you in a sennight, as you asked me to. Yes, please have a house party while I am there, for I would much prefer to meet the kind of friends Simon has to the ones to whom I've been introduced by Madam. You know very well what I mean.

You are living proof that it's worth it to hold tightly to the teachings of the Bible, and everything Aunt Claracilla trained us to hold dear. Madam is still mad at her. She says she interferes excessively much, but I do not agree. I hope our dear aunt will stay in London and help me through any trouble I may have with men, if that day ever dawns.

Lenora and Jerome send their love and kisses. I send you one, too, and also to that good-looking Captain Laurence of yours. Tell him congratulations on his promotion. Isn't he moving up awfully fast? He is wonderful, and you deserve him, and he deserves you.

I am thankful and proud to be

Your sister,
Genevieve

PS: Will Lord Ashby be at your party?

Arabelle smiled delightedly at Simon. "Will he?"

"If he hears that she is coming, I expect we shall see him darken our door, dressed in his best."

Their family's visits had begun with Uncle Trent, Lord Bastwicke, Genevieve, Lenora, and Jerome. The little ones brought a basket and plunked it together onto the Persian carpet in front of Simon. Lenora had Jerome hold the basket top shut until they had Simon's attention. Then, with a portentous look, she told Jerome to open the lid. She plunged her hands inside, picked up a white kitten with black markings, and put it ceremoniously onto Simon's lap. "This is for you," she said in a hushed voice.

Jerome jumped up and down and cried, "The best one! The best kitten! We saved it for you, Simon!"

He was very touched. He lifted it up, looked into the kitten's round green eyes, smiled at Lenora and Jerome, and cuddled his present under his chin. "For me? How can I ever thank you?"

Arabelle put her hand on her heart as she watched them all: the children's delight, and the joyous way Simon acknowledged their special gift. He played with them and the kitten for the next hour.

Lady Bastwicke was conspicuous by her absence. She did not visit. She did not even send a message. Lord and Lady Shepley came twice, and Lord Ashby called in several times for dinner. All had been happy parties. Arabelle loved being the mistress of Simon's home.

Captain Ligonier, though having granted Simon a six-week honeymoon leave, arrived one morning. After he apologized for intruding, he conferred upon Arabelle's husband the rank of Captain. It was for his triumphant espionage, he said. He invited them both to a banquet honouring Simon, to be held at Court, with military brass and the King's courtiers to laud his victorious exposé of Lord Rutley's crimes.

Having finally regained Captain Laurence to herself on this bird-chirping morning, Arabelle felt a slight regret when Simon suddenly alerted and asked, "Did you hear that rumble of wheels?"

"I do. Who is coming, Simon? Are you expecting someone?"

"Not someone, but some*thing.*" He hustled her off his lap. "Do take your lovely form up to the first floor until I call you." He kissed her with a hunger that left her longing to stay, but then turned her toward the stairs with a mysterious smile. He strode back to the door, past the startled servants, to silence the person on the other side of the knocker.

Arabelle grinned in wonder and fled up the curving staircase until she was out of sight of the white marble hall.

Serenely she strolled from room to charming room, through their bedchamber with its light aqua walls of silk, its arched white doorways, and on to their yellow sitting room. From there, she wandered through her pink sewing room and into his library. She sat in his throne-like Restoration chair, her hands gliding over the smooth old wood of its arms. Wondering what was going on below, she moved a vase of snowdrops from an *escritoire* to a Baroque *bombé* chest, and then twitched back a silk print curtain to view the orchards. Apple and filbert trees in rows dotted the rolling hills beyond the formal flower gardens. Later this spring and all through the summer, the fountain would splash in the midst of a colourful display, Simon promised. So far, crocuses and daffodils were peeping out with the first purple and yellow bud ends.

He enjoyed showing her their domain. He had taken her arm-in-arm through the garden walks, past the green hedges dusted with snow, to the barns where his sheep and ducks, his horses and cattle lived cosily through the winter in the spacious barns and stables. He gave her a horse of her own, and they rode to visit the tenants. Simon pointed out his fields, told her their crops, and cantered by her side down one of his favourite rides between two orchards of mature, spreading trees. They stopped and kissed repeatedly, and fingered the yellow catkins that would bring them filberts in the autumn.

Arabelle felt supremely happy. She could do so much here. She could even prune, if she took the fancy.

Waiting for Simon to summon her downstairs, she breathed in pleasure and closed the window in her sewing room. She had smelled spring on the breeze.

A goggle-eyed maid summoned her when she had resumed work on her embroidery of Bodiam Castle. She dashed into her boudoir and gave a last swipe of her brush to her unbound hair. *This is the way Simon likes it,* she told her reflection. In the privacy of their home, she would often wear it down for him.

She lifted her pink and blue silken skirts by her panniers and glided through her boudoir doorway and down the stairs, full of anticipation. Simon was nowhere in sight, but a maid and footman kept glancing toward the drawing room, trying not to, but making it obvious, that the secret was *in there.*

Arabelle walked curiously into the room. The only difference she saw was that the long silver and red velvet curtains were tasseled back at every window, letting the sunlight stream in. Seeing no one, she turned back to look for Simon on the settee, where he and she had taken to reading the Bible or plays or prose, or singing to the tune of his viola in the evenings. Across the room, in the spot where he said they needed a large painting, there hung one!

A flood of surprise soared through her. She stood stock still; it took her breath away. There she was, in the painting Lord Chesterfield had commissioned Miss Agathon to paint. Next to her, of all unbelievable transformations, was a full-length, swashbuckling painting of *Simon!* With his head cocked at a flirtatious angle, he had his arms folded in his blue-coated military uniform with silver epaulettes. He fixed his sparkling, admiring eyes on Arabelle, who looked joyous and alluring on the other side of the Corinthian pedestal.

She thrilled to her toes with the romance the scene portrayed. "Oh my! It's so *real!*"

"Do you like it?" he asked, startling her as he rose from behind a chair. He had been crouching there, observing her through the holes in the carved back.

Arabelle threw him an ecstatic look. "Oh, Simon! Miss Agathon is an absolute genius! She has caught you to perfection." She ran and hugged him with rapture.

"At least she's a genius of persistence," he said with a smile and a kiss.

"She said she was dying to paint you full-length! How did this happen?"

"After she heard how Corisande back-stabbed you, Miss Agathon lamented over the portrait she had done of you two, and called it a wasted effort. I told her not to think so; that I planned to buy the painting from Lord Chesterfield, which I did. I had in mind this slight change, you see, and she expressed herself most willing to comply." He gave Arabelle a saucy grin.

She poked him in the ribs. "How jealous I am that she studied you from all angles, so intimately!" She gazed at his long, sleekly muscled legs in the pale breeches. Even his dimple in that odd spot in his cheek was perfect, and his long fingers lovingly reproduced, with his wedding ring prominent. "Oh! I *love* it!" she exclaimed. "It's you! Thank you, thank you!"

Simon laughed low, and possessed her amorously around the waist.

She returned her eyes to the picture even before their breathless kiss was over.

Noting this, he threw back his head and half-laughed, half-groaned. "Now I have *another* rival in myself!"

"Oh yes," Arabelle agreed, twinkling at him sidewise. "Thank you very much for doubling my pleasure."

"Does this mean you like my wedding gift?"

"Yes, husband, I am in ecstasies over it." She gazed at the pair of them depicted on canvas, each so obviously in love. "But how audacious of you! Corisande is painted completely out of the picture!"

"For that," said Simon, giving Arabelle a dazzling smile as he wrapped her in his arms, "I will be thankful all my days. Come, my sweet, let's plan our party. I know! Shall we take inspiration from Lord Chesterfield, and unveil a new picture?"

"Oh, yes!" said Arabelle, her eyes a-glow as they roved from Simon to his compelling likeness next to hers within the golden frame. "This time, it's a picture of bliss."

The End

"Life is not measured by how many breaths we take, but by how many moments take our breath away."
Author Unknown

If you enjoyed this book, please look for Mellyora Ashley's other works.
You may one day discover a sequel featuring Genevieve.

Glossary

Armoire—A wardrobe, cupboard, or ambry with a front door, usually made of wood, and often embellished with carving or a looking-glass front. Sometimes locked with a key. Often the interior had hooks and later, a rod, for hanging garments, and/ or drawers and shelves. Could be the height of a person, or massive and stately.

Bag wig—Adopted by civilians from the military, bag wigs may have started with common folk because horses' tails were often covered with protective bags. Bag wigs were fastened at the top with drawstrings to protect clothes from the grease and general filth of their hair. Fashion then made the bagged queues popular in a variety of wig styles.

Baldric—A belt or girdle, usually of leather and richly ornamented, worn pendent from one shoulder, across the breast and under the opposite arm, and used to support the wearer's sword, bugle, etc.

Échelles—French for ladder. A form of bodice decoration fashionable in the late seventeenth and eighteenth centuries, where ribbon bows, often diminishing in size from bosom to waist, decorated the centre front of a gown's stomacher.

Escritoire—A writing desk made to contain stationery and documents.

Farthingale—An extensive framework of hoops, usually of whalebone, worked into cloth, worn to extend the skirts of women's dresses, especially at the sides.

Fichu—A triangular piece of light fabric or lace, worn by ladies as a covering for the neck and shoulders; often tied or pinned with a brooch low on the bosom.

Fortnight—A period of fourteen nights, or two weeks.

Girandole—A branched holder for several candles, either in the form of a candlestick for placing on the table or as a bracket projecting from the wall.

Jabot—The frill of lace that surrounded the neck of a shirt and cascaded over the top of the waistcoat.

Justacorps—Men's outer body-coat, reaching to the knees, worn in the seventeenth and eighteenth centuries.

Ostler—A man who attends to horses at an inn; a stable-man; a groom.

Panniers—Side hoops to hold out the skirt of a gown, made of reed or whalebone. They were covered with cotton or linen, and the two halves tied together in front and back at each of the bone semi-circles to form an oval line for the gown.

Parures—A matching suite of coordinating precious gems which could include a necklace, a comb, a tiara, a diadem, a bandeau, a pair of bracelets, pins, rings, drop earrings and/or cluster stud earrings and possibly a belt clasp.

Passementerie—Trimming of gold or silver lace in elaborate designs, often decorating men's coats of this period.

Pattens—Overshoes made to raise the ordinary shoes out of mud or wet.

Petticoat—An underskirt of rich, decorative fabric, visible as the gown skirt was open in front to display it. When gowns were no longer designed with an open front, the petticoat became an undergarment. From about 1800 onward, the term referred only to underwear.

Queue—A hanging tail of hair at the back of the head, secured by a ribbon at the nape of the neck. Sometimes tied into a pigtail. It could also be contained in a bag.

Rapier—A long, pointed, two-edged sword for cutting or thrusting; mostly used for thrusting. The rapier was the weapon of a gentleman, and symbolized that he had status and wealth, and that he was proficient with the sword. While it was often used on the battlefield, it was more readily associated with court, dueling, and fashion. Many had delicate, intricate designs.

Robe a la française—The so-called "Watteau" gown, derived from the early 18th century *contouche,* a *sacque* (sack) gown, with a fitted waist in front but flowing loosely over an immense hoop at back and sides. The neckline was low and wide, the bodice defined with the stomacher and *échelles* in front. Sleeves were elbow-length in pagoda style. The *robe a la française* was of the same style, but the back was designed with large box pleats that extended from neckline to hem. Sleeves ended in a cuff at the elbow, below which depended the lace flounces of the chemise. These gowns went by various names including *robes volantes and robes battantes.* Despite the change in pannier shape in the mid-century, the *robe a la française* continued fashionable until the 1770s, when it was relegated to formal court wear.

Robe de chambre—A dressing gown.

Robe ronde—A gown open in front from the waist down. A separate corset was rarely worn underneath the bodice because the lining of the gown was practically a corset. The fastening of the bodice of this *robe ronde* was always in front, and the material and trimming of the under-dress worn with the *robe ronde* were always the same as those of the *robe, or gown.*

Sennight—A period of seven days and nights; a week.

Smallsword—Developed from the rapier near the end of the 17th century, the smallsword was a civilian weapon and an item of dress for every gentleman. It also acted as a dueling sword. Intended solely for thrusting, the smallsword had a stiff triangular blade. When wielded by a skillful swordsman, it was a deadly fencing weapon. The handguard consisted of a small cup, and finger and knuckle guards. Often magnificently decorated, smallswords reflected the status of their owners.

Viscount—(vi-count) A member of the fourth order of the British peerage, ranking between an Earl and a Baron.

Viscountess—(vi-countess) The wife of a Viscount.